VALLEY

— OF —

THE KINGS

The 18ᵗʰ Dynasty

VALLEY

— OF —

THE KINGS

The 18th Dynasty

A novel

TERRANCE COFFEY

Coffey

Valley of the Kings: The 18th Dynasty © 2016 Terry Coffey
Helm House
ISBN-10: 0-692-75658-2
ISBN-13: 978-0-692-75658-4
ASIN: B01EG5NGFA
Ebook version published by Kindle Press
Library of Congress Control Number: 2016911919

For more information, visit:
www.TerranceCoffey.com

Cover Art: Damon Za
Interior Design: T. Coffey
Editors: Ronit Wagman & Dustin Schwindt
First Edition: July 2016

10 9 8 7 6 5 4 3 2 1

HELM HOUSE
PUBLISHING

For those who dare to dream…

PART I

"The plant reveals what is in the seed."
—*Ipet-Isut*

The World of the 18ᵗʰ Dynasty

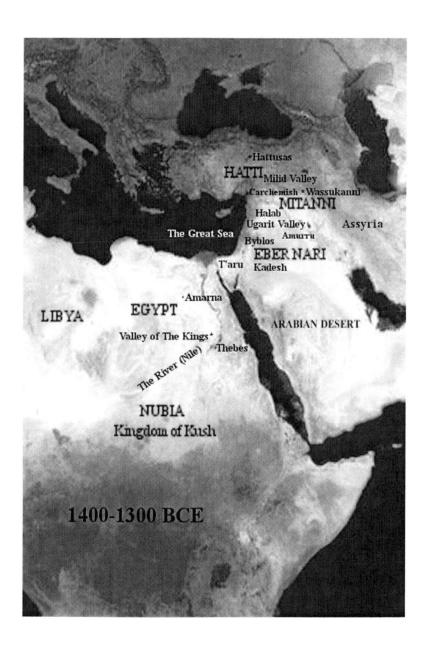

CHAPTER

1

TEPPY BOLTED ACROSS the grainfield like a gazelle fleeing from a cheetah. His linen kilt flapped against his legs, and coarse leaves of wheat thrashed his bare chest. The beast pounced after Teppy, who was too terrified to glance back at the creature that was determined to tear his frail six-year-old body to pieces.

Fixed on his trail, the unseen creature gained momentum while Teppy's heart pounded against his chest. His brother Tuthmosis had warned him not to be afraid, to fight back with all his strength—but Teppy had none left. Fearful the beast intended to rip his head from his body, Teppy kept running through the endless grainfield, calling out for his brother to save him.

Roars erupted, then a wisp of wind brushed the side-lock of hair that hung from one side of his temple. An arrow had cut through the air, narrowly missing his otherwise clean-shaven head. Another arrow sliced through his kilt, burrowing into the flesh of his thigh. Teppy stumbled to the ground, anticipating the coming pain. Before it occurred, Teppy heard the thunderous roars again. He turned his head away from the sight of the wound and yanked the arrow from his thigh. Teppy grimaced, staggered back to his feet and ran until he cleared the field.

In front of him now, rising up among the three great pyramids, was the figure of Horemkhat. With its monumental lion's body and the head of their old pharaoh Khafra attached at the shoulders, the statue stood over forty cubits high, painted in vibrant shades of red, yellow, and blue.

Teppy dashed toward it. *I'm almost there . . . almost safe,* he thought.

His body gave out when he reached the tip of the statue's paw. Gasping, Teppy collapsed in the sand, causing more blood to flow out from his wound.

An ominous shadow spread across the statue until it had enveloped Teppy and the open area around him. He looked toward the sky, searching for the source of the shadow towering above, and was relieved to discover that the beast appeared to be only a man dressed in regal clothing. He carried a sickle in his hand and a bow with a quiver of arrows slung over one shoulder. His face was hidden in silhouette against the blinding orange sun. When the figure shifted its body, its head came into view—the unmistakable head of a ram. It roared again at Teppy, and saliva dripped from its canine teeth. The beast dropped to his knees and grabbed his victim by the throat. Teppy screamed but no sound emitted from him. Easing the grip around Teppy's neck, the beast raised the razor-sharp sickle above his head. Teppy shut his eyes, expecting the swipe of the blade that would slit his throat. Silence followed, however, and a moment later Teppy felt something odd, not the blade slashing through his neck, but a sudden lightness as air rushed into his larynx. Teppy's eyes popped open. His body slowly fell away beneath him, and drops of blood sprinkled the twitching limbs of his headless body. He screamed and flailed about until his brother shook him out of his nightmare.

"Teppy! What is it?" shouted Tuthmosis.

Teppy lurched awake in his bedchamber.

Eased by the familiar surroundings, he cried. His chamber had always been a source of comfort for him, a place where he felt protected by the golden statues of animal gods that towered over his platform bed and the many pottery jars that lined his floor, painted with his father's war scenes and conquests. The guards always kept the torches in Teppy's bedchamber illuminated so that he could see the hieroglyphics covering the walls from floor to ceiling. The inscribed pictures represented incantations meant to prevent evil spirits from entering his dreams at night, though none of it had been enough to stop the beast of that night's dream.

Tuthmosis sat down next to his brother and wiped away his tears with his hand. "Stop crying. It's alright. Tell me what happened."

Teppy took a moment to calm himself. "He was chasing me."

"Who was chasing you?"

"Amun. He shot an arrow in my leg, and he cut off my head."

Tuthmosis pulled the bedcover back. "Look, no arrow, not even a wound."

Teppy sat up and examined his lower half. Other than his right hipbone protruding slightly more than the left, his legs were unblemished and intact.

"And I promise," continued Tuthmosis, "I'm looking at your head, and it's still attached to your body."

Teppy cradled his head with both arms just to be sure.

"What have I told you? You mustn't reveal your fear of him. You have to be brave and fight back. If he kills you three times in your dream, you'll never find your way back from the afterlife. And now look, it's already the second time."

"I can't fight him. He frightens me," Teppy whimpered.

Tuthmosis put a protective arm around Teppy, a gesture that always made his little brother feel safe. At age sixteen, ten years older than Teppy, Tuthmosis was caring, smart, and adamantly brave. He protected his younger brother from everything, even crocodiles. Teppy dreamed of having broad shoulders and muscular arms just like his brother and a side-lock as long as his, too. This, Teppy knew for sure, would make him brave.

Tuthmosis removed an amulet from around his neck and placed it around his brother's neck. "Yes, you can fight him. This will help you," he said.

"Your Aten amulet?" Teppy asked, unable to contain his excitement.

"Now it's yours," Tuthmosis answered.

Teppy rubbed his fingers across the gold-plated disk. Although he was uncertain about the amulet's significance, he remained enthralled by it. The engraving depicted a man with a crown on his head seated and bathed by the rays of the sun. "What does the picture mean?" he asked.

"Aten is the sun, the god that gives us light. Without him, we would have no morning, only the darkness of night. Look, the amulet shows the scene of Aten shining his power down on the pharaoh of Egypt. It will give you power and strength over your enemies as well," said Tuthmosis.

"Even Amun?"

"Yes, even the Amun god. Promise me you'll always keep it with you and never let it leave your sight."

"I promise," replied Teppy. "But if I have it, what will protect you?"

Tuthmosis gave his brother a self-assured look, tapping his chest. "I don't need it. The Aten is always with me. Now get up. It's time to dress and greet mother in her chamber."

Teppy sluggishly rolled his body out of bed with a disappointed look on his face. "Can we go swim in the river instead?"

"You know that father forbade us to swim in the river," Tuthmosis reminded him.

"But he won't know if we never tell him."

"Teppy, you know we can't."

"Please? We hardly ever get to swim in the river."

Teppy pouted. All he would have to do now is hold his defiant facial expression just a little bit longer and Tuthmosis would give in to his wishes.

Just as Teppy expected, a sly grin appeared on his brother's face. Tuthmosis handed him a hooded cloak. "Then we won't tell him."

Teppy shook his head while mimicking his brother's mischievous smile. He was going swimming in the river with his big brother, and there could be nothing better in the whole world.

The boys made their way down the corridor and slipped out of the palace, being careful not to be detected by their father's guards.

From an open window, Ay, the pharaoh's trusted confidant, watched his two young nephews sneak out of the palace grounds before he continued down the corridor to the pharaoh's chamber.

Ay entered as Pharaoh Amenhotep was in the midst of his prayer to the Amun god—the one he would always recite before he went off to war:

"Amun, my god of sustenance, my lord is my protector, who answers the one that calls on him. Amun, the king of the gods, grant me victory over my enemies, light the path I must follow."

Ay stood silently until Amenhotep finished. The pharaoh was fully aware that someone was standing at the entrance of his chamber because of the shadow cast onto the opaque white curtain separating his chamber from the palace corridor. "Who stands there?" he asked.

"My Pharaoh, it's your most humble servant, Ay."

Amenhotep stepped out from behind the curtain into the outer chamber dressed in his king's robe and *nemes*—the royal striped head cloth. Typically, the pharaoh appeared stout and solidly built, but today he was sweaty, frail, and anxious. *He must be craving it again,* Ay thought. Many moons ago, the pharaoh began to suffer from severe toothaches that couldn't be allayed. The enamel in several of his teeth had worn down and most of the pulp was exposed, causing excruciating abscesses. It was Ay's responsibility to extract the opium from the capsules of the poppy plant and administer the medicine to the pharaoh. If Amenhotep didn't get the opium when he needed it, he would behave like a tyrant, and in recent days his need for *the cure* had turned habitual.

Cradling his jaw in pain, Amenhotep yelled at Ay, "Give it to me!"

He snatched the pouch that Ay was carrying and searched inside in desperation.

"Why is it empty?"

"Forgive me, my Pharaoh. I have not had the opportunity to replenish it."

"How dare you even come to me without it?"

"It was urgent I advise you that General Nasheret has formed the troops. They await your arrival."

"Bring me the cure now!" shouted Amenhotep, disregarding Ay's message.

"As you wish, my Pharaoh."

Ay had become the perfect manservant for Amenhotep. He never questioned the pharaoh and always did as he was told, and though he was the pharaoh's wife's brother, Ay's loyalty to Amenhotep had grown much stronger than his devotion to his sister, Queen Ty. How could this not be when it was Amenhotep and not the queen who rewarded him with a life of royalty?

Before Ay could walk away, Amenhotep grabbed him by the arm. "Where is Tuthmosis? My son has not made an appearance in my chamber to greet me."

"I saw him and Prince Teppy leave the palace, my Pharaoh. They were headed toward the river."

Amenhotep seethed. He'd warned Tuthmosis and Teppy not to go into the river. A crocodile had recently attacked a servant boy out for a swim and devoured one of his legs, and now the rogue creature harbored a taste for human blood. It was dangerous for any citizen to swim in the river, much less the royal sons of a pharaoh. Amenhotep instructed Ay to fetch his chariot, and along with four of his royal guards, the pharaoh rode out to the river in search of Tuthmosis.

CHAPTER

2

THE VILLAGE OF THEBES teemed with merchants and citizens bartering their wares under huge looming monuments of farm animals, macabre beasts, and a colossal statue of Pharaoh Amenhotep. Houses painted in pastel hues and outlined in hieroglyphics stood on either side of a narrow road choked with the noisy traffic of donkey carts and small feral animals running about.

Teppy and Tuthmosis made their way through the village disguised in cloaks. Children of royalty were forbidden to go into the village to walk among the peasants. *"Someone might curse you if they discovered your secret birth name and that you were a prince,"* Tuthmosis had once explained to Teppy.

The boys had a secret name given at birth that was known only to their parents, and Queen Ty, had warned them to never reveal those names to anyone. Without the knowledge of their secret names, they were immune from any villager who might be envious or harbor evil intents against the royal family. It was not possible to conjure a spell of divination against them using their public names—Teppy and Tuthmosis. In any case, Teppy found the pronunciation of his secret name too difficult, so his mother's and Tuthmosis's warnings weren't necessary.

While Tuthmosis made his way through the crowded street with quick deliberate steps, upright and poised, Teppy followed closely behind, hunched forward with a slight limp in his left leg, which dragged whenever he attempted to speed up to his brother's pace.

"We're close. Are you tired?" shouted Tuthmosis.

"No," said Teppy, intentionally giving a one-word answer so that his brother wouldn't suspect he was out of breath and falling behind.

Passing through the village was the only way to get to the river, and it was an exciting journey for Teppy. The village presented a whole new world, a welcome change from his secluded life in the palace. He was fascinated by the bustle of the town and loved seeing the people together with all the different animals, especially cats. One, mangy and bone-thin, was partially hidden under the brush. Teppy stopped following Tuthmosis and walked over for a closer look. The cat tried to lift itself from a lying position but couldn't do it because of a paralyzed hind leg.

By the time Tuthmosis turned back and found his brother, Teppy was holding the ailing cat in his arms.

"It's sick," Teppy said. "We have to take it home and cure it." He gently placed the cat on the ground. It didn't move, and Tuthmosis examined its frail body. "It's too late. The disease has overtaken it," he said.

They had seen the same purplish bruising on the cat's underside many times before on animals that had contracted the *disease*: the purplish mark being the first symptom and an inevitable sign of death to come.

"Can we take it home and try to cure it?" asked Teppy.

"There is no cure, Teppy. If we take it home and it dies, who do you think will get punished for it?"

His brother spoke the truth; still, it hurt to leave the animal, so Teppy sat on the ground and cradled the cat in his arms, caressing the top of its head.

"You're a good brother," said Tuthmosis, "much kinder than me, but you mustn't let others see you show such weakness, for if they do, they will pounce on you like a leopard. Do you understand?"

Although he really didn't understand, Teppy nodded anyway. How could he hide his weakness when everyone can look at his body and see it? Maybe Tuthmosis wasn't speaking of his deformity, he thought. Maybe his brother was talking about what was not visible—the weakness he carried in his heart.

Teppy saw his brother suddenly look worried. He was gazing at a group of villagers who were in turn, spying on them. The villagers coalesced from just three to a group of nine and were mumbling strange words under their breath as they approached them. The group paused and stared at the boys suspiciously before starting their approach again, intent on discovering who they really were. Teppy looked up at his brother as if asking his guidance on what to do next.

"You must do exactly as I tell you," he said to Teppy in a soft but firm voice. "Put the cat down, stand up, and take two steps back from it."

Teppy did as his brother commanded, pushing himself off the ground with both hands until he was able to stand. This had happened to them before: almost being recognized, almost getting caught. The tone of his brother's voice was a warning that they were close to being discovered again. "When I run, follow me," said Tuthmosis.

Teppy nodded.

Tuthmosis directed Teppy to walk straight ahead and not to look back. After only a moment of following his brother's instructions, Teppy gave in to his curiosity. He turned back and saw the villagers had stop following them and had circled the diseased cat. A soldier dressed in his combat uniform with a bow slung over his shoulders, stepped out from among the group and pointed at the boys. "Hey, you two!"

Tuthmosis took off running and Teppy lumbered behind him. As he ran he kept looking back over his shoulder at the soldier, who was now aiming an arrow at them. In an instant it whizzed past Tuthmosis's head.

"Why are they shooting arrows at us?" shouted Teppy. "What have we done?"

"They think we hurt the cat. Don't stop!"

The boys were fast approaching the river when Teppy began gasping for air. His struggle to keep up with Tuthmosis had exhausted him, and now he lagged behind at a slow and unsteady pace. This was not a dream where he could run like a gazelle, or hop and jump as high as he wanted. This was real life, and despite his best efforts, Teppy's deformities, his uneven shoulders, protruding hip, and curved spine, would sometimes cause him to lose his balance.

Two hundred cubits short of the river, Teppy fell. He didn't want his brother to notice, so he tried to pull himself up in a hurry and fell again.

"I don't want to run anymore!" Teppy cried out. "Why do we have to run?"

In tears, he lay helpless on the ground. Tuthmosis rushed over and, like so many times before, placed his brother's arm around his neck and lifted him off the ground.

As he carried Teppy, he leaned in to his brother's ear. "Hold your head high. You are a prince," he said, and throughout the rest of the path to the river, Teppy held his head as high as the proudest of royalty.

Once they reached the shore, Tuthmosis and Teppy pulled off their cloaks and kilts and immersed themselves in the cool waters of the river. It was Egypt's sole life sustainer, the flood of Isis's tears of sorrow over the death of her husband, the ancient god Osiris. The river kept the people from perishing due to starvation—the one retreat from the enclosure of the stone walls of the palace and the heat of the searing desert sun.

The boys swam and bathed in silence until Teppy spoke.

"In my dream, I can run fast and tall like you. My legs are strong like an ostrich, and I never fall."

"That's good, but when you dream you must also learn to erase every fear or doubt in your mind and believe with all your heart that there's a sharpened spear on the ground before you. If you truly believe it, one will appear for you as it did for me."

"And what did you do with it?"

Tuthmosis chuckled. "What do you think I did with it? I used the spear to slay the beast, and he has never appeared in my dreams again."

Teppy was amazed at his brother. "I wish I was just as brave."

"You'll dream again, little brother, and this time you'll be brave and kill the Amun beast. I'll show you how to use the spear to do it." He swam up close to Teppy. "But, first—"

Tuthmosis grinned before he flailed his arms and splashed water across Teppy's face. The boy shrieked and laughed as he tried to splash back, but Tuthmosis's arms were longer and faster. Their faces dripped with river water, and they were drowning in laughter until they heard their father's familiar shout.

"Tuthmosis!"

Amenhotep ambled angrily toward them trailed by his royal guards, and the boys' smiles disappeared. The pharaoh stopped right at the shoreline, exasperated. His sudden appearance made Teppy nervous, but Tuthmosis was unshaken. Then again, their father was not directing his stern gaze at Tuthmosis; he directed it at Teppy.

"Whose plan was it to defy my rules? Was it you Teppy?" said Amenhotep.

Before Teppy could speak the first word of his confession, Tuthmosis cut him off. "No, it was not him. My brother is innocent. It was me, Father. I wanted to cool off from the heat. I forced him to come."

Teppy trembled, guilt-ridden that his brother had taken the blame. But when Tuthmosis flashed him a wink at the very moment their father looked away, it calmed him.

"You were warned not to go into the river, were you not, Tuthmosis?" asked Amenhotep.

Tuthmosis waved his hand dismissively at his father. "The river is fine."

"The waters are infested with crocodiles, and where are the guards to protect you?" Amenhotep snapped.

Tuthmosis shook his head at Amenhotep and in a blatant act of rebelliousness, submerged himself in the river. Teppy watched his father swallow his anger at Tuthmosis by looking at the ground and grinding his teeth. A moment later Tuthmosis came up for air. "I'm not afraid of a stupid crocodile, Father. I would welcome the pleasure of killing it right here in the river with my bare hands. The Aten god protects me."

"Tuthmosis, you are the high priest of Amun. You have responsibilities to the temple."

"What about my responsibility to my own brother? Three times a day you make me go to that place and suffer. The Amun priests don't want me in their temple, Father, they treat me like dung."

"You belong there. You were divinely appointed."

"Appointed by you, and they despise me for it. Obviously, there's nothing divine about your appointments," said Tuthmosis.

Teppy could never speak that way to his father—if ever he had, he would be punished severely for it, even if his mother tried to intercede. He never understood why his father found it so easy to punish him while just as easily forgiving Tuthmosis. No matter how much Teppy tried to please his father, or how much he tried to show his affection for him, Amenhotep never loved him as much as he loved Tuthmosis.

Teppy quickly forgot about his grievances when creases formed on his father's face. Amenhotep doubled over, grasping his jaw. His guards rushed toward him, but he waved them away.

"What's wrong? Are you all right?" asked Tuthmosis.

"My son, please, come out of the water."

Tuthmosis waded onto shore and approached him. Amenhotep stood up straight but moved with difficulty.

"You are so much like your mother, always challenging me."

"Not her. I'm actually more like you. No one is more stubborn than you father."

Amenhotep forced a smile and motioned for Tuthmosis to come closer. He silently obeyed.

Teppy studied the interaction between his brother and father as they stood next to each other. Their faces were similar, but he shared no resemblance to either of them. While his face was narrow with a prominent nose, thick lips, and protruding chin, Tuthmosis's round face and pinched nose looked identical to their father's. It was surely the reason why his father loved his brother so much, so all Teppy would have to do to change this is to alter his face to appear more like them.

"It is written that you must fulfill your term as the high priest of Amun before you can become my co-ruler. Do you understand?" Amenhotep asked Tuthmosis in a weakened voice.

"I'm a far better warrior than I could ever be a priest," Tuthmosis remarked.

"Tuthmosis, do you understand?" his father repeated.

Tuthmosis was reluctant to answer. He despised being the high priest. Teppy didn't quite know why, except that the leopard-skin cloak that his brother had to wear smelled awful.

"I'll fulfill my term to the Amun god as you wish, but in my heart, I serve the Aten," said Tuthmosis relenting.

Amenhotep kissed him on the forehead. Jealousy stirred in Teppy. He waved at his father to get his attention.

"Good morning, Father," he said to him with a smile. Amenhotep glanced at him but addressed Tuthmosis instead. "Take him back to the palace and make your way to the temple," said Amenhotep, grasping his jaw again as he tried to contain the pain. He trudged back to his chariot with his guards, moaning with every step.

Teppy melted at the sight of his brother looking down on him in pity. It only affirmed what he had always felt—he wasn't worthy of acceptance by his father, and like it had been since his birth, he would forever be invisible to him.

CHAPTER

3

AMENHOTEP CRINGED in pain as Ay struggled to fasten his armor breastplate around his bloated torso.

"Stop! I can't continue with this!" he demanded. "Administer the cure now!"

For the healing properties of the cure to be effective, it needed to be administered by a priest. A former Amun priest such as Ay was sufficient enough for Amenhotep. He waited with bated breath as Ay retrieved a poppy plant he had hidden away in a pouch inside his garment. With a razor, he made an incision in the pod. A milky-white latex oozed from the capsule. Amenhotep opened his eager mouth wide so that Ay could squeeze every drop of the opium cure into it.

Watching them silently, Queen Ty stood at the entrance of Amenhotep's bedchamber dressed in a translucent, fine-pleated linen garment, adorned with semi-precious stones of turquoise, carnelian, and lapis-lazuli—the hair of the gods, as she called it.

She wore an ornate black wig, woven with gold and jewels. Shiny solid-gold jewelry hung from her neck and wrists, and her face was embellished with heavy makeup. Though the queen was adept at presenting herself extravagantly, her physical beauty had faded with age.

Ay closed the pouch the moment he saw her, bowed, and left the room. Amenhotep fastidiously put on the rest of his armor, purposefully depriving his wife the attention she craved.

"Why the war garments?"

Amenhotep didn't answer. He fastened the last buckle of his armor, grabbed his spear and shield, and shuffled away. Queen Ty followed him out of his bedchamber and down the winding palace corridor. "You're traveling to Nubia, aren't you?"

Amenhotep refused to acknowledge her.

"This was not the appointed time. Where is Tuthmosis?" she asked, the desperation rising in her voice. "Answer me!"

He turned and looked her in the eye. "He's where he should be, in the temple of Amun."

"You swore our son would join you in the Nubian battle."

"Tuthmosis will serve as high priest at the temple until the Montu god chooses him for war," he replied.

"Exactly when will that happen? After one of your mistresses becomes pregnant with a male child to take his place?"

Amenhotep walked out of the palace and down the steps to an ornate war chariot equipped for the most powerful ruler in the known world. Six uniformed Egyptian guards on horseback awaited him. Queen Ty strode after Amenhotep, close on his heels.

"He's a prince. The people need to see him as a victorious warrior. Please, let him go with you. It would make him so happy."

"I've made my decision," Amenhotep snarled back at her. "Tuthmosis will service the temple of Amun."

"A prince serves Egypt and should stand alongside his father in war!"

Her outburst had no effect on him. Amenhotep stepped into his war chariot that was amply suited for one driver and three passengers and turned back to the queen. "When the gods call for Tuthmosis to ride with me into battle, that's the day it will occur, not a moment sooner. For your own well-being, don't speak to me of this again."

He lifted his hand in the air, and Amenhotep and his guards dashed south toward the kingdom of Kush. Queen Ty scurried up the palace stairs and into her brother's chamber, desperate for his help.

The temple of Amun contained the sanctuary where the Amun god resided. The structure was built of white sandstone worked with gold, and its floors were purified in silver. The doorways and thirty-cubit-tall columns were made of electrum, an amber-colored alloy of silver and gold. Colorful banners hung from cedar poles perched atop red granite pedestals. No sunlight could penetrate the imposing darkness of the interior of the temple.

Tuthmosis was completing his duties as high priest there when twelve Amun priests entered. Their heads were clean-shaven, and they were all dressed in the same flaxen-hued robes. The priests knelt around an altar side-by-side and chanted as seven other priests entered, carrying burning incense. These seven priests encircled the shrine's doors.

Tuthmosis stepped up in his leopard-skin cloak and lit the torch of the shrine. He then broke the clay seal off the doors with his fist, knelt, lifted both hands in the air, and recited the Opening incantation:

"The gates of heaven open. The gates of earth are undone."

The massive doors of the shrine opened to an inner sanctuary. A gilded silver statuette of the Amun god—a soldier with a ram's head—sat on the altar. This represented the despicable god that desired to control his life. Unable to conceal his contempt for it,

Tuthmosis stepped inside, waited for the doors to close, and when he could see that no one was there in the inner sanctuary with him, he then stepped up to the statuette and spat in its face. It was the first time he had acted on the impulse. Satisfied, he continued on with the ceremonial "Feeding of the Gods," as was the duty of the high priest, by pouring out a blood-colored wine from the sacred vase into the first of seven bowls that surrounded the statuette.

Before he could fill the second bowl, a black mamba leapt out of it and slithered onto the floor.

Tuthmosis was so startled that he fell backward and dropped the vase, which shattered into tiny pieces. He glanced around the room searching for the snake, but it had disappeared. As he stood, all eyes were on him. Two Amun priests, the identical twins Sia and Neper, the leaders of the Amun priesthood, observed him intently from the entrance. They were bald and had shaved their bodies to be completely hairless; they had even shaved off their eyebrows and eyelashes. They were the Lector priests, the most powerful of all the priests in Thebes, distinguished by the pure white floor-length robes they wore.

"It was an accident," Tuthmosis murmured.

The priests did not respond.

"I underestimated how heavy the vase would be," Tuthmosis tried again.

The twins seemed unconvinced.

Amenhotep had taught his son that the twin priests wielded a superior form of magic that extended beyond this world into the afterlife. But Tuthmosis believed what was written in the scrolls of the former pharaohs of Egypt. Twins were an abomination. Only those who come from a line of immoral descendants could read each other's thoughts and finish each other's words as they could do. Was it possible they were reading his thoughts? Could they tell when he was lying to them? Or worse, did they witness him spit on the Amun statue?

It was when he turned to leave the inner sanctuary that the twins spoke.

"The illusion you saw of the snake—" said Sia.

"Is a premonition of what is to come," Neper finished.

Tuthmosis pondered their foreboding message as he stepped out into the outer sanctuary where he continued his duties of feeding the god he so vehemently despised.

Ay darted past the musicians into the entrance of the temple so that he wouldn't have to hear them playing their instruments. All music reminded him of the love he had lost. His wife, a flautist who had enchanted him with her ability to play beautiful melodies, had died six seasons before, thrown from her horse. Ay and his two young daughters were devastated and miserable without her. Ay searched for a new wife and mother to his children and found Teyla, an older woman who had no children of her own.

After Teyla and Ay married, Mundi and Sete, who had become withdrawn and mute because of the death of their mother, were speaking again. But Ay now despised the joviality of music and Amun's temple grounds were thick with harpists, lutenists, and flautists playing ritualistic melodies, musicians whose eyes had been singed shut with burning hot coals, so that the Horus god would reward their blindness with a total command of their musical instruments.

Once inside, Ay stopped in front of the ablution tank and washed his arms, hands and face. He spotted Tuthmosis exiting the inner sanctuary from across the room. On an urgent mission from the queen, he hurried up to him and whispered her message into his ear. Tuthmosis's eyes widened at the news, and the boy quickly undressed out of his leopard-skinned cloak and left the temple.

When Ay returned to the ablution tank to wash again, the twin priests, Sia and Neper, approached him from opposite sides.

"You now speak for the pharaoh?" Sia asked.

"No one speaks for the pharaoh. I am his manservant," said Ay.

Neper dropped a satchel at Ay's feet. Lapis-lazuli stones spilled out on the floor. "Then you should advise your master—"

"To give his petty stipend to the Aten priests." Sia finished his brother's thought.

"But if he wants the blessings of Amun—" Neper continued.

"Then he must give us a respectable tribute that's worthy of the highest of all the gods," said Sia.

There was no difference in the sound of the twins' voices, both were identically soft-spoken, and the timbre was hollow and raspy. Every word they said, no matter how harsh or benign, exuded authority. Ay crouched down on the floor and collected the stones one by one into the satchel trying not to appear intimidated. "The pharaoh says the war with Nubia will yield an abundance of gold and ivory for the temple of Amun," he said.

"Really? The pharaoh promises many things, but if this one does not occur as he says—" Neper warned.

"Then we will cease our prayers and offerings to Amun on the pharaoh's behalf," Sia concluded.

Taken aback by this threat, Ay looked up at the priests. "That is unnecessary. The pharaoh's word is honorable."

"We will see," said Sia.

Ay placed the last lapis-lazuli stone in the satchel and walked away. Though he still bore the appearance of an Amun priest himself—a shaved head and a tall, thin, and frail body, Ay never cared for piety. He had abandoned his loyalty to the priesthood the moment of his appointment as manservant to the pharaoh, a service of its own divine calling.

Outside the palace, another royal chariot awaited. This one was smaller, with room for only a driver and one passenger. Tuthmosis ran to the chariot and smiled at his mother who stood there waiting for him.

"I've dreamt of this day for so long, Mother," Tuthmosis said as he fastened the leather strap of his copper war helmet under his chin.

"So have I, my son," replied Queen Ty eagerly assisting him to put on his gear.

It had been an easy decision for Ty to defy her husband and tell her son of the campaign in Nubia. Her position as queen and chief wife to Amenhotep would be surely sealed by a son that was known as a warrior at the side of his father. Any queen who had given birth to such an heir would be revered by the people of Egypt as the divine mother who had birthed a god.

"Be brave and courageous and return your father home safely to me," she added.

Tuthmosis kissed his mother's cheek. "I'll be his right hand. No harm will come to him, I promise."

Tuthmosis mounted his chariot. "When you see me again, Egypt will have its victory. Tell my little brother I'll be back for him."

Queen Ty kissed his hand. "Go, son, quickly."

Tuthmosis raised his hand, and the chariot sped away.

"Wait! Tuthmosis!" Teppy shouted, racing down the steps after him. When he reached the last stair, he stumbled. Queen Ty caught him in time to break his fall.

"Let him go," she said to Teppy holding him tightly.

"Where is he going? I want to go with him."

The queen embraced him. "Your brother has gone to war against the Nubians."

Teppy frowned.

"Why are you sad, my little prince?"

"I didn't get to say goodbye."

"There's no need for goodbyes. He'll soon return, and when he does, he will be co-ruler of Egypt alongside his father, forever revered by the people."

Queen Ty and Teppy stood together, in each other's arms as they watched Tuthmosis's chariot disappear in the distance.

CHAPTER

4

ACROSS A VAST STRETCH of the Nubian Desert, five thousand Egyptian soldiers stood in battle formation, two thousand horse-drawn chariots lined in front of them. Each chariot held a shield man, a bowman, and a driver. Two thousand infantrymen carried spears and leather shields in the rear of the formation. The exhausted army remained still as Amenhotep reviewed the front line from his royal chariot.

Nasheret, his general, a bull of a man and nine years his senior, stood next to Amenhotep as the driver directed the chariot along the path. The general's face was heavily scarred and blotches of skin on both his arms protruded in places where it had been sewn back together but had never completely healed. Nasheret's battle wounds were like an amulet of honor to the general, and no one was more proud of Nasheret's wounds than Amenhotep.

"Here we are again," said Amenhotep, looking out in the distance. "You would think after three wars they would just pay us the tribute."

Nasheret spat on the ground. "A degenerate people like the Nubians will always prefer death over concession."

"That would be an admirable quality, general, not a degenerate one," said Amenhotep.

He took a closer look at the front line of his army. "Our infantry looks like plucked birds, especially the Libyans that you've positioned throughout the front line. Have you drained them of all their strength?" asked Amenhotep.

"I assure you that because of my reputation, the Libyans are more than eager to fight for Egypt."

Nasheret's bumptiousness irritated the pharaoh, though he knew it was useful in motivating the army. On this day, however, because of his toothache, he had no patience for the general's boasting. "Eagerness alone does not win a war, general."

"My Pharaoh, I have trained this army extremely well in the art of engagement. As you are aware, I've led them in three battles against the Nubians and was easily victorious."

A sparrow hawk returning to its nest in a nearby willow tree interrupted their debate when it flew above their heads with its prey captured between its claws.

"As a child, general, did your father tell you the story of the little bird and the crocodile?"

Perplexed by the question, Nasheret squinted at the pharaoh. "No."

Amenhotep nodded. He'd told the story to Tuthmosis and Teppy once before.

"There was a little bird that wandered into a marsh where a lone crocodile lived. The crocodile was friendly, and soon the bird would perch on the crocodile's snout and take rides across the river. Every day this would happen. The bird perched on the crocodile's snout and the crocodile swam around the river. One day, the little bird told his father about the friendly creature. The father bird was skeptical, so he flew to the marsh to see if what his son was telling him was true. The little bird told his father to watch. It then perched on the crocodile's snout and in the blink of an eye, the crocodile devoured it. The distraught father asked the crocodile why he ate his son when many times before he had been friendly with him. The crocodile replied, 'You should have taught your son, there's always a risk of being eaten when riding on the snout of a crocodile.'"

Amenhotep checked Nasheret's face to make sure he had understood the message. "We're always on the nose of the crocodile, general," he said before signaling his driver to stop. The effectiveness of the cure was fading and Amenhotep's toothache grew more severe. He moaned as he placed his hand against his cheek.

"My pharaoh, if you're not well enough to fight. I can lead this army alone and have a remnant circle you for protection."

Repelled by the general's suggestion, Amenhotep stood up straight and ignored the pain. "I'm forever strengthened by the gods Amun and Montu."

Nasheret stepped down from the pharaoh's chariot and bowed to him. "And may Amun and Montu fight our battles, and may you, my magnificent pharaoh, live—"

The rumbling sounds of war drums in the distance interrupted him.

On the far side of the battlefield, the Nubian army emerged from the cliffs three thousand men strong—a little over half the size of the Egyptian army. The one thousand horse-drawn chariots they possessed were inferior to the workmanship and ingenuity of the Egyptians' two thousand chariots whose axles were covered in metal, reducing the friction between the wooden parts. This lightened the load on the horses and improved their performance far beyond the all-wood construction of the Nubian chariot.

A thousand Nubian spearmen on horseback rode in front, followed by a thousand bowmen on foot and another thousand spearmen marching behind them. The Nubians formed within twelve hundred cubits of the Egyptian army, unintimidated by Amenhotep's grand display. Suddenly, all became quiet.

Nasheret stepped into his chariot and faced his troops. "We battle for our great Pharaoh Amenhotep!" he exclaimed. The army rattled their swords and shields. Amenhotep turned and faced them as well, shouting, "We battle for Amun and Montu! We battle for Egypt!"

The army roared. Amenhotep nodded at Nasheret. When the general raised his shield, the army charged full speed toward the Nubians.

Tuthmosis's chariot arrived at the northern bluff during the initial attack. The Egyptians charged toward the Nubians, and Tuthmosis raised his shield and alerted his driver to speed them toward the battle.

Below, the Egyptians' mighty chariots ripped through the Nubian front line, striking down the Nubian infantry to just a quarter of its original size. Those who were fortuitous enough not to be trampled or speared by the onslaught scattered into open areas where they were struck down by the hundreds of arrows from the Egyptian archers. The Nubian archers returned arrows as best they could, but the volleys were easily deflected by the Egyptian army's copper shields. Amenhotep pointed to specific areas of the battlefield and barked orders, urging his men on and guiding them as they impaled, decapitated, or dismembered the Nubian soldiers with their spears and battle axes.

Once the Nubian lines broke, the battle descended into chaos, and Amenhotep went to spearing Nubians from his chariot. Their arrows shot at him, but his shield man blocked them as the pharaoh continued killing enemy soldiers. Amenhotep had come close to death many times, but he had always emerged from battle unharmed. He proclaimed this was the work of Montu, the god of war that protected him.

His chariot driver instinctively made a 180-degree turn. A Nubian spotted him and shot an arrow into the horse's belly. The horse neighed in agony and rose on its hind legs, hurling Amenhotep out. The pharaoh tumbled in the dust as another Nubian warrior rushed over with a spear in hand. As Amenhotep turned over, the warrior raised the spear above his chest ready to thrust it in for the kill.

There was a muffled sound of impact. Drops of blood sprinkled on Amenhotep's face. The pointed tip of an arrow jutted out of the Nubian's chest, just before the warrior dropped dead to the ground. Amenhotep tried to make out the identity of his savior but only the rear of the soldier's chariot was visible as it raced back into the heart of the battle.

The battle with the Nubians wound down as the desert sun sank behind the horizon. The fierce confrontation was over, and hundreds of dead bodies littered the field and bled into the cracks of the dry sand. Egypt had lost many of their soldiers to the carnage, but it was a negligible loss compared to the number of dead Nubians. A party of Egyptian soldiers was left with the task of combing the grounds and spearing the hearts of the wounded Nubians still squirming or moaning among the corpses. This was Amenhotep's grandest act of mercy.

The healthiest Nubians were spared and taken prisoners, bound by rope at their waists, ankles, and wrists and made to stand in a single-file line for inspection. Exhausted, Amenhotep and Nasheret strolled along the line together examining each one of them.

"There's over two hundred of them. The rest are wounded and desperate for their death blow," said the general, proud of his coffle.

They paused in front of a Nubian outfitted in red and yellow, a salient difference from the blanched uniforms of the other prisoners.

Under his kilt, his thighs and calves were unusually thick and muscular and his forehead and cheekbones pronounced. His sinewy body was covered with smooth and unblemished skin that was dark as the night. He jerked at his rope restraints, unaffected by the pharaoh's presence.

"I suspect he's an officer," Nasheret said.

Amenhotep stepped up to examine him. Without warning, the Nubian lunged forward the one-half cubit that his rope restraints had allowed him. Nasheret took one step back and unsheathed his dagger.

"No need for that, general," said Amenhotep. "His restraints will hold him."

The Nubian's sudden act of aggression intrigued Amenhotep. He stepped up close to the prisoner and faced him.

"So what are you? A general? A captain?"

The Nubian eyed the pharaoh but didn't answer. His vibrant garment was tattered and his arms thoroughly tattooed. The symbols made no sense to Amenhotep; it was a language he did not understand.

"This carnage could have been avoided if you would have listened to the Mitannians and paid us the tribute," Amenhotep said.

The Nubian prisoner remained silent. The pharaoh assumed him incapable of communication in any tongue but his own pagan language. When he took a step to leave, he discovered differently.

"You foolish little man," the prisoner said in perfect Egyptian. "Do you really think the Hittites and the Mitanni will continue to honor your frivolous peace treaties? We will all unite against you one day; the Hittites, the Mitannians, and my Nubian kingdom will unite to bring Egypt to its knees. And when we tear you from your country, pharaoh, and throw your worthless corpse to the dogs, know that your precious Egyptian people will celebrate your death with us."

Nasheret was enraged at the Nubian's every word. "Let me carve the eyes out of his head for you, my Pharaoh," he pleaded and unsheathed his dagger again. Amenhotep stopped him with a raising of his hand.

"No," Amenhotep answered. Then he turned and walked away.

Confused, Nasheret returned his dagger to its scabbard and trailed him. "So what shall I do with him?"

"Unbind him. Let him return to his land of Kush."

"That would be madness! Why would we do such a thing?"

"His king needs to know what to expect if he doesn't release the tribute to us."

"We can go there and take the tribute."

"No. They will give it to us. Willingly."

"My pharaoh, he's a valuable prisoner of war. He could even be an officer."

Amenhotep's patience with Nasheret had come to an end. He stopped and faced him.

"Did you understand my order, general? Let him go."

Nasheret spat on the ground again before trudging back over to the Nubian and staring him in the face.

Amenhotep had recognized the Nubian captive as his equal in rank and demeanor. What sort of man kills a restrained opponent and feels victorious? Honor to Amenhotep was like the air he breathed. He couldn't survive long without it, and he granted it liberally to even his worst enemy.

Nasheret unsheathed his dagger and cut the Nubian's rope restraints. The Nubian shot a furtive glance at Nasheret.

"Don't be mistaken. I would've loved to have slaughtered you instead," Nasheret said, as he lifted his kilt and urinated in the Nubian's direction.

The harsh sound of Amenhotep's shrill voice calling out to him took his attention from the Nubian captive, and after he shook himself off and ordered additional guards to preside over the remaining prisoners, Nasheret rushed back to his pharaoh's side.

A hundred cubits away, a damaged Egyptian chariot approached slowly. The driver appeared injured. His right arm was in a sling and wrapped in bloodstained bandages from his wrist to his shoulder and tied around his neck. Another soldier walked alongside the chariot, directing its famished horse through the maze of dead bodies and body parts scattered throughout the battleground. The driver's bruised and scarred face was familiar to Amenhotep.

"The dust in the wind has weakened my eyes. Identify those two soldiers for me," he said to Nasheret.

"The man walking alongside the chariot is Horemheb, one of our best-skilled captains. The soldier driving the chariot is the one whose arrow saved your life today, my Pharaoh. It is your son, Tuthmosis."

"Who? How can that be?"

Amenhotep strained to focus on the soldier driving the chariot. It indeed was Tuthmosis. Stunned and confused, the pharaoh vacillated between gratitude to his son for saving his life and intense anger that he once again had disobeyed him. It was disheartening to see that his son was scarred and injured. But this offense was the worst ever committed by Tuthmosis—a blasphemy against Amun and the war god Montu. It didn't matter he had saved his life.

"You can defy me all you want, my son, but you must never defy the almighty god Amun. You will leave this battlefield now and return to the temple where you will plead for forgiveness at the foot of his statue!"

Weak from his injuries, Tuthmosis struggled to stand straight in his chariot as it continued to approach. He used all the strength he had left to shout back to Amenhotep. "I'm not a priest, Father. I am a warrior. I don't care about Amun or Montu. You're my father. I should be by your side fighting with—"

An arrow ripped through Tuthmosis's neck, and blood sprayed across his breastplate. His defiant expression changed to one of shock. Blood dripped from the corners of his mouth as he fell forward.

Amenhotep screamed and whipped around to find the assailant.

Behind him, the Nubian prisoner bore a proud grin as he nocked a second arrow and aimed it at the pharaoh himself. Still in shock, Amenhotep froze. Before he or Nasheret could react, Captain Horemheb sprinted with the grace of a panther full tilt toward the Nubian with a spear in his hand, launched himself through the air, and, at the pinnacle of his leap, released his weapon. There was a sickening crunch as Horemheb's spear pierced the Nubian's skull. The bow and arrow dropped from the Nubian's hands, and his dead weight fell to the ground.

Amenhotep ran over to Tuthmosis's chariot. "Not my son. Amun, I beg you, spare him, not my son."

Amenhotep prayed it wasn't as severe as it had looked. The arrow couldn't have slashed clean through his son's neck. But all hope vanished when the men reached Tuthmosis.

Nasheret and Horemheb helped lift Tuthmosis's limp body from the chariot and placed the boy in his father's arms. There was a reverent silence as Amenhotep cradled and rocked his son as he had done the day he was born.

CHAPTER

5

THE PRIESTS' majestic healing temple stood adjacent to Amenhotep's palace. It was an uninviting structure, oddly dark and brooding for a temple originally designed to bring good health and rejuvenation. In the center of one of its darkest rooms, Tuthmosis lay suspended on a platform hung between four cat-shaped columns, with a cloth wrapped around his neck and arm. Hundreds of lit candles flickered around the perimeter, yet the light was not enough to completely illuminate the unconscious figure.

Meri-Ra unwrapped the bandages and replaced them with new ones. He was a priest of the Aten god and much younger than the Amun priests who practiced at the temple. Dressed in gray hooded robes, the Aten priests were the only faction of priests Tuthmosis had respected and even revered. They were the gatekeepers of his almighty sun-god, the Aten.

Meri-Ra placed a concave vessel down on the platform next to Tuthmosis. He dipped a cloth into it and washed Tuthmosis's wounded arm with ox blood. It was not a familiar treatment for a puncture wound, and Amenhotep was skeptical of it.

"This is not the ritual of the Amun priests," Amenhotep said to him.

Without pausing from his work, Meri-Ra responded. "Were you not aware your son despised the Amun god? I am Meri-Ra, a priest of the Aten, my Pharaoh. I am not an Amun priest."

"Then promise me that the Aten god will save him," said Amenhotep.

Meri-Ra stopped for a moment. He glided his hand over Tuthmosis's chest area. "Where is the Aten amulet?" he asked. "It should have been around his neck."

"What amulet? I've never seen him wearing one."

"The Aten high priest gave him the amulet to wear for his protection."

"Enough with the amulet!" Amenhotep shouted. "Can the Aten god save him?"

Before Meri-Ra could answer, Sia entered the room with Neper, carrying a burlap sack, right behind him.

"There is no power greater than Amun," Sia said. "Have you forgotten what was written in the scrolls, my Pharaoh?" he asked.

Amenhotep shook his head. "No, I have not."

Sia glared at Meri-Ra. A sneer spread across his face. "Why is this Aten priest here in our sacred home?"

"The combined power of Amun and the Aten will surely heal my son," said Amenhotep.

"You're mistaken, Pharaoh. Neither the Aten nor its priests possess healing powers inside the temple of the almighty Amun god," Sia replied.

Meri-Ra expected the pharaoh to admonish Sia for the interruption or at least admit that he had given him permission to do his healing work. Amenhotep did neither, so Meri-Ra picked up his vessel and exited the room.

The twins took Meri-Ra's place at the altar.

Neper removed pieces of raw oxen flesh from the sack and placed it on Tuthmosis's neck and chest. Sia touched his limbs six times with a bronze snake wand. As he touched them the seventh time, he recited a healing spell:

"Punish the accuser, the master of those who allow decay to seep into this flesh, this head, these shoulders, this neck—"

Neper continued the incantation. *"I belong to Amun, says he. It is I who will guard this man from his enemies—"*

In the corner of the room, a nine-cubit-high solid gold statue in the form of an Egyptian pharaoh wearing a double-plumed crown and holding a scepter in his hand shook and rattled. Amenhotep knelt down and prostrated himself in front of the trembling Amun statue. Queen Ty entered the room as the shaking dissipated and Sia completed his spell:

"His guide shall be Thoth who lets writing speak, who creates the books, who passes on the knowledge. We are those of whom the gods wish to be kept alive."

Neper removed the raw oxen flesh from Tuthmosis's body and returned it to his satchel. This was exactly what the queen feared, that the Amun priests would give up on her son too quickly. Queen Ty could not accept such a facile surrender, but Amenhotep would accept whatever the priests of Amun told him.

"Please, you have to try again," she said to Sia.

The priest avoided eye contact with her, so she turned to Neper. "What about the Aten Priests? Let Meri-Ra try."

"The Aten is powerless to the will of Amun," Neper replied. "And Amun has judged Tuthmosis," Sia concluded.

Amenhotep approached Sia directly. "What is the judgment?"

Sia shook his head, and both he and Neper left the room.

Queen Ty's eyes swelled with tears. She went over to Amenhotep and took his hand, although it became clear he had not a glint of empathy for her grief.

"How did he know of the battle?" Amenhotep asked her suspiciously.

Fear made the queen's blood to rush through her veins. "No one was more resourceful than Tuthmosis. The secrets you hid from him he would soon enough uncover."

Amenhotep pulled his hand violently from hers and plodded away.

With her heart in her throat, the queen approached Tuthmosis's platform and caressed his face. "You will live throughout eternity in the afterlife, my beautiful son." She choked back a sob. How would she tell Teppy?

The pharaoh's guards announced that the army had returned from the Nubian battle, so Teppy searched the palace excitedly for his brother. When he didn't find him inside, he peered out over the balcony. A remnant of the Egyptian army carried crates filled with hundreds of Nubian body parts; arms, legs, and heads were all dumped in a massive pile to be burned for the amusement of the citizens. Teppy had witnessed such rituals before and had grown accustomed to them. He had even once seen his father decapitate a man that had disobeyed his commands. 'If your head comes off, it's because you did not do as you were told,' Amenhotep later said. It was the first of his father's laws he memorized.

Two hours had passed since the army's return. Why hadn't his brother searched the palace to look for him? He surmised that wherever he might find his mother, Tuthmosis would be nearby. Teppy asked one of the palace guards about his mother's whereabouts and was told that he would find her in the healing temple. When he found his way there into the inner sanctuary, he saw Tuthmosis laying on the platform with his mother kissing his forehead. Teppy ran over to her and grabbed hold of her hand. He looked up at his brother and frowned. "Why is Tuthmosis sleeping, Mother? Is he tired from his journey?"

Queen Ty was unsure how to respond. Teppy was no stranger to the causes of death, but she had taught him that he and his brother were immune to it. Tuthmosis was the son of the Aten. His life would surely be long and filled with great accomplishments. Royalty was the next step to immortality, a belief the queen had instilled in both her sons from the beginning. She could now only delay the inevitability of telling Teppy the painful truth.

"Yes, he's tired," she finally answered.

"Can I wake him?"

The queen turned her head away from him so that he couldn't see her wipe her teary eyes dry. She took a swallow and masked her voice to sound unaffected by the tragedy. "Not now, my little prince. Your brother has to sleep for a very, very long time."

"Why? He never sleeps for a long time. He's always awake before me."

Queen Ty paused to search her thoughts for an answer.

"I know," she replied. "And starting today he will need to sleep more than he ever has."

Teppy looked confused. He took the amulet from around his neck. "I must give this to him."

"No," she said, and placed it back around his neck.

"He needs it, Mother. It will protect him in his dreams."

She shook her head. "He doesn't need it any longer, Teppy. Tuthmosis is with the Aten now. He is a god among gods."

In her chamber, Ty cleaned Tuthmosis's soldier's uniform, washing and scrubbing it over and over until the skin on her palms chaffed from blisters. It was the one possession the queen had left of her son, and she spent many nights after his death obsessed with it. Ay entered as she once again dipped Tuthmosis's helmet into the ablution tank and scrubbed it with a boar's hair brush.

"My sister, you have to stop this or Amenhotep will sense you are hiding something."

"When he finds proof that I sent our son into battle, he will dispose of me anyway."

"He won't discover what he's never told."

"It doesn't matter what one tells him, Ay. He suspects me."

The queen went back to her work. She wiped the helmet dry and polished it with beeswax and a cloth.

"Tuthmosis was a brave warrior. Your courageous son saved his father's life," said Ay.

He stepped forward and took the helmet from her. "And you, my sister, no matter what you are feeling now, did what was honorable for Egypt."

Unable to hold back her grief any longer, Ty broke down in tears. "He was not supposed to die! God of Bes, forgive me. Forgive me for what I've done!"

Ay put the helmet back into the ablution tank and took her hand. "My queen, his death was not of your doing. The Amun god passed judgment on him."

"Amun passed judgement on him the day he was born. I curse Amun and all his priests! I curse them to my very soul!" she cried out and yanked her hand free of his grip. "They let him die when they could have saved him!"

"My dear sister, his wounds were too severe. No god could have saved him."

Ty grew offended at his continued defense of the priests. "They have deceived you just as they have deceived everyone else in this city, and how much longer before I, myself, am banished from this palace?"

Tears streamed down Queen Ty's face, carrying with them the black kohl that outlined her eyes and the bronze makeup that highlighted her cheeks. It all mixed into a dark-reddish stain on the shoulders of her silk dress. How long would it be before she was replaced by one of his younger and more beautiful wives that would detest her presence, one that was fertile and more than capable of bearing her husband a strong and virile son? Ty wept over what she feared would be her eventual loss of royalty and her consequent banishment because of the death of her son—the heir to the throne of Egypt.

"You are still the queen of this land, and you will remain so," Ay interrupted, trying to ease despair. "You must think of Teppy. He'll need your guidance now more than ever if he is to become the new heir to his father's throne. You have to be strong for him."

In her self-pity, Ty had forgotten about Teppy and that he too was an heir to the throne of his father.

"Yes, Teppy, my beloved son, Teppy," she sighed. "But how can I be strong for him after all that has happened?" she asked.

Ay grabbed his sister by her shoulders and pulled her close. "My dear sister, look at me."

Ty calmed herself enough to look him in the eye.

"You must!" he shouted.

A voice emerged from the entrance of the room. "And what must she do?"

Queen Ty and her brother were startled at Amenhotep standing in the doorway watching them. The queen turned and wiped her eyes dry. If Amenhotep had heard what she and Ay had been discussing, particularly that she had sent Tuthmosis off to battle, she feared he would have her decapitated right there in her chambers. And what then would become of Teppy? She adored him as much as she adored Tuthmosis, and if she was killed, he would be left with no one.

"Go on, Ay. What must she do?" Amenhotep repeated.

The queen saved her brother by speaking first.

"I was reluctant to tell my brother of a dream that haunted me. He thought he could help me decipher the meaning," she said. "But it is of no matter," she added, glancing at Ay.

Ay turned and bowed before Amenhotep. "If that is all, I will take my leave, my Pharaoh."

Amenhotep waved him out dismissively and Ay exited the queen's chamber. Amenhotep began searching the room, rummaging through his wife's clothing and jewelry.

"What are you looking for?" she asked.

Wanting to appear as if she were consoling him, she touched his arm. He pulled away from her and resumed his search.

"Where is his armor?" Amenhotep barked.

The queen retrieved Tuthmosis's helmet from the tank and held it out to him. "You're weak," she said. "You should rest."

"I am not weak!" he snapped, snatching the helmet. He stared at it, dissatisfied. "Where's the rest of it?"

"In his bedchamber."

He turned and strode toward the chamber exit.

"Amenhotep, wait."

Amenhotep paused, his back still turned to her. Despite her fears, Ty needed to make some connection with him in their grief.

"Tuthmosis loved you more than any god or human in this world. There is nothing either one of us could have done to stop him from risking his life for you, and for Egypt. He would've wanted us united in his absence," she said.

Without a word, Amenhotep left her chamber, leaving the queen to wade in her river of guilt alone.

CHAPTER

6

DESPITE THE QUEEN and the pharaoh's somber mood, their royal reception hall brimmed with military captains and soldiers eager to celebrate their victory over the Nubians with a commemoration to Montu, the god of war. For the special occasion, Amenhotep requested the most agile dancers and gifted musicians from the faraway land of Byblos to dance and parade around the reception hall like domestic animals, begging to please their masters in prostration to the Amun god—a ridiculous ritual in the eyes of Queen Ty.

Four female musicians from Egypt were chosen to join the others. They sat on the floor playing indigenous music on double-reed pipes, harps, sistras, and tambourines.

In the center of the hall, at the head of a massive slab that stretched the length of the room, Amenhotep hosted the festivities garbed in his new war armor. Queen Ty sat next to him dressed in her best silk and jewels. On the other side of Amenhotep sat Lady Lupita, Amenhotep's secondary wife, the sister of Artassumara— king of Mitanni.

The remaining seats in the reception hall were filled by military officers and palace officials shouting over the music boisterously. Victory banquets were the types of events the queen could do without. If she had not been told that Lupita would be attending, she would have remained in her palace chamber, away from the debauchery of the soldiers and their desire to be surrounded by nude female servants with oversized breasts, catering to their every whim. This was beneath her, but she could not allow her husband's secondary wife to be seen there without her in attendance. It was necessary for the high-ranking officials to witness her consuming a meal with her husband as a symbol of their unity.

Queen Ty forced a welcoming smile at Lupita who returned her gesture with the same disingenuousness.

The girl was strikingly beautiful and was just fourteen years of age when she arrived a year earlier in Thebes to marry Amenhotep, accompanied by three hundred and seventeen maidservants. Though Queen Ty easily matched Lupita's number of attendees, she could not compete with her youth. The young girl's olive toned skin was perfectly kissed by the sun, and her eyelashes were naturally long and curved above the hazel pupils of her eyes. She had dimples in her cheeks that made her smile even more inviting. Her breasts were perky and her hips appeared overly developed because of her tiny waist. Every one of the young girl's physical features appeared to be molded by the hands of a master sculptor, and what was even worse for the queen was that Lupita's disposition was humble and kind, the abundance of which, along with her femininity, had enchanted Amenhotep. It all made for an alluring combination impossible for Queen Ty to outdo.

The smile she shared with Lupita shifted into a stare of contempt when the young girl turned her attention away from her and toward her animal. Lupita caressed a white cat perched on her lap. His name was Bastian, and he had sea-green eyes and a solid gold collar fitted with a ruby medallion that glistened around his neck.

The queen loathed Lupita's cat as much as she secretly envied her. Its presence at the banquet served as another entity united against her right to happiness with her husband.

At Amenhotep's table everyone feasted on platters of salted fish, honey-roasted gazelle, breads, grains, and fruits. When they finished the wine and beer from their jars, nude female servants returned to refill them. Nasheret was already inebriated. Horemheb sat beside him. The drunken general stood to pay homage to the pharaoh.

"Here, here! My fellow warriors, listen here!" boomed Nasheret. Queen Ty was pleased that no one was listening. The room remained noisy until a soldier stood up from the table and shouted at them.

"My good men, please, let the general speak!" The hall went silent, and the musicians stopped playing. To the dismay of Queen Ty, Nasheret received the attention he sought.

"Let us salute the almighty god Amun for our victory over Nubia and honor the war god Montu with the tribute we bring to them and divide among ourselves."

The soldiers all cheered, and the musicians once again played.

Queen Ty eyed Amenhotep as he placed his hand on top of Lupita's hand, but her attention was drawn away by the troupe of seven female dancers entering the room. They wore gold bands across their hips and gold collars around their necks. They moved through the hall in black wigs with long, thick braided ponytails, their breasts exposed, chanting an incantation as they danced to the music.

Nasheret picked up his jar and slammed it on the table.

"You!" he barked, pointing at a female servant. "Fill my jar!"

"You've drunk too much already," replied Horemheb.

"What business is it of yours how much I drink?" slurred Nasheret as he tried to stand up again. The servant returned and poured more beer into his jar.

"Here! My fellow warriors. Listen!" Nasheret shouted attempting to continue his speech. "May our pharaoh, the living god, Amenhotep the Third, live a thousand years!"

Midway through his salute, Nasheret tilted to the side almost falling over but caught himself.

The soldiers at the table rose to their feet cheering Amenhotep's name. The pharaoh nodded, and they returned to their seats, all except Nasheret. His eyes were fixed on Lupita.

"And behold Lady Lupita. What beauty she brings to Egypt."

Lupita looked away, uncomfortable with the attention. The queen, however, didn't flinch. With those words, Nasheret uncovered her deepest vulnerability—Lupita's beauty. And praising it in front of everyone at the banquet without acknowledging her beauty was insulting and humiliating to her honor.

"He's making a mockery of me," she said into Amenhotep's ear. "He should be removed from this table."

"It's the wine," Amenhotep responded. "Stop your bickering; he's the general of my army."

Amenhotep returned to devouring his plate of roasted gazelle.

Shamed by her husband, Queen Ty contemplated ways she could excuse herself from the banquet without causing a scene.

"May you, Lupita, give birth to many royal children," Nasheret continued, "and bring forth to our pharaoh a new male heir. This time, a courageous one who won't rebel against his own father," he said with a smirk.

Amenhotep abruptly dropped the meat back on his plate. His breathing accelerated. He exhaled and inhaled deep from within his diaphragm while his head hung down, staring at his food.

"Come, let's drink and chant to the birth of royal children!" shouted Nasheret as he gulped down another jar of beer.

Horemheb pulled him down to his seat and whispered something in his ear. Nasheret broke free and stood up again. "I'll sit when I please, and you will address a decorated general with respect, captain."

Amenhotep stood and walked up to Nasheret. He looked him in the eye, smiled, then took a position directly behind him. It appeared odd to Queen Ty that Amenhotep was just standing there like a shadow to the general, staring at the ceiling.

Nasheret acknowledged the pharaoh's presence with a perfunctory bow and returned his attention back to everyone at the table. "Gentlemen, now that the pharaoh is here by my side, let him bear witness to how I speared three Nubian heathens in one thrust. The incompetent beasts were no—"

Before he could say another word, Amenhotep grabbed Nasheret from behind and put him in a chokehold. Nasheret struggled to pry himself free but could not match the pharaoh's animalistic strength. Amenhotep squeezed harder around Nasheret's throat in his determination to strangle the life out of him. After an inordinate amount of time, the general's kicking and grunting ceased, and his body lay lifeless against Amenhotep's chest. The pharaoh sat the dead general down in his seat with his head tilted back and spoke to him as if he were still alive and capable of hearing.

"My son never rebelled against me. He was a courageous warrior, one that will be remembered throughout eternity for his bravery. Your lying tongue betrays you."

Amenhotep took a flint knife from his belt, pried Nasheret's mouth open and with one deft swipe, cut out his tongue. He then turned his attention to Captain Horemheb. "Tomorrow you will go to Nubia and install an Egyptian outpost. Return the Nubian tribute to me, *General* Horemheb."

Astounded by his unexpected promotion, Horemheb stood up and bowed.

"And, general," continued Amenhotep, "if you encounter any resistance from the Nubians, kill them all."

"By your order, my Pharaoh," Horemheb responded.

Amenhotep tossed Nasheret's bloody tongue across the floor and returned to his seat next to a stunned Queen Ty. If she thought her husband had silenced Nasheret in her defense, she might have been gratified, but all he had proven was that her pride didn't matter to him, only his own.

"Pathetic," she muttered under her breath.

Queen Ty leaned into Amenhotep's ear. "How noble of you to defend only your own honor," she whispered.

The queen rose from her seat and exited the room leaving all eyes on Amenhotep. He stood up and gave the musicians a hand signal and they returned to their positions and played again. Everyone else returned to eating and drinking as Nasheret's blood poured out from his nose and mouth. As if by command, over a dozen cats appeared from every corner of the room, jumped one by one onto the table and licked the general's blood. No one dared to scatter them away, for they were the divine creatures of the Bastet goddess that kept the rats from flooding the room and devouring their banquet feast.

Horemheb was not the only one Amenhotep had given strict orders to that day. He had also spoken to Ay, ordering him to appear before the Amun priests, Sia and Neper. Amenhotep wanted confirmation that the priests had performed the customary invocation for Tuthmosis—a prayer and spell to lead his son to a safe passage through the afterlife and to his eventual return to the land of the living.

Only Sia and Neper had the authority and knowledge to recite invocations, a privilege of the lector priests of Amun, the most powerful of the sect. Because the two priests were aware that Tuthmosis despised the Amun god and worshipped the Aten, Amenhotep had to rely on Ay's association as a former Amun priest himself to convince them to forgive his son's blasphemy. Ay gave Amenhotep his word he would not return without Sia's and Neper's assurances that they would complete the invocation. Without it,

Tuthmosis's spirit was destined to be forever lost, unable to reunite with his body.

As Ay approached the courtyard of the Amun temple, farmers accompanied by the eldest of their families began lining up around the perimeter of the complex. This was the first morning of the solstice, an occasion that required that every farmer who wanted to receive the harvest blessing of the Amun god, appear and pay their share of taxes to its priests. Ay navigated through the crowd of roaming animals and donkeys carrying sacks of grain across their backs until he came upon Sia and Neper standing at the head of the line. Sia was checking off a list of names and taxes owed on a sheet of papyrus.

For three days and nights, Ay had rehearsed his plea on behalf of Tuthmosis, confident he could reason with the twins. Yet now that he was face-to-face with Sia, his confidence waned. He was skeptical, and doubted they would even listen to him. Ay had had no real relationship with the Amun priesthood since the day he left the order to become the pharaoh's manservant. He had betrayed their covenant, and because of that, he no longer existed in their eyes. The only way to be *seen* again by them would be if he could offer what they valued the most—the pharaoh's tribute.

Before Ay spoke a word, Sia raised his palm to his face, a sign for him to remain silent. Ay stepped back, intimidated. Sia pointed to the next man in line.

"You, come forward," he ordered him.

An elderly farmer lurched up to Sia, straining to pull his ox on a rope behind him.

"This one from the province of Aluset claims he's only harvested twenty loads," announced Neper.

Sia checked the scroll again, then eyed the farmer as if he were a criminal. "It's written thirty for your province."

"My lord, twenty are all I can spare without starving my family. I've brought you the best of my cattle."

"Amun requires tax on the full harvest. Return with thirty."

The old farmer handed the rope with the ox to Sia and slogged his way back through the crowd. Sia examined the animal, gently petting its head.

Anxious to get his request heard, Ay stepped forward again, rubbing the side of his thigh to settle his nervousness. "The pharaoh has kept his word as I promised you. A bountiful tribute of gold and ivory is at the rear of the temple waiting to be unloaded."

Sia didn't look at him. He continued to study the ox, then turned to Neper. "Secure the pharaoh's tribute," he said.

Neper handed Sia a linen scroll before he exited toward the rear of the temple, and Sia counted the farmers that were in line. It was a blatant effort to dismiss Ay's presence, but Ay, determined to get Sia's attention, stepped in front of him, blocking his view of the farmers.

"The pharaoh desires you to confirm Tuthmosis's invocation into the afterlife," said Ay in a flash of boldness.

Sia exploded with laughter. "Tell the pharaoh we don't perform invocations for spies."

Sia kissed the scroll, knelt on the ground, and unrolled it. Inside was a dagger that glinted in the sun.

"I assure you, Prince Tuthmosis was no spy," said Ay. "His only intention was to service the temple of Amun."

"His intention was to exalt the Aten, never Amun!" Sia shouted.

He ignored Ay's presence, bowed his head and prayed. *"Amun, the god of gods and of Osiris. Empower me through this utensil of your sacrifice, so that I may strike him, who is in the form of an ox who struck you."*

Sia picked up the dagger and slowly circled the ox. Ay watched him, still determined in his mission for Amenhotep. He found his confidence restored.

"As the firstborn of the pharaoh, Tuthmosis deserves all the honor afforded a prince of Egypt," Ay urged. "That is written law."

"Don't speak to me about the law. I *know* the law. Tuthmosis deserved Amun's judgment of death and that is all he will get."

Without warning, Sia plunged the dagger deep in the ox's neck, then yanked it out, severing the animal's jugular vein. The beast let out a choking shriek as a geyser of blood shot out from the wound. The ox teetered for a moment before it fell to the ground.

"My lord, I beg of you," said Ay. "The pharaoh is in deep mourning. Your invocation for his son would bring him a measure of peace."

Rolling the bloody dagger back into the scroll, Sia glared at Ay. "The matter is closed," he said and walked away. Ay stood there unable to move. To admit his failure to the pharaoh would be more shameful than any banishment from palace royalty.

For forty days, Ay presided over Tuthmosis's mummification. The first thirty-nine days they dehydrated the prince's body with natron—a mixture of water and salt. Then they placed the body inside a tent, laid out across a wooden table. Ay had participated in several mummifications as a former Amun priest, including the mummification of his first wife, an experience that rendered him numb to the process. Queen Ty had sent Ay to oversee what she herself was too fragile to witness.

Ay stood stoically in a corner of the tent as a man, taller than normal and wearing a jackal mask, stepped inside. He rolled Tuthmosis's body over on his stomach, and with a mallet and spike, punctured a hole in the back of his head. A speck of Tuthmosis's brain matter landed on Ay's cheek. He didn't bother removing it; there would be more. It was easier to wait to cleanse himself once the embalming was complete.

The masked man pushed a two-cubit-long metal wire up through Tuthmosis's nostril, then vigorously shook it until it liquefied his brain and the dark-gray membranous fluid dripped out from the hole in the back of his head. The man then took a knife and made a "T" incision on Tuthmosis's chest. He broke open the ribs and removed the lungs, liver, and intestines and placed each in separate Canopic jars. In place of the organs, he put sand and linen in the chest cavity, then stitched it closed.

How soon might this be my fate? Ay thought. *And who would I trust to oversee my own mummification?* No one came to mind as he watched the masked man pour the resin liquid over Tuthmosis's face and body. Within thirty days, the entire corpse would be wrapped in small strips of linen cloth, and by the seventieth day, the resin would have set and Tuthmosis's body entombed in the hills above the Valley of the Kings—a long narrow passage between the mountains west of the river.

A day after Tuthmosis's burial, Ay returned to the palace and found Amenhotep stumbling out of his bedchamber into the corridor, naked and screaming Tuthmosis's name. Ay helped him back to his chamber, carrying within his garment what Amenhotep's body yearned for. Having seen the paranoid side-effects the cure had on the pharaoh and the many citizens of Thebes, Ay never had the desire to try it himself. He punctured the capsule of one plant and squeezed the opium latex into Amenhotep's mouth. The pharaoh swallowed it all in a single gulp and sank into his bed.

"You never told me what transpired on your visit with Sia and Neper. Did you convince them to perform the invocation for Tuthmosis?" asked Amenhotep.

Ay paused. The details of his failed mission with Sia at the temple came to mind, and how now despite the care taken with Tuthmosis's mummification and proper burial, the deceased prince had no invocation from the Amun priests to guide him back to the world of the living. Ay couldn't bring himself to look his pharaoh in the eyes and lie, so he focused on a spot beneath the pharaoh's gaze when he responded. "Yes, my Pharaoh. It is done."

CHAPTER

7

TEPPY WHIMPERED when Queen Ty set foot in his bedchamber. He had grown more infirm, and he was sprawled out in the middle of the floor trying to maneuver his body into a kneeling position, so he could stand and walk to his platform bed just five steps away.

Anger surged through the queen's body. Teppy's debility was a hindrance—a reality that tormented her and at the same time demanded her empathy. She not only needed to find a way to help him overcome his curse, but also to reverse the debilitating effect it already had over his body.

Teppy struggled to lift himself, and once again, dropped to the floor. When he gave up and started to crawl, it enraged her. "A prince of Egypt will not crawl across the floor like a helpless infant! You will stand and walk to your bed, Teppy!" shouted the queen.

"I can't if you won't help me," he said.

Teppy reached his hand out to her. She stared at him with a blank expression, refusing to take it. He tried again to lift himself, and this time almost stood erect but fell again.

"I can't," he whimpered.

Frustrated, the queen marched up to Teppy, grabbed him off the floor, and, with a jolt, dropped him down on his bed. When she lifted his chin, there was a pathetic expression on his face. Any acceptance at all of his incapacity would make it grow worse.

"Listen to me," she said grimacing. "Repeat this: 'I am strong; I am a prince.'"

Teppy shook his head. "I'm not strong. My legs are weak."

She slapped him across his face. Teppy stared at her confused, tears forming in his eyes. The queen lifted his chin a second time. "What are you?" she demanded.

He cried out louder. "I'm weak, Mother. It's true."

Teppy had never lied to his mother. She had taught him from infancy how his life would be cursed if he wasn't truthful with her at all times. For the sake of his survival and her own, he would have to lie and believe it with all his heart. So, the queen slapped him again, harder this time. "What are you!" she screamed, raising her voice to the heavens.

"I'm a prince." Teppy sniveled.

"'I am strong. I am a prince.' Say it," Ty demanded.

Teppy did as he was told. "I am strong. I am a prince," he repeated softly as he looked in his mother's eyes for her approval.

"Louder!"

"I am strong! I am a prince!"

Ty was unconvinced and slapped him a third time with the back of her hand. It left a mark on Teppy's face.

"Say it louder!" she shouted again, and finally, Teppy closed his eyes and let go. He screamed out at her with all the pain and anguish he had held inside for so long.

"I am strong! I am a prince! I am strong! I am a prince! I am strong I am a prince!"

The queen lamented as her son broke down in tears. She wrapped him in an embrace and held him close to her bosom.

"Hush now, you *are* strong like your brother, and in time you will overcome this."

She sang him a lullaby, the same melody that had never failed to soothe him when he was an infant.

"I miss him," Teppy said. "He's sleeping too long, Mother; we have to wake him."

Queen Ty caught her breath. Now more than ever Teppy needed to know the truth. "Tuthmosis is not with us anymore. Your brother is dead," she blurted out.

Teppy looked at his mother confused. "No, he's not dead. He's in the temple sleeping."

"Yes, my little one. He is asleep, but in death. Tuthmosis is free to move about as he pleases now. He comes forth by day and assumes any shape he chooses for himself."

Teppy stared at the floor, sensing what his mother told him was dire, but still unaware of the *true* meaning of death.

"He's not himself anymore because he's taken the shape of an animal?" Teppy asked with tears returning to his eyes.

"Yes, any animal he chooses," said Queen Ty.

Teppy wiped his tears away on the sleeve of his garment. "If my brother has taken the shape of an animal, it would be a hyena because they are fearless, quick, and strong."

"You're right, my little prince, that's precisely the animal he would be."

Teppy's demeanor suddenly brightened. "Can I search the fields for him?"

The look of hope in her son's eyes stifled her answer. "No, Teppy," said Queen Ty, holding him closer. "Hyenas are wild and unpredictable. They'll hurt you."

"I'm not afraid of hyenas. If I could see its eyes, I would know if Tuthmosis was in there, and I would be so happy to be with him no matter what. I would take care of him."

Her son's words forced her emotions to surface, causing the queen to do the very thing she had tried so hard to avoid. It was the first time she had cried in Teppy's presence.

"Don't cry, Mother. He would be a friendly animal. Tuthmosis would never hurt us."

"I miss him, my little prince, as much as you do," she confessed, "but he is not an animal in the fields. Your brother is above, watching over us. He is with the Aten when it rises from the mountains."

"Is he happy there?"

"Yes, and when he's looking down upon you and sees that you are strong and brave, that's when he is the happiest. You will be a great king one day, my little prince, and when you take your rightful place as pharaoh of Egypt, you will sustain your mother on the throne as queen."

"I'll never be king," Teppy replied, eager to correct his mother. The conviction in his voice frightened her.

"Why would you say that?" she asked, growing angry again.

"Father told me it was not meant to be."

Queen Ty was rattled. How could Amenhotep have repeated such a cruel thing to their son? She searched for the right response before she answered. "Your father is not well right now. His illness makes him say things he doesn't mean. No one deserves to be king of Egypt more than you, and don't you ever forget that, my little prince. No one."

The queen ignored the confusion in Teppy's eyes, before he nodded his head in agreement.

"Now it's time to dream good dreams for me and your father," said the queen.

She kissed him on the forehead. "The guards will keep the torches illuminated while you sleep, so don't worry."

Teppy retrieved the Aten amulet from under his headrest and kissed it.

"Tuthmosis's amulet protects me. I'm not afraid anymore."

Teppy put it around his neck and settled into his bed. "I hope when I dream, I dream of my brother," he said.

Queen Ty placed the bedcover over Teppy, and he drifted off to sleep. His expression was not of fear this time of what he might see in his dream, but an expectant smile exuding the courage that his brother and the amulet had instilled in him.

Queen Ty walked out of Teppy's bedchamber satisfied the boy had accepted his brother's death and incensed at what Amenhotep had told him.

With a tray in hand, she approached the entrance of Amenhotep's bedchamber, very much aware that it was not her appointed time to see her husband. The period from sundown to twilight was set as Lupita's time to be with Amenhotep, and seldom would it not include copulation. Over the years, Queen Ty had learned to tolerate her husband's sexual desire for his many secondary wives, largely because he had lost the urge for intercourse, but his renewed craving for sexual relations with Lupita were now a threat to Teppy's birthright.

Ty took a step to enter but stopped at the sound of an intimate conversation coming from within her husband's chamber. Keeping herself concealed behind the curtain, she peeked into the room at Amenhotep lying in his bed naked as Lupita stood above him slowly undressing.

"What was it about me that attracted you?" Lupita asked.

"Why do you ask?"

"I'm curious. My father's arrangement did not guarantee you would love me," said Lupita.

"But I did, from the very first day I saw you in the garden. I've never seen a more beautiful flower. How I longed to be surrounded by your goodness."

Behind the curtain, Queen Ty cringed at Amenhotep's confession. He had once told her the same thing, in almost exactly the same words.

Lupita's garment dropped to the ground, and she entered Amenhotep's bed. She straddled him and shared a passionate kiss. The queen wanted to take a step closer to get a better look but was afraid that they'd notice the shadow that her body cast on the floor. So she remained behind the curtain, intermittently peeking in, jealous of what she could see of the perky breasts on Lupita's young, petite frame and how her presence affected Amenhotep—how it changed him and made him feel whole and virulent. She appeared to have restored the self-confidence he possessed in his youth, something Ty was now incapable of doing.

"What about the queen?" asked Lupita. "Did you love her the same way in the beginning?"

Queen Ty's attention piqued at the mention of her name.

"You irritate me now with these questions," Amenhotep snapped.

"We promised we would hide nothing from each other. I've told you everything, Amenhotep."

"No one reveals everything."

"I have to you," said Lupita.

Amenhotep's demeanor softened at her sincerity. "In the beginning, there was intense passion between us. Ty had deep respect for me, and I loved her more than anything."

"And now?"

"Now she spites me by bearing a son who is deformed and weak. The boy is a curse to me and a constant reminder of my own shortcomings," Amenhotep growled just before his face softened again. "In you, my beautiful Lupita, my seed will grow to be strong and courageous, a gift from the almighty Amun."

He kissed Lupita and caressed her slight swollen belly, proof that the queen's suspicion of her pregnancy was true. Queen Ty couldn't stand to conceal herself any longer. She stepped inside the bedchamber with the tray in hand.

Lupita's cat, Bastian, jumped up from the floor onto the bed, arched its back, and hissed at the sight of the queen.

Amenhotep's eyes filled with rage. Lupita grabbed the bed sheets and covered herself.

"What are you doing here? Get out!" he screamed at Ty.

It had no effect. There was a surreal calm about her that could not be shaken.

"There's no reason to be rude. I imagined my husband and his secondary wife would be starving after so much activity."

"My servants will attend to me. I want you out," said Amenhotep.

She placed the tray of fruit, wine, and flowers down on the table. Lupita slid from the bed and dressed herself.

"Don't be foolish," the queen replied. "Who can attend to you better than your chief wife?"

Ty removed a piece of fruit from the tray and divided it into three pieces. She glanced over at Lupita as she put on the last of her garments.

"Lady Lupita, I hope you're not covering yourself on my account, I assure you, I've seen many unshaven parts between a woman's legs in my lifetime. Would you like something to eat?" she asked with a pleasant smile on her face.

Queen Ty held out a piece of fruit to her. Lupita shook her head, so Ty bit into the fruit herself, picked up a flower from the tray, and examined it.

"The lotus blossom. Sublime, isn't it? Because it sinks under the river at night, some call it the flower of death. How unfortunate no one appreciates the beauty of it rising from the river at dawn. I call it 'the flower of life.'"

The queen pressed the flower to her nose and inhaled. "So heavenly," she said, before sauntering over to Lupita and pressing it against hers.

"Doesn't it smell divine, Lady Lupita?"

Lupita trembled as she inhaled the scent. "Yes, it does, my queen."

Queen Ty placed the flower in Lupita's hair and stepped back to admire it. "There. You look beautiful."

"You're very kind," Lupita answered.

Amenhotep looked aghast at what the queen was about to do. "I'm warning you, Ty. Don't!"

She ignored him and pressed her lips against Lupita's in a sensual kiss. The girl appeared stunned and frightened by it. Queen Ty then returned her attention to Amenhotep.

"What would you prefer, my dear husband? Will it be beer or wine for your thirst?"

Not waiting for a response, she poured wine from a vase into a jar and held it out to him. Amenhotep glared at her speechless, refusing to take it.

"Leave us, Lupita," Amenhotep ordered.

When she took a step to leave, the queen moved in front of her.

"By the gods, no, please stay, Lupita."

Lupita caught sight of Amenhotep's furious expression. He didn't have to say a word.

"It's best I go," said Lupita as she picked up Bastian and rushed out of the bedchamber.

Appearing disappointed, Queen Ty returned the fruit and wine back to her tray. Amenhotep was dumbfounded.

"Have you gone mad? It's only by the mercy of Hathor that I've kept you as queen," he said as he rose from the bed and dressed himself.

Ty did her best to quell her anger so that when she asked her most important question she would sound calm.

"How could you humiliate him?"

"Humiliate how?"

"Did you not tell our only son he would never become king?"

"The boy is an abomination."

His words were painful and she shook her head in frustration, but still kept her composure. "He is a prince that cherishes his father," said the queen.

"His deformity could corrupt the royal bloodline. I can't allow that to happen."

"The only corruption is your cruelty to him. You must acknowledge your son."

Hearing the word "son" caused Amenhotep to clench his teeth. The pain in his mouth returned. He snarled back at her. "Tuthmosis was my son. The blood that runs through Teppy is poison."

"The same blood that runs through Teppy's veins runs through yours. You gave him your name, Amenhotep!" she said.

"That was before I knew what he truly was."

Amenhotep's lips pursed, a clear warning for Ty not to press him further. She had seen the same look many times before when Amenhotep made a decision to decapitate someone. Although the chance of losing her life was frightening, losing her son's birthright was more unthinkable. It would be the first step to her being banished from royalty and replaced with the younger, more beautiful, Lupita.

"He's your son," Queen Ty insisted. "You will acknowledge him."

"He is cursed as an abomination."

"Cursed by whom? Sia and Neper? Those despicable twin priests? Can't you see they want to destroy our children so there is no true heir, and when that's done, what do you think they will do next? They will conjure a spell to invalidate all of us to the people. They want to rule Egypt!"

"You truly are mad," he shrugged off.

Ty stepped up to him and caressed his face. "Teppy is just a child, the only son we have left. I have no one else. You can father many children with your mistresses. Teppy is my only reason to live.

Give him a chance to grow stronger. I promise you he will. Don't let the Amun priests take away his birthright. It's all he has."

Amenhotep pulled away from her and fastened the remaining part of his garment.

"With the loss of your fertility, your beauty and sanity have faded. You are the mother of a useless child. Soon Lupita will bear me a son, and he will be my heir. This is the judgement of Amun. Sia and Neper have revealed it to me. Teppy will have no right to the throne."

Stunned by his words, Queen Ty took her hands away from his face, picked up the tray, and walked out of the room, panicked at what terrible fate awaited her and Teppy with the birth of Lupita's child.

CHAPTER

8

AMENHOTEP WAS KNOWN as "the great builder of Egypt," but for Queen Ty, the Colonnade Hall was not one of his greater achievements. The seven pairs of thirty-cubit-high papyrus shaped columns were impressive, yet hardly remarkable in her eyes. The hall was merely an entrance to the Amun temple, the home of its tarnished priests, and an obvious waste of limestone built on the recommendation of Sia and Neper for their own self-gratification, not to honor her husband, nor Egypt.

A year after Tuthmosis's death was still much too soon for the queen to attend a public celebration, but Amenhotep had insisted she attend the hall's dedication. This had been an ambitious project for the pharaoh. During construction, he had changed the dimensions of the hall to be three times larger than what had been originally planned. Consequently, the builders could not complete the eastern walls in time. Instead of postponing the celebration, as the queen assumed he would do, he went on with it. Even unfinished, the hall opening attracted thousands of citizens cheering at the passing of their royal chariot as it led the procession through the crowded street.

Amenhotep had fallen asleep while Queen Ty peered out the chariot window at the Egyptian people, disgusted at how the Amun priests had them all under their control.

An old man balancing himself with a walking stick in one hand led his donkey toward their chariot with the other. One of Amenhotep's royal guards stepped in front of him, preventing the man from reaching them.

"Step back," she heard the guard say.

The old man pointed at the royal chariot, wheezing to catch his breath. "I have to see the pharaoh."

"You have no business with the pharaoh. Move away."

"It's urgent that I'm granted his mercy, please."

"Address your petitions for mercy to the district overseer. Off the road. Now."

The man obeyed and led his donkey away, but the moment the guard turned his attention to the crowd, he trudged back onto the road and right up to Amenhotep's chariot. His sudden presence startled the queen, and she moved back from the chariot's window to avoid having to interact with him. Once she had been attacked by a crazed citizen who had gone mad from an overdose of the cure. The man had broken through her line of royal guards and managed to strike her across the face. He was quickly apprehended and executed, but since that instance, Ty carried a flint knife that she concealed in an inner pocket of her garment for protection.

The queen reached to retrieve it, then suddenly relaxed because the man appeared decrepit and incapable of causing her any harm. He leaned into her chariot window and whispered a message. "I will wait for you a hundred cubits from the rear entrance in a soldier's chariot," he said.

The queen glared at him, baffled.

His manner of speech was that of an official of the city, yet his clothing was tattered and torn like the lowliest of peasants in the village. He had long gray hair that was combed behind his ears and onto his shoulders, framing his clean-shaven face. It was difficult to tell if the old man was a representative of the court of Thebes or just another crazed impoverished citizen.

"Who are you?" she asked.

"If you desire to steal away to the Oracle, this is the only chance you will have before the inundation," said the man. His eyes dotted back and forth between her and the road.

The pharaoh's guard had spotted him again. Furious, he headed back in the old man's direction.

"You must come within the hour if we are to make the journey before sundown. Your brother, Ay, will alert you at the proper moment."

By the time the old man spoke the last word of his message to the queen, the guard had reached and snatched him up by the collar of his garment. His walking stick dropped to the ground.

"What did I tell you, old man?" said the guard sneering at him.

"I will move off the road as you wish, my lord, but have patience with me. I am feeble and slow."

The guard released his grip, and the old man picked up his walking stick and marched off with his donkey around a band of musicians accompanying the procession. The rhythmic music was joined by a troupe of acrobatic dancers all dressed in kilts, holding sticks carved in the shape of a hand at one end. As they performed flips and acrobatics, they repeatedly struck the sticks together. The noise awakened Amenhotep, and his eyes opened to Queen Ty's stare.

The chariot came to a halt at the entrance of the massive hall. Without speaking a word to her, the pharaoh poked his head out of the chariot window and waved at the cheering crowd.

Queen Ty remained quiet, more concerned about the true identity of the old man and why her brother Ay had trusted what appeared to be a peasant with her plan to visit the Oracle. Interrupting her thoughts, Amenhotep stepped out and extended his hand to her. She wouldn't take it. He motioned for her to exit the chariot again; she refused again.

"Step out and greet them, or I'll have your head ripped from your body," he said through clenched teeth, clearly in pain again.

When she didn't immediately react to his command, Amenhotep snatched the queen up by her arm and pulled her out of the chariot. Playing to the enthusiasm of the crowd, he embraced her, and the queen relented to his act, waved, and forced a smile, which was acknowledged with thunderous applause.

Amenhotep climbed the stairs of the Colonnade Hall with a confident stride. He stood in front of a copper-plated podium, which reflected brilliant rays of light out to the citizens. The queen followed, rubbing her throbbing arm where he had grabbed her. She took her position behind him, among his royal guards and advisors.

Three baroque shrines were then carried through the hall on the shoulders of twenty-four Amun priests dressed in white robes. The priests placed each one on a golden pedestal.

Amenhotep pointed at the shrines and addressed the crowd.

"Behold. Before you, enclosed in their sacred shrines, the form of the gods Amun, Mut, and Khonsu."

The people bowed to Amenhotep, all except Sia and Neper. The two priests directed their threatening gaze at Queen Ty before they walked away, leaving her unsettled.

As Amenhotep recited verses from the tomb of his father to the crowd, Ay marched up the Colonnade stairs and took his position next to Queen Ty. He acknowledged his sister with a nod—a sign that what the old man had told her was true and that her moment to exit the ceremony had come.

While Amenhotep continued addressing the crowd, Queen Ty took a step backward and, in a dissimulative fashion, walked indolently toward the rear of the complex, and Ay moved over into the position where she had stood. He would be the one that would offer the excuse of her sudden illness if the pharaoh inquired about her absence.

When the queen reached the Colonnade's courtyard, the old man was waiting for her next to a soldier's chariot without his walking stick. It confirmed her suspicion that his frail appearance and labored gait had been a clever ruse to fool the royal guard.

She stepped inside and took her seat, and he handed her a scarf bundled up in a garment.

"It's commoner clothing that your brother left for you. It would be advantageous that you wear it if your plan is not to be recognized as royalty," he replied.

Queen Ty examined the clothing. It was of poor workmanship and made from unrefined cloth. Ay had supplied her with everything she needed to complete her incandescent visit to the Oracle's home, including the clothing of a peasant.

The old man turned his back to her.

"You're free to change, my Queen. I will remain in this position until you're finished."

To be sure he kept his word, the queen eyed the old man carefully as she changed into her disguise. After her transformation was complete, he tugged the reigns of the chariot horse and they traveled away from the Colonnade Hall at a brisk pace. The old man escorted the queen up a secluded path high in the hills of the village until they came upon a quaint, dome-shaped house made of mud bricks—the home of the Oracle.

It bewildered her that such a supreme one would reside in such a quotidian house. The Oracle was the most powerful priest in all of Egypt, some even believed him to be more powerful than the Amun god. He warned the citizens about the coming plagues and curses in advance so they could prepare themselves. The Oracle delivered justice to the lowly ones who were denied it by the priests or their fellow citizens. It was thought that without him and his prayers to the god Hapi for the inundation, the people would all perish and Egypt would become a desolate wasteland. The queen was convinced that the Oracle would deliver the justice she so deserved.

Ty stepped out of the chariot and the old man remained behind. In the distance, a boy about eleven years of age sat on the ground near the entrance of the dome, holding a stick with a dead rat skewered on the end of it. He held the rat over a campfire, turning and twisting it, trying to get it to cook faster. Eager to satisfy his hunger, the boy took a bite and burned his tongue. He winced and blew on the rat to cool it.

The queen approached him with her head, nose, and mouth concealed by the scarf.

"Is this where I will find the Oracle?" she asked.

The boy glanced at her before taking another bite of the toasted rat. Juices dripped from his mouth, and he wiped them away with the back of his hand.

"Who are you?"

"I am a servant of the pharaoh, here to solicit the Oracle's knowledge for a price," the queen said.

The boy laid the skewered rat on the ground.

"A *price*. Good. Follow me," he said.

Queen Ty followed the boy into the dark domed space where a bald, albino dwarf in a white kilt was sitting on the ground in front of a small fire, his eyes shut. His bare chest and arms were covered with tattoos that appeared distorted because of his wrinkled, sun-scorched skin. No part of his body was left unmarked. A tattoo of a scorpion marred the center of his forehead, and around his neck, the queen noted a black-coiled collar. He was a fragile, elderly man of about eighty-five years of age. According to what Ay had told her, he had served over sixty years as the Oracle.

She took a careful step toward him. The dwarf's collar uncoiled. She gasped. It was not a collar at all, but a black mamba. The snake hissed in her direction and coiled tighter around its host's neck. The dwarf's eyes snapped open and tightly focused on her.

"Why are you here?" he asked.

Despite his old age, his voice did not quiver or shake. It sounded steady and clear, the voice of a much younger man.

"Are you the Oracle?" she asked.

"I am what I am."

"It's been said your power is greater than the magic of the Amun priests and that sorcery and vengeance are not beyond your abilities. Is it true?"

The Oracle didn't respond. Instead, he glanced over at the servant boy.

"Go," he said to him. "Return here at the time of the pilgrimage." The Oracle waited for the boy to leave before he spoke again. "Did you come to ask what you already know, Queen?"

Queen Ty had underestimated the Oracle. Impressed by his ability to see through her disguise, she smiled as she removed her scarf.

"I came to ask if you could help my son. The Priests of Amun have schemed to stop his ascension to the throne. They have committed some manner of sorcery against my husband, such that he follows their every word. If I don't find a way to stop them, I fear they will curse him to his very death. Can you help me? Can you help Egypt?"

The Oracle smirked. "My advice requires an offering." He paused. "A substantial one."

"Of course," said the queen as she removed a gold and sapphire bracelet from her wrist and handed it to him. It was strange to her how he examined it like a foreign object.

"The value of that is far greater than what any king could ever acquire in his life. It is my most cherished piece," she said with pride.

When he tossed the bracelet into the fire, the flames rose and engulfed it. She watched horrified. He spoke out just before she made a move to retrieve it.

"No, let it burn. It belongs to me now," said the Oracle. "On the ground before you lies a piece of string. Pick it up, and with it, tie three knots."

The queen reluctantly took her eyes away from her burning bracelet and focused on a piece of string at her feet. She did as she was told.

"Now untie them and burn the string in the flame," he said.

She untied each knot and held the string over the flame, which consumed it so quickly that it scorched her finger. The queen jerked away causing the black mamba to lift its head in the air at her then slither around the Oracle's neck, repositioning itself as it spewed another menacing hissing sound.

"Prince Teppy will never become pharaoh of Egypt," the Oracle stated.

"I don't understand," said the queen, shocked.

"From where do you think the Amun priests receive their power?" he asked. "I am the source, and I am the way to Amun. You have a choice, Queen. Either accept the will of Amun, or Prince Teppy will suffer the same fate as your other son Tuthmosis."

It was as if she were being crushed alive under a bundle of mud bricks. The queen was trapped by a god that despised her as fiercely as she despised it and with a husband completely under its control. And now, the Oracle—her last chance for salvation, the most powerful one in Egypt, had also proclaimed his alliance to the despicable Amun god.

"You may leave now," said the Oracle.

He folded his hands in his lap and closed his eyes. The snake uncoiled from around his neck, slithered down his body, and disappeared under the sand.

The queen stood there for a moment, unable to move. *Where was her justice?*

She stared at her most cherished possession—her sapphire bracelet, burning among the ashes of the Oracle's fire. In return, he had given her nothing but a future of suffering and death for her beloved Teppy. Something had to be done. She removed the flint knife from her garment and glared at the Oracle. *If he was dead,* she thought, *it would only be natural that his premonition would die along with him.*

While the Oracle's eyes were still closed, the queen rushed up from behind him, and without a second thought, slit his throat. His eyes popped open, and she stepped back and watched as the Oracle tried to stop the bleeding by clenching the wound with his hand. Blood seeped from between his fingers and he fell on his side with a shocked expression frozen on his face, still grasping hold to his neck while he regurgitated blood. The color of it was a deep, dark red, nearly purple, viscous and tainted because of his practice of sorcery no doubt, the queen deduced.

Although he had now stopped moving and appeared to be dead, the decapitation was incomplete, so, in a frenzy, Ty took the knife and slashed it across his neck fifteen times until the head severed from the body and her hands and face were sprinkled with his tainted blood. The completed decapitation would now assure that his spirit was dead and could not return. The queen washed herself in the salted water of the Oracle's ablution tank, then removed her dress and reversed it so that the old man wouldn't see the blood on it when she returned to his chariot.

Once she arrived at the palace, she bathed, then headed to Amenhotep's chamber, brazenly disregarding his orders again that she only appear there at her appointed times. Ty carried a jar of wine from the Canopic branch of the river where the best vineyards grew—Amenhotep's favorite, now the queen's peace offering to him. She stepped up to the entrance, the horror of what she had just done to the Oracle willfully erased from her mind, and listened to see if there was anyone in the chamber with him. All was silent.

"Amenhotep? I've brought wine for you," she said.

After a moment of waiting and not receiving an answer, she entered his chamber. His nemes-striped head cloth was missing from its usual place. It was not uncommon for Amenhotep to travel to some unknown destination on a whim, and because the cloth was not there, she assumed he would not be returning that day.

Disappointed by his absence, the queen lingered in his chamber and found herself searching the room, not sure of what she was looking for. She came upon a small clay tablet with an inscription on it lying on the table. Ty's father was a scribe, one of the few citizens who could read and write. Though it was forbidden, her father had taught her enough inscription when she was a child that she could decipher the fundamentals of the written language on her own.

The queen read the tablet silently to herself. It was a letter from Mitanni informing Amenhotep that Lupita's younger brother, Tazam, had murdered his older brother, King Artassumara, and that they needed the assistance of the Egyptian army in case of an uprising from neighboring kingdoms. This explained Amenhotep's absence, but why hadn't he told Lupita about it? The realization that Amenhotep had kept it secret from his young wife seemed odd at first, but her confusion soon turned to jealousy. His silence was meant to protect Lupita's feelings. He was keeping her unaware of the turmoil brewing in Mitanni to prevent her despair and to keep her from traveling back to her homeland where it would be unsafe. It reminded the queen of bygone days when Amenhotep had protected her in the same way, how he would do anything in his power to keep her heart joyful. Lupita had to be the reason Amenhotep no longer loved her, and as long as the girl remained alive in the land of Egypt, he would never return to her side.

Neper and Sia knelt together and recited a prayer of awakening at the altar of the Amun statue. Footsteps padding on the limestone floor of the temple's outer chamber startled them. The twins stepped out from the inner chamber and found the servant boy on his knees panting.

"My lords, I ran as fast as I could," said the boy.

"Who are you?" asked Neper. "And how did you get past the other priests?" Sia continued.

"I am the Oracle's servant boy, the one chosen to assist him on his pilgrimage to the Great Pyramid of Khufu. I know that you are Sia and Neper, the lector priests. The Oracle once told me you were only second to him as the wisest in the land. It is urgent that you both come with me now to see what calamity has befallen our teacher."

Without questioning the boy further, Sia and Neper followed him to the Oracle's dome. When they arrived, the boy trembled as he pointed at the dome's entrance.

Sia and Neper entered. A lit candle on the floor provided the only illumination. Neper picked it up and carried it with him as they made their way through the darkest rooms of the dome.

"Master, are you well?" Neper called out.

There was no response. When they reached the center of the dome, a trail of smoke ascended from a smoldering campfire. The Oracle was lying on the floor in a fetal position next to it.

"Master you must rise. The time of the pilgrimage is near," said Sia.

The Oracle didn't move. Candle in hand, Neper walked over to him.

"Master?"

Neper shook the Oracle's shoulder. The head rolled off the body and onto the sand. Neper gasped while Sia stood next to him unaffected. Instantly, a horde of rats scurried across their sandals from every corner of the room and descended on the Oracle's severed head, biting the scalp and tearing the flesh off the face. Neper tossed the candle at the ferocious creatures and ran out from the dome screaming.

Sia remained as the flame illuminated a grotesque scene; rats eating the eyeballs clean from the sockets of the Oracle's head. Sia's nostrils flared as he listened to the despicable sounds of chewing and squealing. His breathing accelerated, a reaction not of grief or fear, but of intense anger. Who possessed the insolence to do such a thing? Who could murder the Oracle—the direct connection to the Amun god itself? The life-force of Egypt. Sia suspected the owner of the scarf that lay beneath the Oracle's body knew the answer.

CHAPTER

9

TRAINING FOR the Egyptian army started at the age of fourteen for hand-selected boys of above-average athletic ability. A mastery of wrestling was a prerequisite before Horemheb taught the boys any other combat skills. At the military camp, the young men battled each other for the privilege of becoming his pupils. The newly appointed General Horemheb was a master warrior whose proven skills had surpassed even that of General Nasheret. Horemheb now presided over the training ground where Egypt's future warriors learned the art of war.

In an unannounced visit, Amenhotep arrived in his royal chariot at the base of the camp. A rowdy crowd of boys had circled around two of their group who were mercilessly beating each other. They were bloody and exhausted but continued brawling as the others egged them on.

The pharaoh dismounted and commanded his guards to remain stationed at the chariot. He rushed over to where the boys were fighting and broke the circle just as the smaller of the two fighters was putting the other in a chokehold. The bigger boy's eyelids fluttered as he teetered on the verge of losing consciousness. Amenhotep yanked the smaller boy away from his semiconscious opponent and threw him to the ground.

"Save your killer instinct for the enemy!" he shouted.

It was only a moment before they recognized the man scolding them. The boys prostrated themselves before the pharaoh, shocked into silence at his unannounced appearance.

"Both of you, return to the barracks and tend to your wounds," said Horemheb as he approached from the rear.

The two bloodied and bruised boys rushed off. Horemheb scanned his group of teen warriors and pointed at two.

"You and you, continue."

He clapped his hands twice, and the two young men entered the circle and maneuvered into a wrestling stance.

Horemheb greeted the pharaoh with a smile and bowed dutifully. "My Pharaoh, what an unexpected pleasure. How can I be of service?"

Amenhotep interrupted his gesture and gave him a strong and affectionate rough hug.

"Now that's a greeting worthy of a man who once saved my life," said the pharaoh. "Walk with me, general."

They strolled together across the spacious training grounds. All around them, young boys and middle-aged warriors practiced archery, spear throwing, hand-to-hand combat and stick fighting. Amenhotep surveyed the activities with satisfaction. The scene brought back memories of his own adolescence. He himself had trained there as the son of Pharaoh Thutmose the Fourth, with dreams of becoming a warrior king. It had been decades since he had set foot in one of these training grounds, and the size of it appeared much smaller compared to the enormous grounds pictured in his memory.

"I see you have your hands full," said Amenhotep.

"It's challenging, but I'm not so overwhelmed that I cannot serve my Pharaoh. Is there a task I can do for you?"

"There is a matter in Mitanni we have to deal with."

"What is it?"

"I received a letter yesterday that King Artassumara was murdered by his brother Tazam. And now, because there is no ruler, the Mitanni people are afraid the Hittites are planning to attack them."

"We have a peace treaty with King Suppiluliumas and the Hittites," explained Horemheb. "Would he be so bold as to attack our ally?"

"I would think not. My relations with him have been cordial, but I don't trust him. Neither can I ignore the fears of the Mitanni people," said Amenhotep. "I need you to take an army to Mitanni immediately and, if necessary, defend them from their enemy. We can't risk losing another valuable tributary."

"I can have troops ready to march by dawn," assured Horemheb.

"Most importantly, general, slice off Tazam's hands and bring them to me. I want to present them to Lupita as proof we have avenged her brother's murder."

"Do they know beyond a doubt that Tazam is guilty?"

"He confessed his guilt. There's no one that can account for his innocence."

"It'll be done, my Pharaoh, as you wish."

"I'll wait for the proof before I inform Lupita. If Suppuliumas is planning an attack on Mitanni, it would be much too dangerous for her to return to her homeland now."

A soldier's spear fell flat on the ground in front of them. With a scowl on his face, Horemheb picked it up and hurled it over two hundred cubits back at the soldier. It lodged deep in the earth at the soldier's foot. Horemheb returned his attention back to Amenhotep. "They'll be ready at dawn."

Queen Ty had always been envious of Lupita's special privilege. Her chamber was adjacent to Amenhotep's, and she commingled with the pharaoh whenever she desired. Since the day Lupita arrived in Egypt, Queen Ty was restricted to "appointed times," Amenhotep's biased visitation schedule that she routinely ignored. The day after she discovered the letter in his chamber, she revisited his quarters, though not to see him. She found Lupita sitting in her chamber in front of a polished copper mirror shaving her head with a trapezium-shaped razor.

Lupita's dark brown hair fell to the floor in clumps. She was three locks away from being completely bald when the queen stepped in and took the razor from her.

"It's dull. I have a sharp one," she said.

Queen Ty drew her flint knife and began shaving the rest of Lupita's head. She adjusted her facial expression in Lupita's mirror so that it reflected dread.

"What's wrong, my queen?"

"I have terrible news."

"Tell me. What is it?"

"I'm torn because it's not my place to tell you such things."

"If it's as dreadful as your expression reveals, Queen, you'll only torture me by withholding it," said Lupita.

Queen Ty shaved the last lock of hair from Lupita's head.

"Your brother, King Artassumara, was murdered," the queen blurted.

Lupita gasped.

"It's true, I'm sorry. A messenger from your land of Mitanni delivered a letter sealed by your brother, Tushratta," the queen continued.

Lupita stood up from her seat in shock. "Why? Who would want to murder him?"

"The letter stated that it was your other brother Tazam."

"Tazam? No, there's not a vile bone in his body. He loved our brother Artassumara."

"Perhaps he was clever enough to hide his vileness from his sister," suggested Queen Ty.

Lupita struggled to fight back the tears, and the moment she took her eyes off the mirror, the queen gazed at her own reflection with a smirk. Her plan was working.

"Someone in my brother's house must have forced him into a false confession," said Lupita.

"Then the real perpetrator still slithers like a snake in your brother's house. I grieve for your country," Queen Ty said as she embraced Lupita. "Egypt grieves for Mitanni."

Just as she had planned, the girl was devastated. "It's all my fault," Lupita cried out. "He wanted so much to be with me here in Egypt but I refused his request."

"It's not too late. You can return home, vindicate your brother, and bring him back with you," said the queen.

"Why hasn't Amenhotep come to tell me of this himself?"

"You must understand that war has hardened his heart and rendered him immune to tragedy," she answered. "Amenhotep thought I could better console you during this time of mourning as a mother would."

Lupita looked up at Queen Ty surprised. "My Queen, do you yourself consider me as such?"

"I've always considered you as a daughter," she replied.

Queen Ty opened the box on Lupita's table and removed a black wig woven with gold pieces, jewels, and long braids like her own. She placed the wig on Lupita's clean-shaven head and secured it with a headband. She then removed the lapis-lazuli earrings from her ears and gave them to Lupita.

"You can take these for your journey," she said. "They'll bring you luck from your god Assur."

This act of generosity moved Lupita to tears. They embraced each other and the queen wiped the tears away from Lupita's eyes with her hand and adjusted the young girl's wig so that it was perfectly in place.

"My queen, you have always been kind to me. I hope I haven't caused any contention between you and the pharaoh."

"Amenhotep and I have our differences. It has nothing to do with you. Go ahead, put them on."

Lupita attached the earrings to her ears. She managed a half-smile at her reflection in the mirror.

"How extravagant they look on you," said the queen.

"They're beautiful. How can I repay you for such a priceless gift?"

"You have more urgent things to attend to."

"Yes, there is much to do," replied Lupita. "How many maidservants should I take along with me? Or maybe I shouldn't concern myself with that now. I have nine days to make my decision."

Panic surged through Queen Ty's body. A nine-day waiting period was not part of her plan. She shook her head at Lupita. "Nine days would be much too late. Your family needs you."

"I'm grateful for your help, queen, but I can't just leave on such a journey without adequately preparing myself and my retinue. I will ask Amenhotep for his guidance," said Lupita.

"There is no time, you have to leave now before it's too late," Queen Ty replied, as she grabbed hold of Lupita's hand to get her attention.

"I beg your pardon, my queen, but I will not leave Egypt without the blessing of my husband. It's unthinkable."

Lupita freed herself from the queen's hold and began searching through a stack of clothing on the table. The queen followed her.

"What about Tazam? Your brother Tushratta will surely kill him for what they believe he has done."

"I will vouch for Tazam's innocence to Amenhotep. He'll save him, you'll see. I'll go to him now."

Lupita found the scarf she was looking for and wrapped it around her shoulders. The queen's plan was falling apart and her cracking voice revealed her frustration.

"You should think clearly about this first, Lupita. If you tell Amenhotep now, he'll delay your return to your homeland so that he can send his own messengers there first to kill Tazam before you arrive. King Artasssumara was like a brother to him. He'll seek to avenge his death. That is certain."

"You believe he would murder my brother without my consent?"

"Amenhotep consults no one except the Amun god before he makes a decision of life or death."

Lupita hesitated, and sat down in front of the mirror again, contemplating the queen's advice.

"Perhaps you're right," said Lupita.

"Of course I am. I've known him many years before you and can decipher his way of thinking. You must leave now if you wish to save your brother."

"If you truly believe it's the best way, then I'll go."

"It is, Lupita. I have assembled a Mitanni convoy that can escort you on a short route through the Ugarit Valley to your homeland. You'll find them at the entrance gate of the city prepared and waiting for your arrival as we speak."

Lupita gathered up her jewelry and garments. She scanned the chamber for her cat but didn't see him. "Come, Bastian."

Bastian appeared from his hiding place inside a straw basket and jumped into her arms. Queen Ty attempted to pet the cat's head, and it snarled at her.

"Bastian, no! Forgive him, my queen, he gets nervous."

"It's all right. It hasn't had a chance to get to know me. Once you've had a sufficient head start, I'll alert Amenhotep of your departure so that he'll send his army to shadow and protect you and your convoy."

"Amenhotep will be angry with me. I know it," said Lupita.

"Yes, but he's unable to resist your femininity. He'll forgive you. This is the right thing to do to save your brother. I would do exactly the same for my own brother Ay."

The queen's pronouncement of loyalty to her brother was enough to convince Lupita that she had made the right decision. She embraced Queen Ty again.

"Your wisdom is invaluable. I'll forever remember you for this, my queen. Thank you," said Lupita. "When the time's right, please let Amenhotep know I'll return to him soon."

Queen Ty caressed Lupita's face, sealing her fate with a kiss on her forehead. "I'll do as you requested. Go now, mourn with your family and return to us."

The queen was still anxious but relieved when Lupita finally left the room. *Surely, the inexperienced Mitannian convoy would head straight into the Ugarit Valley and into the hands of the Hittites—a race of heathens known for their brutality and merciless treatment of the Mitannians,* the queen thought. Lupita would not survive, nor would her and Amenhotep's unborn child, the one threat to Teppy's claim to the throne of Egypt.

The great military fortress of T'aru sat on Egypt's eastern border and was twelve days of chariot travel south of the Mitanni kingdom. It was Queen Ty's birthplace, the home that held her childhood secrets and the retreat where she found comfort and solace. It was unusual for Amenhotep to visit such a desolate city, so on the night of Lupita's departure, when the queen had received urgent word from him that they should meet there, she sensed something was terribly wrong. She had no reason to believe that he knew of Lupita's journey to Mitanni or about what she had done to the Oracle, but her extended journey to the fortress gave her an abundance of time to worry about his motives. When she arrived, she rushed up the palace stairs where four guards opened the massive stone doors for her entrance.

"He's in the back chamber, my queen," a guard said to her. "He's expecting you."

Two rats scurried from her path as she continued down the long ornate hall to a room in the back chamber. Before she entered, she blotted dry the moisture on her face, smoothing out the heavy makeup she had applied before she stepped foot in the palace. Queen Ty inhaled and exhaled a deep breath and entered the room. Seated at a table, Amenhotep held a reed brush in his hand, dipping it in ink and writing on a papyrus scroll. It always amazed the queen that the hieroglyphics that had taken her brother Ay five years to master, had taken Amenhotep a mere eighty days. Only a god was capable of such a thing.

"Why have you sent for me?" she asked.

Without taking his eye away from his writing, he answered her. "Tell me what you know of the Oracle."

Fear overwhelmed the queen. She rendered a look of confusion. *How could he possibly know?*

"The Or—Oracle?" she repeated, stumbling over her words. "I know only what you've told me of him. Why?"

"The Oracle is dead, Ty" said Amenhotep.

The queen remained silent for a moment. Her response needed to be believable. "Dead? How?"

"Murdered. Someone severed his head."

"How blasphemous," she said, and placed her hand on her chest feigning shock. "Thieves, most likely."

"It wasn't a thief. Sia and Neper informed me that all the Oracle's possessions were left untouched. What's most troublesome is that the priests suspect the Oracle's murderer was a woman."

This time Ty stifled her gasp. *He certainly knows, but how?* She wondered. Did the old man untangle her secret and betray her? Or could her brother Ay have done the unthinkable? She hoped that Amenhotep would at least reveal the betrayer's identity before he executed her.

"How did they determine it was a woman?" she asked slyly.

"A woman's scarf was found underneath his body."

Inside, the queen berated herself for foolishly leaving the scarf behind. How could she have been so careless?

Amenhotep saved her from her moment of inner loathing. "It was clearly made from the crudest cloth of a peasant—most likely a lowly female commoner murdered the Oracle, the ones he spent most of his life protecting," Amenhotep continued. "Who will warn us now of the plague or the curse?" he asked, meeting her eyes.

"The Amun priests will appoint another. I still don't understand why you summoned me."

"We can mourn the Oracle's death together here."

"We can just as well mourn the Oracle's death in Thebes. Why here?" said Queen Ty, now certain he didn't suspect her.

"Why not here? This city comforts me as it comforts you. I don't have to behave like a mad tyrant here to gain respect from my people. In T'aru, I can be as I am."

His sudden burst of veracity confounded her, and she harbored a sudden sense of pity for him.

"The people of Egypt love and revere you," she said.

Amenhotep placed the brush down and stood. "The people love the *image* of the pharaoh. They can't love me. They don't know me."

He walked toward her, staring at her intently. "What about you? Do you love me, Ty?"

The question stunned her. She had not heard it since the day before they were married.

"You know the answer, Amenhotep."

"No, I don't. Do you or do you not?"

She stepped away from him, suspecting she was being tested. "Why are you asking if I love you? Is that the true reason you had me travel all the way here from Thebes?"

"It's not the only reason. But I need you to answer my question first," he said.

The queen paused. She was nervous in his presence and afraid that his questioning her love for him was trickery to uncover the terrible, but necessary, things she had done. If she lied about not loving him, he would surely see it in her eyes and deem her a liar. She had no choice but to answer him with her heart.

"Very well. The truth is: I loathe you. The way you spew venom at me, it poisons my insides. How you belittle me as if I'm a thorn in your foot is utter cruelty. I hate you even more when you close your ears to my voice and punish me with silence. You have many shortcomings, Amenhotep. Despite them all, I still love you. The sound of your voice, your strength, your courage, soothes my heart. The wisdom that covers you like a fine garment still intoxicates me more than six measures of wine. I fear you, yes, and I despise you even more, but I can't help loving you intensely."

Queen Ty had never said an honest word to Amenhotep in over two decades, but in that moment she spoke her truth. She truly loved him more than life itself, and she hated herself for it. Her love for him was her badge of weakness. *What would he do now?*

She gazed into his eyes and instantly regretted what she had just revealed to him. The thought of it embarrassed her and she waited to hear the words that he would say that would punish her for her honesty. Instead, with passion and tenderness, Amenhotep kissed Ty the way he did so many moons ago at the blossoming of their romance—the kiss she had longed for over a lifetime. She reciprocated almost against her will and relaxed into his extended embrace. He released her and stared at her with sparkling eyes. "I have something for you," he said.

The pharaoh took her hand and led her out of the room and down the hallway to the colossal nine-cubit-high doors at the rear entrance. It was a beautiful dream; she had her husband back, a gift from the Aten god. The man she had fallen in love with twenty-three years before had returned to her, and it had happened there, in the palace of T'aru where they had first embraced.

Amenhotep pushed the doors open and escorted her out onto a balcony adorned with vibrant flowers. Instead of the endless fields of grain she had become accustomed to viewing, there was a spectacular man-made lake surrounding the palace estate, stretching hundreds of cubits beyond the city. The amazement in her eyes provided the reason he needed to feel proud of himself.

"This is Lake Ty, your private lake. These are the waters where you will sail your royal barge whenever you desire," he said.

The queen covered her mouth with her hand. She was overwhelmed and astonished at the beauty of it all.

"It's magnificent, Amenhotep, thank you," she said embracing him. "This is why you traveled secretly? You were coming here to build this for me?"

He kissed her lips again. "I never stopped loving you, Ty. This is how I can show it."

"You are indeed the great builder of Egypt, my husband. I've never seen anything so—"

Amenhotep stooped over, clutching his chest.

"What's wrong? Are you not well?" she asked.

He tried to stand up straight. He couldn't.

"I— I—" Amenhotep uttered, trying to speak, but the strain was too much.

He fell to his knees and collapsed on the ground, unconscious. Queen Ty knelt beside him, pulled his head into her lap, and cradled his trembling body. "Help me! Guards, somebody help me!" she screamed.

CHAPTER

10

THE FORTIFIED WALLS of Mitanni stood tall like a beacon in the distance. This was the land of Wassukanni, the main city of the entire Mitanni kingdom. Horemheb had traveled there before nearly ten years ago as a captain under the command of General Nasheret. Now, he was in command with his own captain, Salitas, galloping alongside. The journey had taken them forty-one days on horseback.

Horemheb surveyed the perimeter of the area. Although the Mitanni walls were impressive; they were also perplexing to the general. *How could an inept and incompetent people engineer such a sound structure without the aid of Egypt?* The Mitannians seemed no better than insects to Horemheb, parasites that leeched Egypt's resources with nothing to give in return. Their kings used the allure of their voluptuous daughters to elicit gifts of gold and jewels from the pharaoh, and, as such, the service of the Egyptian army was at their beck and call. Mitannians seduced, or even bullied, other nations into war, smug that they would not have to face the battle themselves. They assumed Egypt would come to their rescue and fight for them, and their assumption had proven to be correct throughout Pharaoh Amenhotep's reign.

The possibility of his men losing their lives in a war in defense of such a trivial nation as Mitanni sickened Horemheb. Out of respect and admiration for the pharaoh, he kept his hatred of the Mitannians to himself and followed Amenhotep's orders as he swore he would do.

"I've heard stories about Mitanni," Salitas said. "They say its king conspires with the Assyrians in their bribery. Is there any honor here?"

Horemheb smirked. "I'm certain of only two things about this place: the women are voluptuous, and the pharaoh has great affection for this city and its people."

"And his affection for these barbarians doesn't disturb you?"

"It's not my place to question the pharaoh. Nor is it yours, Salitas."

"Certainly, General, I meant no offense," said Salitas.

Horemheb halted the formation before speaking to Salitas again.

"Akure and Menofet will ride ahead with me to the entrance. You'll assume command until I return," said Horemheb.

"By your order, general," replied Salitas.

Horemheb turned his horse around to face his army. He spotted his top-ranking officers, Akure and Menofet, at the helm.

"Akure! Menofet! With me!" he shouted.

The two officers rode up to him, and all three galloped toward the city. They soon came to a sudden stop in front of the fifty-foot walls and startled a murder of crows out of the nearby trees and into the clear blue sky.

Scores of Mitanni archers, previously concealed atop the wall, lifted their heads and then their bows. Their arrows were aimed directly at Horemheb and his two warriors and the general was furious. "Wretched beasts," he murmured to himself.

A slim and pompous adolescent, half the general's age, stood up among the archers. He had a decadent air about him, a confidence that exuded more arrogance than what Horemheb was willing to tolerate. The young man stepped in front of the archers and waved his hand. They lowered their bows, and he disappeared from the top of the wall.

As the gates of the city opened, the man and three of his guards lumbered out to meet the general.

"I am Shattiwaza, the son of the king. He's awaiting your arrival."

Horemheb dismounted his horse. Akure and Menofet followed his lead.

"Is it customary now to greet the general of the Egyptian army with nocked arrows?" asked the general.

"Perhaps if you had sent your troops through the Ugarit Valley, it wouldn't have raised our suspicions," said Shattiwaza.

Horemheb strutted up to Shattiwaza. "Perhaps if you were older and more experienced, you would have known the valley of Ugarit is a Hittite trap and not conducive to an army as massive as the Egyptian army," he responded. "We were told the king of Mitanni was dead."

"He is… very. My father, Tushratta, is the newly appointed king," said Shattiwaza.

"I'm familiar with your father. I am Horemheb, general of Pharaoh Amenhotep's army."

"Follow me, general," said Shattiwaza before he turned back toward the city.

Horemheb followed, and Akure and Menofet kept their eyes glued on the archers at the top of the wall as they all entered the gates of the city and headed toward the Mitanni palace.

King Tushratta was in his bath chamber when the men arrived. He was an obese man with beady eyes and, in Horemheb's view, an untrustworthy face. The king waded in a steam pool and he wasn't alone. Three naked women bathed him while a fourth woman with only her breasts covered knelt between his legs in oral service. The footsteps of Shattiwaza, Horemheb, and his warriors did nothing to interrupt the orgy.

The Mitannians' profligate nature was known throughout Egypt and the neighboring kingdoms. Horemheb found the Mitanni to be nothing more than sexual deviants, existing only to please their depraved pagan god, Assur, a god subservient to the Egyptian gods.

"The Egyptians are here," shouted Shattiwaza as he entered with Horemheb on his heel.

Tushratta pushed the woman's head away from his crotch at the sight of his guests. She rose and left the chamber. The king stared at the general as if forcing his memory to figure out who he was.

"Captain Horemheb? It's been a long time, welcome back to Wassukanni."

"I am the general of the pharaoh's army," said Horemheb, offended.

"My mistake. Congratulations on your promotion."

Horemheb overlooked Tushratta's smugness. He eyed the perimeter of the bath and found no scrolls or any evidence of war planning. It was as he suspected; the Mitannians had no intention of fighting their own battle. It annoyed Horemheb to the bone.

"You have a war brewing on your border, and you're in here bathing with whores?"

"I assure you, general, they're not *all* whores," said Tushratta.

He focused on a voluptuous servant girl standing against the wall nude. "Pyella, don't just stand there. Get the good men something to drink."

Pyella rushed out of the chamber. Tushratta turned his attention back to Horemheb.

"So tell me, General, how is my beloved friend, Amenhotep?"

"This isn't a social visit, Tushratta. What defenses have you implemented against the Hittites?"

"No need to get overly concerned about that, general," Tushratta replied as the remaining servant girls resumed washing his body. "I've already deployed a majority of our troops to the northern province of the Amurru kingdom. This is most likely where they will attempt their crossing."

"That makes no tactical sense," Horemheb replied.

"If you have a better plan, I'm open to hear it."

"The Amurru kingdom has proven to be a formidable barrier between you and the Hittites. Why would you station troops there?" asked Akure.

Without answering him, King Tushratta and his three female servants stepped out of the pool. Tushratta spread his arms as the women picked up cloths from the floor and dried his body. While Akure and Menofet were amused by such a flagrant display. Horemheb was not. His patience with the Mitanni king was already waning.

"King Suppiluliumas has tried many times to subdue the Amurru to gain a more strategic route into Mitanni. I fear he has finally succeeded," said Tushratta.

"Even so," replied Horemheb, "he's not likely to risk taking just one route here. We'll reposition your troops."

Pyella, the servant girl, returned with a tray of jars filled with beer. She handed a jar to both Akure and Menofet, but when she offered one to Horemheb, he refused it.

"Oh, did she bring you beer, general? Pardon her ignorance."

Tushratta winked at Pyella before correcting her. "Only the best of wines can enter the stomachs of Egyptian royalty, Pyella."

Pyella grazed Horemheb's body as she sauntered past him and smiled.

"Are you sure I can't get you and your men something else, general?" asked Tushratta.

"You can inform me where the Hittite army has encamped," replied Horemheb.

"I will, when I'm comfortable. Give me a moment."

Horemheb suppressed his desire to strangle Tushratta in front of his royal retinue. Such actions, however, would not be in the character of a celebrated general, and losing his temper would be a sign of weakness to the pharaoh. He kept his composure as the women assisted Tushratta into his robe and dressed themselves. Tushratta finally took a seat at a table at the end of the room. Horemheb nodded at his men, and they joined the Mitanni king at the table.

"Many days ago, I sent out spies to intercept the Hittites. As of yet, they haven't returned to me," said Tushratta.

"But they have to me, Father," Shattiwaza interrupted as he strode over to Horemheb and handed him a scroll. "The Hittites retreated to their homeland. They apparently had no true intentions on our kingdom after all."

Because he did not possess the abilities of a scribe, Horemheb pretended to read it. He relied on his intuition, and it served him well.

Shattiwaza was clearly delighted with what was written on the scroll. "I would hate to think your journey here was all for nothing, general, but I'm afraid it was," he said.

Horemheb rolled the scroll up and handed it back to him.

"I have other business here," he said.

"Really? Are you now going to teach us the most tactical way to clean our backside?" asked Shattiwaza flippantly.

"Shattiwaza!" Tushratta exclaimed, appalled at his son's words.

"Father, we've defeated the Hittites before without the help of these dictators. Why are you so quick to call on them?"

"Your son is wading in dangerous waters," Horemheb said to Tushratta.

"Forgive my son, general, he's not informed about our arrangement."

"And what 'arrangement' would that be, Father?" said Shattiwaza.

"The arrangement doesn't matter," said Horemheb. "Where are the conspirators who murdered your King Artassumara?"

"The conspirators were put to death," replied Tushratta.

"And Tazam?"

"Tazam is imprisoned in the palace holding chamber."

"He's still being kept here alive in the palace?"

"Yes, he is after all my brother," Tushratta explained.

"He will be put to death as well," said Horemheb.

Shattiwaza grumbled. "No! My uncle will pay for his crimes in prison."

"He'll pay with his blood. The pharaoh has spoken. Where is this holding chamber?"

Not waiting for an answer, Horemheb and his men rose from the table and headed toward the exit.

Shattiwaza rushed up to his father.

"Father, you can't let him kill your own brother. This is not their business."

Tushratta rose and followed Horemheb out of the chamber and down the hall.

"General, please," said Tushratta. "The people of Mitanni have seen enough bloodshed. They are content with Tazam's imprisonment. His ear and nose have already been cut off. Let him wither away in his cage, I beg you."

Tushratta's entreaties did nothing to slow Horemheb's pace. "You'll either execute him yourself," he responded, "or you will give me the order to do it. King Artassumara's death will be avenged properly by the order of the pharaoh."

"You cannot expect me to execute my own brother!" Tushratta shouted.

"Isn't that what just happened here? A brother murdering his own brother? We're merely continuing your country's tradition," replied Horemheb sarcastically as he turned and spat on the wall.

When the general reached the end of the corridor, he spotted the entrance to the holding chamber and unhinged the lock and entered.

Tazam's expression resembled a thief being caught in the act when Horemheb and his officers barged into the room where he was being held. Instead of withering away in a cage as King Tushratta had described, Horemheb found Tazam in a palace chamber complete with every form of luxury a person could desire. A bit of his ear and just the very tip of his nose had been cut off—that part at least was true, but it would hardly cause enough pain to be considered torture. The bandage that covered them had not even a hint of blood on it.

The following day at the rising of the sun, Akure and Menofet escorted a shackled Tazam to the execution barracks. Shattiwaza, King Tushratta, and several Mitanni officers stood in the royal tiers above, stone-faced and somber. Tazam stared up at Shattiwaza with a horrified expression among the jeering crowd of Mitannians who had gathered there to witness the execution of the one who murdered their beloved king.

"Shattiwaza, who are these people? Why are they doing this to me?" Tazam shouted.

"Your own brother has given you up to the Egyptians," he shouted back.

Tazam turned his gaze to King Tushratta.

"Please, my brother, don't let them do this, I am of your blood," said Tazam.

Tushratta looked away, too ashamed to face him, abashed that in his own kingdom he had to cede his sovereignty to the general of Egypt. Tushratta was emasculated as Horemheb proceeded with the execution. The crowd jeered louder, and Akure and Menofet secured Tazam's bound wrists to the pillory apparatus with chains.

Horemheb approached Tazam with his battle ax in hand. He glanced at Tushratta standing up in the royal tiers.

"Give me the order," said Horemheb.

"Wait! Shattiwaza, tell him!" screamed Tazam.

King Tushratta looked to his son, waiting for him to explain Tazam's remark. "Tell me what?" asked Tushratta.

"He's delirious," Shattiwaza answered.

"The order!" Horemheb repeated.

Shattiwaza stood up in front of his father and stomped his foot on the ground. "Don't give that arrogant brute the blessing to kill your brother."

Tushratta hesitated. There was no way around it. The decision had to be made. Torn between loyalty to his blood and his need of Egypt, he sighed as he made his choice. "May my god Assur forgive me," he said before raising his hand in the air.

Tazam was terrified at the sight. "No! You don't know the truth! Shattiwaza, confess—"

Before Tazam finished his plea, Horemheb sliced through his wrists. An explosion of blood splattered across Horemheb's face as the two severed hands fell with a thud, and Tazam dropped to the ground convulsing. The horror of it had no impact on Horemheb. He collected both severed hands into a satchel while the crowd burst into cheers and applause, elated at their murdered king's retribution. Shattiwaza eyed his father with contempt and stormed away. Tazam's convulsing abated until all the blood once inside him had pooled around his body in a sea of crimson.

CHAPTER

11

IT WAS NEARLY a month after Queen Ty and Amenhotep reconciled in T'aru when his illness became more severe. Confined to his bedchamber in Thebes, he yearned for the cure like an infant for its mother's breast. It was an insatiable thirst, that, when quenched, did nothing to improve his condition now. The more Ay administered it to him, the more Amenhotep heard and saw things that weren't there. The cure had to be the reason why he acted as if their reconciliation had never occurred. Queen Ty was devastated by his memory lapse, and his repeated requests for Lupita filled her spirit with a volatile mixture of jealousy and anxiety. How soon would it be before he discovered she was missing?

There had been times when Lupita had gone days without visiting Amenhotep's chamber, notably during her menstrual cycle. Queen Ty had made herself available, tending to him during her absence, so his mind would be eased of any concerns for her. When he asked her to bring Lupita to him, he had hallucinations during which he couldn't decipher if it was Lupita or the queen standing before him.

After seven consecutive nights of confinement in his bedchamber, Amenhotep's entire body twitched, and sweat poured from his brow. Ay was summoned again to administer the cure, and the pharaoh soon settled back in his bed, satisfied for the moment.

"I saw him," said Amenhotep.

"You saw who, my Pharaoh?" asked Ay.

"My son, Tuthmosis. He hasn't crossed into the afterlife. He was standing before me bleeding."

"It was just a bad dream."

"There are no bad dreams, only omens. Sia and Neper didn't perform the invocation. The Amun priests abandoned him," said Amenhotep trembling at his own words.

"My Pharaoh, I was assured by Sia that the invocation was carried out. Your illness brings about delusions."

"It's not a delusion. The gods had not ordained my son to fight in the war, yet I couldn't stop him from doing it. I failed. I betrayed the law of Amun. I caused my son's death."

"My Pharaoh, a Nubian killed Tuthmosis. We're powerless in the hands of fate."

"No. Amun let him die in order to punish me," replied Amenhotep.

Queen Ty stepped out from behind the curtain and excused Ay from the room. She approached Amenhotep, lifted his hand to her lips, and kissed it.

"Ay spoke the truth, it was a Nubian possessed by fate that killed our son"

Amenhotep stared at the queen, searching her facial expression for something. She avoided his interrogating look and used the cloth of her garment to wipe away the sweat drenching his face.

"You stare at me with such contempt. Why?" asked the queen.

"Prove to me it wasn't you who told Tuthmosis about the Nubian battle," replied Amenhotep.

The queen looked at him, stunned that he still suspected her. In the many years that she had been his wife, her *ways* had never changed. Perhaps Amenhotep had memorized her fears, and what would trigger her guilt, even her confession, and no matter how hard she would try to conceal her emotions, in the end, he would know that she was hiding something.

"I'm innocent. I have nothing to prove," she said defiantly.

"Then where is my Lupita? Why has she not come to me!" he demanded.

The queen wiped his brow with the cloth of her garment again. "Maybe she's menstruating."

Amenhotep grabbed her by the arm and pulled her down to him. His face filled with rage. "What have you done?!"

After Tazam's execution, Horemheb and his men hastened to return to Egypt. King Tushratta and his guards stood at the entrance of Mitanni's fortified walls as the Egyptians readied their horses for the return to their homeland.

Horemheb felt not a tinge of regret for carrying out the order of his pharaoh. Only the bloodstain on his breastplate irritated him. In vain he tried to wipe it away as he mounted his horse.

Tushratta scoffed at his efforts. "I apologize that my brother's blood has stained your otherwise pristine uniform, general," said Tushratta. "Nevertheless, I have a gift for the pharaoh."

From inside the fortified walls, a girl around eleven years of age approached on horseback. Her face was masked by a sheer black veil, and behind her, an eight-foot-tall figure covered by a cloth was being pulled on a sled by three horses. Her convoy came to a stop beside Tushratta. He caressed the girl's hand, then rubbed the nose of her horse.

"My daughter, Kiya, will return with you to Egypt. May her marriage to Amenhotep be a symbol of alliance between us. And please tell him that if he doesn't marry her, he cannot impregnate her."

Tushratta stepped to the rear of the sled and removed the cloth from around the eight-foot tall figure—a limestone statue of a Mitannian goddess.

"I'm loaning the pharaoh our statue of Ishtar. I understand he's ill, and she will cure his sickness. But unlike my daughter, I want my statue returned to me once he's cured," said Tushratta.

Tushratta enjoyed the looks of amazement on Horemheb's men's faces as they gazed upon the intricate work of art. Horemheb was not impressed. Tushratta was bartering for something.

"So be it," Horemheb replied, waiting to hear what the king wanted in return.

"And remind him I'm expecting a generous amount of the gold reserves he promised me. Especially in light of recent events here."

Horemheb grinned. Again, his intuition about the Mitanni king's motives proved true. He turned his horse to leave without responding.

"Wait. One last thing, general. You didn't mention what hour my sister will arrive."

"Lady Lupita? She's not traveling here," said Horemheb.

"Are you sure? I received a letter from her some time ago that she was returning for Artasssumara's funerary rites."

"She's not aware of his death," replied Horemheb.

"Indeed, she is, general. She sealed the letter."

"The pharaoh would never allow her to travel without my protection."

Horemheb did his best to conceal his trepidation. If Lupita traveled secretly without telling the pharaoh, then she could be somewhere vulnerable and at the mercy of the Hittites.

"I swear to you, she said in the letter she would be taking the Amurru route here with her Mitanni convoy," said Tushratta.

This information made no sense to Horemheb, and his facial expression betrayed his concern.

"Something wrong?" asked Tushratta.

"The Amurru route passes through the Ugarit valley."

"Exactly. Which is why she should have arrived here before you and your men."

Horemheb thought about demanding to see Lupita's letter, but how would he verify its authenticity when he was incapable of reading it? He turned his attention instead to Akure and Menofet. "A third of the army will remain here with you. The rest will go with me. Escort Kiya and the statue to Egypt." And with that, Horemheb raced off with his army in search of Lupita.

At the palace in Thebes, Amenhotep plunged deeper into hysteria. Only a day after assaulting the queen, then accusing her of harming Lupita and sending Tuthmosis to battle in the Nubian war, he had forgotten the entire incident. His last memory was of T'aru. He remembered being there awaiting her arrival, but still had no memory of their reconciliation, or of the days that followed. Queen Ty worried that in this new state of disorientation her husband might sign a declaration imparting Teppy's birthright to someone else: a soldier, one of his guards, anyone. She had destroyed the threat of Lupita and silenced the Oracle, but she was powerless to stand in the way of Amenhotep's madness.

Her only recourse now was to create *new* memories for her husband—to endear Teppy to his father with gifts of his favorite things. So Teppy limped down the palace corridor hand-in-hand with his mother toward Amenhotep's bedchamber. At the entrance, Ty dropped to her knees, eye-level with her son and lifted his chin.

"Remember, your father is very ill, so when you speak to him, hold your head up high. He needs to see that you're a strong boy that's worthy of his birthright."

"Yes, Mother," said Teppy.

She handed him a ripe pomegranate. "He hasn't had one in a long time because of the drought. Give it to him; he will love you for it."

The queen kissed Teppy on his forehead and left him alone at the entrance to his father's bedchamber. Teppy was apprehensive at first until the thought of his father's smile when he would hand him the fruit gave him the spark of courage he needed.

Teppy entered Amenhotep's bedchamber and found the pharaoh asleep with a sad expression on his face. He had aged dramatically. His skin appeared tough as leather and worn with wrinkles. *Father is much too old to be fighting wars against Nubian slaves,* he thought.

Teppy reached out and touched his father's hand, making sure to hold his head up high as his mother had instructed him. Amenhotep opened his eyes and gazed at his son, but he didn't seem to recognize him.

"It's me, Teppy, Father."

There was no reaction from Amenhotep, only a blank stare.

Maybe he hasn't fully awakened, so Teppy shook his father's shoulder. "Father, wake up. You're still dreaming."

Amenhotep reached out and caressed Teppy's face. "Tuthmosis? Is that you?"

"No, Father, Tuthmosis is not with us anymore. He's with the Aten in the mountains. It's me, Teppy."

Amenhotep looked over his son's head and eyed the perimeter of the room, teary-eyed, as if he didn't recognize his surroundings. "Where am I?"

It startled Teppy to see his father weeping. This was his chance to be like Tuthmosis, the one who had always comforted him when he was afraid.

"You're in your bedchamber, Father. Don't cry, you're safe. I will protect you from the beast."

Amenhotep gazed at him. "I'm so sorry, my son. I couldn't save you, forgive me. Can you please forgive me?'

"Save me from what? I'm here, Father. I'm alive and well."

Amenhotep reached out and rubbed Teppy's chest and arms.

"You *are* alive," said Amenhotep. "But how can that be when you're dead?"

"I'm not dead, Father. I don't want to die," said Teppy, confused.

"You're already dead, Tuthmosis. Look at you. Can't you feel the blood dripping from your eyes and the corners of your mouth? Amun has taken you away and cursed me. Let me cover your neck wound, my son, so that the blood will stop flowing from it."

Amenhotep sat up in his bed and reached out to grab Teppy around the neck.

Afraid, Teppy stepped back. "Stop it, Father. I'm not Tuthmosis."

"You are dead. You should have ascended into the afterlife, my son," he said with his eyes widened and his left hand quivering.

"I'm not Tuthmosis I said! I'm Teppy!"

His scream snapped Amenhotep out of his delusion. He now saw that it was his son Teppy standing in his chamber, and he looked disgusted by it.

"It's you who plays these tricks of sorcery on me, pretending to be Tuthmosis." Amenhotep growled.

"I'm not playing tricks, Father. I only came to bring you a pomegranate, see?"

He held out the fruit to his father. Amenhotep snatched it from his hand and threw it across the room. It smashed against the wall, staining it red before the bloody rinds landed on the floor. Teppy limped over to where the fruit had landed and retrieved it. Amenhotep glowered at his son.

"Your birth has cursed me. Get out."

Amenhotep tried to rise from his bed and stand. The simple task was difficult for him as he started to heave and take quick breaths. Teppy froze in place with the pomegranate in his hand. The fruit was meant for his father and he wanted so much to be the one to give it to him. Instead, he heard Amenhotep shouted at him again as he fell back into his bed.

"Ay! Get him out! Get him away from me!"

Teppy dropped the pomegranate and ran out of the room and down the palace corridor sobbing.

"You told me he would love me! He doesn't love me. He hates me!" cried Teppy.

Though his legs were growing stronger, and his falls had become less frequent, he lost his balance that day and fell hard. Ay spotted him and rushed over to help. When he reached out his hand, Teppy refused it.

"No, I am strong. I am a prince," he said to Ay.

Teppy wiped the tears from his eyes, and with all the strength he could muster, he lifted himself up from the floor and limped away down the palace corridor.

In the days that followed, Amenhotep's voice was barely audible, his speech garbled, and at times nothing he would say made any sense. In her desperation to help him, the queen did something she swore to herself she would never do. To appease Amenhotep, she called on the Amun priests, Sia and Neper. She wanted to save her husband at any cost, even if it meant in the end she would regret her decision.

Sia and Neper entered Amenhotep's bedchamber while Ay and the queen waited outside, hopeful that the Amun god's judgment of the pharaoh would be favorable. When the twins exited the bedchamber after a remarkably short period of time, the queen presumed the news would not be good.

"Tell us. Can his illness be cured?" asked Ay.

"We can't do anything more for him here. We need to transport him to the healing temple— " said Sia.

"And lie him next to the statue where the Amun god himself resides," Neper finished.

"He won't go. He's petrified of the healing temple," said the queen.

"The pharaoh needs the blessing of Amun now, Sia replied."

"You can bless him here. Help him!" Queen Ty shouted.

The twins responded to her demands with the same eerie calm they portrayed after the death of Tuthmosis. "You will watch him die in his chamber…," said Neper, "—if you don't allow us to take him to the healing temple," Sia warned.

Their words infuriated her. Clearly, it had been a horrible mistake to allow the Amun priests to see Amenhotep. To be humiliated again after what they allowed to happen to her son Tuthmosis was intolerable.

The queen looked at Sia and Neper with disgust. "The both of you are worthless. I will not threaten my husband with your lies."

"Sister, please," Ay interrupted. Queen Ty ignored him.

"For many years, Amenhotep and I sacrificed everything to your Amun god: our gold, our precious jewels, and our best livestock. All of it to a god that delights in its own greed. We have received nothing in return for our generosity except more premonitions of turmoil yet to come if we don't provide it with more offerings. Amun has no power to bring goodness," she snapped, "only evil, and so it is with its priests."

"Your words are blasphemous, Queen," said Sia.

"You may soon regret them," Neper finished.

"I regret my husband didn't put an end to your priesthood a long time ago."

The queen directed her attention back to Ay. "Escort them out of this palace," she said as she strode away down the corridor into Amenhotep's chamber.

The moment she left, Sia approached Ay face-to-face. "It seems the pharaoh's fate has been sealed by his queen. If you wish to save Teppy from the same fate, then you must bring him to us at once-"

"We will cast a spell that will cure the prince so he walks like a pharaoh when the time comes," said Neper.

"The queen would never allow it," said Ay.

Sia pressed the palm of his hand against Ay's chest.

"Consider the benefits of your loyalty to the Amun priesthood—" he said.

"And the consequences of your disloyalty," Neper added.

Sia removed his hand from Ay, and he and Neper drifted down the corridor and out of the temple. Ay was left with a tingling sensation under the skin of his chest. He opened his garment. A bruise the size of a fist covered the area where Sia had touched him.

CHAPTER

12

KING TUSHRATTA hurled razor-sharp discuses at a statue of Isis, as he waited in his chamber for his son to arrive.

"I wonder if the Egyptians know you use their sacred statue for target practice," said Shattiwaza entering the room.

"It's no worse than what they'll do with our statue of Ishtar," responded Tushratta as he hurled another copper discus at the statue. It lodged across the bridge of the nose.

"Then why did you give it to them?"

"I didn't give it; I loaned it. It's worthless anyway. Sit."

"I'll stand. Why have you sent for me?"

"I need a word with you in private."

Tushratta stood up revealing his naked, obese body. Shattiwaza looked sickened by it. "For the sake of the gods, why can't you put on a garment?"

"This is my palace; I'll be as I please."

Tushratta stepped over to the ablution tank, cupped water in his hand, and splashed it on his face. "Your rude behavior in the presence of my guests was beyond disrespectful."

"What rude behavior?"

"How quickly you've forgotten how you shamed me in front of the Egyptian general."

"If I were you, Father, I'd be more concerned about the shaming of your sister Lupita. Have you forgotten that she's out there somewhere in the Ugarit Valley unprotected? If the Hittites get to her first, they will do unspeakable things."

"They wouldn't dare harm her. She's a wife of the pharaoh," replied Tushratta.

"A pharaoh of Egyptian vulgarians who have no right to come to our kingdom and dictate who should live and who should die. Why can't you stand up to them like a true Mitannian?"

"A true Mitannian?" Tushratta smirked. "What do you know about being a true Mitannian?"

"I know your greed for Egyptian gold Father, has rendered you spineless. I'd wager the trait is not part of Mitanni's legacy. "

His temper rising, Tushratta sat down and hurled more copper discuses at the Isis statue. One arm shattered, and terra cotta pieces crumbled on the floor. "I've built kingdoms while you were in the womb, led Mitanni armies into war, and judged over countless disputes between men, all while you were merely carried in the pouch that hangs between my legs. You have much to learn before you can question my motives."

"Your motives are as predictable as the sun rising in the east," said Shattiwaza.

Tushratta rose and stepped close to his son, staring him in the eye.

"If your mother was alive, she would be disappointed at what an insolent you've become. Just a useless waste of her breast milk."

"How can a whore be disappointed?" said Shattiwaza.

In a fit of rage, Tushratta shoved his son against the wall and strangled him. Shattiwaza tried to push him away, but his father's grip on his neck only tightened. Shattiwaza's face turned pale as Tushratta lifted him up off the ground.

"She sacrificed her life to save yours, you ungrateful brat."

The king released his grip, and Shattiwaza dropped to the floor gasping for air.

Tushratta wrapped himself in a robe, picked up a scroll off the table, and threw it at Shattiwaza. It landed on the floor beside him.

"You were one of the conspirators," said Tushratta. "It's Tazam's full confession."

Tushratta was not surprised that Shattiwaza wasn't curious enough to open the scroll. He knew of everything in it.

Shattiwaza stood warily. "Uncle Artassumara was making secret treaties with Kadesh and the Assyrians. He would've destroyed Mitanni if he remained king."

"I'll give you till dawn to leave Mitanni," replied Tushratta. "Take all I've given you and go. If I find you here after dawn, you'll be sent to the prison barracks."

"You can't just banish me from my homeland," Shattiwaza said in disbelief.

"Maybe you'll be fortunate enough to find a 'true Mitannian' to help you. I want you out of my sight!"

Shattiwaza trudged to the exit of his father's chamber. "The next time you lay eyes on me, Father, one of us will die."

Tushratta hurled another copper discus at what was left of the Isis statue as Shattiwaza left the room. It toppled over and crashed on the floor in pieces.

For six days, Horemheb led his army along the bank of the river as they searched for Lupita and her convoy, and for six days they found nothing. On the seventh day, one of his scouts spotted vultures circling an area east of the Great Sea. Horemheb ordered a regiment to accompany him and left the bulk of his army at the riverbank as he crossed over the river to inspect the site.

Hidden behind rows of trees, Horemheb found Lupita's convoy: three carriages with empty reins. The horses and camels were missing and the supplies needed to survive their long journey scattered on the ground. Salitas dismounted his horse alongside Horemheb.

"It's suicide for a Mitanni queen to travel this way without the escort of an army," said Salitas.

"She's foremost an Egyptian queen," Horemheb replied.

He turned his attention to the carriages. A line of his soldiers stood ready to draw their swords as he and Salitas peered inside the first carriage, then the second. Both were empty.

"Spread out and search for survivors," Horemheb ordered.

"King Suppululiumas has stolen their horses and camels and taken them prisoners," Salitas suggested. "He doesn't know Lupita is a wife of the pharaoh."

"It is his great error if he didn't know what he should have known," replied Horemheb, as he extracted a Hittite arrow out of a tree. A soldier interrupted their conversation.

"General, over here!"

Horemheb and Salitas rushed over to where a group of soldiers stood still, all of them had solemn expressions as they stared down into a shallow ditch.

The dead bodies of the members of Lupita's convoy were stacked on top of each other, their faces mutilated and their bodies and clothing stained with dried blood. The vultures had all but eaten away most of the flesh around their heads and necks, but from the garments they wore, Horemheb surmised that Lupita was not among them. *Perhaps Salitas was right, maybe King Suppululiumas captured her and will soon return her safely to Egypt.* In his gut, however, he believed otherwise.

"Why would they do this when we have a peace treaty with them?" asked Salitas.

"The treaty is now severed. Gather the bodies," Horemheb ordered.

The soldiers carried the bodies to the chariots, while Horemheb continued searching the area. A tiny object glimmering in the sunlight caught his attention. He walked over and retrieved it—a lapis-lazuli earring engraved with intricate designs, a rare item of jewelry only a queen of Egypt could afford to wear.

Horemheb whipped around at the echo of a twig snapping. Lupita's cat, Bastian, was staring at him from behind a bush. Once it was sure it had Horemheb's attention, the cat trotted away, confidently leading him. Horemheb followed the cat through an area of dense vegetation. Bastian glanced back at Horemheb, and then entered upon an open field.

Pieces of tattered and torn linen lay strewn on the ground. There was no sound of animals, insects, or even birds, only silence and foreboding. Bastian led Horemheb right up to Lupita's body. Naked and lying on her back in a pool of blood, her torso appeared riddled with stab wounds. Bastian licked Lupita's face, staining his milky-white fur blood red. *The cat must have chased away the vultures,* he thought, because her skin and flesh were still intact.

The cat climbed on top of her and lay down on her swollen belly. Bastian peered up at Horemheb with its sad sea-green eyes, as if asking for help.

There was nothing the general could do; Lupita was dead. What made it all the worse was that she had been butchered by his military rival—the Hittites—the very ones he had sworn to Amenhotep that they would be protected from.

Horemheb removed his breastplate and covered Lupita's nakedness. Overcome with guilt, he knelt down beside her and spoke to her aloud, asking for her forgiveness for not reaching her in time. Informing the pharaoh of her murder would not be easy;

however, confronting Queen Ty with the lapis-lazuli earring was something he looked forward to doing.

Horemheb's army was a twenty-one-day journey away from Egypt, and the general worried that the prolonged heat and decomposition would render Lupita's internal organs impossible to preserve. So, as the regiment crossed the river and joined with his army, Horemheb attached a third horse to his chariot, the sturdiest and strongest animal in the convoy, and lay Lupita's body across it. Horemheb left the command of his army to Salitas and rushed off in his chariot, traveling as fast as the horses could carry him.

CHAPTER

13

TEPPY DIDN'T KNOW where Ay was taking him. His uncle had awakened him in the middle of the night, dressed him, and with no explanation, led him into the Amun healing temple. The last time he had set foot there was the last time he saw his brother Tuthmosis alive. Returning to the temple filled him with sadness and dread. Although comforted by his uncle's presence, he was frightened to be there without his mother.

Sia and Neper entered the room, and took turns lighting little candles around the perimeter of the platform. Frightened by the ritual, Teppy tried to hide behind his uncle, but the priests pried him away from Ay and placed him on the platform.

Despite the many candles, Teppy was in darkness. Ay had left the temple, and he was alone with Sia and Neper hovering over him with their foreboding onyx black eyes. Neper reached across Teppy's chest to take the Aten amulet from around his neck. Teppy grasped it with both hands to stop him.

"It's my brother's!" he shouted. "You can't have it!"

Sia glanced over at Neper and nodded. Neper relinquished his hold on it.

"Where did my uncle go?" asked Teppy scanning the room with his eyes. "I have to find him."

Teppy tried to sit up but Neper pushed him back and fastened his wrists and ankles to the platform with leather straps. Sia filled a jar with a red-tinted liquid. He lifted Teppy's head and put the jar to his mouth.

"Drink," he said.

Before Teppy could resist, Sia poured a portion of the liquid down his throat.

Teppy spat it back up. "It stings like a thousand bees."

"Drink it!" Sia shouted.

When Teppy refused to open his mouth, Sia forced it open and poured more of the liquid down his throat. It made him cough, and he spat it up again.

"I can't drink it. It burns. I want my Mother," cried Teppy trembling. He wanted to scream her name but was afraid that the priests might slice his face with a sickle as the Amun beast had done in his dream.

"The queen has given you over to us—" said Neper.

"Because you are weak," finished Sia.

"I am not weak. Mother said that I am strong, I am a prince and will soon be a king."

"What you are is a curse—" said Sia, tightening the straps.

"From the Aten god. An abomination," Neper said, finishing the thought.

Neper handed Sia a linen scroll. He took it to the corner of the room and knelt down in front of the Amun statue. He placed the scroll at the foot of the statue and bowed in prayer:

"Amun, the god of gods and of Osiris, whose skin is of gold and bones made of silver. Empower me through this utensil of your sacrifice, so that I may strike him, who is in the form of a child who struck you."

Sia kissed the scroll and unrolled it. Inside, was a bloodstained dagger. He grabbed it. "Only death can bring us the light."

Queen Ty stormed into the Amun healing temple, as Sia was raising it above her son's chest.

"No!" she screamed, rushing toward the platform where Teppy was strapped.

That night, the queen had found it hard to sleep. Her maternal instincts led her to visit Teppy's bedchamber where she discovered him missing from his bed. A black mamba was slithering across his bedcover in his place. The sight of the snake in Teppy's bed, she believed, was an omen from the Oracle she murdered and his Amun priests.

When she found Teppy lying on the priests' platform, Sia was holding the dagger in one hand and a goose by the neck in the other, stifling its ability to squeal. The queen's sudden appearance alarmed him.

"No need to be concerned. The blood of this sacrifice will heal the boy, so that he walks like a pharaoh," Sia said defending his actions to a horrified queen.

It appeared that the Amun priests' intent was not to harm Teppy, but to cut the jugular vein of the goose and spread the blood over the boy's chest. Still, the queen wasn't convinced. She believed what she witnessed with her own eyes; the Amun priests attempting to sacrifice her son to destroy the only obstacle preventing them from ruling Egypt.

Queen Ty unfastened the straps from Teppy's wrists and ankles. The boy was so overjoyed at the sight of his mother that he cried and flung his arms around her so tightly she could barely catch her breath. She kissed his forehead and assured him that everything would be as it was before.

"Are we going home?" he asked.

"Yes, my little prince. We're going home."

Keeping one eye on Sia, the queen lifted Teppy off the platform and escorted him out. The priest muttered a curse at her for halting their ritual, and she silently cursed him for subjecting her son to their barbaric ritual.

After Queen Ty tucked Teppy into bed, she asked who had taken him to the healing temple. He informed her it had been his uncle, and as soon as he drifted off to sleep, she went to find out why.

Asleep in his bedchamber, Ay awoke to a flint knife pressed against his throat. Queen Ty straddled his chest, breathing erratically, prodding him to make even the slightest movement so she could sever his head without guilt. The knife trembled in her hand and broke the skin on his neck. Ay looked in her eyes, petrified.

"So you secretly wish to give my son over to the evil of the Amun priests?" Ty asked.

"No, I am your brother and the servant to your husband. You know that I'm not of the Amun priests anymore," Ay said squirming.

"You're my brother and I have loved you all my life, but I swear, if you don't give me a reason I can believe, I'll decapitate you right here and now," she said to him.

A drop of blood pooled around the blade as the queen pressed the knife deeper into Ay's throat.

"My sister, Sia and Neper convinced me they could heal Teppy so that he would walk without falling. They swore it would guarantee his ascension to the throne, and that they would bless Teppy's kingship in the presence of the pharaoh."

"Lies!" Queen Ty shouted. "You know how much I despise and distrust them, and yet you took my son to those evil priests? What reason will you give me to spare your life?"

"One reason only, and I swear to you it's the truth. I'm afraid of him. Sia threatened to punish me if I didn't follow the will of Amun and bring Teppy to them."

"How can they punish you when you're protected by royalty?" she pressed.

"I'm not protected from their magic."

Ay slid his garment down, careful not to make any sudden moves.

"This is the curse Sia left on my body when he touched me," said Ay pointing at his chest.

At first glance, the queen saw nothing, but when she looked closer, it appeared. The bruise Sia had left on Ay had spread across his torso to twice the size.

When Horemheb arrived in Thebes days later, he gave Lupita's body over to the Amun priests, and they at once prepared it for mummification. He had succeeded in getting her body there in time, but soon after, collapsed from exhaustion and had to be escorted to his chamber. After consuming seven measures of wine, and pieces of fruit, and meat, he regained enough strength to drive his chariot to the pharaoh's palace.

Horemheb strolled through the corridor with a sack in his hand. Ay ran up from behind and caught up with him.

"General, is there something I can assist you with?"

"No," said Horemheb without breaking his stride.

"If you're here to see the pharaoh, the queen has forbidden anyone to disturb him."

"I'm not anyone. I'm the general of his army."

Ay was worried. The queen had ordered him under no circumstances to let anyone in to see Amenhotep. He tried again. "General, any interruption would only aggravate his illness. The queen advises you confer with her on all matters of state until the pharaoh recovers."

Horemheb ignored him and continued toward Amenhotep's chamber. When he pulled back the curtains, the queen stepped forward, blocking his way.

"Welcome back, general," she said.

"Is he here?" asked Horemheb.

"My husband needs to rest. I can give him your message at sunrise."

"It can't wait until sunrise."

"I am the queen, the great royal wife of Amenhotep, and I'm more than capable of handling the affairs of state on his behalf. What is it?"

"I'm very aware of who you are. This matter is between me and the pharaoh."

The faint sound of Amenhotep's feeble voice silenced them both.

"General? Is that you? General?"

Horemheb stepped around the queen and into Amenhotep's chamber.

Inside it was pitch dark. Balls of incense were set atop burning coals releasing the astringent aroma of myrrh and frankincense. The smoke enveloped the entire chamber, obscuring Amenhotep's face as he sat slouched in the corner gazing back at Horemheb.

"General, you have to stop them. They're coming for me. I can't fight them alone," Amenhotep said in a crackling timbre, his face still obscured in the dark.

"My Pharaoh, who is coming for you?"

"The Nubians. The ones I killed in the war. If you listen closely you can hear them."

"But my Pharaoh—"

"Shhhh, listen General, they're here," whispered Amenhotep cutting him off.

The pharaoh stepped out from the dark corner of the room. Horemheb was shocked. Amenhotep's face appeared gaunt, his body looked half the size it was from the last time he saw him. He had aged beyond his years and was frail and slightly bent over like an old man. His eyes were sunken and dark—the sure look of opium addiction. Horemheb himself had fought his own battle against the cure, and for the most part had won. It was heartbreaking for him to see that now it had hurled Amenhotep into madness. Not only was he losing his pharaoh, he was losing a loyal friend, one who he had come to love and respect as a great ruler and military commander of Egypt.

Amenhotep paced around the chamber in a paranoid frenzy, searching for something.

"Did you hear that? They're here," he repeated. "They're hiding because they're afraid of you, general."

"My king, there's no one here but us. No harm will come to you."

"You don't believe me. Why don't you believe me?" he said pleading. "I'll show you. Yes, I can prove it, general."

Amenhotep ripped the garment from his torso. To Horemheb's astonishment, the letters H-E-R-E-T-I-C were crudely carved into the pharaoh's chest. A scab had formed over it so that the word appeared as though it was written in black kohl.

"Now you see? You see what they did to me?" asked Amenhotep.

Horemheb watched him step over a flint knife as if it wasn't there. The tip of it was stained in blood.

"They've taken my Lupita, and now they're coming for me," said the pharaoh.

Horemheb took his hand and led him back to his bed.

"You have to take me away from here now," he mumbled to Horemheb. "Ty won't let me leave."

Horemheb placed his hands on Amenhotep's shoulders and sat him down on his bed. He didn't want to tell him, especially now, but maybe the truth might bring his pharaoh back to reality, no matter how painful.

"No one has taken Lady Lupita," said Horemheb.

"Then where is she?"

"Lady Lupita is dead."

Amenhotep's eyes widened. "The Nubian spirit killed her?"

"No, my Pharaoh, it was not a spirit. Lady Lupita left Egypt for Mitanni without my army as an escort. The Hittites captured her and her convoy in the Ugarit Valley and slaughtered them all," he said without the slightest restraint.

Amenhotep shook his head. "It can't be. For what purpose would she go there without telling me? I never told her about her brother's murder. Did you, general?"

"I'd never betray what we speak in confidence."

Amenhotep buried his head in his hands weeping over Lupita's death. It was enough to keep Horemheb from divulging his suspicions about Queen Ty.

"My sweet, gentle Lupita," Amenhotep cried out. "She was pregnant with my child, my heir."

"You'll have vengeance, my Pharaoh."

"The Hittites have broken the peace treaty and spat on me like a dog. Swear to me, on the oath of Amun and the god Montu, that you will find the ones responsible."

"I swear to you amidst the glory of the highest god Amun that they'll pay an equal price for what they did to Lady Lupita. You have my word."

Amenhotep reclined back into his bed, and for an instant, it seemed his pharaoh was having a moment of clarity.

"General, if they come to take me away, I trust only you to carry Egypt and my people forward as pharaoh, not my queen nor Teppy. You are the courageous and noble overseer of Egypt. I'll draw up a declaration today and place the scroll with the priests of Amun for safekeeping," said Amenhotep.

His declaration moved Horemheb. They had always shared a mutual admiration for each other, but he never imagined the pharaoh looked to him as his equal. Amenhotep, the great ruler and builder of Egypt, had complete confidence in him to lead his glorious country in his absence. Overwhelmed by the honor, Horemheb prostrated himself before the pharaoh. "I'm humbled and honored to serve you and my country, but no one is coming to take you away. You will live a thousand years, my Pharaoh"

Horemheb laid the sack he was carrying on the bed next to Amenhotep, bowed to him, then exited his chamber, knowing that when the pharaoh opened it, he would find Tazam's severed hands cut off at the wrists and bound with string. Although it meant nothing to Horemheb now that Lady Lupita was dead, it would mean everything to Amenhotep that he had kept his oath to him.

CHAPTER

14

QUEEN TY REGRETTED sending Teppy in alone to see his father. The cruelty brought on by his delusions had caused Teppy to fear him. This time she would be there to assure his protection.

The queen dressed Teppy in a miniature soldier's uniform that she had especially tailored for him, thinking that if Amenhotep envisioned their son as an Egyptian warrior king, it might change his heart and persuade him to give Teppy a chance at claiming his divine destiny as heir to the Egyptian throne. She believed this would happen only if she continued to be tenacious.

"Is this all mine?" asked Teppy excitedly as the queen fastened the scaled-down breastplate around his chest.

"It's all yours. You are your mother's brave little warrior."

"Can I show it to Uncle Ay and cousin Sete?"

"Let's put your helmet on first," she said as she removed a war helmet from a burlap sack and placed it on him. Teppy laughed because it swallowed up his entire head.

He lifted the helmet above his eyes. "I can't see. It's too big."

"I know. You'll grow into it soon."

The queen hesitated. There was another presence in the room. When she turned around, General Horemheb was studying them from the entryway in silence.

"What're you doing here?" she asked.

"I was directed here by your maidservant," said Horemheb, wry-faced at the sight of Teppy in a miniature replica of his army's uniform.

Queen Ty took the helmet off Teppy's head.

"This is my son's bedchamber, general."

"I know where I am. My guards protect your son's bedchamber."

"Teppy, go to your Uncle Ay's quarters," said the queen.

"Can I play the twenty-squares game with cousin Sete too?"

"Yes, you may if your uncle gives you permission. I'll come and get you soon," she replied with a forced smile before kissing the top of his head. As soon as Teppy left the room her smile changed to a scowl and she turned her attention back to Horemheb, perturbed at his ill-conceived entitlement to enter any royal chamber at will.

"What is it you want, general?"

Horemheb handed her the lapis-lazuli earring he had found near Lupita's body. She was jarred by the sight of it but adroitly masked her reaction.

"It appears to be of royalty. Is it yours?" asked Horemheb.

The queen glanced at it again, pretending to be perplexed by the sight of it. "It's been missing from my cosmetic box for many days. Where did you find it?"

"It was lying near Lupita's mutilated body."

He searched for a reaction in the queen's eyes. There was none. She placed the earring in her pocket and began to braid the locks of her hair.

"I would never think that she would steal from me," replied the queen nonchalantly.

Horemheb sneered at the absurdity of her answer. "It would be senseless for a mistress of the pharaoh to steal, my queen, when she could as easily request anything she desired directly from him."

"No matter how she obtained my jewelry, what does this matter have to do with me?"

"Would you really be interested in hearing my speculation?"

"No, though I'm certain that won't stop you."

The queen walked over to the ablution tank and slowly washed her hands and arms—a perfect excuse to have her back turned to him while he spoke.

"I could be far from the truth," said Horemheb, "but I would guess someone discovered that Lady Lupita's brother was murdered and went to her and told her of it. Because she was young and naïve, this 'someone,' was able to convince her to travel back to her homeland without informing me or the pharaoh, knowing that she and her Mitanni convoy would be an easy target for the Hittites."

Horemheb peered over the queen's shoulder to see if she was paying attention to him before he went on speaking more of his accusations.

"The earrings, I would surmise," continued Horemheb, "were used to win Lady Lupita's confidence, a parting gift for an ill-fated journey."

Horemheb impressed the queen. She now understood it was not just because of his combat skills that Amenhotep praised him so but also because his perceptual abilities were profound. She chuckled as she grabbed a cloth from the table and dried her arms and hands, the only reaction possible to rebuff the general's accusations. "I pray to the gods you find and punish the savages that attacked her, the ones who are truly responsible for her death."

"All who were involved have Lady Lupita's blood on their hands and should suffer the punishment. Would you not agree?"

"I agree that everyone should receive what they deserve," said the queen.

"Do you know of any other purpose she would leave Egypt for Mitanni without informing me or the pharaoh?"

"I can assure you Lady Lupita never thought of me as her confidant if that is what you are so absurdly suggesting. Is there anything else?" Queen Ty turned away from Horemheb and placed Teppy's helmet back into the burlap sack.

"Yes," said Horemheb. "Have you prepared living quarters for the girl?"

"Girl?"

"Lupita's niece, Kiya, the princess of Mitanni. She's eleven years of age, and I would imagine very fertile. King Tushratta has given her in marriage to the pharaoh along with their statue of Ishtar. They have arrived and are waiting at the entrance of the palace. I must admit, intense beauty proves to be a consistent trait of Lupita's family. What living quarters are prepared for her?"

Stunned to hear such news, the queen smiled at Horemheb to disguise the affliction the general had brought on her. "There are none at the moment because I was simply not aware of any of this," she explained. "I'll have my servants prepare a special place for her soon, but for now my concern is for my husband's recovery."

"I assume you will make her feel as comfortable as you did Lady Lupita," said Horemheb.

Horemheb's sly remark revealed how much pleasure he received from taunting her. His presence made her nervous, and there was no relief until he bowed and left the room. Her mission became even more urgent now.

Hand-in-hand, Ty walked Teppy in his soldier's uniform down the long, winding corridor. When they reached the entrance to the pharaoh's chamber, she straightened his miniature armored breastplate and kissed him on his forehead.

"Look at you, my little warrior," she said, beaming with pride.

The queen escorted Teppy into Amenhotep's chamber, illuminated by a single torch, and led him right up to his father's bedside. There Amenhotep lay sound asleep, breathing silently through his nose but exhaling an intimidating snore from his mouth.

When she took another step toward him, a white cat jumped out from under the pharaoh's bedcover. It was Lupita's cat, Bastian, and it hovered over Amenhotep like his protector, pacing back and forth across the bed. With no fear, Teppy walked toward it, and before the queen could pull him back he petted the animal's head. Bastian purred in affection.

"Don't be afraid, Mother, it's a nice one," said Teppy. Astonished by her son's bravery, Queen Ty approached the animal herself, but when she put her hand out to pet it, the cat hissed at her. The queen grabbed Teppy's hand, and they slowly stepped back from the bed, and out of Amenhotep's chamber.

After she returned Teppy to his room, she took her concerns to Ay. He was painting a carved relief on his chamber walls, dipping his reed into a jar of water then onto his scribe's palette filled with red and yellow ochre, malachite, orpiment and carbon black pigment powder. She was silent at first as he painted the scene of him and his family kneeling in worship to the Aten. The vibrant carving was framed with a long prayer inscribed in hieroglyphics.

"He brought her cat back to torment me," said Queen Ty, expecting a response from her brother. Ay was more interested in painting his symbols perfectly.

"I could see the contempt in his eyes," she continued. "Anyone else that disrespected a queen of Egypt as such would be put to death on the spot, but Amenhotep does nothing but spew out accolades about his beloved general."

Her brother kept his silence.

"Are you listening to me?" she asked.

"General Horemheb is a man of war. I don't believe his intentions are against you. His desire is to please the pharaoh."

"Yes, to please the pharaoh and to destroy me."

"You have him all wrong, my queen," said Ay, his eyes still focused on the wall as he brushed another stroke of his reed onto the carving. Queen Ty lashed out and jerked his arm away from it, making him deface a large section. Now she had Ay's undivided attention.

"I want Lupita's cat out of this palace! Return it to the beasts of the fields from where it came," she said.

Ay put down his brush and turned to her, his voice shrouded in empathy.

"Queen, I would be put to death if I harmed a cat in the slightest way, you know that. And the Bastet goddess would curse us both throughout eternity."

"I'm not asking you to harm it," she replied. "Just get rid of it."

At that moment, a palace servant entered, surprised to see Queen Ty, and bowed in front of her.

"Forgive me for the intrusion," he said, before turning his attention to Ay. "My lord, the pharaoh is suffering and calling out for you."

The servant left the room, and Ay put on his linen cloak.

"I'll come," said the queen.

"No. Wait here, I will return," Ay replied removing the lid from a large pottery jar.

He reached inside, pulled out three pouches and rushed out of the room to the pharaoh's chamber.

The queen believed Ay's reluctance in allowing her to join him was not of his own volition, but connected to Amenhotep's insistence that she not witness their ritual with the cure. So she sat in Ay's chamber and waited as she was instructed.

As King Tushratta bathed with two of his female servants, three of his guards barged into his bath chamber. Tushratta teetered onto his side to stand and the women wrapped a robe around him. He welcomed the soldiers, expecting to see his son Shattiwaza, along with them.

"Where is he?" asked Tushratta.

Ornus, the captain of his royal guards, stepped forward. Military captains were almost always chosen based on their combat skills and above-average height and size. Ornus was the exception; a short man with a diminutive stature, chosen by Tushratta because of his cleverness to outsmart his military rivals.

"He's gone," replied Ornus with his head down.

"I ordered you to follow him."

"My king, we followed him as best we could, but he switched horses and tricked us. We thought he would travel east to the Assyrian province but didn't find him there."

"Then where is he?" asked Tushratta, his anger rising. "And I suggest you not tell me you don't know."

Tushratta dislodged one of his copper discuses from the wall. The razor-sharp edges were still intact. Ornus looked fearful.

"A merchant on the main road claims they saw him riding north," Ornus mumbled.

"North?" repeated Tushratta. He flipped the razor-edged copper discus back and forth across his fingers, a habit that would surface whenever he was anxious or angry. "Do you know what lies to the north, Ornus?"

"The Milid Valley, Sire."

"Yes, Ornus, the Milid Valley. Of the Hittite province! You're telling me that my only son, Shattiwaza, the prince of Mitanni, is traveling into the hands of our enemy, and you're standing here babbling to me about how you lost him?"

"My king, it would be suicide to ride north into Hittite territory. We're vastly outnumbered. Without help from the Egyptians we—"

Tushratta cut him off. "If you don't return with my son, I'll kill your wives, your children, and anyone else who happens to be a guest in your house. Do I make myself clear?"

Ornus nodded.

"Find him!" Tushratta screamed as he hurled the copper discus at Ornus. It barely missed his head and lodged deep into the wall.

After a third hour of waiting patiently for Ay to return news about the condition of her husband, Queen Ty grew restless. She stared at herself in the copper mirror on Ay's wall and outlined the wrinkles on her face with a finger, then pulled the skin back on both sides to create a temporary youthful appearance. If she were younger, if her skin hadn't been so marred by a life of pain and anguish, Amenhotep would love her again, and he would yearn to be as one with her. If her heart was not willfully kept so guarded, he could reach it and once again gain her trust.

Lupita's demise had been meant to allay the queen's deficiencies in the eyes of her husband; instead, it shed light on it and exasperated his illness. She blamed herself for his deteriorating condition and believed that if she nursed him herself, he could overcome his ailment. No prayers or spells from the Amun priests. No more doses of the cure, only care and nurturing from the one who had always loved him from the beginning.

It should be her and not Ay who was at his bedside administering to her husband. Ty could not wait a moment longer. She rushed out of Ay's quarters, determined to take her rightful place next to Amenhotep. When she entered his chamber, she found a single lit candle on the floor. She picked it up and used it to light the others. They illuminated Amenhotep sitting up in bed, his head down and a bedcover over his legs.

"Amenhotep?"

She walked up to him and lifted his chin.

"Amenhotep?"

His eyes were empty and staring straight ahead at the wall. The queen snatched her hand away. Amenhotep's head fell limp and lifeless. She took a step back and stared at him. "No," she kept repeating over and over again and shaking her head. Ty suddenly ripped her garment and began beating herself in the chest with her fists as she squeezed her eyes shut to stop the tears from flowing. The queen had feared the cure would one day bring about Amenhotep's demise, but there was always the hope she carried that he would conquer the addiction and come to rely on her instead. For reasons unknown, the Aten had judged it not to be.

The queen gained control over her emotions, stepped forward again and caressed his face. His skin was gray and cold to the touch. She closed both his eyelids and tenderly kissed his lips. Her husband, Amenhotep the Third, the great builder, the beloved pharaoh of Upper and Lower Egypt, was dead.

In Amenhotep's lap she counted thirteen pouches and numerous poppy capsules punctured and drained of their opium latex. He was clutching a scroll in one hand, and in the other, a flint knife.

Suddenly, Bastian lifted its head from underneath the pharaoh's bedcover and snarled at the queen. Petrified at the sight of his razor sharp teeth, she froze. The cat lunged forward at the precise moment that Ty grabbed the knife from Amenhotep's hand. She raised her arm to protect her face from the cat's claws and slashed at its torso repeatedly until the animal stopped moving and the sound of its snarling ceased. She would need to dismember the head from its connection to the heart to thoroughly vanquish its spirit. Accordingly, the queen swiped the knife across Bastian's neck until the head was severed from the body. Streaks of blood covered her face and Amenhotep's body, and both her arms were littered with scratches. She paused a moment to calm herself. It was then, in the aftermath, that she felt the sting of Bastian's scratches as if razors had sliced across her skin.

Queen Ty removed the scroll from Amenhotep's hand. In the center of his palm appeared a dark purplish bruise that she could not recall ever seeing before. Ignoring the oddity of it, she continued unrolling the scroll, reading the inscription as best she could. Just as she suspected, Amenhotep had ordained Horemheb as pharaoh over Teppy. A tear rolled down her cheek. Her greatest fear had come to pass, but the Aten god had looked down on her with mercy, and had seen to it that she would visit Amenhotep's chamber at the appropriate time to make things right.

The queen took the scroll and hid it inside her blood-stained garment. She then moved to gather up all the pouches of opium. Once she had it all concealed away, she fled Amenhotep's chamber never to return.

PART II

"Man must learn that what he does will have consequences."
—Precinct of Amun-Re

CHAPTER

15

THERE WAS GREAT fanfare that day as a mammoth crowd gathered in the grand courtyard of Thebes. Twelve years of presiding herself over the land of Egypt after Amenhotep's death, Queen Ty would now anoint her son Teppy, now at eighteen years of age, pharaoh.

As a child-king, Teppy was uninformed on how to speak or behave as a pharaoh. The prayers, the food and animal sacrifices to the gods, the meetings directing the military with General Horemheb, and the "State of Affairs" decisions with the viceroy, were all things as a child he had been unable to do. Not even at sixteen did Teppy prove competent enough to take on the full responsibility of pharaoh. Queen Ty was always there as his co-regent, standing by his side to represent him, to guide his footsteps down the right path. Now on his eighteenth birthday, Teppy had become a man, deserving the title of king, and she would relinquish full control over the country to him.

When she placed the crown of Upper and Lower Egypt on his head and proclaimed him pharaoh, everyone cheered and applauded.

Teppy knew well of General Horemheb's perfunctory support of his ascension. The general stood at the side of his throne applauding with the others. Sia and Neper feigned support as well. Teppy knew better than to trust any of the three of them. He never forgot how maliciously the twin priests had treated him as a child and the disdain they had shown for his brother Tuthmosis, assuring his death. He never forgot the day of his father's interment when Horemheb harassed his mother about a scroll he claimed Amenhotep had written giving the general the throne of Egypt over him. At this moment of his own crowning, Teppy dared not look their way. Instead, he focused his attention on the part of the ceremony that would bring him insurmountable joy—his marriage.

Two women waited to take Teppy's hand that day. One was Kiya, the daughter of Tushratta—king of Mitanni, who had once been promised to his father. Teppy's marriage to her was foremost an act of pity; second, it served to appease Tushratta in securing Egypt's alliance with the Mitanni kingdom as his father had decreed. It was the other marriage Teppy most looked forward to.

Though as children he played with many of his cousins who would visit him in the palace, he was drawn to his cousin Sete the most because of her kindness and gregariousness. Never had she teased him about his physical deficiency or treated him any differently because of it. While the other children would sometimes pity him, Sete paid little attention to his deformity. She was his mother's favorite niece, the daughter of his Uncle Ay, and through the years, as he served as co-ruler with his mother, Teppy witnessed Sete blossom into a woman. In his eyes, there was no one in the world more beautiful than her.

Attended by three of her maidservants, Sete approached Teppy's throne in a procession adorned with mandrakes and perfumes. As she approached, Teppy spoke the name for which she would be called from that day forward—Nefertiti: *"The beautiful one has come."*

Nefertiti bore no feelings of jealousy about Teppy's second wife. She was content that her status and beauty were beyond Kiya's. The Mitanni princess would be an afterthought to her husband while she herself would be the Great Royal Wife.

When Nefertiti's procession reached the base of Teppy's throne, the new pharaoh stood up to greet her, leaning on a wooden cane. Teppy didn't need the cane to stand that day, but he was accustomed to having it with him in case his legs unexpectedly buckled under him. His body changed often, so he needed to be prepared at a moment's notice. Teppy had grown tall and slender, and his hips and belly widened like a woman close to giving birth. His fingers, arms and legs grew disproportionately longer in relation to the rest of his body. Even his face had elongated and narrowed. Teppy resembled no one, human or animal. He believed as his mother told him, he was *evolving* into a god, and the shape of his body was the perfect manifestation of the Aten god itself.

The Aten amulet his brother had given him as a child was still around his neck. He had never stopped wearing it and often wondered if Tuthmosis would still be alive if he hadn't passed it down to him. It hurt too much to think of what he believed was the obvious answer.

Nefertiti stepped up to Teppy, reached out, and examined the amulet, holding it between her fingers.

"You are the pharaoh that the Aten has chosen to shine its light upon," said Nefertiti with eyes that mesmerized him and a presence that healed him. He pulled her body close to his. It was wrong, even forbidden, for a pharaoh to display affection for his wife in front of the Egyptian people. On that day, what the people thought was of no concern to him. Teppy couldn't resist the temptation of pressing his lips against hers. Her mouth tasted of pomegranate and honey, and she reciprocated his kiss with her tongue. The Aten had brought them together that day never to be apart.

TO AMENHOTEP IV (Teppy), king of Egypt, from Suppiluliumas, king of Hatti:

[1]The messages I sent your father when he was alive, and the wishes he expressed to me will certainly be renewed between us. Oh king, I did not reject anything your father commanded, and your father never neglected any of the wishes I expressed, but granted me everything. Why have you, my brother, refused to send me what your father during his lifetime sent me?

Now my brother, you have acceded to the throne of your father, and, similarly, as your father and I have sent each other gifts of friendship, I wish good friendship to exist between you and me. I often expressed this wish to your father. We certainly shall make it come true between us. Do not refuse, my brother, what I wished to receive from your father. It concerns two statues of gold, one standing and the other sitting, two silver statues of women, a chunk of lapis-lazuli, and some other jewels. They are not gifts in the true sense of the word, but rather, as in the majority of such cases, objects of a commercial transaction. If my brother should decide to deliver these, as soon as my chariots are ready to carry the cloth, I shall send it to my brother. What you my brother may want, write to me, and I shall send it to my brother.

Ay finished reading the tablet and handed it to Teppy.

Two years had passed since his marriage and coronation as pharaoh, and Ay, who had been his father's manservant, was now

---

[1] EA 41. A letter from Suppiluiimas, king of Hatti, to Amenhotep IV, king of Egypt. After a French translation by Claire Lalouette, Thebes ou la naissance d'un empire, Fayard, Paris 1986.

his. The uncle who had devoted so much of his life to taking care of him as a child had been honored to assume the grand position as Teppy's confidant and advisor. Ruling over the two regions of Upper and Lower Egypt with its massive construction projects, tax collections, and frequent disputes preoccupied Teppy so much that he rarely had time to be in the company of his wife. Ay lessened his load by prioritizing and scheduling Teppy's obligations so that his life would be manageable. As such, Ay designated the first full moon of the month as the day the pharaoh would review letters from kings of other lands.

"Is it your wish to send him the gold and silver statues, my Pharaoh?" asked Ay.

"Suppululiumas speaks as though we don't suspect him of murdering our Lady Lupita," said Teppy.

"It could have been the Nubians; we have no proof it was him."

"General Horemheb seems to be convinced it was."

"If the general was truly convinced of king Suppiluliumas's guilt, he would've attacked the Hittite regiment he encountered just thirty-three days ago," said Ay.

"Are you not aware that Horemheb is a patient man of honor? *'A royal life for a royal life.'* Those were only Hittite soldiers he encountered, no one of royalty."

"General Horemheb, my Pharaoh, is a man who yearns for war with the Hittites."

"Nevertheless, I find it odd this Suppiluliumas waited twelve years after my father's death to seek out gifts he claimed were rightfully his. Why are the gold and the lapis-lazuli important now?"

"No matter how many years may pass, my Pharaoh, gold and lapis-lazuli will always be like the hair of the gods that only grows in abundance here in the motherland of Egypt and the kingdom of Kush."

"Don't send him a thing. My father would not have agreed to such if he had had all his senses," said Teppy.

"Then why did you agree to send a gold statue to King Tushratta?"

"Tushratta is Kiya's father, Ay."

"Of course, my Pharaoh."

"Furthermore, I will not reward a foreign country that's suspected of murdering an Egyptian queen," said Teppy. "As long as I am pharaoh, Suppiluliumas will never see another piece of Egyptian silver or gold, nor the lapis-lazuli jewel."

Teppy tossed the clay tablet across the floor and it broke in half.

The collecting of Egyptian gold was for King Tushratta, a source of erotic pleasure. He was overjoyed when the Egyptian messengers arrived in Mitanni with his gold statue.

The king unveiled the statue in front a small crowd of his royal family in the Wassukanni palace. A gift from Egypt had always been, for the Mitanni, a major event. Tushratta paced around the statue inspecting and admiring the height and decadence of it. Teppy had had it especially made for him, nine cubits in height and three cubits in width. The Osiris statue was in its usual standing position with its arms crossed on its chest holding a crook and a flail. A crown with two ram horns adorned the head and a curved beard jutted from its chin. The eyes were realistically inlaid with alabaster and glass, and whenever the sunlight enveloped it, the golden statue shimmered.

"Magnificent. Absolutely magnificent. Finally, a gift from the great land of Egypt. The Pharaoh Teppy, the husband of my daughter Kiya, has delivered the gold that his father promised me," said Tushratta. "Mitanni's friendship with Egypt has spanned hundreds of years, but it is because of me and my camaraderie with the Egyptian kings that Mitanni reaps the rarest and most valuable of their golden treasures."

Tushratta's bluster masked the true reason for his joy over the Egyptian gift.

There had not been another sighting of his son Shattiwaza after he had banished the prince from Mitanni ten years earlier. Ornus's search for him in the Milid Valley had proven to be fruitless, so Tushratta had assumed the merciless Hittites had captured and killed him. True to his word, Tushratta had punished Ornus's failure by executing his wife and children and, worse, by keeping him alive to suffer from it as he himself suffered. Possession of the Egyptian gold statue would help assuage his guilt over causing the loss of his own son.

As Tushratta admired the statue, he focused on a small mark on the leg. When he examined it closely, it appeared to be a crack. He poked at it with his finger and right away a fragment of gold broke off from it and landed on the ground. Under the gold plating Tushratta caught a glimpse of stone. The statue was not made of solid gold as the pharaoh had led him to believe. It was a worthless fake and now his shame in front of his entire royal family.

CHAPTER

16

AT THE BEGINNING of Teppy's fourth year as pharaoh, he and Nefertiti were nurturing two young daughters: Meketa and Mayati. By the end of that same year she had given birth to their third daughter, Senpaten. Their decision to name her in honor of the Aten god sparked outrage among the entire hierarchy of the Amun priesthood. Sia, in particular, issued proclamations denouncing Teppy's blasphemy against Amun. He warned that the pharaoh's actions would halt the annual flooding of the river, which could lead to deadly famine throughout Egypt. The Amun priests' plan was to frighten the Egyptian people into revolting against him.

The priests refused to make the customary offering to Hapi, the god of the inundation for the flood, hoping it would trigger a famine in Egypt that they could blame on Teppy. The pharaoh prayed to his god, the Aten, and although the Amun priests had warned the citizens that the needed flood would not occur without the power of their gods Hapi or Amun, the inundation did occur because of Teppy's incessant prayers and the power of his god—the Aten.

Nefertiti had prayed and petitioned the Aten god for a male heir, but in its perfection and wisdom, the Aten gave her not what she desired, but what she needed for her heart to be joyful: their beautiful baby girl, the princess Senpaten. She was a gift of replenishment to Teppy and tending to her was his favorite way to pass the time during the annual flood.

Teppy cradled his daughter in his arms, while Nefertiti and his two eldest daughters swam in the river and explored its treasures. They were known by their birth names, Meketa and Mayati, to the people of Egypt, and only Nefertiti knew their secret birth names of Naeemasha and Sagiramala.

"Father, look, we picked lotus flowers for you," said the four-year-old Meketa. She walked into his chamber hand-in-hand with her two-year-old sister, Mayati from their swim in the river. The girls were the love of Teppy's life, and, along with his wife Nefertiti, made up the world of femininity with which he longed to be surrounded. He had his own family now, one that loved him and would never reject or abandon him.

Nefertiti took Senpaten from Teppy's arms, and Mayati jumped in his lap for her turn of his nurturing. She handed him the lotus flowers, anticipating his kiss of approval.

"They're beautiful, just as you are, my little one," said Teppy as he embraced her and kissed her forehead.

"What about me, Father?" asked Meketa. "I have lotus flowers for you too."

"And I have kisses for you as well, my little princess. Come to me," he replied.

Meketa jumped into her father's lap next to her sister, and he gave them both the longest embrace they could endure. When Nefertiti placed Senpaten down in her little bed, the newborn cried.

"Sing the lullaby to her," said Meketa.

"Yes, sing the lullaby to Senpaten, Father, please" Mayati repeated.

Teppy's singing voice was not pleasant to his own ears, but to his daughters it was like a musical instrument they could make him play whenever they wanted. He would always sing to them the same lullaby his mother, Ty, had sang to him as a child when he would cry. Teppy leaned over Senpaten, and with the help of his two daughters, sang to her softly.

> [2]*Little baby in the dark house,*
> *You have seen the sun rise.*
> *Why are you crying? Why are you screaming?*
> *You have disturbed the house god.*
> *'Who has disturbed me?' says the house god.*
> *It is the baby who has disturbed you.*
> *'Who scared me?' says the house god.*
> *It is the baby who has scared you.*

By the time they had repeated the verse three times, Senpaten had stopped crying and was looking up at her father and sisters with big bright eyes. She was a beautiful baby, one that Teppy predicted from among all his daughters would be a queen of Egypt.

When Ay entered the Amun temple that morning, he was startled by shouts and murmurs. The commotion emanated from the outer sanctuary where the nine-cubit-high solid gold statue of Amun stood. The priests had surrounded it, and fellow worshipers formed a crowd around the towering structure. There were gasps and awes as they witnessed what appeared to be blood dripping from the corners of the golden statue's mouth.

---

[2] One of the earliest lullabies on record, dating from around 2,000 BC. Nina Perry, "The Universal Language of Lullabies," BBC World Service, BBC News Magazine.

"Look, Amun is furious. It is because we have presented him with an animal sacrifice unworthy of him!" yelled a villager.

"We must find who committed this crime and kill him before Amun curses us with disease," said another.

Suddenly, the statue rumbled. A deep sense of fear spread among the throng in the outer sanctuary. No one was sure if it was better to flee the temple or hide in one of its many rooms. Their fear was calmed when Sia and Neper entered, dressed in their ceremonial robes.

"Help us!" a villager implored Sia. "Help us appease Amun."

In perfect sync, Sia and Neper knelt in front of the statue, raised both their hands in the air, and bowed their heads. Ay was there when the rumbling sounds from the Amun statue subsided, and the blood stopped dripping from its mouth. Sia and Neper stood up and faced the people.

"It is not because of a sacrifice that Amun has become angered. It is because the people are building a new temple in honor of the Aten god, a place much grander than the Amun temple," said Neper.

"The construction of the Gempaaten temple is blasphemous in the eyes of Amun," Sia continued, "the building of this temple must stop for your own sake!"

With that, Sia and Neper led the crowd out of the Amun temple grounds and toward the Gempaaten construction site.

Teppy had commissioned the building of the Gempaaten temple in the second year of his reign in praise of his god, the Aten. It would be a site of grand beauty—a much needed improvement over the old dilapidated Aten temple near the Colonnade court.

Three times the size of the Amun temple, Teppy's new temple had been specifically designed so that the massive structure would receive the most rays of sunlight directly from the Aten, and at night, hundreds of torches would keep it illuminated so that it would never be in a single moment of darkness. It would be a place of happiness and rejuvenation, contrary to the Amun temple that reminded him of death and despair.

Now, three years later, the Gempaaten temple had been half completed when Ay reported to Teppy that the Amun priests had halted its construction. The workers were vacating the site because of curses from the Amun priests and their worshippers. Teppy was riled and quickly mounted his royal chariot en route to Gempaaten.

Sia and Neper delighted in assisting the exodus of thousands of the pharaoh's workers. The ones that had refused to leave, the priests taunted and threatened with premonitions of a forthcoming catastrophe they said came from the mouth of the Oracle himself.

"This temple you were deceived into building pays tribute to the Aten, an enemy of the god of all gods—Amun," said Neper.

"If you do not stop construction, your children, your animals, and the river will be cursed. The Amun god has decreed this, and I am his only messenger," said Sia.

Neper turned and glared at Sia, surprised at the failure to include him in his proclamation.

"*We* are the only messengers," Neper corrected.

"Are we not as one, my dear brother?" asked Sia.

Meri-Ra stepped forward and interrupted their exchange.

"In essence, you are instructing these workers to disobey our only living god, the pharaoh Teppy, who does, in fact, have the power of the almighty Aten at his command," Meri-Ra said, adjusting his robe and collar necklace.

"The pharaoh would be wise to accept what has always been known since the beginning of time: the power of Amun is much greater than the Aten," said Sia.

"Perhaps you can tell him yourself. His royal chariot has arrived at the entrance," replied Meri-Ra.

As Teppy dismounted his chariot, his temple workers were gathering their belongings and departing in droves. The sight of it made his anger boil. When the people set their eyes on the pharaoh, they dropped what they had in their hands and bowed. Assisted by his jeweled walking cane, Teppy limped up the staircase to the top of the platform. All movement ceased, and there was no sound except that of the wind and of birds chirping. Teppy's voice echoed off the unfinished walls.

"Don't be fooled by what you were told. Why should you be afraid? I am the pharaoh, the living god of Egypt. Just as my father, Amenhotep, was the great builder, we will be the builders of even greater things. If you, my citizens and my workers, return to building the Gempaaten temple, I will double your compensation, and you will be supplied with beer three times daily. The Aten is the god of the sun-disk, the god of the light. He will give us all what we desire, and you, my people, will build the temple and the statue where he will reside with us for eternity."

Teppy stepped off the platform and descended the stairs. He had no sense of whether the workers had actually listened to him and would return to building the temple or not. What he wanted most was to confront Sia and Neper privately, and it wasn't long before they came to him, greeting the pharaoh with a perfunctory bow followed by a warning.

"What you're doing is blasphemous to Amun," said Sia.

"Who appointed you and your brother the judges of what is blasphemous? As a living god, I, Teppy, have the authority to do as I please. You, on the other hand, insist on challenging my sovereignty as pharaoh of Egypt. If I choose to name my beautiful baby daughter and my temple in honor of the Aten, it will be done. I'll not continue to tolerate your interference, priest," replied Teppy.

"We do not answer to the Aten. Amun is our god, and the god of this country. He has condemned the building of your temple as sacrilege."

"Your Amun god is a beast with the head of a ram, a god of the night where evil lurks but cannot be seen. My god, the Aten, is the sun-disk, a bright light that brings about goodness in full view of the people. We can survive without the beast that hides in the darkness, no one can survive without the life-giving rays of the sun," said Teppy.

"Amun was the god of your father, Amenhotep, and of your father's father. What evil do you accuse them of, Pharaoh?"

Unable to look Teppy in the eye, Neper stared at the ground, his hand twitching. Teppy sensed the priest was having second thoughts about the enmity his twin was creating between him and the Amun priesthood.

"This will all be settled at the Sed-Festival," said Teppy. "With the power of the Aten, I will prove my worthiness in making all decisions concerning Egypt to whom it matters the most—the people of Egypt."

Nefertiti removed all her clothing and lay on her stomach as she waited for her maidservant to enter and rub her limbs with oils and her favorite lotus-flower perfume. This was the ritual she participated in every night in their bedchamber while Teppy visited the children's chamber and sang them to sleep with lullabies. She looked forward to her husband's physical reaction when he would return to their bed to find the room filled with the sweet scent of her body. It was such a delight to him, and she knew the softness of her skin was as delicate as a blossoming flower.

Someone entered Nefertiti's chamber and began pouring the oils on her back. Feminine hands massaged them into her skin, but instead of the gentleness she was accustomed to, these hands made rough and aggressive movements.

"I would prefer the gentle touch you always provide," said Nefertiti.

"This is the way Teppy prefers it."

Nefertiti turned over and discovered that it was not her maidservant but Teppy's secondary wife, Kiya.

"What are you doing here?"

Kiya picked up the bottle of perfume, but before she could pour it, Nefertiti grabbed her wrist and didn't let go.

"I asked you a question," Nefertiti said. "Why are you here? And where is my maidservant?"

Nefertiti released Kiya's wrist, and the girl placed the bottle on the table.

"My husband, Teppy, sent your maidservant to his mother's chamber to assist her. He asked me to take her place here because I am familiar with sweet oils and massage," replied Kiya.

"Your husband?" mocked Nefertiti. "You are just a secondary wife, a mistress, an afterthought."

"An afterthought that's fertile and capable of bearing Teppy a son, something he deserves, and that you cannot give him. You are only good for birthing meaningless daughters."

Nefertiti slapped Kiya across her face. "Get out and take your sweet oils with you!"

Kiya picked up her oil and perfume bottles and slowly took backward steps away from Nefertiti, concerned of what the queen might do to her next.

"You will never lay your hand on me again," Kiya warned.

Nefertiti sneered at her and Kiya rushed out of her chamber.

CHAPTER

17

AT THE MIDNIGHT HOUR, Teppy entered Nefertiti's chamber drunk with lust and yearning to be as one with her. She lay in bed veiled by a cloth that hid the jewels of her body. Her stare was hypnotic, and he undressed himself in a hurry to join her. Without saying a word, Teppy kissed her, but this time, there was no reciprocation. He persisted, engulfed in his own desire, touching her and removing the cloth revealing her breasts. Before he could kiss them with his lips, she covered them.

"Promise me now you won't send that woman to my chamber again," said Nefertiti, holding the cloth over her body as collateral.

This was unusual treatment from his sweet Nefertiti. She had always returned his passion and in some instances, initiated it even in the face of Kiya.

"Why do you call her 'that woman'? I sent her to relax you with massage and sweet oils as she has done many times for me."

"She has nothing but contempt for me. How can you not see that?"

"She is still my wife."

"A secondary wife is no better than a mistress, and I loathed the presence of your envious mistress in my bedchamber," replied Nefertiti.

"Fine."

Teppy tried again to remove the cloth, but she gripped it even tighter.

"Swear to me under oath of the Aten god that you'll not lie with her in her chamber again," said Nefertiti.

Teppy sat up, baffled by her request.

"How many times must you be reminded that she is my secondary wife?" he countered. "Why would I promise you such a thing?"

"You would if you truly loved me."

"There was never a question about whom I love Nefertiti. I don't dream of Kiya, I dream of you."

Teppy reclined back into bed without giving her the answer she wanted. He refused to lie to her under any circumstance. Nefertiti sensed there were much heavier concerns weighing on her husband's heart, so she dismissed the quarrel for the moment.

"What's really disturbing you?" she asked. "Tell me so I can help you."

"There's nothing you can do."

"I'm your wife, and I have the wisdom of my father."

Teppy nodded. As his chief wife, she indeed had the right to know.

"It's the priests of Amun. They keep challenging my sovereignty," he said.

"How?"

"They halted the construction of my Gempaaten temple, convincing the workers that the Amun god will curse them and their children with disease if they continue to build it. The Amun statue was even seen rumbling and blood dripped from the corner of its mouth. Again, in this new year, they're threatening not to pray to the god Hapi for the inundation of the river."

"Have you tried speaking directly to the workers?" asked Nefertiti.

"I offered them double compensation, even beer three times daily, but their fear of Amun stifles them."

Nefertiti caressed Teppy's brow with her hand. "The Amun priests are wicked and greedy, and because they're never taxed, they continue to accumulate wealth and power." She removed the cloth revealing her oiled and perfumed body and straddled him. Her movements were slow and deliberate.

"The Sed-Festival is where you'll prove your vitality," she said. "After the people witness your regeneration from the Apis bull, the workers will return to building the temple in honor of you and the Aten."

Teppy was aroused by her movements across his body and the warmth of blood rushing into his extremities. She quickened her rhythm as Teppy grabbed ahold of her, and the two moved and moaned, groping each other, until his ecstasy gave way to climax. Nefertiti collapsed on Teppy's chest, and from the twilight till the morning sun, he held her close in his arms.

When Teppy and Nefertiti awoke, they began the day by teaching their two daughters hieroglyphics as their newborn Senpaten slept soundly in her bed. Teppy trusted no one else to tutor his children, afraid that someone might discover their secret birth names if they were taught outside of their presence. While Nefertiti taught Meketa and Mayati the meaning of the symbols, Teppy taught them how to draw them on a papyrus scroll. They both delighted in creating pictures of all the flora and fauna they had seen the day before on their trip to the river. Teppy's time with them reminded him of treasured moments from his childhood, when Tuthmosis would teach him to draw animal pictures.

Ay halted the children's teaching session when he came to inform Teppy that General Horemheb needed to speak to him urgently. Speaking to Horemheb was something Teppy tried to avoid. He was not versed in the tactics of war, nor capable of leading an army due to his deformity, thus he avoided contact with the general.

Ay and Nefertiti escorted the children from their chamber and sent Horemheb in to see Teppy. The general was dressed in his officer's uniform with his breastplate and helmet polished and shined. He looked valiant and poised to conquer. His size and muscularity intimidated Teppy, and the scowl on the general's face was evidence that he would not like what he was about to hear.

"Pharaoh, your order to execute the rogue Nubians that attacked our outpost and killed our viceroy has been carried out. However, some members of their tribe escaped and joined forces with the Libyans in halting our shipments of gold. They're attacking more Egyptian outposts in the other surrounding lands. We must act soon before we lose control of the entire region."

"Act how?" Teppy replied.

"By sending a regiment of our forces out into the kingdom of Kush where they have taken refuge."

"What is stopping you, general? Subdue them."

Teppy went back to drawing hieroglyphics on the papyrus scroll. He had no interest in war; it only brought misery and death. War was why his brother had never returned to him. War was evil, and it was sure to drain the royal treasury.

"My warriors are afraid to fight because the priests of Amun proclaimed they will no longer petition the war god Montu in ensuring our victory against the Nubians," said Horemheb.

This inflamed Teppy, but he refused to let the general see him angry. The Amun priests were succeeding by flaming superstitions and fear mongering. They had taken control of his people, his workers, and now with their warning to the army, threatened the potential wealth of Egypt. Teppy was trapped. The only thing left he had control over was his demeanor. He turned to Horemheb, trying to appear calm and unaffected.

"Then you should execute the Egyptian warriors that refuse to follow your orders," Teppy said as he stood up and rolled up the scroll.

"If I were to do as you say, my Pharaoh, Egypt would be without any warriors. Most of them are afraid of the Amun priests' curse."

"If what you're asking me, general, is to give in to wicked priests; that'll never happen. Let each Egyptian soldier pay the price for his rebellion against Egypt."

"Pharaoh, are you not aware that the Hittites are a looming threat to the stability of Egypt's tributaries? I need all my men," said Horemheb.

Queen Ty walked into the room and interrupted him.

"I would wager that our general is more concerned with avenging the death of Lady Lupita with a war against the Hittites than he is of stabilizing our tributaries," she mocked.

Horemheb ignored her. "Pharaoh, we'll continue our discussion when it can remain private," he said before he gave the queen a flippant look and walked out of the chamber.

Queen Ty stepped up to Teppy. "He's not to be trusted. The general is a traitor of his own country," she said taking her son's hand and kissing it.

"No, mother," he replied, pulling his hand away. "General Horemheb worships his country, and father worshiped him."

Teppy moved away from his mother and took a seat at his table.

"Enough of Horemheb," she said. "Have you sent the gold statue to King Tushratta as your father requested in his last will and decree?" asked the queen.

"It should have reached him many days ago. Why?"

"I received this from a Mitanni messenger today."

The queen removed a scroll from her garment, opened it, and read it out loud:

[3]*To Queen Ty, lady of Egypt, thus speaks Tushratta, king of Mitanni.*

Everything is well with me. May everything be well with you. May everything go well for your house and your son. May everything be perfectly well for your soldiers and for everything belonging to you.

You are the one who knows that I have always felt friendship for Amenhotep, your husband, and that Amenhotep, your husband, on his part always felt friendship for me. The things that I wrote and told Amenhotep, your husband, and the things that Amenhotep, your husband, on his part wrote and told me incessantly, were known to you. But it is you who knows better than anybody the things we have told each other. No one knows better.

You should continue sending joyful embassies, one after another. Do not suppress them. I will not forget the friendship with Amenhotep, your husband. At this moment and more than ever, I have ten times more friendship for your son, the pharaoh.

You are the one who knows the words of Amenhotep, your husband, but you have not sent me yet the gift of homage which Amenhotep, your husband, ordered to be sent to me. I had asked Amenhotep, your husband, for massive gold statues, but your son has sent gold-plated statues of wood. As the gold is like dust in the country of your son, why have they been the reason for such pain, that your son should not have given them to me? Neither has he given me what his father was accustomed to give.

---

[3] EA 26. A letter from Tushratta, king of Mitanni, to Ty, lady of Egypt. After a French translation by Claire Lalouette, Thebes ou la naissance d'un empire, Fayard, Paris 1986.

Teppy was silent.

"Is it true?" she asked. "You have disregarded your father's decree and have only sent a gold-plated statue to king Tushratta?"

"My dear father-in-law continues to raid and steal from our Eber-Nari tributaries while he pretends to nurture a friendship with us. Why should I keep enriching Mitanni with our treasures?" Teppy said.

"It serves your father. It was his will and decree."

"Father is dead. He is not the pharaoh anymore, Mother. I am."

The unfinished pillars of the Gempaaten temple cast broken shadows on the silent construction grounds as Neper approached Meri-Ra. The Amun priest had requested to meet with him in seclusion.

"I couldn't risk being discovered," Neper said as he removed the cloak concealing his face.

"Why have you summoned me? And why is it necessary to hide?" Meri-Ra asked.

"I fear the pharaoh is in great danger.

"In danger?"

"There's a plan to overthrow him," said Neper.

Meri-Ra's attention was aroused at the audaciousness of Neper's revelation, though he instinctively doubted the veracity of an Amun priest.

"And what evidence do you have of this?"

"Are you aware of the Amun statue in our temple?"

"I am."

"The blood dripping from its mouth, the thunderous sounds it makes, it's all tricks to manipulate the people into fearing us," said Neper.

"But I've seen it myself with my own eyes."

"You saw an illusion, made from contraptions that engineers have built for us and hidden beneath the temple itself."

Meri-Ra looked unconvinced and wondered instead if Neper had devised a plan against him.

"I can prove to you that it's true if you're willing to meet me at the Amun temple. I will show you there in private, the contraptions, how it's done," said Neper. "Sia will be away administering to the Mut god."

"What does this have to do with a plan to overthrow the pharaoh?"

Neper exhaled before speaking again. Meri-Ra hoped it was the coolness of the night that made Neper tremble so.

"The one who is planning to overthrow pharaoh Teppy is my twin Sia. He is being assisted by the other Amun priests. That is the reason he has threatened the people with curses from Amun and using illusions from the statues. What I'm telling you is the absolute truth. You must warn the pharaoh before it's too late," said Neper.

"Why are you revealing this to me? You are an Amun priest yourself, and I am a priest of the Aten. There's hatred between our gods."

"It is written in the old scrolls that twins are blasphemous and despised by Amun. I fear that my twin is conspiring to kill me so that there will only be one of us, as it was meant to be from the womb," said Neper.

The priest's nervousness and paranoia now made sense to Meri-Ra. If Sia planned to overthrow the pharaoh and his twin was found to have revealed his secret, his life would indeed be threatened.

"I'll come to you by dawn tomorrow," replied Meri-Ra.

Neper covered his face with his cloak and exited the Gempaaten temple leaving Meri-Ra concerned for his own life. The Amun priests were known to be volatile at the threat of their discrepancies being exposed. Because they wielded unlimited power over the people of Egypt, a common citizen could be induced by them to stab or even stone Meri-Ra to death.

That night, Queen Ty found it hard to sleep. She got up, sat down in front of her mirror, and while shaving her head, a noise of metal crunching against metal startled her. Ty stepped out into the palace hallway and found it vacant. Within a moment of returning to her seat, an image of Lupita flashed across her mirror. Ty lurched around. No one behind her.

Afraid someone was hiding in her chamber, she rushed out into the hallway again. It was still quiet with Teppy's royal guards standing post. The only sound was from her own erratic breathing.

"It's the wine," the queen whispered under her breath. She walked back into her chamber trying to convince herself of it. An object gleamed on the floor, and she reached down to retrieve it. Perplexed by its appearance, the queen held it tight in her hand. It was not a wine-induced figment of her imagination. It was the matching lapis-lazuli earring she had given Lupita.

CHAPTER

18

QUEEN TY ARRIVED at Horemheb's military camp just days after their confrontation. She assumed the general would expect that it was nothing more than her desire to continue their dispute.

Women were not allowed at military training camps, and certainly a refined queen would never want to be tainted with the smell and sweat of war. Nevertheless, Queen Ty's chariot thundered in, and she stepped out from it in awe at the hundreds of young boys practicing archery, spear hurdling, sprinting, and wrestling. She had seen drawings of this on the palace columns and pottery jars, but it didn't appear as fascinating as it did in the flesh.

Horemheb marched in front of her, disrupting her gaze. "My queen—"

"I came to speak with you general," she said, her eyes still fixed on the young boys engaged in their training exercises.

"This is not the place for a female, not to mention a queen," said Horemheb.

"You have no authority to tell a queen where she can or cannot appear."

"I do have the authority to act on behalf of your well-being. The training grounds are dangerous," replied Horemheb.

The queen interpreted Horemheb's advice as another instance of his blatant disrespect for her.

"If I need your advice, General, I'll ask you for it," she said, handing him a leather pouch.

Confused, Horemheb opened it and pulled out what appeared to be her lapis-lazuli earring.

"Why have you brought me this? This is Lupita's earring that I returned to you," said Horemheb.

"I have the one you returned to me, general. It's put away. This is the matching one you planted in my chamber last night to frighten me into your extortion."

Horemheb handed it back to her. "There was only one earring found, and I gave it to you."

"If it wasn't by your hand, then it was by someone you convinced to carry out malicious deeds on your behalf," said Queen Ty.

Her purpose was not to quarrel, only to inform him she knew of his machinations. "Whatever scheme you are conjuring against me," she purposefully left the sentence unfinished and returned to her chariot.

"I am the general of this army, not a conjuring priest, nor do I have time for childish games," said Horemheb. "

"Make sure we have a sufficient amount of guards at the Aten temple for my son's Sed-Festival."

"I know nothing of a Sed-Festival, that would be senseless. Sed-Festivals are celebrated in the thirtieth year of a pharaoh's reign, not the fifth as it is with pharaoh Teppy," said Horemheb.

"You have been made aware of it now," she replied, motioning her driver to pull away.

Queen Ty understood why Teppy needed to prove his vitality early in his reign. The Sed-Festival would offer proof of his strength and a confirmation of his right to rule, demonstrated in front of Horemheb and the Egyptian citizens. As a mother aware of the limitations of her child, she worried if Teppy had the physical ability to endure it.

Three days later, in the Colonnade court of the old Aten temple, Teppy appeared in front of the massive crowd of Egyptian citizens, dressed in a short cloak that reached the length of his knees. Teppy appeared confident along with his royal wife Nefertiti and his daughters, Mayati and Meketa, in attendance. Their faces were filled with pride as they waved at the crowds and received thunderous roars of applause in return.

Teppy shuddered inside—vulnerable and preoccupied with what Meri-Ra had told him just hours earlier. He would have to be alert and cautious at all times in the company of Sia and the Amun priests. If they could rig statues to perform illusions in the face of the people, how much more possible that in an audacious move they might attempt to overthrow him during the Sed-Festival itself? The additional one-hundred and fifty royal guards posted throughout the Colonnade court were meant as a deterrent to any such uprising.

Compounding his concerns, a row of tenebrous clouds moved across the sky, obscuring the sun. It worried him that the Aten god's presence might be blocked from sight during his run. He kissed his Aten amulet, and the engraving of the sun's rays shining down on the pharaoh reassured Teppy that the clouds would soon dissipate and he would have the courage of his brother Tuthmosis.

The Colonnade temple courtyard was flanked on one side by a chapel dedicated to the Aten god and the image of the jackal. On the opposite side stood the double throne of Egypt, the finish line of his run. The competition began in the open space between the rows of shrines, a one hundred twenty-five-cubit course with spaces evenly separated by three markers.

Meri-Ra bowed in front of Teppy holding the royal scroll in his hand. It represented the pharaoh's sovereign right to rule and his ownership of the two lands of Egypt, Upper and Lower. The priest said a prayer to the Aten and handed Teppy the scroll. He looked up into the sky, nervous and apprehensive that the clouds still obscured the Aten's rays. *How can I complete the seven times around the course without the power of the Aten?* Teppy paced back and forth, thinking it would mask his fears from the people. If they had no faith in him as a physically fit living god, it would only be a matter of time before the Amun priests could justifiably rally the citizens to their side, shaming him and his family from royalty.

The roar of beating drums and the cheering of the crowd grew. Teppy rubbed the Aten amulet, and turned to face the course. He took one last look at his wife and his daughters, vowing that he would never let them see failure.

After a silent prayer, he began running the boundaries of the field with the royal scroll clutched tight in his hand. Though his pace was slow, the crowd cheered him on. His euphoria from their enthusiastic support was not enough to stop his legs from weakening, and when his heart pounded against his chest and his breath quickened, panic struck him. He had abandoned faith that he could even make it past the first round of the course, and before reaching the first marker, Teppy's legs collapsed under him.

As he fell to the ground out of breath, the sound of the crowd dissipated, and all that was left was silence—the emptiness of being alone in the world, alone without his brother, Tuthmosis, to carry him from this nightmare, alone without his mother to help him back to his feet and make the pain go away.

Out of respect for himself and his family, Teppy tried to lift himself from the ground, but each time he fell back down. Nefertiti sprang from her seat and ran across the field toward him carrying his cane. She had tears in her eyes when she reached her hand out to help him. Suffocated by her pity, he pushed her away.

"I am strong, I am the pharaoh," he said to her.

With what little pride he had left, Teppy pushed himself up from his elbows and back onto his feet. The crowd, not sure of how to react, remained silent. Nefertiti handed Teppy his walking cane. He took it and limped the rest of the way to the finish line in front of the double throne.

As was traditional, an Apis bull was brought forward by the hand of the Amun priests, Sia and Neper. They had adorned the black bull calf with flowers and jewelry, and Sia said a prayer over it before leading the animal to the pharaoh and walking away. Both priests avoided looking Teppy in the eye during the ceremony; however, when Neper, the twin with the scar on his neck, strolled past the pharaoh, it appeared from his gaze that the priest wanted to reveal something to him. Teppy witnessed Sia glance in Neper's direction, causing the nervous priest to abandon his urge.

Teppy refocused his attention on the eyes of the bull. There was nothing there except fear. He rubbed its head to calm the animal's spirit and shouted the words of praise from the scroll:

"It is you, the great Apis bull, the god Osiris that will regenerate and ordain me, the pharaoh of Egypt with a long and prosperous reign. With this offering of food, you accept and honor my request!"

Meri-Ra reached into his sack and handed Teppy a slab of raw oxen flesh and a dagger. Teppy sliced off a piece of the flesh and fed it to the bull. The animal turned its head away refusing to eat it. The more Teppy tried to force it into the beast's mouth, the more the beast rebuffed him. A deafening crack of thunder roared, then the rain sprinkled the courtyard. It had to be the work of the Amun god, conspiring with the Apis bull and Seth, the god of the storm, Teppy deduced, all part of the Amun priests' plan to humiliate him in front of the crowds and his family. Without the Apis bull's blessing, how could he gain the respect of the people?

After three more failed attempts to feed the Apis bull, Teppy relented. He tossed the oxen flesh to the ground and limped out of the courtyard, shamed and humiliated as the rain poured down on him.

❧❦❧

For three days and nights Teppy spoke not a word to Nefertiti or his children, secluding himself from everyone except his mother, the one who had always comforted him with her strength and wisdom. Now broken, he needed to be convinced of his worthiness and reassured of his connection to the Aten god.

When he entered his mother's chamber, he walked right into her arms without saying a word and wept. The queen welcomed him with a full embrace as she had when she protected him as a child. Teppy rested his head on her shoulder, ashamed to look his mother in the eye.

"I am as my father said I was—an abomination," Teppy said.

"How dare you repeat such a thing! It has been your destiny since the day you were born to be pharaoh of Egypt. Not even the deficiency of your body parts could stop what the Aten god had planned for you. You are a son *not* of your father, but of the Aten. You are strong Teppy, you are a god."

His mother's words were like rays of sunlight. Why should he act defeated when he still stood strong, chosen by the powerful Aten? Teppy wiped his eyes dry with his garment.

"The Amun priests are strengthening their authority over me. I have to stop them," he said to her.

"My son, the authority of the priests relies on the people's faith in the power of their gods. If you reduce the power of the Amun god to nothing, the priests will cease to have influence over the Egyptian people."

"What are you saying?"

"You told me before the Sed-Festival that the Amun priests uses trickery with their statues to appear more powerful, did you not?"

"Yes."

"Then destroy the statue where their Amun god resides. Every god they worship, destroy its statue, and you will destroy the Amun priesthood," said Queen Ty.

Her words of wisdom jarred Teppy's memory.

"When I was a child I remember you telling me a story. It was about the Habiru people who were enslaved by Egypt in the time of our great pharaoh, Thutmoses the Third, in the cities called Pithom and Raamses. Do you remember the story, Mother?"

"Vividly."

"You told me how one of the Habiru slaves was raised to be as Egyptian royalty, and how he grew to resent them, longing to free his people. He was a prophet with the power of one god, and he returned to Egypt to challenge the pharaoh's gods for the freedom of his people. And when the pharaoh refused to free them, the Habiru's god plagued Egypt tenfold with unspeakable plagues until he finally allowed the Habiru slaves to leave."

"Your memory serves you well," said the queen.

Teppy's excitement grew.

"So this one singular god of the Habiru defeated all the Egyptian gods? Including Amun and his magic-practicing priests?"

"It was the story that was written and passed down to my grandmother."

"Then tell me, Mother, if I was to do as you say and destroy their gods, do you believe the people would be more inclined to accept the Aten as their one true god as I have?" asked Teppy.

"My son, though the story came to pass over a hundred years ago, there are many among the people that will remember it and will embrace the Aten as their one true god as you have."

His mother's affirmation invigorated him.

"I have told no one this, not even my wife Nefertiti, but for many days I've had this vision of the Aten. It appeared to me, Mother, not in its form of the sun-disk, it was in the form of a man, a mysterious man who glowed like the sun. He instructed me to sail north, away from Thebes until I find the place where the two mountains cradle the sun. And there, he told me that I must build a new city to the Aten, where no other god will be served and worshiped. He said my loyal ones will follow me and abandon Thebes, this evil city of the Amun priests."

Teppy gazed into his mother's eyes. "I will destroy their gods, then we will leave this city. I will build a new capital city, Mother."

Queen Ty caressed Teppy's face. "My dear son, you don't have to abandon this city in order to destroy their gods. Thebes is our home."

"It is not our home," Teppy snapped. "It belongs to Amun and its wicked priests. We will have our own city where the Aten will be our only god. Will you stand with me, Mother?"

Queen Ty hesitated before she answered. "Always," she said and kissed him on the lips. "Carry out what is in your heart to do, my dear son."

CHAPTER

19

REELING FROM THE humiliation he had endured at the Sed-Festival, Teppy still found it agonizing to be in the company of his family. To prevent the children from pressing him for attention, Nefertiti took them with her on a short chariot ride to her father's home. When they arrived, her sister Mundi and stepmother Teyla greeted them all with flowers, fruits, nuts, and kisses.

Nefertiti embraced her sister and stepmother and presented them with gifts of perfume and gold jewelry. They were pleasing things to Mundi, but what Nefertiti craved most of all was to be alone again with her sister.

It was rare that she and Mundi could share their time and secrets with each other. Becoming a queen of Egypt brought Nefertiti isolation from her old family that weakened the bond she and Mundi had shared as children. So, while Senpaten slept and Meketa and Mayati played with their grandmother, the sisters found a moment to steal away into a private chamber. At once, Mundi bowed perfunctorily in front of her sister. "So what may I bring you to eat and drink O' great 'Queen Nefertiti'?" Mundi teased.

Nefertiti laughed. "Oh stop it. Don't call me that."

"But you *are* Queen Nefertiti."

"Maybe to everyone else, but to you I'm just Sete," said Nefertiti.

Mundi sat on the platform bed and Nefertiti sat next to her.

"You first," said Nefertiti, eager to hear about the developments in her sister's life.

"No, you must tell me first," replied Mundi.

"I'm a guest now in your home, so I get to choose, and I choose you."

Mundi smiled. "Fine, I'll tell you, but you can't tell anyone else, not even our stepmother. Agreed?"

"I'd never share your secrets," said Nefertiti.

Mundi moved closer to her sister. "I have a lover, and we're planning to marry."

Nefertiti looked shocked. She had always known her sister to be particular about suitors, often critical and fault-finding. It surprised her that Mundi had settled for someone after so many years of celibacy.

"Who is it?" she asked.

"Not yet, it's your turn now. Tell me your secret," replied Mundi.

"And you promise not to share it, right?"

"I'd never."

"We are leaving Thebes," Nefertiti blurted.

"Where will you be visiting?"

"It's not a visit. We're leaving this city permanently."

Mundi's eyes widened. "Why? It's the only city of royalty. Where would you go?"

As quickly as Nefertiti had blurted it out, she regretted telling her. Now she would have to reveal the whole sordid story of the

Amun priests and their plan to overthrow Teppy. It was depressing news she'd rather not repeat. Fortunately, Teyla entered the room interrupting their conversation and gave Nefertiti a way out.

"Nefertiti, your husband has sent a messenger here requesting your return to the palace immediately."

"But why should she leave us now when she has only just arrived?" said Mundi.

It concerned Nefertiti that Teppy would order her return to the palace so soon after their departure. Had the priests tried to retaliate? Or did they possibly need to escape the city sooner than they had planned?

"It's all right, Mundi," Nefertiti sighed in relief. "I imagine it's because he misses the children already. I'll return to you soon and explain everything."

With questions still unanswered from both sisters, Nefertiti gathered her children and returned to the palace as Teppy had ordered.

Meri-Ra was speechless at the sight of Ay in the Aten temple. The pharaoh's chief adviser was known to be a servant of the Amun god, and no follower of Amun dared set foot inside the temple where the Aten resided.

"I know you were not expecting me," Ay said, "especially here, but I need your help."

"Why would a worshiper of the Amun god need the help of an Aten priest?"

Ay ripped his garment open, revealing the bruise Sia had left on his chest long ago. It had spread downward to his abdomen over the years.

"Can the power of the Aten reverse a spell of an Amun priest?" asked Ay.

Meri-Ra barely glanced at it before responding.

"Why would an Amun priest conjure a spell against one of its own?"

"I am not of the Amun priests. I am a manservant and advisor only to the Pharaoh. Please, tell me. Can the Aten god remove this bruise from my body?"

Meri-Ra scanned Ay's torso. "There's nothing there."

"You don't see it?" asked Ay, pointing to his chest. "It's right here, the mark of the twin priest, Sia. Can the Aten god remove Amun's curse or not?"

"There is nothing there," Meri-Ra repeated.

Befuddled by his reply, Ay looked down at his chest and abdomen to make sure it was there. "I'm not mad, my chest is covered with a bruise that's spreading, and it will soon kill me. It's been said that only a magic-practicing priest taught by the Heka god itself could conjure such a thing."

"You must listen precisely to what I tell you," said Meri-Ra, resolute in his instruction. "There is no *real* bruise on you, nor magic from the Heka god. The Heka cult disappeared from Egypt hundreds of years ago, and their teachings have been long buried and lost. What you're seeing is what Sia convinced you was there. If you allow yourself to believe what I am telling you now, you won't see it. Look again, it's not there."

Ay looked again. The bruise was still in its place.

"It would be better for you to admit that you have no power from the Aten god than to be proven to be an imposter," said Ay.

When he turned to leave, Meri-Ra shouted at him. "Remove the image from your mind!"

It startled Ay and he stopped in his tracks. Ay closed his eyes and imagined the bruise was not there. He then opened them and glanced again at his chest. And just as Meri-Ra had told him, it was gone. The bruise that had once appeared to be spreading from his chest to his abdomen like a plague had completely vanished.

"You mustn't allow yourself to be fooled by what you can or cannot see. The Amun priests have no such power," Meri-Ra said as he handed Ay a new garment. "They can deceive you with illusions because you were once loyal to them. It's part of the same trickery they employ to control the people of Egypt," he said.

"I don't understand. My sister Ty saw the bruise as I did."

"Because you unknowingly placed in her mind the same suggested illusion they had placed upon you," Meri-Ra replied.

Ay put on the garment, enchanted by Meri-Ra's knowledge of the Amun priests' secrets.

"So that you can be assured that I no longer have loyalty for the Amun priesthood. I will tell you the pharaoh's plan," said Ay. "He has made an order to destroy the rigged statue in the Amun temple, and furthermore to strike down any Amun priests that are harboring statuettes of gods related to Amun. Today, at the setting of the sun, the Amun priests' days of trickery and illusions will be over."

Instead of expressing exuberance for the pharaoh's decree, Meri-Ra shook his head, looking concerned.

"Is not this the day of salvation that the Aten priesthood has yearned for?" Ay asked.

"You must postpone it," answered Meri-Ra. "The Amun priest Neper is defecting from his twin, Sia, and the Amun priesthood. I am assisting him in his conversion to the Aten priesthood. He's making one last visit to the Amun temple to gather his belongings. He must be spared from the pharaoh's order."

Ay nodded. "I will advise the pharaoh to postpone until the next day as you requested."

Ay had no intention of speaking to the pharaoh. Teppy's orders were already set in motion. He had instructed his guards to post scrolls of his proclamations throughout the city of Thebes declaring his rejection of the Amun god and all the other gods that were worshiped along with it. Ay had delivered Teppy's petition directly to the citizens, inviting them to sail the river along with the royal family in discovery of a new land far away.

At sunset, Teppy's five hundred and fifty royal guards were dispatched throughout the city fulfilling his orders to cut down the statues of Amun, Mut, and Khonsu with their battle axes and hammers until not one remained. Wherever the name of Amun was found engraved or written, it was to be carved out or defaced. Once the false gods and its priests were destroyed, they would have no power to retaliate. The people would be free to make their own choice without fear, and Teppy believed that most of them would choose to be loyal to him and follow him to the new land of the Aten.

When the guards reached the Amun temple, the priests were scrambling to hide the smaller statuettes. They were powerless at the hands of the pharaoh's guards, who searched every cubit of the temple until they found them all and crushed them. The last remaining idol was the nine-cubit-high gold Amun statue, the treasure of the priesthood, and the source of their many illusions and trickery against Teppy and the citizens. A squad of Teppy's guards struck at it until the base cracked.

Neper raced into the temple, his loyalty to the Amun god reignited. "No!" he shouted.

The destruction of the statuettes he had worshiped his entire life gave rise to paternal instincts to save what had always been part of his family. Neper flung himself in front of the golden Amun statue, shielding it from the swing of an enraged guard's ax.

CHAPTER

20

A FLEET OF FERRYBOATS cluttered the banks of the great river. Thousands of Thebans and their families gathered up all their possessions and placed them into the sailing vessels. Massive barges had been loaded with building materials of limestone, granite, marble, and alabaster that would be used to build the new capital city. Livestock and grain were loaded on storage boats as pilots, helmsmen and oarsmen prepared to navigate through what was mostly treacherous waters.

The royal riverboat was a pleasure boat with multiple decks that featured lavishly decorated cabins and dining rooms; even the oars were made of ebony and decorated with gold. The pharaoh's children were the first to board, excited to embark on the great adventure. Queen Ty escorted them, mimicking their excitement in a ruse to hide her anxiety over leaving Thebes. She wanted to be supportive of her son, but in her heart she believed they were making a terrible mistake. Only the thought of never having to see another Amun priest consoled her.

The queen caught a glimpse of Teppy's smile the moment he arrived on the boat. She returned the gesture by placing her hand over her heart and nodding at her son with the same loving smile.

Teppy took his position at the helm, and spoke out to the citizens that could hear him, encouraging them with words inspired by the Aten god itself.

"This is not my revolution, it's yours!" he yelled. "You must abandon your statues of Amun and all the other useless gods who have enslaved you. Their oppressive priests claim to have power from the gods but instead they have used illusions to deceive you. This city of Thebes is infected with their corruption. We have the Aten: the sun-disk, the only god we need. We will sail to a glorious place where we can build our new capital city, a land unaffected, and of unimaginable beauty. The Aten will give us all a better life."

The people cheered at Teppy's declaration. It was a welcome revelation to see how many of the citizens of Thebes supported him against the Amun god and its priests.

Nefertiti encouraged the children with her own display of cheers and excitement at Teppy's declaration to the citizens, but like Queen Ty, she hid her angst about leaving Thebes, fearing what could happen to them if the new land turned out not to be as Teppy envisioned.

Nefertiti was comforted by the sight of Mundi stepping onboard the ship. Now at least she would have the company of her dear sister on their long journey. *But where are her belongings?* Mundi's hands were empty.

"Where are your things?" asked Nefertiti.

Mundi was hesitant to respond. Nefertiti could tell her sister had been crying.

"Mundi, what's wrong?"

"I can't go with you."

"What do you mean? The entire royal family is going: Father, our stepmother, everyone."

"I know they are, but I can't."

"Why?"

Mundi paused before revealing the last thing in the world Nefertiti expected to hear from her. "I'm in the third month of pregnancy."

Her confession jarred Nefertiti. The pain of it swelled throughout her body. It was unthinkable that her sister would wait for months before sharing the secret of her pregnancy—an occasion sisters yearn to share with each other from the beginning.

"Who is the child's father?"

"General Horemheb."

Nefertiti dropped the sack she was carrying. Her reaction made Mundi nervous.

"Please, you mustn't tell Aunt Ty," Mundi begged.

"So Horemheb is the lover from the secret?" Nefertiti asked.

Mundi nodded. "We're in love. I can't leave him, sister. It would be a sin against my heart."

Nefertiti cherished the all-encompassing emotion of love, and though her feelings were hurt, she understood Mundi's unwillingness to leave behind the father of her unborn child.

"I won't speak a word to Aunt Ty. You will when you're ready. But tell me, Mundi, how do you know for sure whether Horemheb truly loves you or is just using you to gain a position of royalty? He's most certainly an ambitious man."

Mundi looked astonished by her sister's remark. "I may not be as beautiful as you, but I am worthy of love, Nefertiti."

"You are, Mundi. That's not what I—" She broke off and reconsidered her tactics. "I don't want your heart to be misled by anyone, that's all."

"He loves me," said Mundi, stoic and firm. Her defensiveness caused Nefertiti to refrain from speaking another word about Horemheb. Instead, she masked her true feelings about him with words and expressions of joy that would comfort Mundi.

"Let the sweetness of love embrace you both," said Nefertiti, "as it has embraced me and Teppy."

Nefertiti hugged Mundi, and they kissed each other on the cheek. "Go now," said Nefertiti, wiping her sister's tears away.

Mundi turned for one last look at Nefertiti before walking off the barge. Nefertiti waved good-bye, distressed that she might never see her sister again.

Neper was missing. The former Amun priest had failed to come to the pharaoh's royal barge at the designated time of departure. Concerned, Meri-Ra boarded a chariot and made his way to Neper's home in the healing temple of Amun. When he arrived at the temple's courtyard, he was confronted by three Amun priests, curious to why a priest of the Aten had come to their home. Instead, they directed him to the Amun temple, an hour chariot ride away, where they had seen Neper and Sia together.

The ax swing intended for the Amun statue had sliced into the flesh of Neper's leg. The priest had collapsed, falling backward onto the ground as Teppy's guards continued striking their axes against the statue's base until the colossus monument had finally toppled. Neper had cried out as an elbow of the massive golden structure broke off and landed across his chest, pinning him down, just before the entire Amun statue had fallen on the limestone floor in a thunderous crash.

As quickly as the guards had arrived and desecrated the temple, they fled into the night. Neper was left inside, alone and trapped. He glanced down at his leg, the blood was pulsating out of his body with every breath he took. He tried to push the fractured piece of statue off his chest with his arm, but it was much too heavy and the loss of blood was continuing to weaken him. He thought that if no one came for him soon, his body would be completely drained of it.

In the distance. Footsteps.

"Help me!" shouted Neper.

The sound of footsteps grew louder. Soon, Neper was relieved to see his twin Sia standing over him.

"My brother, help me; the pain's unbearable," said Neper.

Sia attempted to lift the statue off his brother's chest.

"No, it's much too heavy," said Neper. "You have to find someone to help you lift it or I'll die here."

Neper cringed at the sight of the blood pooling around his leg wound. It intensified his labored breathing.

"Stay calm, I'll return," replied Sia, before rushing away and out the temple doors.

Within minutes, Sia returned. Neper was wary to see that his twin was alone.

"Where are the others?" he asked.

"Have patience," replied Sia, "Help's coming."

There was something tainted about Sia's voice—a tone of deception that only an identical twin united in blood could detect.

"No one is coming, are they?" asked Neper.

Without uttering a word, Sia shook his head. The whites of his eyes turned bloodshot and suddenly his skin perspired. He removed the rope that held his robe around his waist and knelt down beside Neper, staring at him through dilated black pupils.

"For your betrayal of Amun—" said Sia. Neper finished his thought. "He has struck you down and judged you for death."

Sia smiled, amused that even in his brother's last moment of life, he was still capable of finishing his thoughts.

Sia wrapped the rope around Neper's neck and pulled both ends. Neper's eyes widened in horror.

"Can the Aten save you now, my brother?" asked Sia as he pulled the rope tighter, causing it to constrict deeper into his brother's throat.

Neper tried to speak, but there were only gasps as he struggled at first, grinding his teeth and trying to squeeze his fingers between the rope and his neck to stop the excruciating pain. He kept squinting at Sia as if begging him to stop but to no avail. The rope tightened around his neck so hard that it disappeared into his skin. Neper had always believed that he and his brother were physically the same. That day he discovered how wrong he had been. Sia's inhuman strength was grotesque and unrelenting, and finally Neper gave in to the inevitability of death.

Sia witnessed Neper go limp. His life-spirit left his body and Sia kissed his brother's lips, taking into his mouth, Neper's last breath.

"You and I are as one now," said Sia. "The way it was meant to be from the beginning."

The sound of footsteps trampling over debris quieted Sia, and he hastily removed the rope from Neper's neck, tied it back around his waist and rushed toward the entrance of the temple. Sia stopped dead in his tracks at the sight of Meri-Ra plucking Neper's priest wand from the debris. He had entered the Amun temple alarmed to see it had already been ransacked. Ay's promise to persuade the pharaoh in postponing the temple's desecration was worthless.

"That belongs to my brother," said Sia, pointing to the priest wand in Meri-Ra's hand.

"Where is Neper?"

"Neper is dead," said Sia without a hint of emotion.

Meri-Ra froze in shock. "How?"

"The pharaoh's guards murdered him."

"The pharaoh's guards were ordered only to destroy statues."

"So you knew of the pharaoh's planned atrocity?"

"If a priest was killed it was because they were protecting an Amun statue," said Meri-Ra; his way of justifying Teppy's orders to slay Amun priests—a course of action he would never condone.

"It was as you say," Sia replied.

"Neper wouldn't give his life to protect a statue of Amun when he had made the decision to convert to the Aten priesthood."

Sia sneered. "You think you know my twin better than I do, priest of the Aten?"

"I want to see his body," Meri-Ra demanded.

He walked over more debris and headed toward the direction of the toppled Amun statue.

Sia stepped in front of him, blocking his way and his view of Neper's corpse. "He's being prepared for mummification," Sia replied.

Meri-Ra thought to challenge him but assumed it would be useless, so he turned to leave.

"You are aware that the Apis bull refused to eat from Pharaoh Teppy's hand during the Sed-Festival. It is written if the bull refuses the food offering, one is not fit to be pharaoh," said Sia.

Meri-Ra faced him. "That is the law of Amun, not the law of the Aten."

"And Amun will have his vengeance against the pharaoh and all who follow him out of Thebes."

Meri-Ra ignored Sia's warning. The Amun priest had threatened him many times before, even when he had been an adolescent priest of the Aten. It was the habit of the Amun priests to intimidate anyone who didn't follow their explicit instructions with a curse from the Amun god.

"Pharaoh Teppy has ordained me as the Aten's lector priest, and I have no fear of Amun," said Meri-Ra, as he walked away.

"I don't believe you," replied Sia "You should put down Neper's priest wand. It's scorching hot."

In an instant, he heard a sizzling sound, then a tingle sensation in his fingers morphed into intense heat. The smell of burning flesh caused Meri-Ra to drop Neper's wand. He gasped at the sight of blackened skin across his fingers as if they were burned by fire. This was indeed the ancient magic Meri-Ra had assured Ay that Sia could not possess; the same form of magic that has frightened the Egyptian people for hundreds of years. Meri-Ra was wrong. Sia was indeed one of the elite conjurors from the long lost cult of the Heka, endowed with power stronger than illusions. Meri-Ra ignored what looked like pus-filled blisters forming in the palm of his hand, and faced Sia head on.

"You cannot stand against the Aten. You cannot stand against the Aten," repeated Meri-Ra. "To me belonged the universe before your god had come into being. You have come afterward because *I am Heka*, and you cannot stand against the Aten."

Sia's smirk melted when his legs suddenly buckled beneath him, and he collapsed to the floor.

Sia discovered he was not the only priest who had learned the ancient cult of magic from the writings of the Heka god, and from that day on, it would be an unrelenting battle between the priesthood of the Aten and that of the god Amun.

As a third of the population of Thebes boarded the boats that would take them to the land of the Aten, others gathered near the bank of the river to witness pharaoh Teppy's departure, and to see who had chosen to follow him.

Horemheb stood in the forefront of the crowd, watching, as the largest barge, at one hundred twenty cubits in length, carried the obelisk that once stood tall at Teppy's unfinished Gempaaten temple. There were rumors of the pharaoh's plan to leave Thebes, but Horemheb had refused to believe them until he learned that

Teppy's guards had raided and ransacked the Amun temple. It inflamed Horemheb that an act of aggression by the pharaoh's royal guards, an extension of his army, was not brought to him first for his approval. How unthinkable that an Egyptian pharaoh would leave the capital city and curse to damnation the gods that existed in Egypt since the beginning of time. Standing on the bank of this grand departure, it became clear to Horemheb that Teppy was the heretic abomination that his father accused him of being.

Alongside Horemheb stood his younger half-brother, Kafrem— a tall, slender, lanky man twenty-two years of age. He had drooped shoulders, skinny legs and a concave chest that he would stick out whenever he was in the presence of Horemheb.

To hide his premature balding, he wore a wig made of date palm fibers that were shaped and curled by waxing. The fibers were shoulder length and tinted with henna and juniper berries.

The brothers had different fathers, with Horemheb's father being of a poor family of farmers, and Kafrem's father's lineage from wealthy descendants of royal scribes, that which Horemheb assumed his brother had gained his warped sense of entitlement. The Amun priesthood had ordained Kafrem mayor of Thebes just days before the Amun temple was raided. Horemheb suspected his brother's appointment was meant to soften the blow that the priests had planned to challenge his right to regency of Thebes. Kafrem would be expected to overlook their unlawful acts, unwittingly, a pawn under the Amun priests' control.

Both Horemheb and Kafrem gazed in silence at the enormous fleet of ships floating in the river. It was a grand spectacle that filled Horemheb with both anger and awe.

"Do you believe the pharaoh and his followers will return?" asked Kafrem.

Horemheb grinned. "I once saw the word 'heretic' carved in his father's chest. I never understood why Amenhotep mutilated himself in such a manner until this moment."

Kafrem turned to his brother, eager to hear the answer why.

"He was carving his son's destiny into his skin with a flint knife," said Horemheb.

"Had he gone mad?"

"Premonitions are not born of madness. Amenhotep was a great man, a noble man, and a courageous warrior. Teppy is not of his father. He cannot prevail without us. He'll return. I guarantee you, he and his followers will come crawling back to us."

The general smiled at his prediction as the massive fleet drifted downstream. Mundi appeared and walked into Horemheb's open arms in tears. He lovingly consoled her, comforting her with words of assurance of the pharaoh and Nefertiti's inevitable return.

CHAPTER

21

THE FIRST THREE DAYS of sailing for the great fleet were uneventful. While the royal family gorged themselves on sweet breads, fruits, and Egypt's best Canopic branch wines, time passed by fleetingly. Teppy and Nefertiti did their best to keep the children amused with games of twenty-squares, while they enjoyed their own board game of Senet.

Teppy so cherished seeing the joy on his sweet Nefertiti's face when she would win that he never tried to be victorious in the game himself. It was satisfying to see the dimples in her cheeks when she smiled after removing her last piece from the board ahead of him, cementing her triumph.

At night they all sang jubilant songs together. Queen Ty, Ay, Teyla, the children, Nefertiti, and Teppy, the entire royal family all sang and played musical instruments that mimicked the sounds of birds. The children danced for their parents and were happy and exhausted by the time they were put to bed. After they had fallen asleep, Nefertiti found herself walking about the deck alone after twilight, watching the group of forty oarsmen turn their oars in perfect unison. The rocking of the boat sickened her, making it nearly impossible for her to fall asleep. Four nights into their voyage and she was without a full night's rest. The fatigue from it all caused her to overlook Halima. She had not seen or spoken to her most favorite maidservant since the day they embarked on their voyage. Nefertiti made an unannounced visit to Halima's cabin that night, and was horrified to see her prostrating in front of a statuette of Amun; one she had hidden away before the purge.

"What are you doing?"

Halima was startled out of her trance. Before she could stand up on her feet to answer, Nefertiti marched up to her and struck her across the head, knocking her back onto the floor.

"Get up!" ordered Nefertiti.

Halima stood up disoriented.

"If my husband found out about your blasphemy he would have you executed on the spot. It's only because you're a vital part of my children's lives that I'd even think of sparing you from his wrath.

"Please forgive me, Queen. I am so ashamed."

"Listen to me Halima, because I'll only tell you this once. You will hide the statuette in your garment and when no one is watching, you will toss it overboard into the river. Is that clear?"

Halima nodded.

"There is no other god here but the Aten. None!" shouted Nefertiti. "I have always shared a predilection for you, but if you are seen again with any statues or images of gods from Thebes, I myself will harden my heart and give you fifty blows of the whip before my husband cuts off both your hands."

"My queen, I'll do as you ask. Praises to you and the Aten for your undeserved mercy." Halima held the statue inside her garment and meandered out to the deck with her head down in shame.

The following night, Nefertiti slept soundly. The river had changed its course and the wind became almost non-existent.

Though the boat had ceased the drastic rocking that had kept her awake, the absence of wind created treacherous sandbanks and some of the ships ran aground. By the sixth day, it had become a dangerous journey that when coupled with the darkness of night, became all the worse.

Queen Ty summoned Teppy to her cabin. When he entered she kissed his cheek, a tentative kiss that drew attention to her distress. His mother was not dressed extravagantly as he was accustomed to seeing her. She wore no makeup, nor any of her precious jewelry. Her garment had a tear on the sleeve, a minor inconvenience for anyone else, but highly unusual for a meticulous Queen Ty.

Because her eyes were glassy, it concerned Teppy that the rocking of the boat had sickened her as it had Nefertiti.

"Let me send in a physician to see you," he said. "You don't appear well."

Ty took the scarf that was around her neck and tied it around her head. "It's not physical," she replied and seated herself on the couch. Teppy followed and sat next to her.

"Then what is it?"

Before she answered she took his hand. "When you were a child someone had taken your favorite toy. It was a wooden hippopotamus with jaws that opened and closed. You adored it. Do you remember?"

Teppy nodded.

"You were sure the thief was one of your cousins and you cried and screamed and refused to play with them ever again. Of course they were hurt because they loved you and enjoyed coming to the palace to play with you. It was months later when you found your hippopotamus toy. You had hidden it away in one of your straw clothing baskets and had forgotten. I remember how you worried if your cousins would forgive you for abandoning them, but when they returned to the palace to play with you again, it was as if it had never happened."

The Queen placed her hand gently on Teppy's face. "My dear son, it's not too late. We can return to Thebes with our pride still intact, the people will forgive us. It's where we belong," she pleaded.

Her desperation caused Teppy to crease his forehead. He moved his mother's hand away from his face and stood up. "For the remainder of this journey, don't speak another word to me," he said, menacing.

Teppy left his mother's cabin disgusted by her vile words and her unfaithfulness to the Aten. He would immediately have to pray for her forgiveness, so that the Aten would not curse her or the remaining days of their voyage.

By the seventh day, the children were restless and yearned to be on solid ground. Sailing into shoals was a common occurrence, but Teppy's prayers to the Aten were answered and by nightfall they had succeeded in navigating all their vessels away from the treacherous shoals of the river and into calmer waters.

Finally, after eight days and nights of sailing, Teppy's vision was illuminated at the first sign of dawn. He opened his eyes and witnessed it again—the same vision the Aten had revealed to him before they embarked on their journey. Above the flatlands in front of him, the sun was rising between two mountains: a testament that they had arrived at the divinely chosen destination. He raised his hands to the sky in praise of the Aten.

"You appear beautiful in the horizon of the sky, oh living sun disk," Teppy shouted at the top of his lungs. "When you rise in the eastern horizon, you fill every land with your beauty. You're the beginning of life, beautiful, great, resplendent, and exalted over every land. Your rays encompass the lands to the extent of all things which you have made. You bring them all and make them subject to me, your beloved son. This is the horizon of the Aten!"

The massive fleet of ferryboats and barges anchored along the eastern riverbank. Over twenty-five thousand of the pharaoh's followers disembarked onto the fertile land that stretched beyond their range of vision, anxious to explore its hidden gifts from the Aten. With excitement and fanfare, servants carried Teppy and Nefertiti off the boat on the royal litter with their children. When Teppy's bare feet touched the ground, the spirit of the Aten surged through him. Its rays of sunlight shone upon his face and he was overcome with gratification. Teppy had merged and become as one with his father, the Aten. There was one god and one mission: to construct and build what would be called the city of Akhetaten, known as Amarna, the new capital city of Egypt in honor of the Aten.

The first challenge was to protect themselves from the elements. In the days that followed, hundreds of tents were set up around the proposed construction site. Architects drew plans of the city's layout based on Teppy's vision and presented them to him for his approval. The foundation of the city was to be established within fourteen markers that he set forth upon the cliffs on both sides of the river.

To speed up the construction, most of the buildings were to be made from mud-brick and then white washed. The Royal Palace and the Great Temple of the Aten would be the only exceptions, faced with limestone and granite and the first structures to be completed. Over a hundred scribes drew hieroglyphics on every standing structure while more building supplies were brought in from Thebes.

After two years of diligent construction, only the foundations of the Aten city had been completed. Yet in Teppy's eyes, Amarna had been born, and even in its unfinished state, it shone as a glorious place, grander than the city of Thebes could ever wish to be.

One day, while strolling near the entrance of the Great Temple of the Aten, Teppy gazed upon the two unfinished statues of himself that stood on either side. Bek, the royal sculptor, was busy instructing his workers on the carving of the pharaoh's image into the stone. The statue had a muscular chest and shoulders not bearing the least resemblance to Teppy's thin, womanly body. The next day, he summoned Bek to his chambers.

"The likeness you have carved of me is deceptive," Teppy said.

"I don't understand. The depiction is muscular and strong. My only wish is to honor you, my Pharaoh," Bek said, cowering under the pharaoh's accusation.

"We're no longer in Thebes, Bek. You can honor me by not hiding my true features. As the royal sculptor of Amarna, you will sculpt exactly what you see or what I tell you. My physical appearance is perfect the way it is."

Bek studied Teppy's appearance and nodded. "It is, my Pharaoh, my apologies. I'll do as you wish."

Months later, Nefertiti was mesmerized as she observed Bek put the finishing touches on the new version of her husband's statue. This one now included Teppy's perfect deformities that mirrored the shape of a god: his elongated head, neck, and fingers, his newly formed potbelly and wide feminine hips—differences that set him apart as the true son of the Aten. Though Nefertiti and his daughters did not have his physical features, she ordered Bek to sculpt her and the children's images in the same manner, so they all would appear as part of her husband's god-like appearance.

Throughout the city of Amarna, engravings and statues of the pharaoh and the royal family were depicted with the same wide hips, elongated heads, drooping breasts, and sagging abdomens, perfect deformities from Teppy, the descendant of a god.

After three years of construction, the royal family celebrated the inauguration of the city with an appearance in front of the people of Amarna.

From the palace balcony, the pharaoh's family could peer out over the people and greet them on special occasions. They called this balcony their "Window of Appearances," and on that day of inauguration the crowd applauded and roared when the royal family stepped out and waved at them. When the cheering abated, Teppy spoke directly to all his Amarna citizens.

"We are here in this magnificent new land, given to us by the only true god, the Aten. I am his only son, and I am the only way through to him. Any tributes of worship will be made to me and the royal family to please the Aten. No tributes or taxes will be paid to the Aten priesthood, only to me through Maya, our treasurer. The Aten god—the sun-disk—is the only god of Amarna and anyone harboring a statue or object of any other god from Thebes will be severely punished. You are part of a great revolution. You are the chosen ones, blessed to live in the glorious light of the Aten for eternity."

Teppy paused for a moment before he made the next announcement. He touched Nefertiti and each one of his daughters' faces so they would know that what he had to say next was meant for them as well.

"There is no more Teppy; my name has changed. From this day forward and into the afterlife, I will be known as Aken*aten*, a name that represents my devotion to the Aten. I make an oath to you today that neither the royal family nor I will ever leave the boundaries of Amarna. This is our capital city, and we will reside here forever, even when we return in the afterlife. I am Akenaten."

The applause and cheers soon changed to roars and then chaos when Nefertiti tossed gold bracelets out to the people one-by-one. In mass hysteria, the crowd screamed and pushed one another about trying to catch them.

After leaving the Window of Appearances, Ay and Teyla took the children on a chariot tour of their new city. Akenaten wanted his daughters exposed to the people and the animals, never to be confined behind the palace walls as he had been as a child in Thebes. He had built the city of Amarna for his family so they would thrive and live forever under the sunrays of the Aten.

Since the year that Akenaten had become pharaoh, Egypt had not seen one day of war. There had been threats brewing from the land of Kush, Libya and even the Hittites, though no motivation for combat existed until after the third year following Akenaten's exodus from Thebes, when General Horemheb heard reports of raids and sneak attacks posed on Egypt's borders. He sent letters to Amarna informing the pharaoh of the threats and had never received a response. Akenaten had closed his eyes to it and left the task of war to his god, the Aten.

The pharaoh's refusal to allow Egypt into war did not halt Horemheb's stringent military training schedule for his young warriors. At the military camp, the boys trained incessantly every morning until sundown, led by the hand of Horemheb and his military captain, Salitas. Egypt would be ready and prepared with formidable warriors whenever the pharaoh returned to his senses.

Horemheb was teaching an archery class of one hundred and fifty boys when his brother Kafrem walked across the field and approached him. The general stepped away from his students to learn the reason for his brother's visit. Kafrem met him half way, glancing at the warriors training on the field and running the track.

"Why do you even bother with this? He's not going to give you your war," said Kafrem. "You'd be better off at home making beer."

"What do you want?" asked Horemheb.

"I want you to stop procrastinating and do something before our country is taken over by foreigners. We must have the gold tributes. How else are we to make trade for the wood we need and the lifestyle we're accustomed to?"

Horemheb was irritated by his brother's response. Even his mere presence on his training grounds irked him.

"Leave. I have work to do," said Horemheb, before turning and walking away. Kafrem followed him across the field.

"The people want a pharaoh they can see. You control the army; you should be their pharaoh. Why are you allowing him to make a mockery of Egypt?" said Kafrem. "If you destroyed Amarna along with the pharaoh and his queen, Thebes would become the capitol again and you would reunite—"

Before Kafrem could finish his thought, Horemheb turned around and punched him in the nose so forcefully that he was lifted off the ground, catapulted backwards and dropped flat on his back.

"We are not a family of traitors," said Horemheb. "The pharaoh will come around soon enough."

Kafrem got up and walked over to where his wig had landed in the sand and placed it back on his head. His nose bled and he covered it with his hand to stop the flow. "You said he would come crawling back to us. It's been three years. He's not coming."

Horemheb watched his brother tear a piece away from his garment and use it to absorb the blood from his nosebleed.

"If you don't do something," warned Kafrem, "Sia and the Amun priests will. They have already discussed separating upper and lower Egypt where they will rule the lower portion, and Teppy the upper. The decision will be made without you."

Sharing a rare moment alone away from the children, Nefertiti poured herself and Akenaten both a jar of pomegranate wine to relax their senses. Nefertiti drank a generous portion, but it failed to relax her, and Akenaten sensed something was occupying her thoughts.

"The wine cannot help you hide what's clearly there for me to see, my love," he said.

Her face blossomed in a loving smile.

"You know me all so well. There is news, great news."

"Tell me."

She gently stroked his hand. "I am with child." she said, beaming with joy.

Those words—the same four words she had told him three times before, were no less beautiful than the first time she had uttered them. Akenaten kissed her forehead and held her close to his body.

"The Aten has blessed me twice today."

Nefertiti pulled away, curious. "What other blessing have you received?"

"Kiya came to my chamber this morning to tell me of her own pregnancy," said Akenaten.

An uneasiness spread across Nefertiti's face.

"Why didn't you tell me of this earlier?"

"I thought you would become jealous, but now there's no reason to be."

"Why would there ever be a reason I should be jealous of her, when she is insignificant to you, as you say. On the contrary, Kiya has many reasons to be jealous of me," said Nefertiti.

Akenaten had been right to expect her adverse reaction to Kiya's pregnancy. Yet, their pregnancies fulfilled his dreams of more beautiful children. For Nefertiti, it would be a race between which wife would bear the pharaoh's son first, insuring to one, the most coveted position for a woman of royalty—mother to the heir of the throne of Egypt.

CHAPTER

22

KING SUPPILULIUMAS was a physically imposing man, a warrior king that stood a cubit taller than the tallest Hittite and weighed almost twice as much. His massiveness was due to the excessive amount of food he would devour and the muscle he acquired from lifting stone and iron daily. He had a receding forehead and a prominent curved nose. His black hair was gathered into a long pigtail, and the king, whose eyes were slightly slanted, spoke with a strong jaw. As was the custom for many Hittite men, he shaved his face; when he reached the age of sixty-six, it would be acceptable to grow a lengthy beard. Suppululiumas was proud and confident, and he raised his sons to be the same. They were known as the three princes of Hatti: Telipinus, Piyassilis, and Mursili II. The eldest was Telipinus, who, along with his brother Mursili, was sent with an army by his father to contain the rebels in the lands of Eber-Nari.

To prove his loyalty to King Suppululiumas, Shattiwaza, the banished prince of Mitanni, accompanied the two princes on their campaign, and now all three had returned to the Hattusas palace in Hatti to a grand celebration of their conquest.

"Shattiwaza, I have to admit, I see you much differently than I did before," said Suppululiumas.

"It's all meaningless, my king, if you don't see me as a son-in-law," replied Shattiwaza.

"A daughter of a king should marry a king. Why should I allow my only daughter to marry you?"

"Carranda loves me, and I believe it's quite obvious that I'm enchanted by her. Second of all, I'm only one barrier away from being a king. With your help, that barrier could be eliminated."

Suppululiumas chuckled. "I thoroughly enjoy your absurd ambition."

"And this coming from a king that has schemed against and conquered every country in the vicinity except Egypt."

"I have no desire to conquer Egypt," replied Suppululiumas.

"I think your desire would awaken if you knew of a way to do it. I, my king, can help you, if you're willing to help me."

"Help you overthrow your own father? Was not your uncle enough?"

"Both were traitors to the legacy of Mitanni, and because I wouldn't go along with their treachery, I was banished from my own country," said Shattiwaza. "If your Hittite army conquered it, how simple it would be for you to install me as the new king. As the prince of Mitanni, I am, as you know, the rightful heir."

Shattiwaza's exile from his own country intrigued King Suppululiumas. When the Mitanni prince was first captured crossing over Hatti's borders, he was thrown in the Hittite prison to await execution as an invader.

There, he was given only a ration of bread and water three times a week and pieces of fruit once every seven days. His cell was dark and wet from the excessive rainfall that would drain down into the prison cells, flooding them every thirtieth day and beyond. Fighting to keep his bread and fruit from the rats was part of his daily struggle to survive the most miserable conditions a son of a king could fathom. His Hittite captives had not spoken a word to him until one day in the tenth year of his captivity, a guard appeared and unlocked his cell door.

"You're free to go," he said and tossed a small pouch at him.

Shattiwaza caught it and looked inside. The pouch was filled with gemstones. Shattiwaza stood up from the floor, suspicious of this sudden act of kindness. *It must be some kind of trick*, he thought.

"What is this?"

"Carnelian. Take it and go," said the guard, holding the cell door open for him.

"Go where? I can't return to Mitanni. They'll kill me."

"That's none of our business."

"I want to see King Suppiluliumas," demanded Shattiwaza.

The guard laughed. "Now why would the king agree to see you?"

"I am a Mitannian prince. I know secrets about the Egyptians that King Suppiluliumas would find immensely valuable. More valuable than this," said Shattiwaza as he tossed the pouch of carnelian jewels back to the guard.

After he bathed and was given a clean garment to wear, Shattiwaza was brought before King Suppiluliumas in his Hattusas palace. The king took a glimpse at Shattiwaza and went back to eating his evening meal without saying a word to him.

"I want to make a trade with you," said Shattiwaza, breaking the awkward silence.

"Your voice is whiny like a pregnant woman. Speak up!"

Shattiwaza took a step closer to the king and lowered the pitch of his voice. "I said I would like to make a trade with you."

"I don't trade with Mitannians, I kill them, and if it wasn't for the fact that you're a Mitanni prince that conspired and killed your own king, you certainly would be dead and returned to dust by now," said Suppiluliumas.

"I've been withering away in your ghastly prison for ten years. It took you that long to discover I had confessed the truth about who I was and what I did?"

"Actually it took only two; I threw in the extra eight for good measure," replied Suppiluliumas with a smile.

Shattiwaza noticed a woman dressed in a red silk garment standing at the entrance staring at him.

"Come, Carranda, sit and share a meal with your father," said Suppiluliumas.

The woman kept her eyes locked on Shattiwaza as she took a seat opposite Suppiluliumas. She wasn't particularly attractive, but there was something about her that intrigued Shattiwaza—most likely her relation to the king.

"I can reveal to you every secret trade route the Egyptians are using through the Ugarit Valley including the entire Eber-Nari if you allow me asylum here in your country," said Shattiwaza to the king.

"Or I could just torture the information out of you then slice off your head," Suppiluliumas replied. "It would be so much simpler."

"And foolish," Shattiwaza snapped. "I'm more valuable to you alive, and I would bet my life you're not a foolish man."

"We have a peace treaty with the Egyptians. Why would you think we'd want their secret trade routes?"

"Every king wants the Egyptians' secret trade routes," answered Shattiwaza.

In the end, the Mitanni prince had successfully bargained with King Suppiluliumas and was granted asylum in the Hittite country.

Now, in the two years since his release from their prison, Shattiwaza had ingratiated himself with Suppiluliumas and his sons, even volunteering to assist them in their campaigns of war on neighboring kingdoms.

One afternoon, as Suppiluliumas was consulting with his viceroy, his wife Tawanna entered the room hand-in-hand with their youngest son, Zenanza. The little four-year-old bolted from his mother's side and climbed onto his father's lap.

"Father, I want you to play a game with me," he said.

The boy held a ball made of leather skin, filled with dried papyrus reeds and tied together with string. He handed it to Suppiluliumas, who regarded it with disdain.

"The moment is approaching when there will be no time for games," he said to his son, "only time for you to prepare to become king over a foreign land as your older brothers have done."

Suppiluliumas crushed the ball within his palm. The boy cried out at his crushed toy. Tawanna, riled by her husband's interaction with her son, grabbed Zenanza by the hand and took him from his father's lap.

"How dare you! He's still a child and will be treated as such," snapped Tawanna.

"Within the next ten years our son will be a man and maybe a king," replied Suppiluliumas.

"If he becomes king, it will be here on this soil as king of Hatti, not of some distant kingdom like you sent your son Piyassilis to so that we never see him again," replied Tawanna.

"Do I need to remind you, my wife, about proper etiquette in front of the Mitanni prince?"

"My great king, please, never mind me," Shattiwaza interrupted. "The queen is welcome to speak as though I'm not here. It makes me feel like part of this big happy family."

Neither Suppiluliumas nor his wife found Shattiwaza's comment as humorous as he did. Tawanna stepped up to him and stared into his expressionless face.

"Why my daughter finds herself attracted to you baffles me," she said. "I myself can't find one redeeming quality about you. Your character is irritating, your hair resembles the feathers of a rooster, you smell unpleasant, and your smile is so crooked it exposes your deceitfulness. Not even a cow in heat would find you appealing. Undoubtedly, you'll be the worst mistake of my daughter's life."

Shattiwaza sneered at Tawanna before she turned and rushed out of the room, dragging the young Zenanza behind her.

A villager and his wife were escorted by guards inside the Amun temple to receive a judgment from Sia. After the announcement of the married couple's arrival, Sia exited the outer sanctuary and went out to the entrance doors to greet them. The sixty-two-year-old man gripped his twelve-year-old wife's wrist tighter when she tried to pull away from him. Her clothing was soiled as if she had been dragged through the mud. Sia cringed at the sight of their uncleanliness, and wouldn't allow them a step further than what they had already taken into the temple. His intention was to resolve their case as quickly as possible so they would leave his sacred temple. "Stand here and tell me what's the urgency?" he said.

"My lord, my wife committed adultery and must be condemned so that I may be divorced from her," said the man.

The girl jerked her wrist free and backed away from him.

"I swear my innocence to you my lord before the Amun god himself," she said to Sia. "I'm not guilty of what my husband is accusing me. It's a ruse for him to be rid of me to marry another," the girl replied.

"If there is no witness to the adultery, you cannot condemn her," said Sia to the man.

"But I do have a witness my lord."
The man opened the temple doors and Kafrem entered. "He is my witness."

Both the girl and Sia looked astonished to see him.

"What is this?" asked Sia, dubious of Kafrem's involvement.

"I am the witness. I'm the one she seduced into copulating with her," Kafrem said.

The girl shook her head, bewildered. "My lord I have no idea who this man is, except that I've seen him speaking to my husband in the past. I have never been with him."

"I am the mayor of this city, you know very well who I am, adulteress," said Kafrem.

"No my lord, he's lying and both he and my husband are conspiring together against me."

"Give me the scroll," said Sia.

The man handed him a papyrus scroll. Sia unrolled it, dipped a reed into red ink and wrote his proclamation, all without asking the girl questions that could verify her innocence. He then rolled it up and returned it to the man.

"You are divorced from your wife and she will have her nose cut from her face," said Sia.

"No! They're lying! Please, my lord you have to believe me!" she shouted.

The Theban guards shuffled her away and out of the temple as she kicked and screamed for mercy.

Kafrem and the man had just stepped outside the temple door when Horemheb arrived. The general saw the man hand Kafrem a pouch before he hurried away at the sight of him.

"Are you now accepting compensation from citizens as part of your duties as mayor?" asked Horemheb.

Kafrem stashed the pouch in his garment and shrugged. "I'm a witness to his wife's adultery, and he offered me a token of his gratitude. It would be an insult not to accept it," Kafrem replied.

Horemheb didn't believe him. His brother most likely accepted gold for bearing false witness against an innocent woman, simply because a man wanted a lawful way to leave his wife for another. Horemheb knew of the scheme, but never considered that Kafrem would succumb to such heartless bribery and greed. Disgusted with his brother, he marched past him into the temple.

Sia spied Horemheb's entrance and his march through the nave on his way to the outer sanctuary. He stepped in front of his path and held out his arm to stop him.

"This is my home—the sacred temple of the Amun god. You will wash yourself before you come any further," said Sia.

Horemheb capitulated and returned to the ablution tank at the temple's entrance and washed his face, arms and hands. Sia passed him a linen cloth, and the general used it to dry himself.

"This will be brief," Horemheb said. "I was made aware that you're inciting a separation of Upper and Lower Egypt among our citizens. Is it true?"

"Egypt must move on without the pharaoh. A separation is the best way to do it," replied Sia.

"You're ignorant to the ways of men. Even a rumor of separation of Upper and Lower Egypt would cause every kingdom in the known world to suspect that we have a weakness in our military. It would be the most fatal mistake Egypt could make. Your rhetoric is very dangerous to this country."

"You, general, are the one to consult for hand-to-hand combat advice. You should leave the intellectual decisions to those who have the capacity for intellect. I know what would make the Egyptian citizens joyful," replied Sia.

"And I know what would keep them alive." Horemheb countered. "Were you aware, Sia, that the Hittites are now encroaching on our boundaries in T'aru? Do you even know what that means?"

As Horemheb expected, Sia remained silent.

"I make it my absolute priority to be aware of every threat there might be to my country," said Horemheb. "If king Suppiluliumas thinks that Egypt is not united, he will use it against us in a war, that at this moment, we're not prepared to fight."

"More the reason we should have a vote and elect a pharaoh for Upper Egypt that will make the necessary decisions for Thebes," Sia replied. "I'm certain that most citizens along with every priest here will cast their vote for me—their lector priest."

Horemheb stared at Sia with extreme contempt. "There are tens of thousands of soldiers in my army, alert me when you're ready to have that vote," said Horemheb, as he exited the temple.

In her palace chamber in Amarna, Queen Ty sat in front of her copper mirror wiping away her makeup with a linen cloth when she was once again interrupted by a loud clang—the same horrible sound of metal striking metal she heard years before in Thebes palace. What sort of curse could follow her as far away as Amarna?

She opened her door and walked down the corridor; there was no one but members of Akenaten's royal guard standing post in sections alongside the wall.

"Did you hear the noise?" she asked a guard.

"No, my queen, I heard nothing," he replied.

What if her son's own guards were conspiring with Horemheb, attempting to deceive her into believing she was mad? *Some were highly ranked in Horemheb's army. It's possible they maintained their loyalty to him and not her son,* she thought. Her paranoia had risen to a point of no return and there was not a word anyone could say to her that would calm her spirit.

When the queen returned to her chamber, her door was closed. She had no doubt she had left it ajar when she went out to speak to the guards. With caution she cracked it open, and—*hisssssssss*—a white cat with sea-green eyes peered out from behind her door with its back arched, ready to attack. Around its neck was a solid gold collar with a ruby medallion. The queen slammed the door shut. She ran from the room and down the corridor.

The guards tried to help her, but the queen, suspicious of a conspiracy with Horemheb, refused to speak to them. Instead, she had her servant drive her the short distance to Ay's home where she woke him and Teyla from their sleep.

"My brother, you have to help me. It won't let me rest," she pleaded in a quivering voice. Ay tried his best to soothe her, massaging her hand as Teyla brought her a jar of wine to calm her nerves.

"You must come to my chamber," she said, refusing the wine. "Lupita's cat is haunting me."

Ay had seen the same redness in Amenhotep's eyes many times before; it was from the effects of the cure, but since the queen dreaded her husband's addiction, Ay assumed she would never conceive of taking it herself. He was saddened to conclude his sister was on the fringe of some other kind of madness. Still, he appeased her by following her back to the palace.

Queen Ty stood behind Ay, and the royal guards watched as he pushed the door open to her chamber and peered inside. The room was silent and appeared vacant. Ay searched it and confirmed that the cat was gone, or most likely had never been there at all. Cautiously, Ty entered after him.

"I swear to you Lupita's cat was here," she said pointing at the doorway. "The guards must have let him out."

"My dear sister, as you know, Bastian died next to Amenhotep. He most certainly killed the cat before he died himself. There are many cats that roam the palace night and day. It's possible you saw one that resembled Bastian," said Ay.

"I know what I saw, and it was Bastian. He wore the same gold and ruby collar that Lupita put on him. One of the guards must have let him in my chamber then released him."

"I would never accuse you of being mad. Perhaps what you saw was a *mut* spirit," replied Ay.

"What is a mut spirit?"

"I learned of them when I was an Amun priest. Because Lupita could not give birth to her child, she refuses to journey into the realm of the dead. She and her cat are wanderers between this life and the afterlife, searching for a way to avenge instead of accepting their fate. You must protect yourself from such an evil spirit," warned Ay.

"But how?"

"I'll travel back to Thebes and consult the Oracle for you. He will give me the ingredients for the spell that I can pass on to Meri-Ra, the Aten priest, to rid you of the mut spirit."

At the mere mention of the Oracle, Queen Ty's eyelids fluttered. Surely, the new Oracle would know she caused his predecessor's death. Though her life might depend on it, she would be foolish to ask for his help.

"The Oracle helps those who worship Amun. Do not consult him on my behalf," she said to Ay.

"You're the queen mother of Egypt, my sister. The Oracle is sworn to uphold your honor."

"His honor is only for the Amun god. That is where his true loyalty lies. Bring me, instead, four live scorpions that I can use to represent the Oracle's power for my own spell."

"Spells are meant solely for the priests to cast. Should I consult Meri-Ra or Panhessy?" asked Ay concerned that his sister had indeed lost her senses.

"No, the spell is not of the Aten, but one I overheard spoken by the Amun priests."

Ay gasped.

"My sister, it would be sacrilege against the Aten to recite a spell from the Amun priests here in Amarna."

"Bring me the scorpions, Ay," she barked. The queen's menacing tone startled her brother.

Ay left the queen's chamber uncertain of what he should do. If he brought her the scorpions, it might give in to her delusions, and she would undoubtedly recite a spell to Amun committing unforgiveable blasphemy against the Aten. Worse, the scorpions could poison her if she didn't handle them correctly. But if he didn't bring them to her, she would find another way to get them and have him punished for his disobedience.

That night, Nefertiti suffered from her own insecurities as her concerns over Kiya intensified. The young queen had convinced herself that she would never become jealous of a secondary wife whose beauty could not compare to her own, but now that Kiya's pregnancy was showing, jealousy overwhelmed her. Akenaten's interaction with Kiya appeared more loving and affectionate than it had before. The chance that his secondary wife might bear him a male heir before her was distressing. If it was determined that Nefertiti was only capable of giving Akenaten female children, how much longer would she go unchallenged by a more capable replacement? Queen Ty would be the most sympathetic to her plight, so she went to speak to her in private.

When she walked into Ty's chamber, she made a conscious effort to ignore the queen's pale and emaciated appearance.

Queen Ty welcomed Nefertiti with a warm embrace.

"I need your guidance, my queen," said Nefertiti. "You have always given me invaluable advice. I pray that you can help me."

"You're more than just a daughter-in-law. You're as my own daughter. Have you prayed first to the Aten for his direction?"

"I have, but I feel the need to prove to our god that I can help myself when I am able," Nefertiti answered.

Queen Ty invited Nefertiti to sit beside her. She accepted and held the queen's hand as she spoke.

"I'm concerned about Kiya's jealousy of me and her infatuation with my husband. It's not reasonable," said Nefertiti.

"A mistress is never reasonable," replied the queen. "Yet, she is his secondary wife."

"I'm aware of that, and I'm also aware that you faced the same predicament with your husband, Amenhotep, and his second wife, Lady Lupita. Kiya revels in taunting me. How would you suggest I deal with her cruelty?"

"It's not my place to get involved with matters of the heart when it comes to my son, but I understand your fears," Ty said. "You're worried that Kiya will give birth to a male heir before you. And yes, you should be very concerned, my daughter. If she does give birth to his male heir first, her son will certainly grow to be king over your children, and he will banish you and make his mother, Kiya, the queen of Egypt. It's what kings do," she affirmed.

Nefertiti was visibly shaken by her bluntness. Queen Ty stood up and retrieved a pouch from a Canopic jar. She put it in Nefertiti's palm and closed her hand over it.

"What is it?" asked Nefertiti.

"It's what you need. Your instincts will direct you as to how you should use it."

Queen Ty kissed Nefertiti's forehead. "Go now. I must contend with my own predicaments. And when you see my son, tell him I wish to make a trip to my homeland of T'aru," she said.

"My queen, I don't wish to alarm you, but you appear too ill to travel such a long distance."

"Perhaps I am, but T'aru is where I mourn my son, Tuthmosis, where I imagine all the great works he might have accomplished if he had been allowed to live. T'aru is where my husband, Amenhotep, once loved me with such passion that he built a lake for me there in my honor. Love can heal, my dear Nefertiti, even in the form of a lake," said Queen Ty.

"I will do as you ask," Nefertiti said before she left Ty's chamber with the pouch held tight in her hand.

Speaking with her daughter-in-law was like reliving her past life in Thebes. Ty saw so much of herself in Nefertiti that it saddened her that the young queen was experiencing the same turmoil that had once deprived her of her dignity.

Queen Ty went to her mirror and unsealed her last remaining pouch. She released the scorpion into a bowl and crushed it alive with a stone before it could scurry away. In a vase filled with wood scraps and linen, she sprinkled the severed scorpion pieces and topped it with pounded frankincense, then set the concoction on fire. Queen Ty recited the spell she overheard from the Amun priests in Thebes but adjusted it slightly so it would affect the mut spirits of Lupita and her cat.

[4]*Down upon your face, evil spirits. You are thrust down into the flame of fire and it has come against you. This flame is deadly to your soul and to your spirit and to your body. This fire will prevail over you, the flame is piercing, it devours you and there is no escape. Your soul has shriveled up and the names of Lupita and her cat Bastian are buried into oblivion, silenced, and will not be remembered or will ever live again. Your spirit has come to an end, driven away and forgotten, forgotten, and forgotten.*

The queen blew out the flames and pounded the ashes into a fine powder. She then mixed it with water. After a short period of contemplation on whether she was making the right decision, she consumed it all.

Moments later her eyelids were heavy and she drifted off to sleep in her bed. The hour had not even passed before she suddenly opened her eyes again. Something had stung her, shocking the queen from

---

[4] Certain passages are from the document "The Book of Overthrowing Apep," originated in the Ramessid period (1307-1070 B.C.E.)

her sleep and directing her attention to the wall. Moving across it were the sinister shadows of Lupita and Bastian, and finally the Oracle himself exiting her bedchamber, one after the other in slow and measured steps. She tried to rise from her bed, but her legs and arms wouldn't move. She screamed, but no sound came from her mouth. The queen gasped in pain from another sting that seized her already paralyzed body. Queen Ty fell into a fixed stare of death as a black mamba slithered from beneath her bedcover onto the floor.

CHAPTER

23

AKENATEN BELIEVED it was the Aten who rendered the judgment of death against his mother, not a mut spirit as Ay argued, nor the scorpion's poison. The queen had dared to recite a spell she overheard from the Amun priests, and the Aten had punished her accordingly.

Akenaten could not in good conscience allow himself to dishonor the Aten's judgment of his mother's death with a public display of grief. Reciting a spell from the Amun priests was blasphemous, and he shuddered to admit that his mother deserved her punishment. Yet, during the seventy days of her mummification he had had not a moment's rest fighting back the despair over losing her in his life. If he could just shed a tear for her, beat his chest in anguish, maybe the pain would subside, instead of festering through his innards like poison. The queen embodied the pinnacle of Akenaten's life, and he knew from that day forward, no one would ever love him again the way she had loved him.

Queen Ty, the grand queen of Egypt, chief wife of Amenhotep the Third, and mother of the Pharaoh Akenaten, was mourned for seventy days by the people of Amarna, then interred in her son's tomb hidden deep in the cliffs above the city. Never will he forget the one who had nurtured him to be the great pharaoh he had become.

While Akenaten was able to hide his grief for his mother internally, Nefertiti struggled. She mourned the death of Queen Ty the same as she had mourned the death of her own birth mother as a child. At times she'd burst into tears at the memory of the queen being interred in her tomb or when Akenaten mentioned her name in passing. She craved for her husband's consolation, and when she tried to gravitate closer to him, he would pull away, widening the divide between them.

With her mentor and confidant gone, Nefertiti now had to contend with Kiya alone.

Both wives were in their eighth month of pregnancy, with Kiya expected to be the first to give birth. To divert Nefertiti's attention away from Kiya's pending day of childbirth, Akenaten commissioned a bust to be made of her beautiful face by Dutmose, who, along with Bek, was one of the finest sculptors in Egypt.

For her sitting, Nefertiti wore her favorite blue crown. It featured a golden diadem band looped around like horizontal ribbons, joining at the back, and a cobra over the brow. Around her neck hung a broad collar with a floral pattern on it, similar to the pattern on her dress—a dress much too sheer for a queen to wear in the presence of a commoner.

As soon as Akenaten stepped into Dutmose's workshop, he was disturbed by Nefertiti's appearance. He stood there in silence while Dutmose carved the stucco layers around the limestone core of the bust, appearing more captivated by Nefertiti's beauty than by the image he was forming. It was precisely what she wanted to happen, and once she determined that Akenaten's jealousy was thoroughly provoked, she pretended to be surprised by it.

"Is there something irritating you, my husband?" she asked, while casting a flirtatious smile at Dutmose.

"Do you think your attire is appropriate in the presence of a commoner?" replied Akenaten.

"I see nothing inappropriate with it," she responded, and turned her attention again back to Dutmose. "Do you see anything unbecoming of my attire?"

Dutmose shrugged, afraid to say anything that might insult the pharaoh or the queen.

"It doesn't matter what he thinks," Akenaten said, clenching his teeth.

Nefertiti desired more than the reaction he gave her, so she continued on with her prodding.

"You're right, my dear husband, this dress is inappropriate for such a special occasion. Perhaps it's best without it," she said, and with that, she pulled it off her shoulders and down to her waist, revealing her breasts. Akenaten was appalled, abashed, and furious all at once.

"Put the dress on and return to your chamber," Akenaten said, restraining the tone of his voice.

"You commissioned him to create this bust of me and that is what he'll do," she replied.

"Nefertiti!" he shouted.

The stirring up of her husband's emotions pleased her. Finally, she received the attention she craved from him.

"Tell me, Teppy, what are you feeling? It can't be any worse than what I feel when I see you and Kiya together frolicking about as if I didn't exist. Go on, tell me. What are you feeling, Teppy? Describe it. I'm curious to know, Teppy," she said, intentionally repeating his birth name to get under his skin and spite him in front of Dutmose.

To Nefertiti's astonishment, Akenaten rushed up to her and grabbed her around the throat with both hands.

Dutmose dropped his carving utensil and fled the room.

"You'll not ever again as long as you are alive address me by that name. My name is, and will always be, Akenaten. Is that understood?"

He tightened his grip around Nefertiti's throat, stifling her ability to answer. All she could do was nod. Never had she seen him so filled with rage, as if possessed by the evil of the Apep god—a miscreant force truly capable of killing her.

Akenaten caught sight of the fear in his sweet Nefertiti's eyes, and what was worse; that he was the cause of it. His manner softened as suddenly as it had turned violent. Akenaten removed his hands from Nefertiti's throat and slowly backed away from her.

She pulled her dress back onto her shoulders and glanced at her reflection in her metallic hand mirror. A bruise had formed around the entire circumference of her neck. She sighed as she looked up into her husband's face. The way he put his head down in shame while he limped out of the workshop was proof enough that he regretted what he had done. It was her behavior that provoked him and Nefertiti blamed no one but herself for pushing him to his limit.

Akenaten had reassured her numerous times that she had no valid reason to be jealous of Kiya, that he loved her more than any woman he had ever known, that it was only empathy he shared for Kiya and her unborn child—never love. Still, Nefertiti found many reasons in her heart to doubt him, and as long as Kiya carried her husband's child in her womb, her mercurial behavior toward him would continue to slip beyond her control.

In the thirty-third week of her pregnancy during an evening meal, Kiya buckled over and screamed. A severe pain had surged upward from her groin into her abdomen so excruciating that she could barely stand on her feet. Ay witnessed the liquid bursting from her womb and spilling out over the ground. The birth had come prematurely.

Teyla helped Kiya to a birthing chamber equipped with a wooden stool so that the child could be delivered. Because males were not allowed inside, Ay remained in the entryway as his wife, Teyla, helped position Kiya in a squatting position over the stool. Praying for a fertility blessing from the gods Bes and Hathor was forbidden in Amarna, so Teyla spoke only a part of the prayer, repeating, "Come down placenta, come down," over and over again.

"It's dying; I can feel it. My child is dying!" screamed Kiya.

Blood seeped from her vagina as Kiya bore down in haste to push the baby out in time to save it.

Ay pretended to be concerned for the well-being of Kiya and the child, but his only interest was for his daughter, Nefertiti. He had purposely neglected to inform Akenaten of the birth so that the pharaoh wouldn't insist on being present during the child's delivery. A male heir born from Kiya would not only diminish his daughter's standing as chief wife to Akenaten, but as the queen's father, his position of royalty might be challenged as well.

Teyla pushed down hard around the outline of Kiya's abdomen, massaging it, hoping to help ease the release. Instead, it made her scream louder as more blood dripped down onto the stool.

"Push!" Teyla shouted. "Push! It's coming!"

Kiya pushed with the last bit of her strength. It felt like the child was reaching up inside of her, pulling, twisting and squeezing her internal organs. The sudden strain triggered a blood vessel in Kiya's left eye to hemorrhage. It stained the white of her eye bright red. The child's head had not tilted down toward its mother's pelvis where it could push on the birth canal and free itself. Instead, the child had curled up against it, causing the shoulder to emerge first. Teyla quickly repositioned the child and the head passed through, then she gently turned the child's shoulders again to help them move past the pelvis. After the abdomen and legs passed through, the baby dropped down into Teyla's waiting hands; a boy that was silent except for a creaking noise he made, like that of a pine tree bending from the wind. Teyla cut the umbilical cord with a flint knife and pinched the baby's arm. There was not another sound from him. Moments later, there was no sound from Kiya either. Ay sighed in relief and left the entryway thanking the Aten god.

The pharaoh's firstborn son had died in childbirth, and the child's mother, Kiya, who desperately tried to give him life, had lost her own.

It was the will of the Aten that Kiya and Akenaten's son did not survive in Amarna. Ay accepted the child's death as fate and advised the grief-stricken pharaoh to do the same. Ay never speculated about the real cause of Kiya's early labor and death in childbirth. Though he suspected his daughter, Nefertiti, had a role in the tragedy, he remained content that no such proof of it existed. The second scorpion pouch that he had given to Queen Ty had long disappeared.

It had been four years since Akenaten left the city of Thebes. In the first year of his absence, the capital came under the control of Sia, Horemheb, and his brother Kafrem—the priest-appointed mayor. Rumors of Queen Ty's death in Amarna had spread throughout the city, and Horemheb made plans to travel to Amarna under the guise of paying homage to her. The true reason being to quench his curiosity of whether the rumors of Kiya's and Nefertiti's pregnancies were factual and to see with his own eyes the city the pharaoh had built in reverence to the Aten god.

Horemheb loaded gifts of lapis-lazuli and talents of gold onto a sailing barge, and with a boat crew of twenty men, he sailed the river seven days and nights until they came upon the shores of Amarna.

He was astonished at how meticulously the new city, though still incomplete, was planned out with its foundations set up on markers above the cliffs. Most shocking to him, however, was how all the statues, art, and drawings of Akenaten scattered throughout the village depicted his body the way it actually appeared. His curved feminine hips and ample potbelly were blatantly displayed and not altered as they had been for his statues in Thebes.

When Akenaten was informed of Horemheb's arrival, he sent Ay and Ranefer—the captain of Akenaten's guards, out to greet him, specifically to learn the motive for the general's visit.

Ay and Ranefer approached Horemheb as he guided his crew off the barge and onto the banks of Amarna.

"It's quite a surprise to see you here, general," said Ay. "The pharaoh would like to know the reason for your visit."

"Queen Ty is dead, is she not?" asked Horemheb as he continued directing his crew in unloading the shipment containers.

"The queen is entombed here in Amarna," replied Ay.

"Then that would be the reason I'm here. Tell Pharaoh Teppy that I have brought gifts of gold and lapis-lazuli for the queen's tomb and for the newborn children of Kiya and Nefertiti."

"How is it you know so much about the state of affairs in Amarna?"

"Why does it matter? Though we are two separate cities, we are still one country."

Ay capitulated, telling the general what he wanted to know. "Kiya and her newborn died in childbirth, and Nefertiti has yet to give birth to her child."

The news alarmed Horemheb, but not enough to warrant a reaction.

"And the pharaoh is no longer known as Teppy. His name is Akenaten," added Ranefer.

"Who is this?" asked Horemheb, pointing at Ranefer as if he were a mere servant.

"He is Ranefer, Pharaoh Akenaten's captain of the royal guard," replied Ay.

"Akenaten?" repeated Horemheb with a smirk. "His father named him Amenhotep the Fourth, and he is known throughout every country and kingdom as Teppy."

"Here he's known as Akenaten, and as long as you are a guest in this city, that is how you will address the pharaoh. Any other name will be considered a sign of disrespect," said Ranefer.

Horemheb ignored him, and after his crew unloaded the last shipment container, he ordered them back to the barge.

"Would you like to speak to the pharaoh before you depart?" asked Ay.

"No, but you can make sure he receives the talents of gold and the lapis-lazuli stones in honor of our departed queen mother and the coming birth of Nefertiti's child."

"Your thoughtfulness is surprising, general," said Ay. "It's no secret you and my sister, Ty, shared a mutual animosity for each other."

"Regardless of our supposed animosity, she was the chief wife of Amenhotep and will always have the right of respect as the queen mother of Egypt," said Horemheb.

With that, Horemheb gave Ay and Ranefer a scroll with one last message.

"The scroll is a letter for Nefertiti from her sister, Mundi, my wife. Please tell this 'Akenaten', as you call him, that when he's done tinkering with his primitive capital city, we'll be waiting for his return to Thebes, the known and established capital of Egypt, with welcoming arms."

"Pharaoh Akenaten has vowed never to take a step outside the boundaries of Amarna," said Ay.

"And I made a vow never to set foot here. Vows are broken as often as bones, Ay," replied Horemheb.

Days later, Nefertiti was overcome with birth pangs and had to be prepared for childbirth. Premonitions that her unborn child would be stillborn haunted and frightened her. Though relieved at first by Kiya's death, she pitied the death of Kiya's child, an innocent life that never had a chance to be nurtured in the way that it so deserved. There was a special place in Nefertiti's heart for children—all children. The chance of Kiya's child becoming Akenaten's heir threatened her, but if it had survived, she would have loved it as if it was her own. Kiya and her child's death was supposed to bring Nefertiti solace, yet in the end, the horrific manner in which they died caused her to suffer even more anxiety about her own life and the mortality of her unborn child.

Nefertiti squatted over the birthing stool and prayed for a boy, but expected another girl. Akenaten entered her chamber before the moment of birth. It was unthinkable for a pharaoh to stand in the same room at the actual birthing of his child, but after the shock of Kiya's death, Akenaten couldn't stay away from his Nefertiti. If he lost her in childbirth it would be unbearable. He went to the birthing chamber to make sure that whatever happened to their child, that at least his sweet Nefertiti would survive.

Not long after he said a prayer to the Aten for her and the child's health, their baby pushed out unencumbered from the womb into Teyla's waiting hands. Nefertiti cried tears of joy as her stepmother severed the umbilical cord and the infant was freed to be placed in her arms. Nefertiti had given birth to the son she so badly wanted.

Her excitement so overwhelmed her that she had no concern that his tiny foot was deformed and he appeared to have a slight cleft palate. His boisterous cries were like music to her ears and confirmed the boy thrived with good health.

Nefertiti handed the newborn to Akenaten, and for the first time he cradled his son in his arms, crying tears of joy. His heir was the son of a god, and that day he named him Tutankhaten—the living image of the Aten.

CHAPTER

24

NEFERTITI AND AKENATEN sat together in the grand Amarna courtyard along with their daughters Mayati, Meketa, and Senpaten, who had all grown up to be beautiful young girls resembling their mother. They watched with bated breath as Tutankhaten's arrow hit the target precisely in the center of the gazelle's picture. His sisters jumped up from their seats applauding and cheering him.

Over the years, Akenaten had the pleasure of watching his son mature into a valiant hunter, so unlike him, and much more like his uncle Tuthmosis. The pharaoh had never imagined that he would know joy with his son as he had with his daughters, but in the nine years since his birth, Tutankhaten had become the best part of his life and the reason his heart remained young and vibrant. The slight cleft palette and deformed foot that plagued his son at birth had all but vanished within a few years—sealing the Aten's blessing that his son's deformities would never be carried into his adulthood as had been the case for him.

Tutankhaten was a brave and skilled nine-year-old boy for his small stature, and Akenaten watched him, filled with pride as his son balanced himself in his chariot while preparing his bow. Tutankhaten's driver guided his horse, wrestling with the animal to keep it aligned with the speeding chariot that shadowed them. Tutankhaten loaded an arrow, took aim at the moving picture of the gazelle and released. Akenaten, Nefertiti and their daughters all chanted 'Go Tut Go!' in exhilaration.

Everyone called Tutankhaten Tut,' but not because it was a shortened version of his name. It was in honor of Tuthmosis, because Tut's courage reminded Akenaten of his brother.

Akenaten kissed his brother's Aten amulet that he still wore around his neck day and night. Seeing his son mastering his chariot brought back childhood memories of Tuthmosis riding off for the last time in his war chariot. Although the memory of his brother depressed him, he found a way to appear cheerful so that Nefertiti wouldn't question why he was melancholy at such a jubilant occasion.

Akenaten had never grieved for his brother because he had never accepted the finality of his death. Tuthmosis had been ripped from his life, and young Teppy always expected his older brother to return. Thirty-two years had passed and the pain of it still cut just as deep. Akenaten was still there, in the same state as he was as a child, waiting for a sign of his brother's return from the afterlife. Only when Tut dismounted his chariot and approached them, did Akenaten free himself of the memories.

His daughters were so proud of their little brother; they each took turns embracing him.

"You were so good, Tut, a real gazelle would be of no challenge to you," said Mayati.

Meketa squeezed Tut's bicep.

"It's not getting any bigger but your head is growing much too thick for your neck to hold," she said as she pulled on his side-lock of hair that had grown halfway down his back. Meketa would get a certain gratification out of taunting her younger brother.

Tut took it all in stride, but Nefertiti was not so amenable.

"Meketa, stop it. Leave your brother alone so he may rest from his training. Return to the palace."

Meketa stormed away and Mayati followed behind her. Everything Meketa and Mayati did, they did together. The two were inseparable. Senpaten remained with her parents and congratulated Tut with a gold bracelet. They were the closest in age and had deep affection for each other.

"One day, Tut, you will be a great warrior king and all the people of Egypt will honor you," said Senpaten.

A chill went down Akenaten's spine, and before he could couch his words, he shouted back at his daughter.

"My son will not become a warrior! He will be honored because he is a son of a god. And you, keep your foolish words of war and warriors to yourself."

Tears formed in Senpaten's eyes. Never in her life had her father raised his voice at her. He had always treated her delicately, believing she was the most fragile one of his daughters. While Meketa and Mayati both had hearts of iron, Senpaten was acutely sensitive, with a heart as soft as linen. Nefertiti eyed Akenaten as she took Senpaten in her arms and consoled her. She then escorted her daughter to the palace, leaving Tut and Akenaten in the courtyard.

Senpaten encouraging Tut into war highlighted Akenaten's debility and was a reminder to him that because he was not a warrior king, he might never be truly honored as a god-pharaoh. War meant death and suffering. War was darkness and pain. The Aten would never allow war to visit Amarna. Tuthmosis died from the horror of war, and Akenaten was determined that his son, Tut, would not suffer the same fate.

Though there were rumors emanating from Thebes that his unfinished city was plagued with disease and political turmoil, Akenaten was proud of Amarna's growth. From what he observed, all was well there in the city of the Aten.

For the annual meeting of his court, Akenaten brought gifts for his advisers. Ranefer, Ay, Meri-Ra, Maya, and his newly appointed lector priest, Panhessy, sat around his grand table as he praised them for their achievements in organizing the city. Akenaten gave each of them a gold necklace as a token of his approval, then waited for their report, pleased with his generosity. He was not prepared however, for the news they had to give *him*.

"We are concerned about the stability of the city's wealth, my Pharaoh," said Maya, the city's treasurer. "Because the inundation did not occur this year, the crops were not fertilized properly, and now our grain stores are extremely low. Normally, we would trade with other kingdoms, but our supply of gold has not been replenished."

"General Horemheb has sent letters here requesting your approval to wage war against Nubia so that they'll return to paying Egypt the tribute of gold and grain," said Ay. "It might be wise, my Pharaoh, to reconsider and grant him your blessing."

"In the meantime, my Pharaoh," added Ranefer, "we can order Kafrem, the mayor of Thebes, to send us grain supplies immediately and also the gold they have collected in storehouses across the city. That way the people here in Amarna may survive."

Their talk of gold, grain, and war made Akenaten's temper rise.

"Raise the amount of taxes here on the people, Maya, if that's what you must do, but Egypt will not go to war with anyone. Amarna is the city of peace and plenty, and the Aten gives us all that we need."

"But, my Pharaoh," said Maya, "The city of Thebes will deliver to us whatever you command."

"We will not beg for anything from Thebes!" shouted Akenaten.

Panhessy, who had been silent, spoke out. "There are other matters, my Pharaoh. Many of our citizens believe the purple death, so feared in Thebes, has come to Amarna. The disease has made some sick with fever and purplish bruises over their bodies. They murmur that this scourge is a curse from the gods, and if—"

"Why are you repeating rumors from Thebes, Panhessy?" interrupted Meri-Ra. "There is no scourge here in Amarna, nor the purple disease. Those who are sickened are because they failed to cleanse their food properly before consuming it."

"More importantly than cleansing their food, it would be in the people's best interest to make a grand offering to the Aten, proving their loyalty to me—the manifestation of the sun god," proclaimed Akenaten.

"Panhessy and I will both immolate a ram in your honor, my Pharaoh, and a calf bull at the altar of the Aten," said Meri-Ra as he eyed Panhessy.

"Let the people fear the Aten, not a disease. The Aten will always prevail against the machinations of false gods," replied the pharaoh.

Irritated by their lack of faith in the Aten, Akenaten concluded the meeting and left his counselors to bicker amongst themselves.

The grand temple of the Aten was where Akenaten became one with his god, rejuvenated by its rays as they shone throughout the temple from the many openings in the ceiling and walls. There, in the light of the sun, in the heart of the Aten's power, Akenaten would make his animal sacrifices.

But that day in the temple, he was not alone. His son, Tut, accompanied him. The day marked his tenth year of life, his coming of age into manhood and the beginning of his dedication to the Aten. Tut entered before his father, nervous and afraid.

"It'll be all right, my son," said Akenaten. "Did you bring with you the honey and the linen strips?"

Tut handed him a satchel. Inside was a jar filled with honey and several pieces of linen. He wouldn't look at his father, thinking he would be ashamed of how frightened he appeared. Akenaten embraced Tut and kissed his forehead as his mother did for him whenever he was afraid.

In spite of his fear, Tut put on his bravest face.

"I am accepting to what must happen, Father. Still, I would like to know, will it be painful?"

Tut knew the answer to his question but yearned to hear any advice from his father that would soothe his fear.

"There will be pain, but not so much that you cannot bear it," Akenaten said to him. "When you have healed, you'll find pleasure beyond anything you have ever known."

His words were only a mere sense of relief for Tut, just enough to relax his anxiety.

Tut removed his kilt and stood before his father naked. Akenaten washed Tut's penis with water and natron, then took the base of it in his hand and squeezed the foreskin above the tip, until he was clenching the excess skin between his thumb and forefinger. Tut tensed up as he gazed upon what his father was doing.

"Listen to me. Do not look down. Keep your eyes focused straight ahead at the sight of the sun-disk. Under no circumstances should you glance at what is occurring. This will be quick and over soon," said Akenaten, still clenching his son's foreskin between his fingers.

Tut peered ahead as his father had instructed, bracing himself for the pain sure to come.

Akenaten retrieved a flint knife from his garment and recited a prayer to the Aten. Without warning, he swiped the blade across Tut's foreskin, severing it clean off.

Tut's piercing scream disrupted his father's prayer, so he repeated it louder.

"To you, the Aten god, my son, Tut, makes his sacrifice. May the unclean blood become clean."

Tut fought the urge to collapse on the floor from the pain. His father was still clenching the severed skin on his penis to control the bleeding. So Tut remained standing, quietly now in front of his father, tears flowing down his cheeks.

"The circumcision is done; the pain will subside in time," Akenaten said.

He massaged the honey over his son's penis and wrapped it in the linen pieces. The bleeding stopped though the pain continued. Tut sat on the floor and rocked back and forth trying to contain the inner cries of agony.

"You'll remove the linen pieces every morning at dawn and wash with water, then reapply the honey for twelve days, after which it will be fully healed."

Tut nodded, clenching his crotch. Even in the midst of intense pain, he wanted to prove to his father that he was strong.

"The Aten has cleansed you," said Akenaten, "clearing the way for your ascension to high priest that you will soon share with Meri-Ra. And as you have sacrificed your foreskin to him today, you must also sacrifice a clean animal to him during the days you appear here at the Aten temple. This has to occur twenty-four times before you can become my heir to the throne of Egypt."

Akenaten helped Tut to his feet, and the two left the temple.

Once Meri-Ra was sure that the pharaoh and his son had departed the temple grounds, he turned to the three commoners who had arrived in their donkey carts.

"Did anyone see you come here?" Meri-Ra asked.

"No, my lord," one of the men answered.

"There are reports of six dead somewhere in Amarna. You will seek these diseased bodies out and take them in your carts to the burial pit at the edge of the village."

"We have heard the disease is contagious. How will we protect ourselves?" asked another of the men.

"If the purple bruises are visible on the body, lift them by their garments without touching the skin."

Meri-Ra handed each of them a nugget of lapis-lazuli. "Tell no one of what you see or do today."

The men nodded, returned to their carts, and drove away.

The revelation that the disease was spreading in Amarna would reflect badly on Meri-Ra's ability to appease the Aten god, exposing his weakness as a high priest to the pharaoh. It was necessary to keep the devastation of the purple disease a secret from Akenaten until it subsided, or until he could at least conjure up the right incantation that would annihilate it from the city.

CHAPTER

25

AKENATEN OFTEN SURVEYED his grand city of Amarna with a daily stroll in his royal chariot. Every morning he wrote down on a scroll how many new foundation structures were laid each day and at what stage of completion was each statue and monument. Seldom would he direct his driver to travel away from the center of the city into the village where most of the Amarna citizens lived.

To quench his sudden curiosity, he changed his course and made an impromptu visit to see his people in their daily course of life. He expected most would be farming, making pottery jars or even weaving clothing for themselves and the royal family—thriving from the abundance of the Aten god. Instead, there was hardly anyone attending to the animals nor farming the vegetables or fruits, only crowds of people appearing at dozens of funerary rites performed throughout the village. When Akenaten questioned Meri-Ra about the abnormally high death toll, the priest dismissed his observations as a mere timing coincidence and assured him he had no reason to be concerned. It wasn't until he encountered Panhessy at the entrance of the Aten temple that he would hear what Meri-Ra had kept secret from him.

"Pharaoh, before you enter, it's my sworn duty as your lector priest of the Aten, to inform you of what's really occurring here in Amarna," said Panhessy.

"What's occurring that I'm not already aware of?"

"My pharaoh, can you not smell the putrid stench of dead bodies that has enveloped our entire city? It's not just from the dung of dead animals seeping in from the village. The people are becoming sick and some are even covered in bruises. Dead bodies are being discovered and buried in mass graves throughout the village. The afflicted are being ostracized by their own families, and left roaming the village streets scavenging for food. Our food supplies have dwindled and the people have come to me mumbling that the disease has reached Amarna because we have angered the gods of Thebes."

"And what was your answer to them?" asked Akenaten, holding in the anger of hearing Panhessy's undesirable news.

"I had no answer."

"There is but one god, the Aten. The false gods of Thebes have no power or place here in Amarna. Tell the people this, Panhessy: If they continue not to put their faith and obedience in the Aten, he will not heal them. If they are sick and indeed dying, then it's because their offerings and sacrifices to the Aten were not to him alone, but shared with other gods in their hearts. The Aten requires unconditional loyalty and devotion from them all if they truly want his blessing."

Akenaten left Panhessy and entered the temple, content with his condemnation to a faithless people, yet the news of mass graves and death deeply concerned him.

Nefertiti knew of the onslaught of famine and disease spreading throughout Amarna. Ay had told his daughter about the shallow graves and the enormous number of Amarna citizens the disease had most likely killed. What was actually occurring there was contrary to the wonderful prosperous life that Akenaten had promised his citizens. Her husband's blind devotion to an untested god made her hesitant to discuss the reality of their predicament with him. Nefertiti's faith in the Aten waned though she dared not tell Akenaten and provoke his anger. Something had to be done to help feed and care for the people or they would surely revolt against her husband and harm her children. Even if it meant disobeying Akenaten's decree not to request supplies from Thebes, the risk of an uprising justified her disloyalty. The surplus crops and wealth of the capital city belonged foremost to the royalty of Egypt, and Nefertiti would have whatever part of it whenever she desired. So, without Akenaten's knowledge, she wrote a letter to Horemheb and had Ay deliver it by messenger. She then went and sat by the river to watch her daughters swim.

It was a hot and humid day that for Meketa and Mayati could only be relieved by a playful dip in the cool water of the river. They both reveled in challenging each other to see who would be brave enough to swim out the farthest. The game frustrated Ay. One of his many responsibilities was to search for crocodiles while the royal daughters swam the river. The further they ventured out into the water, the more strenuous it was for him to spot the threatening creatures. He warned the girls many times not to stray far from the shore, but rarely did they obey him. The challenge of the dare proved irresistible, and the girls found it humorous watching their grandfather scramble back and forth across the shore like a madman stalking them.

It was Meketa's turn in the dare, and she swam out into the river farther than any of them had ever before.

"Meketa, return to the shore now!" shouted Ay.

"We're the only creatures in the river today, grandfather. Calm down," replied Meketa, as she swam out even further.

"Listen to your grandfather and return to the shore Meketa," Nefertiti repeated.

Mayati had remained near her mother, close to shore, where she could stand up in the water whenever she wanted.

"C'mon Mayati, it's not over yet. Don't be afraid," shouted Meketa.

"I'm not afraid. I don't want to go out that far."

"Then I guess that makes me the winner again."

Meketa submerged herself in the river and when she surfaced a moment later, there was something floating toward her. It had no features of an animal or flora, but resembled a dark opaque mass swirling slow and aimless in a circular motion.

Curious, Meketa swam toward it.

"Meketa!" screamed Nefertiti. "Return to the shore!"

Meketa suddenly stopped when the identity of the object became clear. Hundreds of duck carcasses had floated together forming a large ring-shaped mass of death, and along with it, a putrid and sickening smell.

Meketa cringed and swam toward the shore as fast as her arms and legs would take her. The splashing noises awakened a slumbering crocodile and it entered the river after her. Mayati ran screaming back to her mother that the animal was after Meketa. Nefertiti turned and yelled out to Ramose—the pharaoh's butler and master of horses who patrolled the river. Ramose ran into the water with his spear in hand. It was up to his waist as he trudged through it trying to reach Meketa. Nefertiti went into the river after her, but Ay pulled her back. Meketa swam wildly toward the shore, and in a frenzy, took water into her lungs. The sight of it terrified Nefertiti. Her daughter was only twenty cubits away from her grasp when the crocodile opened its mouth to devour Meketa's leg. Nefertiti screamed just as Ramose appeared and plunged his spear through the creature's snout all the way through the bottom of its jaw. The crocodile slowly sank to the bottom of the river as Nefertiti helped pull Meketa onto shore.

Unaware of what was happening to their siblings in the river, Tut and Senpaten were in the palace chamber playing their parents' favorite board game of Senet. It had now become their favorite game and they would play it together for hours.

Most times the pair chatted while they played, but that day, Senpaten was unusually solemn. Tut was astute enough to know that something plagued his sister.

"Are you feeling sick?"

"I'm fine," said Senpaten, avoiding eye contact with him.

"Don't be sad, sister, it's only a game. Perhaps I'll let you win next time."

The playful taunts that had made her smile in the past, failed to stir a reaction from her. Senpaten was silent, then all of a sudden—

"Are you fond of Grandfather Ay?" she asked, looking up into Tut's eyes anxious to hear his answer.

"Yes, of course, why?" replied Tut.

"He's old and strange, and I'm afraid of him."

"He's old because he's our grandfather. Why would you be afraid of him? He takes care of us."

Senpaten didn't answer him.

"Senpaten, why? Tell me."

"I see him sometimes watching me when I'm changing into my garments."

Senpaten went silent again before meeting Tut's eyes.

"And there was a time he even caressed me," she mumbled.

"You mean like an embrace? He embraces all of us because he loves us."

Senpaten looked directly at him now.

"No Tut, it was not like an embrace. He frightens me."

"Senpaten, Grandfather Ay means no harm to you. He has always been good to father and me, and he wants to be good to you, too."

Their conversation was cut short by the commotion in the palace corridor. Tut and Senpaten stepped out from their chamber in time to see the guards rushing out of the palace and toward the river.

Akenaten entered Meketa's room to find his daughter sweating and shivering as Meri-Ra administered a liquid cure of aloe, honey, and dried poppy seeds. Nefertiti had informed him how their daughter had developed a fever after being nearly mauled by a crocodile and almost drowning.

Akenaten kissed Meketa's forehead and began to thank the Aten god for saving her life. Nefertiti interrupted his prayer with questions.

"What sort of bruise is that on her arm? Could it have come from her ordeal in the river?" she asked.

Akenaten examined his daughter's left arm, then the right. There were purplish bruises on both. It looked eerily similar to what he witnessed as a child on the skin of sickened animals.

"It resembles the mark of the—," Akenaten caught himself before he said the word 'disease.'

"The mark of what?" asked Nefertiti.

"It's not of Amarna," replied Akenaten. "It's of the city of Thebes."

The fear grew in Nefertiti's eyes, and she received no consolation from the despair she glimpsed in his. Meri-Ra examined Meketa's entire body before making his own diagnosis.

"These marks are caused by a powerful spell," said Meri-Ra.

"A powerful spell from whom?" demanded Akenaten.

"A spell like this could only emanate from the Oracle himself."

"It's not possible. How could it reach Amarna?" said Nefertiti.

"Does anyone know your children's secret birth names?" asked Meri-Ra.

"No, not even I know their secret names. Only Nefertiti knows," said Akenaten.

"I've told no one, I swear. Why has this happened to her?!" Nefertiti yelled.

Panhessy entered carrying a tray with a cooked mouse on it. He fed as much of it to Meketa as she could eat, then wrapped the bones in linen. He tied seven knots over the cloth with a string and secured it around Meketa's neck.

"Give it time to heal her," said Panhessy, before he walked out of the room. Mayati, Tut, and Senpaten rushed past him and into Akenaten and Nefertiti's arms. They all stood by Meketa's bedside in shock.

CHAPTER

26

I AM YOUR QUEEN NEFERTITI,
Queen of Upper and Lower Egypt, royal wife of the pharaoh
Akenaten. May all be well with you in the city of Thebes General
Horemheb. I am writing to you on behalf of my husband and
the citizens of Amarna. We are in need of gold and grain
supplies. I am aware the storehouses in Thebes are full and have
a surplus, so I am commanding you, general, to send more talents
of gold and sacks of grain immediately so that the royal family
and the people here will have a respite from the threat of famine
that has befallen us this year. I will expect the shipment to arrive
here by sailing vessel no later than nine days and nights, time
enough for you to gather a competent boat crew to load the
supplies requested. Be aware also that I have not heard word
from my sister, Mundi, for many months now. I am worried
about her well-being. Please mention my concerns to her.

Your queen, Nefertiti.

Salitas rolled up Queen Nefertiti's letter and handed the papyrus scroll to Horemheb.

"Should we ignore her request, general?" asked Salitas.

"We'll give the queen a portion of what she's requesting," said Horemheb. "But you will send it along with this message:

> *This shipment of supplies will be your last. There is no further surplus of gold and grain here, and unless your husband—our pharaoh—grants me his consent to wage war against Nubia and Libya for the tribute, in a short matter of time the entire kingdom of Egypt will be lost to famine and poverty. As for your sister—my wife, Mundi—there is no need to be concerned; she is well and thriving here in Thebes.*

"Make sure she gets the message along with a token of what she requested, but only a token," said Horemheb.

"I will as ordered, general. However, I find it odd that the queen failed to mention anything about the disease that has swept over Amarna. Obviously, the gold and grain shipments cannot cure it," said Salitas as he transcribed the general's message to Nefertiti on a scroll.

"The pharaoh is stubborn. It's the only redeemable trait he inherited from his father," replied Horemheb. "Neither he nor Nefertiti will concede that their beloved city is cursed."

The disease spread throughout Amarna as if it were carried by the wind. Akenaten demanded his royal court search for the cause while he proclaimed that anyone suspected of blasphemy be brought to him for judgment and punishment. He would not allow his daughter, Meketa, to continue suffering alone because of the sins of his people against the Aten, the god that had delivered them to their glorious new land.

In Amarna's grand courtyard, Akenaten prepared to pass judgement on a woman caught worshipping one of the Theban gods.

Nefertiti was seated on the royal tier when the pharaoh entered, leaning on his jeweled walking cane. Citizens had gathered in the courtyard to glimpse Akenaten as he lumbered to his throne and sat next to his queen.

Ramose stepped forward with the accused woman. Her shame kept her focused on the ground beneath her.

"This woman I saw with my own eyes worshiping a statuette of the Tawaret god, my Pharaoh," said Ramose. "I caught her in her own house prostrating herself in front of it."

Akenaten's mind drifted away from Ramose as he envisioned how the Tawaret god must have appeared to the woman while she knelt down before it. In his vision it was not an inanimate statuette carved out of wood, but a massive beast that resembled the hippopotamus toy he had as a child. The animal was alive and breathing, sweating profusely while it stood upright on its hind legs at over three cubits in height. It had a protruding abdomen and full voluptuous breasts with erect nipples. When the beast turned its face to Akenaten, the pupils of its eyes were like black onyx and satiated of evil. It let out a piercing squeal that jarred Akenaten out of his sinister daydream and back to the woman's judgment at hand.

"Why would you commit this blasphemy in the presence of the Aten?" Akenaten asked the woman.

She remained silent, keeping her eyes on the ground.

"Answer me. Why did you have in your possession gods from Thebes? You must have been aware the offense is punishable by death?"

Before he could condemn her for not responding to his questions, her husband rushed forward and bowed at Akenaten's feet.

"My Pharaoh, my wife has miscarried three times, and she was afraid for the life of our unborn child. It was for that reason only that she prayed at the foot of the fertility god, Tawaret."

"Her first and most fatal mistake was bringing the statuette here to Amarna. What she has brought along with it, is pain and death from Thebes. For that she'll be executed," replied Akenaten, his voice cracking and harsh.

A silence fell over the crowd. Both the man and his wife were shocked by his declaration.

Nefertiti, surprised by the severity of the punishment herself, tried to hide it from Akenaten and the people.

"Please, my Pharaoh," the man pleaded. "Take my life instead, but please spare my wife and our unborn child. I beg for your mercy."

When the man received no response from the pharaoh, he turned his attention to Nefertiti.

"My queen, you yourself have given birth to precious royal children. As a mother you must have mercy for my wife's unborn child."

Nefertiti's face bore a salient amount of pity, a reaction she no longer tried to hide. The man's plea affected her, but before she could say a word in his defense, Akenaten cut her off by speaking out his final judgment.

"I have changed my mind," he said to the man.

Nefertiti exhaled a sigh of relief.

"Instead, both you and your wife will be executed," said Akenaten, spitting out the words in disgust.

The crowd gasped and murmured, and the woman collapsed in her husband's arms wailing. Nefertiti shook her head in disbelief.

"Let this be a lesson to anyone who harbors statues of gods from Thebes and worships them in secret," Akenaten proclaimed, addressing the crowd. "You will be discovered and executed immediately. The Aten is our god and there is no other. Disloyalty to him has brought on this disease—this purple death that spreads among us. Take them from my sight!"

The pharaoh's royal guards led the woman and her husband out of the courtyard to the prison barracks to await their execution.

Inside the border of Mitanni, near Carchemish, Zenanza, King Suppiluliumas's youngest son had led his Hittite cavalry across enemy territory. The confident adult prince spied two Mitanni guards in the distance, and without a word, gave chase. His cavalry followed as the guards turned and fled on horseback. The Mitannis' horses were unusually fast and they easily out ran Zenanza and his troops. The young prince slowed his horse and raised his hand in the air to halt his cavalry from the chase.

"Why have we stopped chasing them?" asked the commander. "If they reach their homeland, King Tushratta will surely mount a massive Mitanni counterattack against us."

Zenanza scoffed at his commander's comments. "Tushratta will not send an army against us," he said. "He'll do as he has done in the past: send a messenger to the Egyptians and have them fight the battle for them," replied Zenanza.

Akenaten retired early to his chamber. Nefertiti followed him into bed and caressed his shaved head. When she planted a firm kiss on his lips, he sensed her tenderness was a prelude for something she wanted from him.

"My husband, my sweetest love, I would never take sides against you in front of the people, but please, grant the woman mercy. Ten blows from the whip would be sufficient enough for her repentance.

Her unborn child is innocent of this. Why would you kill them both?"

"What she has done has caused mass death here in Amarna. If she's not punished severely, the Aten will not heal Meketa's illness. I refuse to lose our daughter because of the vile acts of our citizens," replied Akenaten.

Nefertiti nodded. There was nothing more she could say or do that would change Akenaten's judgment. He remained as the queen left their bedchamber to stay the night with Meketa.

The following morning, Ay woke Akenaten to inform him that Meketa's condition had worsened, and that Nefertiti had requested his presence.

When the pharaoh entered the room, Nefertiti was holding Meketa's hand, sobbing. The purple bruises on their daughter's arms had spread across her chest and her breathing was labored.

"Do something!" Nefertiti screamed at him. "Help your daughter!"

Her desperation broke his heart. *There had to be others,* he thought, *more who were hiding statuettes of gods in their homes, angering the Aten god into holding back his healing powers.* Akenaten ordered every house in Amarna searched and he determined within himself that whoever had done this to him and the royal family would be executed in front of their own children.

In Mitanni, two outpost guards burst into King Tushratta's chamber as he was meeting with his military advisors.

"My king, we have urgent news," said one of the guards, out of breath.

"You're disrupting a private meeting with my military commanders," replied Tushratta.

"This concerns the military, my king. We were nearly captured by Hittite troops in the city of Halab where we saw a remnant of King Suppululiumas's army slaughter over a hundred of our citizens. We narrowly escaped with our own lives."

Tushratta stood up from the meeting table and paced the floor, then seated himself again. He and his commanders all looked troubled by the news.

"Suppuliumas is a scheming miscreant and a traitor to his own word. He for certain has now ignored our peace treaty and has his eye set on Mitanni," said Tushratta. "Both of you will deliver a message to Pharaoh Akenaten saying these words:

> *We are facing an imminent threat of invasion by King Suppiluliumas's army. As your father, Amenhotep, did before, please send a contingent of your troops here as quickly as possible so we can defend ourselves from this Hittite madman.*

The outpost guard transcribed it all on papyrus and rolled it up and placed it in his garment.

"Hurry," said Tushratta. The two guards rushed out of Tushratta's chamber, leaving the king nervous and frightened of what was sure to come.

Dressed in a long-sleeved cloak, with his walking cane in one hand and carrying a live rooster by its legs in the other, Akenaten entered his grand temple of the Aten with one purpose: to petition the Aten god to spare Meketa's life. He trudged toward the altar of sacrifice, but after three steps, his cane snapped in two from his excessive weight, and he fell to the ground still grasping hold of the rooster. The animal squealed and flailed about, trying to escape his grip by pecking his hand. Akenaten tried to stand, only to fall back to the ground, igniting his memory of the feeble and helpless child he had been in Thebes, dependent upon his mother for survival.

The pharaoh dragged his legs across the floor, cubit by cubit, loathing himself for still having no control over his body. He finally reached the altar of sacrifice where he was able to brace himself enough to stand on his knees. Holding the rooster across the platform, he grabbed the flint knife from the altar and slashed the rooster's neck, decapitating the animal. He then drained the blood over the altar so that it dripped down into the pottery jar that had been placed underneath. Akenaten lifted his head toward the temple ceiling in awe of the sunrays that illuminated his blood sacrifice before bowing and reciting his prayer:

> *My god, the Aten, you are the one and only god of Egypt and the world. I am your only son, Akenaten, who brings you glory and a sacrifice of blood to his father. I have discovered the ones who have put a false god in front of you, and they will soon be executed for their blasphemy. I have cleansed your city of the heresy and now I beseech you to shine your power down upon my daughter, Meketa. My father, I ask you to remove this evil from her body. Silence the evil spell of the Amun priests. Meketa is your daughter, a child of a god. Heal her, I beg you, please!*

With his eyes closed, Akenaten stretched his arms up toward the sun's rays in exultation to the Aten god. The sleeves of his cloak slipped down revealing his bare forearms, and when he opened his eyes, there in clear sight was the unmistakable purple bruise of the disease.

CHAPTER

27

AT THE MEETING of Suppiluliumas's court, Shattiwaza and the Hittite military captains gathered for a long-anticipated event—the signing of the treaty that would unify the kingdoms of Hatti and Mitanni. After years of subtle manipulation, Shattiwaza had finally convinced King Suppiluliumas to help him overthrow his father, King Tushratta. The Mitanni prince had managed to receive every concession he asked for from the Hittite king, and with the help of the Hittite army, Shattiwaza would soon replace his father as the new king of Mitanni and finally take the hand of Suppiluliumas's daughter in marriage.

Reveling in his new powerful alliance with the Hittites, Shattiwaza eagerly reached out to attach his seal to the treaty, but King Suppiluliumas pushed him back.

"Not before I'm convinced you thoroughly understand the conditions," said Suppiluliumas.

"I understand them completely, my king. But for good measure, maybe you should remind me again," said Shattiwaza with an obsequious smile.

"I will require exclusive loyalty from Mitanni and its tributaries. A duplicate of this treaty will be kept before the goddess Arinna here in Hatti, and once you return to Mitanni and become king, you'll keep a duplicate there before the Storm-god and the Moon-god where it should be read as a reminder for you and the Mitanni people. If you don't observe the conditions of this treaty, I and the gods of Hatti will destroy you along with the Mitanni people. Do I make myself clear, prince of Mitanni?"

"Please, feel free to call me son-in-law," Shattiwaza replied.

Suppiluliumas was not amused, so Shattiwaza erased the grin from his face.

"All that you ask, great king, I have consented," said Shattiwaza in a more serious tone.

Suppiluliumas handed him the seal. "Then I say prolong the life of your throne, Shattiwaza. Prolong the life of Mitanni by sealing this treaty."

Shattiwaza dipped his seal into the wax and pressed it to the tablet.

"I can't think of any occasion grander than what has happened today, except, for what will happen tomorrow. Today your daughter, Carranda, is a princess of Hatti, tomorrow she will be the queen of Mitanni."

Suppiluliumas feigned a nod of conformity, tolerating Shattiwaza's infatuation with his daughter only at the prospect of having the loyalty of the Mitanni army at his beck and call.

"Will your father step down from his throne peacefully," asked Suppiluliumas, "or will force be needed?"

"My father and I are both reasonable men. There's nothing that can't be resolved by a private discussion between a father and his son," replied Shattiwaza.

Akenaten was a god, the son of the Aten, and the human image of his father—the sun-disk. Although he had the mark of the disease, he refused to believe it could harm him. Instead, his sudden affliction only reaffirmed his commitment to seek out and execute those who hid statuettes of false gods in their homes in secret. For Amarna to survive the curse of the disease, the keepers of this poison had to be rooted out and removed from the city.

Nefertiti did not share Akenaten's zealotry. While the people gathered before the pharaoh in the grand courtyard ready to witness Amarna's 103rd execution for blasphemy against the Aten, Nefertiti wished she had been bold enough to defy Akenaten's order that she attend. She had no desire to be there by her husband's side observing his excessive use of torture. Generally, the executions were carried out in the prison barracks, out of sight of the Amarna people, but Akenaten saved the execution of the pregnant woman and her husband to be an example the people would see with their own eyes.

The executioner came forward carrying a horsewhip, his face hidden under a jackal mask. The woman's husband gasped in fear.

"Spare her please! I'm the guilty one, not my wife and our unborn child," he pleaded.

The executioner ignored him and stepped behind the woman, and without warning, he struck her repeatedly across the back. Her husband flinched at the sight and sound of each strike of the whip slicing through his wife's tender skin. She screamed out at first then went still and silent as the jackal continued striking the horsewhip across her body, causing it to spasm involuntarily. The pain was so intense that the woman collapsed, her body hanging limp from her rope restraints as the jackal went on lashing across her skin. Her back became a maze of cuts lined with blood, bruises, and ripped flesh.

Ranefer handed the executioner a battle ax, and the jackal tested the sharpness of it by rubbing his finger across the blade's edge. Satisfied, he stepped forward and stood over the unconscious woman. Her head hung limp with the back of her neck exposed. He glanced over at Akenaten for approval. The pharaoh stood up and repeated the law he learned from his father when he was a child. "If your head comes off, it's because you did not do as you were told," he proclaimed.

Akenaten gave the executioner the nod of approval he yearned for. At the sight of this, Nefertiti rose from her seat and stormed out of the courtyard. She longed for the Aten to cure her daughter, but she didn't believe the woman's unborn child needed to be sacrificed in order to accomplish it.

The executioner lifted the ax above the woman's head.

"Please! Pharaoh. Grant mercy!" screamed the woman's husband.

"Did you think because I'm innately kind that I wouldn't sentence you both to the harshest of punishment?" asked Akenaten.

"No, never, my Pharaoh."

"Perhaps it was because you thought I was weak, and if you had the chance you would pounce on me like a leopard."

"Pharaoh, I know that you're strong. I would never—"

"You will see just how strong I am," said Akenaten.

The pharaoh nodded at the jackal again.

"No!" shrieked the woman's husband.

The executioner ignored his cries and brought the ax swiftly across the woman's neck. Blood splattered in every direction and her head fell to the ground and rolled until it landed face up with the eyes wide open in a morbid stare. Akenaten smiled in approval at the sight of it.

As the husband was dragged to the post to take his wife's place, Akenaten left the courtyard with Ranefer and Ay and returned to his chamber, convinced that he had done what was necessary to please his god.

"Have you searched every home in the city?" Akenaten asked Ranefer.

"Every home was searched, my Pharaoh, except for those of the royal family," Ranefer replied.

"Search them all, and if any are found to have statues of gods, execute them there in their homes."

Ranefer was shocked. "Your royal family, my Pharaoh?"

"Don't question me when I give you an order. Kill them!" he shouted.

"As you ordered, my Pharaoh," said Ranefer, rushing away to continue the search.

"I assume you have no objections to that, Ay," said Akenaten.

"Not at all, my Pharaoh. My home is yours to search. May you discover and punish all who have committed blasphemy against you and the Aten," Ay replied.

The next morning, as workers filled the royal drinking jars with fresh water for the pharaoh's palace, Ramose spied something floating in the shallow part of the river. He ran along the riverbank to get a closer view. There, clearly visible in the midst of the water, he came upon it—carcasses, of all kinds: fish, ducks, geese, birds, and two crocodiles, all decomposing together in one black putrid heap of disease that stretched hundreds of cubits down the length of the river. Because of mass hysteria triggered by the disease throughout the land, no one had even noticed the poison that was breeding and expanding in the river.

Raucous citizens flocked to the pharaoh's palace. Outside Akenaten's doors, a mob of them cried out for him and his royal family to appear. The curse of the disease was ravaging the people, and in their minds, if the pharaoh, the son of the Aten god, would set his eyes upon their affliction, they would be healed.

Akenaten refused to see them. He had warned that there would be no rest from the curse until every pagan statuette was found and destroyed along with all who committed blasphemy by harboring them. His daughter, Meketa, he contended, remained in her bed suffering because of their sins. How could they expect him to have pity on them?

Still, the crowd kept growing and their cries became unbearable to Nefertiti. It was only to appease her that Akenaten finally agreed to step out into the Window of Appearances by her side.

The citizens roared with exaltation at the sight of the royal couple. Many were sick and emaciated as they begged the pharaoh to appeal to the Aten god on their behalf.

Nefertiti's heart was touched by the sight of so much suffering. She soon disappeared into her chamber and returned moments later carrying a sack in her hand. Without saying a word to Akenaten, she tossed pieces of gold and gold jewelry off the balcony to the people. This created a frenzy of pushing and pulling as each one tried to grasp on to the treasure before the other.

Akenaten looked appalled. "Have you lost your senses?"

"If we don't do something they'll soon revolt against us," said Nefertiti.

"The gold is scarce!" Akenaten shouted back at her.

"Only because you won't give Horemheb his war," replied Nefertiti, as she continued tossing the gold pieces over the balcony. The crowd became like a pack of wild boars striking each other and screaming out for more gold.

Three nights before, the grain and gold shipments Nefertiti had secretly ordered from Horemheb had arrived, along with his message that it would be the last. She believed if she gave what was left of the gold away that Akenaten would have no choice but to consent to Horemheb's war.

As she moved to toss another handful, Akenaten grabbed her wrist.

"General Horemheb does not rule Egypt," he growled. "There will be no consent for war, nor will you give out another piece of my gold to these vile people," he commanded.

Nefertiti didn't look him in the eye as he spoke to her. Instead, she stared at his arm. Her expression was one of utter terror. As he was clutching her wrist, the purple bruises of the disease on Akenaten's arm were visible, bruises that had spread down from his forearm to his wrist.

"What have we done to deserve such horror? You are a god; you are his son. Why has the Aten forsaken you?" said Nefertiti confused by it all.

He had no answer for her, so she rushed away into the palace, leaving the crowd below still crying out and begging for more gold. Akenaten soon followed, abandoning them to their clamoring, and entered his chamber. There was a sickness brewing in his intestines. It was rising from his abdomen into his throat. The sudden pain caused him to slump over and he vomited. *The disease cannot harm me,* he reasoned to himself. He was immune to its poison, and to the fever now raging inside him—all of which he wanted so desperately to believe.

CHAPTER

28

MEKETA'S ENTIRE BODY was covered in bruises, and she dripped sweat from the fever as she slept. Teyla had nursed her throughout the night, constantly wiping her dry with a cloth and reminding her that she was a daughter of the Aten and would soon be healed.

Meri-Ra walked into the room carrying a tray of onions and water that he placed on the platform next to the girl.

"I would think you would want to be at your home while the guards are searching it," said Meri-Ra to Teyla.

"What guards?"

"I'm told the pharaoh's guards are searching every house of the royal family for false idols from Thebes."

Teyla disguised her fear and pretended she knew of the pharaoh's search. "Yes. I'm aware, but perhaps you're right," she said. "It would go easier if I assisted them in their search. I'll return here in the morning."

As soon as Teyla departed, Meri-Ra placed his palm over Meketa's forehead to check the severity of her fever. She opened her eyes and stared at him, bewildered.

"Who are you?" she asked. "Where is my sister, Mayati?"

Meri-Ra peeled three of the onions and squeezed the juice into a jar without answering her. Only when she began to cry because of her delirium did he speak to her. "Your sister will return here soon, but for now this will help rid your body of the evil spirit that's causing your fever," he said comforting her. He gently lifted Meketa's head and helped her to drink.

Teyla arrived home in time to find Ranefer and the pharaoh's guards making their way to her bedchamber. Teyla rushed in front of the chamber's entrance.

"My husband is the father of the queen. You will be reported to the pharaoh if you don't leave my home," said Teyla. "There are no statuettes of gods to be found here."

Her mock display of anger failed to convince the guards.

"The pharaoh has ordered every home to be searched regardless of relation," replied Ranefer. "Move or I will remove you myself," he threatened.

Teyla left her bedchamber entrance consumed with fear. Her copper chest was blatantly visible, and the guards headed straight for it. As they pried it open, she took a step backwards, her heart racing.

Teyla looked away as the guard lifted the lid. When they immediately closed it, she turned back, surprised.

"It's empty," said the guard.

"Indeed," replied Ay, entering the room. "I am the royal adviser to the pharaoh, and the father of the queen. It's preposterous to suspect us of harboring statuettes of gods from Thebes. Leave my home!"

Teyla stared at Ay in disbelief.

"We're all aware of who you are. We will continue the search," replied Ranefer.

On Ay's heel, Ramose entered the room. "As he said, the search is over. You will respect this man," Ramose commanded. "That is my order as the Master of the pharaoh's horses," he said.

Ranefer was silenced, and he and his guards, along with Ramose, finally left Teyla and Ay alone in their home.

Teyla was still staring at Ay, waiting for him to speak—to explain what happened to the statuette she had so carefully hidden away from him in the copper chest. Instead, he went into their bedchamber without saying a word.

Teyla followed him into the room.

"What did you do with it?" she asked.

Ay turned to face her, furious that her only concern was for the statuette and not the catastrophe she nearly caused by hiding it in their home. "Is it your plan to have us both executed? Let me assure you, the pharaoh will spare me. Only you will pay for your blasphemy."

"It's a curse that I have not been able to conceive a child. Hathor is the only god capable of making me fertile again."

"You're an old woman. Your time for bearing children has long passed. How dare you conceal a statue in our home!"

"I regret what I did, but if I could keep it for just three more nights, it would be time enough to heal my womb. Please, my husband, tell me where you've hidden it."

"I burned it and crushed it to pieces. And if you're found caught with another, I will be delighted to assist the executioner in giving you a hundred blows across your back with the horsewhip before your decapitation," Ay replied.

As Meketa continued to suffer from the disease, Akenaten had begun executing children, not because they were found to have pagan statuettes in their possession, but because they made the mistake of unknowingly uttering the name of a god other than the Aten. Akenaten summoned Meri-Ra to make an animal sacrifice to the Aten on Meketa's behalf and to render judgment over her condition. When he completed it, he returned to the pharaoh with an answer.

"My Pharaoh, as I told you before, this disease has to be the work of the Oracle. He would be the only one capable of conjuring powerful magic without reciting an incantation," said Meri-Ra.

"And again, you overlook the fact that we're not in Thebes. What harm could he conjure against us here?" asked Akenaten.

"An accomplice may live among us."

"What you speak is preposterous! The Aten would have revealed his identity to me. Stop with your baseless assumptions and tell me if my daughter can be saved."

Meri-Ra gave him the answer he dreaded to hear.

"No, my Pharaoh, her ailment has been judged untreatable."

Those simple words were enough to crush him. Akenaten had never considered that he could lose his daughter in death. The Aten would certainly intervene before death occurred, and she would be healed as the royal daughter of the Aten so deserved. The shock of it all flooded his mind. How would he tell his children that their sister, whom they love dearly, would die? How would he console his sweet Nefertiti and explain to her that she would no longer have the embrace of her beloved daughter? Akenaten struggled to contain his grief as he went to inform his family of Meketa's fate.

To help lift their spirits, Nefertiti had allowed the children to go horseback riding along the riverbank. Senpaten and Tut enjoyed riding more than anyone and would often ride together escorted by Ramose. As always, Mayati lagged, nervous from the animal moving beneath her. Riding on the back of horses was not one of her favorite things to do, but it was a chance to cavort with Tut and Senpaten, a substitute now for her dear Meketa.

Her brother and sister led the way, guiding their horse easily through the mud and silt.

"Who do you love the most, Senpaten?" asked Tut.

"The answer is easy. Mother and Father," Senpaten replied.

"Then who do you love second most?"

Senpaten pondered for a moment before replying. "I'm not sure. Who do you love the most?"

"Hard to say."

"Why? What about Mother and Father?"

"Second most."

"If you know whom you love second most, then you must know whom you love foremost," said Senpaten.

What she said made perfect sense to Tut, and no matter how awkward it might be, he had to give her an answer.

"I think I love you the most," he said.

"No you don't. Stop teasing," she giggled.

"Really, Senpaten. I mean it," Tut said, now with a serious look on his face.

Senpaten was quiet. It was the reaction Tut feared he would receive. To release himself from the embarrassment, he laughed. "I'm kidding. I love Father and Mother the most," he said, so that Senpaten wouldn't see through his lie.

Up ahead was a fisherman kneeling on the ground and digging holes in the dirt around the river's edge. Defying Ramose's rules, Tut and Senpaten dismounted their horses and went over to the fisherman to get a better view of what he was doing. The man stood up quickly and bowed when he recognized the garments the children wore.

"For what purpose are you digging those holes?" asked Tut.

The man hesitated before he answered.

"The river water is cursed with disease. Fresh water can only be extracted from deep holes in the earth where it is cleansed," replied the fisherman.

Tut was surprised at the man's candor. It was known that the wells in Amarna were yet to be completed and that the citizens received their water directly from the river.

The river water was life sustaining. It would be blasphemous to believe the Aten poisoned the very thing that gave them life. Nevertheless, digging holes along the riverbank, the man had created small makeshift wells for himself to circumvent it. He filled his pottery jar with one last scoop of water and hurried away, visibly nervous that the pharaoh's children might report his blasphemy to the guards.

The day after Meri-Ra's woeful judgment of Meketa's illness, a messenger from Mitanni arrived in Amarna demanding to see Akenaten. Ay intercepted him at the entrance and was handed a scroll.

"King Tushratta sends urgent word to the pharaoh. We need Egyptian troops quickly before the Hittites invade our kingdom," said the messenger.

Ay unrolled the papyrus and read it for himself. "The pharaoh has not made a decision whether to take Egypt into war or not," he said. "The prince of Byblos has also made a request to the pharaoh for troops and the answer to him was the same. I'll ask the pharaoh again. In the meantime, you should return to your kingdom and tell your King Tushratta to organize his own defenses," said Ay.

After the messenger left, Ay searched the palace for Akenaten, but instead found Nefertiti walking out of Meketa's room.

"My queen, do you know where I can find the pharaoh?" he asked.

"You'll find him there in Meketa's room," she answered.

"How is she, my queen?"

Nefertiti didn't respond. As if in a trance, she walked away down the palace corridor.

Ay waited outside the entrance. Through the sheer curtains Akenaten was standing above Meketa's bed.

"My pharaoh, King Tushratta has sent word requesting Egyptian troops to help fight the Hittites that are encroaching on their kingdom. The Byblos king also awaits word for military help against them as well. What would you like me to do?" asked Ay.

Akenaten stepped from behind the curtain. "I would like for you not to mention Tushratta or the Byblos king to me ever again. If you do, I'll cut out your tongue."

The pharaoh trudged past him and limped down the corridor. Ay entered Meketa's chamber and discovered what Nefertiti and Akenaten had just learned—their daughter, Meketa, was dead, and from the look of Akenaten's dank face, his fever was rising.

CHAPTER

29

IT WAS NOT the first time since Kafrem was appointed mayor of Thebes that Horemheb had to search the village to find him. Only days after his appointment, Kafrem had become corrupted by the Amun priests and was known throughout the city for accepting bribes. Horemheb regretted promising their mother before her death that he would look after his younger brother and wouldn't judge him harshly for his expected missteps. His own reputation had now come under question by the Theban people because of his brother, and Horemheb was rapidly losing his patience for him.

As he searched the village, he encountered a woman standing at the entrance of her home staring at him in a peculiar manner. A blue veil covered her face, and an erect phallus jutted from the top of her door—a symbol of the perversion allowed in her residence. Horemheb thought her inquisitiveness meant she had seen his brother.

"Has there been one like me traveling here today?" he asked.

"Like you? No," said the woman as she removed the veil. Her lips glistened with bright red glossy paint and the pupils of her eyes were an amber and yellow copper tint accentuated by the thick outline of black kohl. Her face was more than attractive, it was alluring, and it took more than a moment before Horemheb could overcome the distraction caused by it.

"I'm speaking of one that is known as an officer of Thebes," he said.

"Are you referring to your brother Kafrem—the mayor of Thebes?"

Her awareness of who he was surprised him. Most citizens knew the name of Horemheb but few had ever seen his face.

"You know of my brother? Where is he?"

"He's on a spiritual journey and would prefer not to be disturbed by a brother who's obviously jealous of him," she replied.

Horemheb had to restrain himself from assaulting her. Instead, he spoke to her calmly. "You'll tell me where I can find my brother, or I'll slash your throat right here in front of your immoral house."

Horemheb's expression didn't alter in the slightest with his threat. His stare frightened her so much that the woman covered her face with the veil again.

"We are *The Sacred Women of Bes*. Your brother is cohabiting with us," she said.

"Where?"

"I'll take you."

She directed Horemheb to an unfinished mud-brick home. The door was barely visible behind the overgrown shrubs and vines that concealed it. When Horemheb pushed it open, he found Kafrem naked and entwined with four ample women clad in blue faience-beaded fishnet dresses. They had tattooed breasts and their lips were painted as bright as the woman's. Kafrem sat up straight at the sight of his brother. Red stains from the lip paint covered his entire body.

Kafrem appeared inebriated, his eyes bloodshot and his speech slurred as he ordered them to leave the straw mattress.

"You're pathetic," Horemheb snapped. "Are you paying these 'sacred' whores with the gold you extorted from your bogus divorces?"

The women all turned their heads and glared at Horemheb offended.

"Our work here is divine, sanctioned by the god, Bes," the largest of the group said. "Never have we accepted payment for the spiritual services we provide," she added.

Horemheb picked up Kafrem's garment from the floor and tossed it at him.

"Go home to your wife," he said. "We leave for Amarna at dawn."

"Amarna?"

"We will verify the rumor that the royal daughter Meketa has died and the pharaoh is gravely ill," replied Horemheb.

The women looked shocked. "The royal daughter is dead?" one of the women asked. "She is but a child," another said in despair. Horemheb and Kafrem ignored them.

"Whatever calamity has befallen the pharaoh in Amarna was caused by his own heresy," replied Kafrem, still suffering from slurred speech.

"He is the son of Amenhotep," Horemheb corrected. "You, and every soul here in Thebes, will respect and honor his birthright."

Kafrem nodded as he struggled to put on his garment. The lack of beer and wine in the room led Horemheb to believe that his brother could not be intoxicated. He had long suspected that Kafrem was addicted to the opium cure. Still, even with the poppy plant capsules scattered across the floor confirming his suspicions, he closed his eyes to it as he had to pharaoh Amenhotep's addiction.

As Akenaten lay in bed ravaged with fever and bruises, he refused to succumb to what had afflicted his father before him—the temptation of the cure. What his heart yearned for was an answer from the Aten. How long would it see him suffer? When would it deliver him from the sins of the Amarna people?

His precious daughter, Meketa, was dead, and the pain of it was excruciating to the point that Nefertiti had become inconsolable. In retaliation, Akenaten had executed mothers, fathers, men and women, young and old, all who had hidden or were suspected of hiding statues of gods against the name of the Aten. Still, the pharaoh had no answer from the sun god on why the disease continued to spread.

Mayati's sudden appearance in his chamber calmed his anguish. At fifteen years of age, Mayati had grown exquisite to him, a duplicate of her mother. He sensed the uneasiness in his daughter's expression when she looked closely at his face. Sweat dripped from his brow and she stared at the deep purple bruises that had spread to his neck and arms.

Mayati was carrying a pottery jar too heavy for her, so Akenaten rose from his bed and struggled to help her place it on the floor.

"What's in it?" he asked, out of breath.

"The river water is unclean, father, so Tut, Senpaten, and I dug holes deep in the earth and brought you fresh water."

If anyone else had done such a thing, Akenaten would have accused them of blasphemy, but because it was his dear children, it touched his heart that they would gather together on his behalf.

"Father, promise me you will not die and leave us like Meketa."

"The Aten is the almighty god, and I am his son. He will protect me from the disease because I am like him," he replied.

Mayati walked up to her father and clutched the Aten amulet that hung from around his neck. "Is this the amulet that protects you?" she asked.

"From my brother," Akenaten said and kissed her forehead. "Do you love me, Mayati?"

"Of course I love you, Father."

He kissed both her cheeks and pulled her close to his body. He had to know for certain how *much* she loved him.

"More than anything?" he asked.

"More than anything."

Akenaten stooped down and kissed her lips. The taste of it was sweet as honey, like that of his Nefertiti. Mayati took a step back from her father, uncomfortable and confused.

"Do you truly love me or not, Mayati?"

"I do, Father."

"More than you loved your sister, Meketa?"

Mayati paused before lying to him. "Yes, Father, more than anyone," she replied.

Akenaten pulled her to him again and caressed his daughter through her garment, kissing her lips with the same passion he shared with his wife Nefertiti. It didn't matter that her answer was untruthful. In his delirium, he heard only what he wanted to hear.

At first there was a slight resistance, then a feeling of her giving in to him. The next thing he felt was Mayati being jerked away from his embrace.

Nefertiti now stood in front of their daughter, drenched in anger, shock, and pity. "What are you doing to her!" she shrieked.

Ashamed, Mayati buried her face in her hands and remained behind her mother as if she were her fortress.

Akenaten balked at Nefertiti's interference. "She is my daughter and I'll do what I wish with her."

"The disease is spreading in you, Akenaten. You have to fight against it or it'll take over your mind," pleaded Nefertiti.

Akenaten started vigorously scratching his shaven head, causing it to bleed. "I know what you're doing. You're trying to get inside my head, then next my heart, so that you can manipulate me," he said. "I won't let you."

"I'm doing no such thing my sweet husband. You are very ill and what you're attempting with our daughter is not right."

Akenaten looked at Nefertiti thoroughly confused. "Is it not right in the eyes of the Aten to show affection for those whom you truly love?"

"No, it is not with our daughter," said Nefertiti.

"I love her."

"She knows you love her, Akenaten. You don't have to show her in that manner. I'm here for you."

Akenaten expression softened. He paused and stared at Nefertiti. She thought that maybe it was a sign that his senses were returning. She was wrong.

"This is not of your concern, Nefertiti. Leave us," he said with renewed vigor.

Left with no other choice, Nefertiti began removing her garment.

"Why are you undressing?"

Nefertiti ignored Akenaten's question and finished removing her garment along with the precious jewels that adorned her body. Completely naked and bare, she turned her attention to their daughter.

"Take off your garment," she said to Mayati.

"Why, Mother?"

"Take off your garment, Mayati!" Nefertiti shouted.

With a tear falling down her cheek, Mayati complied. Both of them now stood in front of Akenaten unclothed. He glared at Nefertiti.

"I'm warning you for the last time to leave us," said Akenaten.

Nefertiti was unbowed.

"If it's your plan to have sexual relations with our daughter," she stated, "then you'll have them with the both of us together."

This was the only way Nefertiti could stop Akenaten from his intentions with their daughter. He couldn't love Mayati in front of his wife, and never would he think of loving them together. Without a word, he left his chamber so that Nefertiti and his daughter could dress themselves in private.

Nefertiti was greatly concerned about Akenaten's state of mind and the unrelenting fever from the disease, so she went to the grand temple to pray directly to the Aten for his healing. When she arrived at the entrance, her father, Ay, stopped her at the door.

"Where are you going?" he asked. "You can't go in there."

"I must look in the eye of the Aten and beg him to heal my husband," said Nefertiti.

"My daughter, you know it's forbidden for you or any woman to enter the sacred temple. It's sacrilege."

"My husband's body and mind are dying, Father. I have to do something."

"The pharaoh is the son of the Aten. He will be spared from death, but you, my daughter, if you enter his temple, you'll not be forgiven."

"What does it matter? Half of my heart died with my sweet Meketa. If my husband dies, there will be nothing left of me to forgive."

Nefertiti shoved past Ay and entered the temple. She knelt down at the altar of the Aten, in the face of the sun-disk, and prayed for Akenaten's life. Dismayed, Ay left her there alone in the temple where the queen remained until the sun set between the mountains.

Asleep in his Mitanni palace, King Tushratta awoke to an eerie stillness enveloping his bedchamber. Faint voices sounded off in the distance and he lay still to listen. Suddenly, a shadow moved across the torch-lit wall. Tushratta knew from its unfamiliar shape that it was not one of his royal guards.

The king reached under his bed and retrieved a dagger and a razor-sharp copper discus. Just as the three uniformed Hittite soldiers converged on him, Tushratta sat up from the bed and in one swift move hurled a copper discus at one of the soldiers. It struck the first one in the center of his forehead, and he collapsed dead on the floor. Tushratta unsheathed his dagger and hurled it directly at the second soldier, penetrating his chest and lodging into his heart. There was an audible gasp before the man fell to the ground. The third soldier waited not a moment longer and threw his dagger at the king. Though obese, King Tushratta was unusually agile and he could maneuver himself as well as any fit man. He moved away from the path of the soldier's dagger just before it found its way into the wall.

Screaming at the top of his lungs, Tushratta charged him like a wild ox. He knocked the soldier flat on his back, straddling and then strangling him. The soldier tried as hard as he could, but was not strong enough to pry Tushratta's thick fingers from around his neck, nor the enormous weight of his body off his chest. Within minutes the soldier fell limp.

Tushratta stepped out from his bedchamber into the palace halls out of breath and exhausted, carrying a dagger in his hand. The bodies of his private guards were strewn about the floor riddled with stab wounds. Blood was splattered across the walls and more pooled on the floor. Stepping gingerly around the slaughter, Tushratta searched his palace for signs of life. He caught sight of someone walking down the corridor toward him, their face obscured in the darkness.

"Who are you? Identify yourself!" shouted Tushratta.

"It is I," someone shouted back.

Tushratta recognized the voice. His first thought was that it was his imagination fooling him, brought on by the chaotic confrontation with the Hittite soldiers. It sounded eerily similar to Shattiwaza's voice, the last voice he had ever expected to hear again.

"Shattiwaza? Is that really you, my son?"

As the man stepped closer, the torches illuminated his face.

"It is," Shattiwaza replied. "You speak as if you weren't expecting to ever see me again."

The voice sounded like his son, though the pitch was a bit lower.

"Come to me," said Tushratta. Prove that you're flesh and blood and not a trick of my imagination."

Tushratta dropped his dagger and opened his arms wide in anticipation. Shattiwaza stepped up to his sobbing father and was met with a full embrace.

"After all these years, you escaped the Hittites, and they came here after you, didn't they?" said Tushratta, still holding onto his son. It didn't matter that Shattiwaza never answered his question, Tushratta was overcome with emotion. His son was alive and had survived his ordeal with the Hittites.

"All this time, I assumed you were dead," said Tushratta. He finally released his son from his embrace so he could get a good look at him from head to toe. "But you're not dead. You're standing in front of me very much alive!"

Overwhelmed with sentiment, Tushratta embraced Shattiwaza a second time.

"Obviously they're not competent enough to kill a mouse," replied Shattiwaza, staring at the Hittite soldier lying dead in his father's chamber doorway. "It's time we had a *true* father and son discussion."

"I know that I was wrong to banish you. I can only hope that you can forgive me for it," said Tushratta, stepping back to look him in the eye.

Shattiwaza smiled. "All is forgiven, father." He reached down to pick up his father's dagger from the floor. "You dropped this," he said, and before Tushratta could react, Shattiwaza stabbed him three successive times through the heart so fast that Tushratta never saw it happen. Only when he looked down and glimpsed the handle of the dagger protruding from his chest did he realize he was dying.

"The discussion is over," Shattiwaza sneered.

Tushratta looked stunned as he crumpled to his knees.

"Remember when I told you, Father, the next time we laid eyes on each other, one of us would die? I will wager it never crossed your mind that it could be you."

Tushratta fell over on his side, his blood spilling out and pooling around him. In desperation, he reached out for his son once more.

Shattiwaza kicked Tushratta's hand away and the life drained from his father's eyes.

"Neither you nor your brother Artassumara were fit to be king," said Shattiwaza spitting on his father's corpse.

Ornus peeked out from behind a column at him.

"Ornus, my father is dead," shouted Shattiwaza. "Would you prefer to join him or pledge your allegiance to me?"

Ornus approached Shattiwaza.

"Your father butchered my family. *King* Shattiwaza," he replied.

Shattiwaza perked at the sound of his new title as more Hittite soldiers stormed the palace corridors and searched the rooms for other Mitannian guards to kill.

CHAPTER

30

"I have weakened . . . where I once was strong.
I have fallen . . . from where I once stood erect.
And I, Akenaten, in the form of a god, am dying."

H IS BLOOD WAS like streams of tiny needles piercing his
veins, causing his whole body to spasm. Akenaten writhed
from the burn of the fever in his head and at the same time
shivered from the chill as a cold sweat poured from his bruised skin.

Nefertiti lay warm cloths over her husband from his neck to his
feet to absorb the excessive moisture and held his hand in hers. The
loss of fluids had left him severely dehydrated.

In the waking hour, Ay summoned the physicians to Akenaten's
bedside: one to treat his fever, another to treat the pain inside his
body, and a third to treat his bruises.

The physician treating the pharaoh's fever fed him breast milk
from a mother who had given birth to a boy, a proven remedy for
cooling and soothing from the inside out. However, there was no

change in his condition. The physician for his pain peeled a fresh clove of garlic, wrapped it in a muslin cloth, and pinned it to the pharaoh's undergarment, while the physician for his bruises combined cumin and coriander with wheat flour and water and rubbed the mixture over his body. None of it had any effect. The fever and pain only grew more intense.

Meri-Ra never believed that herbs and potions ingested and rubbed on Akenaten's body would heal him. A spell had overtaken the pharaoh—a possession of his body by an evil entity conjured up by the Oracle. Akenaten needed a superior magic to rid his body of the disease. The only cure was to drive it out with an incantation that would cleanse the body from its spell, something that only Meri-Ra himself had the power to carry out.

Meri-Ra had searched the mystic writings from *The Book of Coming Forth* and had come to Akenaten's chamber with the knowledge to conjure up his own spell. Once the physicians departed, he removed the bedcover from Akenaten's body, exposing his bruises. Meri-Ra then raised his priest wand over Akenaten's head while he recited the incantation:

> *Only you, the Aten—the sun-god Ra, omnipotent in your power, can prevail over this evil spirit who hacks the heart, who allows decay to seep into his flesh, the pain and the fever, as something entering into his body, who causes the seven openings in his head to ache, as something entering into his skull. Who knows all but the Aten? Who is greater than him the almighty? The evil ones of Amun bruise the body with charcoal. May the Aten seize this god from his innards so that the pharaoh becomes healed and anew.*

Meri-Ra touched each of Akenaten's arms with the wand and repeated the incantation three times. He then touched Akenaten's legs with it and repeated it twice. There appeared to be an excessive amount of moisture on his legs compared to the rest of his body.

Meri-Ra crouched over his lower extremities to study it. The pharaoh's sweat looked tinted, but most likely because of the scarcity of light in the room, Meri-Ra thought. To be sure, he wiped a large portion of it away with his hand and brought it up to his face for a closer look. Meri-Ra was horrified. It was not his imagination. Akenaten's legs and torso perspired blood. He had never witnessed a spell that could induce blood shedding. Whoever had cast it against Akenaten possessed an indomitable ability of sorcery that frightened Meri-Ra to the core.

In haste, he covered Akenaten's body with the bedcover. A spell combined with a ritual of magic needed to be cast immediately, not to help the pharaoh (nothing more could be done for him), but to save himself and the people of Amarna. Once again, Meri-Ra would have to consult the writings from *The Book of Coming Forth* and cleanse himself of Akenaten's tainted blood in the temple of the Aten so that the infection wouldn't spread through his own body. Before he could leave the pharaoh's chamber, Nefertiti stopped him, desperate to know what he had learned.

"Tell me. Can his illness be treated?" the queen asked.

Meri-Ra was ashamed to tell her what he knew. How soon would he be blamed for the gravity of the pharaoh's illness because of his incompetence to heal him? So the priest kept his head bowed when he responded.

"I'm sorry, my queen. His illness has been judged. It cannot be treated."

Meri-Ra rushed out of the pharaoh's chamber and into the palace corridor. Nefertiti followed behind him, seething.

"You're sorry?!" she shouted as she stalked him down the hallway.

"There's nothing more I can do."

"You are the high priest of the Aten," she pressed. "Don't let him die like this. You must do something to help him."

Meri-Ra stopped and turned to face the queen. "I am incapable," he said, shaking his head.

Nefertiti strode up to him, face-to-face. "I swear to you, as the queen of Egypt, I will have you slaughtered if you don't return to his chamber and help him."

Meri-Ra ignored her and continued down the corridor again toward the exit doors of the palace.

"You will return to his chamber now, Meri-Ra!" screamed Nefertiti.

Meri-Ra faced her, driven to the pinnacle of enragement.

"I can't help him!" he shouted. "What else would you have me say? That the Amun priests are stronger than me? Does my confession now bring you contentment?"

Nefertiti was speechless. Never had anyone dared to say that Amun was stronger than the Aten god, and worst of all, this admission had come from the mouth of the Aten's highest-ranking priest.

"It doesn't matter what you do to me. What the disease will do is a thousand times worse. I expect it to enter me next," said Meri-Ra.

He bowed and left the palace, leaving Nefertiti uncertain of what to do next.

She returned to Akenaten's chamber and took his hand again. Breathing had become arduous for him, and with each inhalation and exhalation he struggled. Nefertiti ignored the blood-sweat on Akenaten's legs and wiped the moisture from his eyes with a cloth so he could open them again without the salt stinging him. The sight of his gaunt face triggered her emotions. Unable to hold them back any longer, she broke down in tears.

"Hold on, my dear husband," she said softly. "The Aten is rising into the sky and its rays will heal you. He will not abandon his son. He cannot abandon his son. You are strong, you are a god," she said.

"I am strong," Akenaten repeated back to her, his voice fading and feeble.

Nefertiti wiped the moisture from his face again and started to kiss his lips. In a moment of lucidity, he placed his hand to her mouth to stop her.

"No, you mustn't, the disease could enter you as well," said Akenaten.

She ignored his warning and kissed his lips.

"You are my husband. We are one," she replied.

Tut and Senpaten entered the room. They glanced at their father's face. The look of it frightened Senpaten.

"Father, you'll be well soon, won't you?" she asked warily.

When he didn't respond, she turned to her mother. "Father will get well, won't he?"

"You can't remain here. You have to leave and let your father rest," said Nefertiti, avoiding her daughter's question.

"Tut will stay. I want to speak with my son alone," said Akenaten.

Nefertiti wanted to object, but obeying her husband, she took Senpaten's hand and escorted her out of the chamber.

Tut was afraid. He stared at the dark bruises covering his father's neck and chest. The pharaoh pushed himself up in bed so he could face Tut eye-to-eye.

"Come closer," he said.

Tut sat on the bed next to him, teary-eyed.

"Don't feel pity for me, son. The Aten has not forsaken us. I'm still his son, and you are of his offspring. You must promise me you'll continue to worship him."

"I will," said Tut.

"Your reign as pharaoh will bring an end to this curse and Amarna will flourish for a thousand years."

Akenaten removed the Aten amulet from around his neck and placed it around Tut's.

"My brother, Tuthmosis, gave it to me when I was young as you are now, and it has always protected me from the beast that brings about death. The time has come for me to face him, but it's your time to live, my son. Wear it always. Never let it leave your sight. It will protect you."

"I'll do as you wish, but what will protect you, Father?"

"The Aten is always with me," said Akenaten.

He kissed his precious son on his forehead. In his eyes, Tut was the most profound gift that the Aten had ever given him.

"Have I ever told you how proud I am of you and your skills as an archer?"

"Many times, Father," Tut replied.

"The Aten has chosen you to be the next great ruler of Egypt. I love you, son, more than I love my own life."

"I love you too, Father. When will the Aten heal you so that we can be together in the courtyard again?"

"He will heal me in the time he chooses. For now, you must go. Send your mother here to me," said Akenaten.

Tut left his father's chamber firmly clutching the amulet.

When Nefertiti returned, Akenaten was shivering more than ever. With some difficulty she helped him sit up in bed and dressed him in his king's robe: an elaborate pleated garment made of the finest weaved linen and dyed in royal purple. The collar was adorned with feathers and precious jewels, a favorite garment of his father, Amenhotep, handed down to him after his death.

"If I were as unblemished as our son, Tut, my father would have been proud of me," said Akenaten as Nefertiti helped him back into his bed and under the bedcover.

"You're a good man, a wonderful husband and father, a god of the Aten, and the people of Amarna love you dearly," said Nefertiti. "If your father was alive to see the beauty of what you have created here in this glorious city, he would be enormously proud of you, my husband."

"No. My body carries more than just the weakness. I am blemished from the inside and unworthy."

The barrier Akenaten had taken a lifetime building around his heart had burst. Tears flooded his eyes, and he lost all control. "Why would you have me believe that I could be acceptable to him?"

Nefertiti was silent. She struggled to contain her impulse to cry for him again, an act of pity he despised.

Though he lay on his own deathbed, weak and near discovery of the afterlife, his father's approval was still the one thing that her husband longed for.

Nefertiti tenderly caressed his face and whispered. "You are more than acceptable, my sweet husband."

She lifted Akenaten's head to help him drink from a jar of wine. He could only muster enough strength to take one swallow. His body tensed. His legs and arms would not move at his command anymore. It was about to happen, and he needed to tell her everything before he embarked on his journey.

"Promise me with your whole heart that you'll never leave Amarna—that you'll keep my people here safe from the tyranny of the Amun priests. This is now *your* city Nefertiti."

"I promise I will do everything you ask," she replied.

"Are you truly *listening* to me?" They'll come here and attempt to force you and the Amarna people back to Thebes. Fight them. You are the queen of Egypt, and they must abide by your rule," said Akenaten, struggling not to lose consciousness.

He reached up and touched her face. "My sight is fading."

"Can you not see me?"

"It's cloudy, like a fog-mist rising from the river at dawn," replied Akenaten.

Nefertiti took his hand from her face and kissed it. "I will love you into eternity, my husband."

As Akenaten's eyelids fluttered shut for the last time, he found himself in a familiar place. He was Teppy again, a six-year-old boy running terrified through an endless grainfield. There was a roar in the distance as the beast pounced after him. The nightmare that haunted his childhood had returned.

Akenaten ran like a gazelle fleeing from a cheetah, his linen kilt flapped against his legs as coarse leaves of wheat thrashed his bare chest. Suddenly, a voice called out to him. A familiar one.

"Teppy! Teppy, wait!"

Akenaten stopped running and collapsed in the sand. A shadow spread quickly across the area around him. It was in the form of a man dressed in the regal clothing of a pharaoh. He carried a sickle in his hand and a bow with a quiver of arrows slung over one shoulder. His face was hidden in silhouette against the blinding orange sun. When the figure shifted its body, its head came into view—the unmistakable head of a ram. It roared again at Akenaten, and saliva dripped from its canine teeth. How could the beast be the source of the soothing familiar voice that had called him by his childhood name? No one would dare call him Teppy, man or beast, except his brother. And before Akenaten could scream at the sight of the ram-headed creature, Tuthmosis miraculously appeared from behind him. "Don't be alarmed, Teppy, it won't harm you," said Tuthmosis as he took Akenaten's hand and lifted him up onto his feet.

Tuthmosis had not aged a day since the last time Akenaten had seen his sixteen-year-old brother in the healing temple before his death. His face was golden, and his eyes, vibrant and filled with life. Akenaten could only stare at his older brother, speechless, yet overjoyed.

"Tuthmosis," he said timidly, unsure if it was safe to unleash his emotions.

"Yes, it's me and I have returned for you my little brother."

At this, Akenaten threw his arms around Tuthmosis's waist and clung to him as tight as he could. "I missed you so much. Why did you leave me?"

"Now is not the time for sadness, Teppy. We're together again, and look . . ."

Tuthmosis peeled his brother's arms from around him and removed what now appeared to be a mask of a ram's head off the shoulders of the beast. Under it was their father, Amenhotep. "I told you, little brother, you don't have to be afraid of him."

"My son, come to me," said Amenhotep, his arms extended.

Amenhotep embraced Akenaten, and in that moment, all the weight of Akenaten's life's despair fell away. He was accepted, and no longer invisible to the father he had always cherished.

When Akenaten turned around, he saw his sweet Nefertiti standing alone, barefoot in the desert sand, only a hundred cubits away, distraught at watching their reunion. Her long white linen dress flowed effortlessly in the wind, and her skin glinted like polished copper. She was as beautiful as the day he had married her. Nefertiti held out her hand, silently entreating Akenaten to return to her instead.

Tuthmosis interrupted his gaze. "Come, Teppy, we have to hurry before the Aten rises between the mountains."

"Are we going to the river to swim again?"

"Not this time, Teppy."

Tuthmosis pointed to the white light that gleamed a short distance ahead of them and expanded over the Aten's horizon. It was sublime, with prisms of colors brighter than the sun. The time had come for Akenaten to embark on his journey. He was now a young boy again, able to run like a gazelle and hop or jump as high as he wanted. His legs were as strong as those of an ostrich, and there was no need for a walking cane. Akenaten turned away from the image of his dear sweet Nefertiti and took the hand of his brother, Tuthmosis, and his father Amenhotep. The three of them walked across the desert sand together as one, hand-in-hand, into the light.

CHAPTER

31

THE YEAR WAS 1334, the year of Pharaoh Akenaten's death, and at only ten years of age, Tut was forced to accept that he would never again hear his father's voice or feel his embrace. He would never see him beaming with pride when he dismounted his chariot after precisely hitting a moving target. It was the worst pain of all to lose the one he believed cared the most for him.

His sisters, Senpaten and Mayati, couldn't stop crying. They still grieved the loss of their sister Meketa, and now their father's death had only compounded their anguish. Akenaten was the son of the Aten—an omniscient god, not only to his children, but even more so, to the citizens of Amarna. He implored his people to depend solely on him, and now that they were without their pharaoh to appease the Aten, a blanket of trepidation covered the city.

Hordes of women screamed and wailed outside the palace doors as the village mourned the pharaoh's death. Men beat themselves in the chest and tossed dirt over their bodies. "Akenaten! Akenaten!" they all shouted over and over again. Others secretly welcomed his death, hopeful that Akenaten's cruel executions would stop.

Nevertheless, it frightened the royal children to hear the people wailing and cheering, and there was no chamber in the palace free from the sound of it.

Tut was determined to hold back his tears for the sake of his sisters. He thought if he maintained his composure, they would soon be calmed.

His mother's behavior proved to be the most disconcerting. Nefertiti withdrew from her children, adding to their feeling of abandonment. Tut tried to console his mother but failed to get through to her. Nefertiti had remained in bed with Akenaten's corpse for days after. Tut turned to his grandfather for help, and when Ay entered the pharaoh's chamber, he found his daughter lying next to Akenaten's body under the bedcover. The smell of death in the room was unbearable, yet Nefertiti appeared unaffected by it. Worried about the state of her sanity, Ay awakened his daughter by snatching away the bedcover. He covered his mouth and nose with his hand to mask the putrid smell.

"My daughter, please. We have to prepare him," said Ay.

Nefertiti looked past her father. "He'll come back into his body, you'll see. Just give him more time," she replied. "He will come back to me. He'll return to his children."

"Time has run out for him, daughter, he has begun the transition. As it is written, you have to let the priests prepare his body for mummification, or he won't complete his journey into the afterlife."

"No, he's coming back."

"If you don't release his body to the priests, you'll anger the Aten and cause even more harm to this city. Allow Akenaten to make the journey so he can live again!" yelled Ay.

His shouting shook Nefertiti from her trance, and life began to return to his daughter's eyes. He reached his hand out to her, and she took hold of it. Nefertiti rose from Akenaten's bed and covered his pasty gray face with the bedcover. "All he wanted was to see the city he dreamed of completed. How could the Aten deny him of that?" she said. Ay embraced his daughter, and she cried there on his shoulder.

Horemheb's ferryboat arrived on the shore of Amarna seven days later. Ay was suspicious of the timing because the general's visits aligned with the death of royalty. First, Queen Ty and Kiya, and now Akenaten and Meketa.

Ranefer escorted Horemheb and his brother Kafrem to the Amarna palace where Ay sat at a table inscribing the pharaoh's death proclamation, to be sent out by messenger to their tributaries.

"General, your visit here again is unexpected. I assume you're surprising the queen with shipments of gold," said Ay.

"It's impossible to give you what we don't have," replied Horemheb. "The queen was informed some time ago that there would be no more shipments of gold until the pharaoh grants me the authority to wage war against our enemies."

"Then why have you come? No such authority has been given."

"We're concerned about the stability of Amarna," replied Kafrem.

"Your concern should be for Thebes," said Ay, "not Amarna."

"We know of the famine in this city and the lack of grain supplies," said Kafrem. "The disease has killed many citizens here, has it not?"

Ay was annoyed at being questioned about Amarna, especially by Kafrem. "You may be a mayor in the city of Thebes, and a brother to the general, but here you are irrelevant."

Ay dismissed Kafrem and turned to Horemheb.

"We have adequate grain supplies here and the spreading of the disease has slowed. Amarna is grateful for your concern general, however, it's not needed. You're welcome to return from where you came," said Ay.

Horemheb stood his ground. "Is the royal daughter Meketa dead?"

Ay paused, not sure how he should answer. Nefertiti would be outraged to know that Horemheb's motive for coming to Amarna was not to bring gold or supplies, but to spy on their city. Still, Ay had no choice. The general would find out soon enough.

"Yes, Meketa has died," said Ay.

"Was it the disease that took her life?" asked Kafrem.

"Possibly."

"I want to speak to the pharaoh now," demanded Horemheb.

Ay looked at the general skeptically. "You've heard no rumors about the pharaoh?"

"What rumors? Take me to him."

"That's beyond my ability to grant," Ay replied.

"I am the general of his army, and I'm ordering you to take me to him."

Ay put down his reed brush and rose from the table. "Very well, as you wish, general. Follow me."

Ay escorted Horemheb and Kafrem outside the palace to an elaborate tent adorned with jewelry and precious stones. An enormous image of the Aten sun-disk was drawn with red and black ink onto the fabric. Ay stopped at the entrance.

"What is this?" asked Horemheb.

"This is where you will find the pharaoh," replied Ay. "I'll wait."

Horemheb and Kafrem entered the tent and were at once confronted with Akenaten's naked, bloated body laid out on a platform. Horemheb was speechless.

As they looked on, the lector priest, Panhessy, continued performing the embalming procedure, inserting a long wire into one of Akenaten's nostrils, while a viscous fluid drained out from a hole in the back of the pharaoh's head.

Horemheb ignored the smell and stepped closer to examine the dark purple bruises that covered the pharaoh's body.

"It was the disease that killed him," Horemheb said to Kafrem, turning back toward the entrance.

"The city of Thebes will celebrate the heretic pharaoh's death, and welcome you in his place," whispered Kafrem as they left the embalming tent.

Ay was still waiting patiently outside the tent's entrance. He searched Horemheb's stoic face for a reaction. Nothing.

"Where is the queen?" asked Horemheb.

"Queen Nefertiti has left explicit instructions not to be disturbed until after she speaks to the people of Amarna today."

"We're dying to hear what she has to say," said Kafrem.

Ay led them to the northern side of the palace below the Window of Appearances where it was noisy and crowded with villagers who anxiously awaited the queen's arrival.

The murmuring of the crowd penetrated Nefertiti's palace chamber. Outside her door, the anticipation of her appearance caused pandemonium among the citizens. It confirmed that what she had planned to do was necessary to save Amarna. Tut was too young to succeed his father as pharaoh, so instead of becoming her son's co-regent as Queen Ty had done with Akenaten when he was a child, Nefertiti opted for a permanent solution.

In order to calm her Amarna citizens and give them a god they so desperately needed, Nefertiti sacrificed her identity for one who would be more like her husband, the son of the Aten. A transformation would be the only way she could assert and align her authority with an image that the people could recognize as strong and formidable.

Seated in front of the mirror, Nefertiti handed Halima a trapezium shaped razor and she cut off the locks of Nefertiti's shoulder length hair until only stubble remained. Halima heated a mixture of sycamore juice, crushed bird bones, oil and gum, and applied the warm concoction over Nefertiti's head. After the mixture cooled, Halima pulled the hardened layer from Nefertiti's scalp, removing the hair stubble and leaving her scalp smooth. She used a copper razor to shave Nefertiti's eyebrows completely off.

Halima assisted Nefertiti in attaching a false beard to her chin. Made of goat's hair and plaited like a braid with the end jutting forward, the beard fastened around her head with a cord.

Nefertiti dressed herself in a masculine kilt and Halima placed the pharaoh's striped nemes crown on her head. Her reflection in the mirror cast an identical image of the only queen of Egypt ever known to be a pharaoh in her time—Queen Hatshepsut, the great queen of Egypt who had transformed herself into a male-god of great power and wisdom over a hundred years before.

Before her accidental death, Nefertiti's mother had told her the story of Queen Hatshepsut. Though the inscriptions of Hatshepsut's reign as pharaoh were erased by her stepson, the women of royalty passed down the story to their female children, keeping the queen's memory alive throughout generations.

When Nefertiti stepped out onto the balcony of the Window of Appearances holding a flail in her hand, the crowd quieted. It was the first time she had appeared there without Akenaten by her side. The initial contact frightened her. Conquering her fears would be part of her transformation.

Horemheb and Kafrem were as amazed with her appearance as the enormous crowd standing around them. Not until she spoke her first words did the people accept that it was their queen, Nefertiti.

"Don't despair my people because of his death. My husband, the pharaoh of Egypt, the great Akenaten, has embarked on his journey into the afterlife. Be jubilant for him. His transition to the

Aten will be successful and his return to the living world expedient. Praises to my beloved Akenaten," Nefertiti declared.

The people exploded with applause and. Nefertiti waited until they calmed before continuing.

"Look at me and behold. I am no longer your queen, Nefertiti. Just as my appearance has been renewed by the Aten, so has he renewed my name. I am Smenkare, *the vigorous soul of the Aten*. I am now a male and your pharaoh, and in the coming days before the setting of the sun, I will prove my vitality at the Sed-Festival. I welcome all to come and witness the strength of your pharaoh Smenkare at the Amarna pavilion. Praises to the Aten," said Nefertiti.

The crowd prostrated themselves, bowing and raising both their hands in the air toward her feet. Nefertiti glanced at the crowd, her face expressionless and her eyes empty. Despite her own self-doubt, she would have to remain impenetrable so that no one would discover her one vulnerability—her concern for her children.

Immediately after Nefertiti's appearance, Horemheb and Kafrem pushed themselves through the crowd, and with the approval of the pharaoh's guards, entered the palace.

"Either the people here have become severely ill from the disease, or their worship of the Aten has driven them all mad to the point of no return. No citizen of Thebes will accept a woman as pharaoh," said Kafrem as they walked down the corridor in search of Nefertiti.

"It's obvious that Thebes is not part of her plan," replied Horemheb.

Nefertiti's guards directed them into her chamber where she was conferring with her father, Ay, who had not had a chance to warn his daughter of their arrival.

"Queen, we share your grief on the loss of the pharaoh," Horemheb said. "If we had known of his death before we left Thebes, we would have brought preparations and gifts for his funeral."

"That's surprising general when oddly you appear to know the timing of every major event that happens here in Amarna. My father was just informing me yet again of your timely visit, and that you have once again come empty handed. What really brings you here?" asked Nefertiti. "I assume you haven't come all the way from Thebes to offer condolences to a pharaoh of the Aten, a god you and your Amun priests despise."

"I have no allegiance to any priesthood. My allegiance is to Egypt," Horemheb replied, getting to the point of his visit. "We can help you prepare for your return to Thebes."

Nefertiti sneered.

"There will be no such return," she said. "This is the city built by my husband and chosen by the Aten god itself. I and the people will never abandon Amarna."

"For your own good and the lives of the people here, we ask that you reconsider," said Horemheb.

"Have you lost your hearing? I am the pharaoh of Upper and Lower Egypt, from the desert sands to the banks of the Great Sea. I have made my intentions known, and the people have chosen to remain here in Amarna with me."

"The people are dying from the disease," Kafrem interjected. "Thousands of them are stricken with it. It's likely you yourself are afflicted."

His accusation riled Nefertiti, but her anger was quelled by the startling entrance of her sister Mundi.

Mundi had accompanied Horemheb on his voyage to Amarna, and had agreed to stay on the ferryboat until he returned to escort her into the palace. She found it impossible to wait any longer to see the sister she had not seen since the day Akenaten had taken her from Thebes. Mundi wholeheartedly embraced Nefertiti, shedding tears of joy. She suppressed her confusion at the sight of her altered appearance.

"My beautiful sister, I've missed you so much," she cried. "Please, save yourself and the people here. Return with us to Thebes; it's the only way. If you don't, you'll die here from the disease. Please, Nefertiti, the gods of Thebes will forgive and bless you. They will give you the life that you deserve."

Nefertiti freed herself from Mundi's embrace and slowly stepped back from the sister she had loved dearly since her childhood. *It had to be her marriage to Horemheb that had changed her. How else could she become like an enemy spouting offensive things?* Nefertiti thought.

"If the gods of Thebes are so powerful and benevolent to their people," said Nefertiti, "then why have their fertility gods Hathor and Bes not made you pregnant, Mundi? My god, the Aten, has given me daughters and a son, and his name is Tut. You are still barren, and you'll remain that way in your corrupt city of Thebes."

Mundi stared at her sister in disbelief and left the room. Nefertiti words were meant to cut her sister through the heart, and for just a moment she was satisfied that she had succeeded. Though the urge was resilient, Nefertiti remained determined not to betray weakness in the presence of men by going after Mundi and consoling her. It could never be known she still had the heart of a woman.

Her new found masculine identity did not sway Horemheb. He approached her and stood only an arm's length away from her face.

"Without the mercy of Amun, the disease will kill everyone here in Amarna. He will not even spare you if you don't return to Thebes."

Nefertiti wanted to close her eyes to the reality of the disease and how it was ravaging the city; yet, the possibility of losing another child left her conflicted. Would the Aten god remove it from the city before it spread to the rest of her children? She questioned her faith, but not enough to abandon the promise she had made to Akenaten—that she would never leave the boundaries of Amarna, and that she would keep the people safe from the tyranny of the

Amun priests of Thebes. Nefertiti's expression turned to stone as she moved in closer to the General, now only a finger's length from his face.

"Get out of my palace and leave my city," she said chillingly calm and firm.

Horemheb and Kafrem followed her orders and returned to their ferryboat where Mundi awaited. As Horemheb prepared the boat to depart from the Amarna shore, a crowd of villagers gathered in front of it, curious to why the general of Egypt had come to their city. From the deck, Horemheb took the opportunity to spread his warning.

"Listen, you must tell everyone, your families and even your enemies: if you, the people of Amarna, return to Thebes and to the worship of its gods, Amun will forgive and wipe away the disease from your body. Amun can cure you. The Aten is powerless!"

The crowd started to mumble. A fraction of them yelled at Horemheb to leave, while others stepped closer to his boat, swayed by his proclamations. Meri-Ra stood in the midst of the crowd infuriated with a counterargument.

"I am the high priest of the Aten, the god of all gods. Neither Queen Nefertiti nor our beloved Pharaoh Akenaten would ever dare to forsake the Aten or its city of Amarna. Don't listen to him; it's a trick to deceive you! The Aten god itself will remove the disease from us in due time. We must remain patient and loyal to him," said Meri-Ra, "and he will reward us."

Though tempted, Horemheb refused to challenge the priest in a shouting match. Mundi needed her husband's comfort more than ever after reeling from distress of her and Nefertiti's confrontation. Aware their presence would not be welcomed at Akenaten's funeral procession, Horemheb and Mundi left the shores of Amarna.

Nefertiti interred Akenaten at the royal Wadi tomb in the river valley. She and her daughters, Senpaten, and Mayati stood together as Tut led the *Opening of the Mouth* ceremony on the seventieth day after his death. Panhessy slaughtered two bulls and cut off one of their legs and handed the severed bull's leg to Tut. As instructed by Meri-Ra, Tut touched the mouth of his father's mummified body with it while repeating the incantation for his return:

"You are young again, you live again forever."

At the conclusion of the ceremony, Meri-Ra and Panhessy recited a prayer from the five sacred scrolls. Akenaten's mummy was then moved into a solid gold coffin where Nefertiti placed a fitted gold mask over his face. Jewels were inserted between his linen cloth wrappings and his coffin lowered into a yellow quartzite sarcophagus and sealed shut.

CHAPTER

32

THE TIERS OF THE PAVILION were only half filled to capacity. A third of the Amarna citizens had died or remained at their homes still sickened by the disease. Nefertiti appeared in front of the subdued group dressed in the traditional attire of male royalty: a pleated kilt and a knee-length cloak. No matter how scarce in attendance, the Sed-Festival would be her way of proving to the people that she was accepted by the Aten as more than a queen, that she had made the complete transformation into a male-god pharaoh.

From the front row tier, Nefertiti's children waved at her. Aware that the audience scrutinized her every move, she nodded at her children in return, void of any expression of emotion.

Nefertiti glanced up at the weary faces of her citizens. They were her devoted ones who traveled to the pavilion in support of her ascension, even though many of them were weak and broken. Nefertiti's children dominated her thoughts and to keep them calm, she tried her best to appear confident of completing the run. Out of the corner of her eye she saw Tut kiss his father's Aten amulet that he now wore proudly around his neck, hoping it would bring her luck.

Meri-Ra recited a prayer to the Aten and handed Nefertiti the royal scroll. Her children grabbed a hold of each other's hands, anxious for what was to come.

Nefertiti scanned the opposite side of the field where the double throne of Egypt stood. At the first beat of the drum, she bolted toward the boundaries of the field holding the scroll tight in her hand. Her gait was quick and her agility high, owing to her slender frame and muscular calves. Nefertiti's adrenaline surged and she inhaled and exhaled at the same erratic pace of her heartbeat. Images of Akenaten running in the Sed-Festival flashed in her mind: the moment he collapsed, her rushing across the field to hand him his walking cane. But unlike, Akenaten, Nefertiti remained strong on her feet, and Meri-Ra's prayer was answered when she touched the third and final marker with the scroll after running the course the required seven times. Nefertiti was drenched in sweat, exhausted and gasping to catch her breath. She had completed the run victorious.

Tut and his sisters stood up and cheered their mother's triumph along with the crowd. It had been years since Nefertiti had seen her children so excited and happy. The joy it gave her, however, needed to remain hidden from the eyes of the Amarna people.

"I am Smenkare, your pharaoh!" she kept repeating out loud.

The crowd hushed as she stepped in front of the double throne—the finish line of the race.

Meri-Ra brought forward a black bull calf adorned with flowers and jewelry. He said a prayer over it before leading it to Nefertiti and handing her a dagger to cut the fruit for the bull's consumption. She rubbed its head to gain its spirit and recited aloud the words from the scroll.

"It is you, the great Apis bull, that will regenerate and ordain me the pharaoh of Egypt with a long and prosperous reign. With this offering of food, you accept and honor my request."

Nefertiti cut open the fruit, and when she attempted to feed it into the bull's mouth, it refused by turning its head away. The more she tried to force the feeding, the more the bull resisted, its mouth closed tight and jerking its head away from her grasp. The queen remembered how the animal had refused to eat the offering from Akenaten's hand and how it had turned out to be a bad omen and curse for him. She could not allow it to happen to her. If the bull would not partake of her food offering, then she would partake of the bull.

In a streak of rage, Nefertiti took hold of the dagger she'd used to cut the fruit and shoved it deep into the bull's neck. As the blood gushed from the wound, she carved a chunk of flesh from the animal and consumed it in front of the stunned crowd.

"I, Smenkare, the pharaoh of Egypt, have captured the power of the Apis bull. I am your god, the son of the Aten!" shouted Nefertiti, with a growl unlike anything her children had ever heard.

The bull collapsed to the ground with its jugular severed. Nefertiti stood over it so that the upward spray of blood saturated her garment. She appeared intoxicated by it, and smeared the blood all over her face until it was covered in a hideous mask of red. Senpaten and Tut gasped at the sight. This was not the mother they knew. The children watched her toss the dagger to the ground and abruptly leave the pavilion while the villagers cheered her new name, "Smenkare! Smenkare!"

Three days after the Sed-Festival, Nefertiti called on Maya, the city treasurer, to her chamber to answer for the state of Amarna's affairs. There was something urgent she needed completed and only Maya would know if Amarna had the resources to help her achieve it.

"You have yet to give me a report on the state of affairs of this city. Why?" asked Nefertiti.

Maya was surprised.

"My pharaoh, are you not aware that we're still experiencing grain shortages and famine here in the village? The state of affairs hasn't changed," replied Maya.

"You're the keeper of the taxes, are you not? Raise them if you have to."

"Pharaoh, I have raised the taxes six times already. They have nothing more to give."

"I'm not concerned about grain. What quantities of gold do we still possess? I have commissioned Bek for a solid gold statue in honor of my husband to be placed at the foundation marker of the city."

"There are no gold reserves. There are barely any grain reserves left. I'm not sure we can even sustain the people through the flooding season, my Pharaoh. We need the help offered from Thebes. Perhaps we should consider what General Horemheb proposes and return there before more die here from the disease," said Maya.

"No one is leaving Amarna. The Aten will cure us in time," replied Nefertiti. "Send a messenger to Thebes with my orders that Horemheb deliver more talents of gold here to our city."

"But, my Pharaoh, he has explained to us many times that they have no more gold reserves in Thebes either. Without Pharaoh Akenaten's consent, he had no authority to wage war against the Nubian's and the Libyans for their gold tributary."

"I am the pharaoh now. Tell him he has my consent to wage war against whoever he chooses as long as he delivers the gold to me quickly."

"Thank you, my Pharaoh, thank you. You'll see it was the right decision. Your wisdom will save the people from starvation. I'll send a messenger to Horemheb immediately," said Maya, stuttering in his excitement as he rushed out of her chamber.

Agreeing to war against Akenaten's wishes overwhelmed Nefertiti with guilt, but she saw no other way Amarna could survive without giving in to Horemheb's lust for combat and his bullying coercion of tributes from weaker kingdoms. War was abhorrent to Nefertiti as it was to Akenaten, but in this case, it was necessary. Gold had become scarce in Egypt, a place where it once was abundant. The only way to acquire it now was to take it by force.

Her reversal was not an acknowledgement that she had completely abandoned her faith in the Aten god's ability to sustain Amarna, only that she was helping to speed up the process. After consuming the flesh of the Apis bull days before, she had taken in the power of a god. By delivering the people from their curse of pestilence and famine, Nefertiti desired to prove that she was as powerful as any male pharaoh of Egypt. If the Aten could not deliver Amarna in the necessary time period, then the gold and her divinity would.

That night, Nefertiti awoke to find her twelve-year-old daughter Senpaten standing over her.

"Senpaten? What are you doing here in my private chamber?"

"I can't sleep, Mother, I'm afraid."

"Go back to your room. I'll send Halima to watch you while you sleep."

"I don't want Halima. Can I sleep here with you in your chamber?"

Nefertiti was inclined to refuse her. For the good of the people she had vowed to maintain her new identity as a stern male pharaoh even to her children. Her desire to quell her daughter's anxiety deadened (for the moment) the spirit of Queen Hatshepsut, and Nefertiti surrendered to her need to comfort her child.

"You may, but only for this night," Nefertiti replied.

Senpaten eagerly climbed into her bed.

"Tell me what you're afraid of," said Nefertiti.

Senpaten was silent. Nefertiti sensed her daughter was in deep fear, withholding a secret she longed to reveal.

"You can tell me, Senpaten. Why are you afraid? Is it because of me?"

"No, Mother, it's because of Ay."

Nefertiti sat up in her bed. It was not at all what she expected to hear.

"Ay? Your grandfather?" she asked.

Senpaten looked terrified at the mention of Ay's name. She finally nodded her head.

"My precious daughter, why are you afraid of your grandfather? You must tell me now."

Ashamed, Senpaten closed her eyes and answered her.

"He touches me in a way a husband touches his wife, and when I refuse him, he says that I'm insulting the will of the Aten. I do love the Aten god and I would never intentionally insult him, Mother, but Grandfather is an old man, a husband of your stepmother, Teyla."

Nefertiti took a deep breath and exhaled—a reaction intended to keep her calm. First it was Akenaten who tried to have relations with Mayati only days before his death, and now to discover her own father had attempted the same with her youngest daughter was painful and infuriating. Ay had no illness. There was no sound reason that she could think of, or blame for her father's depravity against her daughter. Nefertiti's maternal instinct to protect her child was ignited. She had to be careful of making Ay's indiscretion appear as egregious to her daughter as it truly was for herself.

When Nefertiti looked at Senpaten, she displayed no signs of anger. Instead, she spoke to Senpaten soothingly. "It's good to tell me these things," she said. "Whatever it may regard, you can come to me."

"Yes, Mother."

"Your grandfather Ay, will never touch you again in that way, I promise you. You don't have to be afraid anymore."

Nefertiti kissed Senpaten's forehead and rubbed her braided locks of onyx black hair.

"It's safe here, my daughter," she whispered. "Sweet and happy dreams to you."

The queen waited for Senpaten to drift off to sleep before she left the bedchamber. She strode the corridor with a dual purpose in mind. First, to confront her father. Second, to pray for forgiveness at the Aten temple for what she had planned to do to him.

It had been three months since King Suppiluliumas's army invaded Mitanni, and the Hittite king finally entered the city to inspect what they had conquered.

Shattiwaza greeted him at the fortified walls unable to conceal his distress and irritation at the king's much delayed arrival.

"We have been sitting here counting birds while this city goes to ruin without a king to shepherd it," said Shattiwaza.

"It's your homeland. Shepherd it," replied King Suppiluliumas.

"You must be aware that if I'm not ordained king by you, it means nothing to the other kingdoms, nor to these people."

"Where's he imprisoned? I would like to have a word with your father before I ordain you."

"He's dead," replied Shattiwaza.

Suppiluliumas pursed his lips in an attempt to holdback his temper. "And why is he dead?"

"That's a question you'd need to ask of your guards. They're the ones that killed him."

"My guards are wise enough to know that you don't murder a king no matter how treacherous he might be. You capture and imprison him," replied Suppiluliumas.

"Perhaps your guards are not as wise as you think, my king."

King Suppiluliumas searched Shattiwaza's eyes for deception. He saw nothing there but emptiness. "Was there a witness to Tushratta's murder?" he asked.

A voice emerged from behind him. "I saw the slaughter of Tushratta, but the assailants ran away before I could catch a glimpse of their faces, however it was clear they wore Hittite uniforms," said Ornus, as he walked forward and stood next to Shattiwaza.

"And who is this?" asked Suppiluliumas.

"His name is Ornus. He's an experienced military captain of my Mitanni army," replied Shattiwaza.

Shattiwaza gave Ornus an approving glance cemented with a smile that made King Suppiluliumas suspicious of them both.

"Take me to where you're keeping his body," Suppiluliumas ordered. "I'll perform the coronation there."

The king followed Shattiwaza as he walked through the palace corridor into King Tushratta's chamber.

"Now that we have conquered Mitanni, it's only natural that our next conquest will be the great land of Egypt," said Shattiwaza.

"You have conquered no one," said Suppiluliumas.

"But I helped you, my king, by giving you their secret trade route."

"And I'll tell you again, the route is of no use. I have no intentions of war with the Egyptians."

"None I'm sure you would want to share with me," replied Shattiwaza. He reached into a pouch that was hidden beneath the bedcover and tossed the contents at Suppiluliumas. With a quick reflex, the king caught it and peered inside. He was aghast to see it was a severed finger with a king's ring on it.

"What is this?" asked Suppiluliumas, his face painted with disgust.

"It's what it appears to be: my father's royal ring," replied Shattiwaza. "You didn't expect me to keep his entire bloated body here on display for three whole months did you?"

"I would expect you show some display of reverence for the spilled blood of your father," Suppiluliumas answered.

He pulled the ring off the severed finger and handed it to Shattiwaza. "With this ring I ordain you king of Mitanni under the laws of our treaty."

Suppululiumas turned and walked away down the palace corridor. Shattiwaza followed behind him confused. "So that's it? Where is my blessing from your Storm-god?"

Suppululiumas stopped in his tracks and faced him. "How could I be so foolish as to forget your blessing?" Suppululiumas said as he patted Shattiwaza on the shoulder. "My daughter and her maidservants will arrive here within the next eleven days for your wedding. If you humiliate her in any way, I'll slit your throat myself. That is your blessing from our Storm-god. Welcome to our family, son-in-law."

Tut was awakened in the middle of the night by his sister Senpaten shaking him. When his eyes adjusted to the light in the room, he saw the panic in her face. "What's wrong?"

"I can't find Mother," Senpaten answered.

"She's not in her chamber?"

"No. I was with her in her chamber and now she's gone. I've looked everywhere."

Tut and Senpaten awakened Mayati and together they informed the guards, who immediately searched the palace grounds.

After hearing of his daughter's disappearance, Ay instinctively went to the Aten temple. Only he was aware that Nefertiti was defying the traditional laws and would pray directly to the sun-disk itself. And it was exactly where he found her, cold to the touch, lying dead in front of the statue of the sun-disk.

In a state of confusion, Ay picked up her lifeless body and carried it out of the temple without shedding a tear. The royal guards were shocked to see their queen was dead, but dared not ask Ay a word about it. They assisted him in placing her body in the royal chariot for the short ride back to the palace.

Tut, Senpaten, and Mayati looked perplexed at the sight of their mother being carried through the palace. Ay instructed the guards to lay her body on the bed in her chamber while he returned to the corridor to address her children.

"What's wrong with Mother?" asked Senpaten, on the verge of tears.

"Is she sick? Does she have the disease?" Mayati continued.

Ay remained silent.

"Grandfather tell us! Why is our mother being carried?" shouted Tut.

Senpaten grabbed Mayati and Tut's hands and they were all staring at Ay, afraid of what his answer might be.

"I am so sorry, your mother has died from the disease," said Ay. "My beloved daughter is dead."

Senpaten's scream pierced Tut's heart. "No, she can't be," he said shaking his head in disbelief.

Tut released his sisters' hands and stepped toward his mother's chamber, but Ay pulled him back.

"How could she die from the disease when she never had the mark on her?" asked Tut, trembling.

"I was with her the whole night," cried Senpaten. "She was never sick."

"Most likely the mark was even hidden from her," Ay replied.

Senpaten and Mayati were crying profusely, holding onto each other for strength when Tut took hold of their hands in an attempt to console them and to hide his own fear. His sisters' grief was enough to bring tears to his eyes, but he suppressed it to appear strong in the presence of his grandfather.

A messenger approached them and Ay instructed him to ride to Thebes to inform Horemheb of Nefertiti's death and to request ferryboats for the people of Amarna. Then Ay turned his attention back to the children.

"Heed my warning," he said. "We have little time. General Horemheb and the mayor will be here within days to return us all to Thebes."

"Noooo! This is our home!" Mayati shouted.

"Mother and Father would never want us to leave Amarna," said Senpaten.

Ay focused a stern gaze at Tut.

"Your sisters will be judged and punished for blasphemy if you do not have them do exactly what I tell you. Do you understand?" asked Ay.

Tut didn't respond. The thought of returning to Thebes was frightening.

Ay firmly grasped Tut's shoulders. "I asked you a question, do you understand?"

Tut wanted to refuse his grandfather, but knew his mother, above all things, would want him to protect his sisters; they were all he had left. "I do," he answered reluctantly.

"Good. You will renounce the Aten as your god and we will return to the worship of Amun. You must dedicate yourself now to the Amun god. Never will you mention the name of the Aten again. The Aten god is dead. Amun lives forever. All of you, repeat it back to me," ordered Ay.

"Why must we abandon the Aten?" asked Tut. "The Amun god knows nothing about us, nor do we know anything about it. The Aten has always been our god. Why do we need to pretend that he's dead?"

"If you defy me Tut, the Amun priests will see to it that your sisters are punished, and it will be all because of your stubbornness. The Aten god is dead, Amun lives forever. Repeat it. All of you" demanded Ay.

Tut perfunctorily repeated it as he looked Senpaten and Mayati in the eye, leading them to do the same.

The next morning, Tut accompanied Ay as he gathered the people of Amarna under the Window of Appearances and told them of Nefertiti's death, informing them that they would be returning to Thebes and from that day forward would once again worship the many gods of Amun. Ay brought Tut onto the balcony so the citizens could see him. He was petrified and intentionally looked over their heads so they wouldn't see the fear in his young eyes.

"Prince Tut is the heir to the throne of Egypt and he himself has proclaimed that you, the people of Amarna, should follow him back to Thebes, where there is no curse, and many gods that can bring you food, prosperity, and relief from the disease!"

Everything was happening so fast for Tut. He stood there, still and afraid, praying to the Aten for the moment to be over. When Ay finally released him and he was out of sight of everyone in the palace, including his sisters, Tut went to his bedchamber where he cried for his mother and for the return of his father from the afterlife.

Ay took Nefertiti's body to the embalming tent so that Meri-Ra could begin the process of her mummification. When he returned the following day, the priest revealed that he and the physicians had all examined Nefertiti's body and found no bruises or marks of the disease. Meri-Ra confessed to Ay that Nefertiti's death appeared suspicious.

"You more than anyone should be familiar with the magic of the Amun priests," Ay responded. "As you once told me yourself, Meri-Ra, 'one should not be fooled by what you can or cannot see,'" he said.

In three weeks' time, Horemheb and a fleet of ferryboats arrived on the Amarna shore to transport the people back to Thebes. Weary from famine and death, most of the citizens agreed to return and boarded the boats with all the belongings they could carry.

Tut, Senpaten, Mayati, Teyla, Maya, Panhessy and Halima, were all escorted by Ay onto the royal riverboat for their grand return to Thebes. Ay reminded Tut and his sisters that they must never speak of the Aten or their father again and to remember everything he taught them of the worship of Amun. Their lives depended on it.

Tut huddled together with his siblings. It was just the three of them now without a mother or a father to protect them, on their way back to a land they knew nothing about, and to a people who had never before seen them. There were many questions, and Tut had no answers. Would they be accepted as royalty in this new land of Thebes? Or would they be hated then killed because they were children of the Aten and of their father Akenaten? No matter what lay ahead for them, Tut was determined to protect his sisters to the end.

PART III

"There is no one who deceives who is not deceived."
—*Ankhsheshonq*

CHAPTER

33

FTER TEN DAYS and nights of sailing, the fleet of Amarna ships arrived on the shores of Thebes led by the royal riverboat. Tut and his sisters remained huddled together in one of its many cabins while the oarsmen dropped anchors in preparation for docking. Theban citizens lined up along the banks of the river, anxious to see who would step out first.

The children walked out onto the deck holding each other's hands, and Horemheb escorted them onto Theban soil. The people stared at them as if they were an exotic breed of animal they had never seen before. Maybe they sensed how frightened he and his sisters were, or how much they hated returning there. Their father had warned them about the city of Thebes, how the evil Amun priests controlled it and oppressed the people with threats from their false gods. It soothed the children to see their Aunt Mundi there to greet each one of them as they disembarked. Though she had known his sisters as infants, Tut was born in Amarna, and it was the first time he had laid eyes on his aunt. She wrapped her arms around him and his siblings, embracing them as if they were her own.

Ay told them the evil god Sekhmet had left their Aunt Mundi and Horemheb childless, and their arrival in Thebes would be like a gift from the fertility gods Hathor and Bes. Since his mother had spoken of how she distrusted Horemheb, it didn't make sense why any benevolent god would gift him and his sisters to the general unless that god was actually corrupt as his father had warned. Tut didn't believe Ay, but he trusted his Aunt Mundi's love for him and his sisters was genuine, and that their mother would be at peace knowing they were in her sister's care. At Mundi's request, Horemheb agreed to become the children's guardian and protector, promising Mundi that no harm would come to them at the hands of the Amun priests. A man of his word, Horemheb kept them safe and his guidance made their transition to life in Thebes palatable.

Mundi told them stories about their mother they had never heard, stories of her kindness to young animals and how, when they were children, their mother would make her laugh by painting ghastly masks on their faces with lip paint and black kohl and how they'd frighten their father, Ay, by waking him from his slumber with their distorted faces, screaming as loud as they could.

Tut enjoyed the stories of his mother's life as a child, but it was his father's childhood that he yearned to know more about. Mundi had no stories to tell of him, neither did Horemheb. It was as if his father never existed or had ever lived in the city of Thebes. There were statues, monuments, and inscriptions everywhere of his grandfather Amenhotep, and even more of his grandfather's father, Thutmose IV, yet Tut could find no evidence of his father's past life in Thebes, and no one dared to say his name.

Following the example set before them, Tut and his sisters never spoke their father's name either. Only in secret did they express to each other how much they missed him.

In a side chamber of Thebes palace, Senpaten and Mayati gathered up the ingredients they needed to make a batch of lotus perfume. The royal children had moved from Mundi and Horemheb's home and were now living in the palace along with their many servants and guards. Their aunt and uncle would travel by chariot from their home nearby to visit them, assuring they had everything they desired to live a comfortable life, including the ingredients they requested to make their perfume, something new that they were excited to try.

Senpaten filled a pot halfway with oil and goat-fat, and Mayati added myrrh, frankincense and blue lotus flowers into the mixture. The oil absorbed the scent, creating a fragrant perfume they could rub on their bodies. When the floral aroma filled the chamber, Mayati saw how it affected Senpaten. Her sister sat on the ground and cried and Mayati sat next to her.

"What's wrong? Why are you crying?"

"The scent is like the one mother wore. It makes me think of her."

"It's okay to be sad. I think of her too. It's a beautiful scent, and she was just as beautiful," said Mayati.

Senpaten looked away. "It's my fault she's gone."

Mayati gazed at her sister thoroughly confused. "Mother's death was not your fault at all. Why are you saying that?"

"I know why she left her chamber the night she died."

After years of harboring the guilt of Nefertiti's death, Senpaten felt brave enough to tell her sister.

"Have you kept secrets from me? Tell me what happened," said Mayati.

"I told mother about grandfather Ay."

"What about him?"

Senpaten took a deep breath and exhaled before she answered. "I told her how he touched me like a man touches his wife, and how I was afraid of him when he would stare at me as I changed my garments. I think mother waited for me to fall asleep and went to search for him. Don't you see Mayati, if I had never told her about grandfather, she would never have left her chamber that night. She would be alive with us today," said Senpaten.

Mayati cradled her sister in her arms as she cried, rocking her back and forth. "I'm sorry that you felt you had to keep it to yourself," said Mayati. "You could have told me what grandfather did to you, and I could have been there to comfort you, just as you could have comforted me if I had gone to you, and told you what our father had done to me," said Mayati.

Senpaten looked up into her sister's eyes stunned. "Father?" she said. "What did father do to you?"

"He was very ill and not himself. It's okay, I didn't feel anything," said Mayati, her eyes watering. "He was always good to us and he didn't mean it."

That day, Senpaten learned that her sister held her pain inside and had locked it away as she had. The revelation that they had suffered the same defilement had brought them closer than they had ever been. Mayati was the one who needed to be consoled the most, so Senpaten suppressed her feelings of guilt about her mother's death to comfort her sister. She gently stroked Mayati's hair to soothe her.

"You and I will make a vow that never again will we be afraid to share our fears and secrets with each other," said Senpaten, "as I will forever share mine with you."

Senpaten and Mayati locked hands.

"The Aten seals our bond forever," Mayati replied.

The girls had not seen Tut in the royal palace for several days. His absence concerned Senpaten and after she went to Horemheb for advice to where she might find him, he told her that Tut could be found in the Colonnade Hall. A royal guard transported her there in his chariot, and she entered the unfinished structure for the first time, intimidated by the colossal size of the thirty-cubit-high papyrus shaped columns towering the entrance.

Senpaten saw no one inside as she strolled through the corridor. There was an eerie feeling of being watched. It alarmed her to see a man in a flaxen-colored robe and shaved head staring at her and then abruptly walk away in the opposite direction. Nervous by his appearance, she quickened her pace, and when she turned the corner at the end of the hall, someone touched her shoulder from behind. Senpaten spun around and was startled, then relieved to see that it was Tut.

"You frightened me," she said as she caught her breath.

"What are you doing here?"

"I came to see what was keeping you from returning to the palace. Mayati and I were concerned about you."

Tut walked over to the wall and pointed at the intricately inscribed hieroglyphics that covered it from floor to ceiling.

"It's because of this—the many stories of our country, the wars and the strategies used to fight them. The wisdom of the powerful pharaohs that have come before me is here, Senpaten, and there is not enough time in a day to absorb it all."

Senpaten heard little of Tut's response. She was more concerned about the priest who still appeared to be shadowing them.

"Why is that man following us?"

"He's one of the Amun priests. Sia doesn't trust me," said Tut, loud enough for the priest to hear him.

The priest gazed at them again, then turned and walked away.

"Come, I want to show you something," he whispered.

Tut took Senpaten's hand and led her to one of the monumental columns in the unfinished section of the Hall. He first eyed the perimeter to make sure the priest had left the area, then stooped down and directed Senpaten to touch the freshly carved hieroglyphics at the base of the column. When she traced the symbols with her fingers, her eyes widened and her expression was joyful.

"It's mother and father's name and the story of Amarna, the beautiful city father built for us," whispered Senpaten, trying to contain her excitement. "I thought their names were erased from every building and monument in the city?"

"They were," Tut replied. "I've been coming here daily and while no one was watching, I would carve it in little-by-little."

Senpaten embraced Tut, overwhelmed with love and gratitude for her brother. He had prevented their parents' legacy from being destroyed by the Amun priests and secured a path for their return. Only a moment later she realized that what Tut had done was dangerous. Her joyful expression changed to fear.

"If the Amun priests discover what you've done, they will punish you, Tut."

"I don't care if they discover it, and I don't care if they punish me. Our parents deserve to be here among the great pharaohs of Egypt. They are the son and daughter of the Aten and should be remembered throughout eternity."

Senpaten hugged her brother again and they held each other longer than they had ever before. His bravery and determination to honor their parents, no matter how much it might put his life at risk, inspired her and had further emboldened him.

"I want to be pharaoh," Tut blurted out. "It's time."

"Tut, you're too young. Wait until you're older, when you'll be ready."

"I am ready and I have a right to take my position."

Tut's ambition for the throne made Senpaten uneasy. Turmoil, pain and death ensued the life of a pharaoh, rarely would there be moments of joy and happiness. She believed Sia and the Amun priests would fight against Tut's ascension, and Horemheb, who had once challenged her father for the throne, would likely do the same.

Two years had passed, and Tut and his sisters had settled into a daily routine that gave them a sense of security. Thebes palace had become like their palace home in Amarna, and they had developed a comfortable life with Mundi and Horemheb until their grandfather, Ay, paid them a visit and disrupted it.

He informed Tut of an imminent marriage arrangement between him and a princess from the land of Byblos that the Amun priests had ordained. The announcement petrified Tut so much that he went to Mundi for help. Tut pleaded with his aunt that he was not ready for marriage and didn't want to marry someone he didn't know. When Mundi confronted Ay on his behalf, he warned her that if Tut refused to go along with the arranged marriage, that the Amun priests would likely charge him and his sisters with heresy because of their former worship of the Aten god, and there would be nothing she or Horemheb could do to save them from banishment. Mundi relented and for the sake of Nefertiti's daughters, she convinced Tut that it was best to agree with what the priests commanded.

Marriage with a stranger was unthinkable to Tut. His closest sibling was his sister, Senpaten, and they had remained inseparable since early childhood. If he married a foreigner, he would lose more than a sister; he would lose his best friend and the one he loved more than anyone else in the world. This marriage threatened to rip them apart, leaving his dear Senpaten to be alone without him. Tut feared losing her forever. The only way to keep Senpaten by his side would be to marry her instead. Marriage between members of royalty was permitted and practiced throughout the history of Egypt's forefathers. What he didn't know was if Senpaten felt the same way about him or if he even had the courage to ask.

The days passed quickly, and before Tut could gather the nerve to approach Senpaten with the question, Ay was dressing him for his coronation and marriage ceremony to the Byblos princess. Tut was adorned in gold and carnelian jewelry and brought forth in front of Sia and the royal court at the Colonnade Hall. Before the marriage ceremony could take place, Sia, as the leader of the Amun priests, would lead the coronation to ordain Tut pharaoh of Egypt, but in co-regency with him. The priest unrolled a papyrus scroll and read from it:

"Do you renounce the Aten as your god and dedicate yourself now to the worship of Amun and the gods of Egypt?" asked Sia.

Tut glanced at Ay on how to answer. Ay nodded his head—a cue for Tut to recite what he had taught him.

"I renounce the Aten. Amun is my god and the god of all gods. May the gods Osiris and Montu witness my loyalty to him."

Tut answered Sia as if he was reading a list off a papyrus scroll. The priest didn't seem to notice; his concern was that Tut's answers were correct.

"Do you renounce the heresy of your mother and father, Akenaten and Nefertiti?" Sia asked.

It had been a long time since someone spoke the names of his parents. Tut looked over at Ay again for courage to bear witness against the parents he so loved.

"I do renounce my mother and father for their heresy against Amun," said Tut, a declaration Ay instructed him to say if he was ever asked the question. "As I am king, Egypt will return to its former glory from the days of my grandfather, the great builder Amenhotep," he added.

The crowd broke out in a roar of cheers. A thunderbolt of guilt struck through Tut's body. How could he betray the memory of the parents he adored so much? He had to remind himself that he was saving his sisters with his words, and that his parents' spirit would exonerate him when they returned as flesh and bone from the afterlife.

Sia placed the crown of Upper and Lower Egypt upon Tut's head and two other Amun priests covered him with the royal king's robe.

"Your name will no longer be Tutankh*aten*, you are now Tutankh*amun*, the co-regent pharaoh of Egypt. The time of your marriage has come. Bring forth the princess of Byblos," ordered Sia to the palace guards.

In an elaborate procession of dancers and musicians, a woman dressed in exotic clothing of purple and red silk came forward and stood next to Tut, accompanied by thirty of her female maidservants. The Byblos princess looked twice his age, hovering over him almost a cubit taller, gaunt-thin, and cursed with a salient overbite. There was nothing special about her appearance except for the abundance of precious jewels on her body indicating the enormous wealth of her country. Tut's heart broke. He wanted to look over at Senpaten, but feared if he did, he might burst into tears and cause her to do the same. The ceremony would assuredly break them apart if he didn't gather up the courage to stop it.

Before Sia recited the marriage oath, the princess reached out her hand to Tut. He refused it.

"You must take her hand before we can begin," said Sia.

Tut glanced at the Byblos princess and then at Sia. "Why is that necessary? A marriage doesn't guarantee friendship," Tut replied.

Sia looked at him perplexed. "Are you now refusing the marriage mandated by the Amun god?"

Senpaten's attention peaked at Sia's question. Tut sensed her anxiety to hear what his answer would be. After he said a silent prayer to the Aten, he broke his silence.

"If I am the pharaoh of Egypt," he began, "then I can make the decision as to whom I should marry, can I not?" asked Tut.

Sia was taken aback by Tut's boldness.

"No," he said. "The decision has been made. You are obligated to marry the Byblos princess here and now."

Horemheb stepped forward and stood side-by-side with Tut. "Sia, it's your error that you crowned him co-regent pharaoh before he recited the marriage oath, so he most certainly has the right to make the decision as to whom he wants to marry. That is the law."

Tut's opinion of Horemheb changed that day. At the most devastating moment in his life, the general had come to his rescue and saved him from a miserable life with a foreign woman. If anyone in the city of Thebes was trustworthy, it would be his defender, Horemheb. The general had challenged Sia on his behalf and had easily won. Sia had no choice but to capitulate.

"True, you now have the authority to decide" Sia replied. "But what other female among us is qualified to marry a pharaoh?"

"I do not choose the Byblos princess. I choose the one I love foremost, my sister, Senpaten," said Tut, as he finally met Senpaten's eyes, searching for a reaction.

Mumbling and gasps filled the royal court.

To Tut's relief, Senpaten's eyes glistened with tears of joy and affection. It was the confirmation he sought, that his sister shared his feelings. They had loved each other since they were children and now they would love each other as husband and wife.

Tut held out his hand to her, and she joined him, replacing the Byblos princess by his side.

So it was, that at the age of fourteen, in the year thirteen hundred thirty, Tut married his sister, Senpaten, in front of the citizens of Thebes. As the siblings joined hands as husband and wife, the people chanted and roared, "Long live King Tutankhamun and his Queen Senpamun!"

Meri-Ra had remained in Amarna, afraid of what illusions Sia and the other Amun priests might conjure up against him if he returned to Thebes. The sudden and suspicious conversion of the royal family back to the Amun god frightened him enough not to think twice about his decision.

His task from the Aten was to keep Amarna safe and functioning as a living city, no matter how daunting. The prayers and sacrifices to the Aten god must continue as they were when pharaoh Akenaten and Nefertiti ruled. His duties to the Amarna people were clear, but the path to how to complete them, blurred.

Amarna appeared desolate except for the abundance of animals roaming free throughout the city. The farmers that had remained were attending to three times the livestock and crop raising that they were capable of handling now that the others had abandoned the city. The vegetation fields had overgrown and were infested with weeds, the village streets—littered with debris and the buildings and homes, in desperate need of maintenance or repair. The Aten priests now ruled Amarna in place of the pharaoh, and the people were comforted that the disease had not taken another life since Nefertiti's death.

That day, as Meri-Ra crouched on the Amarna shore filling a vase with water for use in the Aten temple, a ferryboat arrived carrying Ay, Horemheb, and several of his guards. Meri-Ra was startled to see the Theban men in his village. He had made it clear to Ay upon his departure that he had no intentions of leaving Amarna. His loyalty to Akenaten and the Aten would not be shaken by promises of a better life in Thebes. Nevertheless, the men had journeyed from Thebes to once again try their hand at convincing Meri-Ra and the rest of the villagers to return to Thebes.

"You won't be able to survive here much longer with the threat of the disease," said Horemheb. "The citizens here will eventually need food supplies. You can convince them it's best to return with us. They'll listen to you," he argued.

"No one here has contracted the disease since you took the pharaoh's children away," replied Meri-Ra. "We're doing quite well raising our own food and living an honest life. Why would we want to return to a city ruled by corrupt Amun priests?"

"The boy Tut rules Egypt. He is pharaoh," said Ay.

"You know as well as I that he is pharaoh in name only," answered Meri-Ra. "The Amun priests will never relinquish control of Egypt to a boy-king."

"The priests do not control Egypt, and we're not here to quarrel with you Meri-Ra. Take us to the Aten temple," ordered Horemheb.

Horemheb's request was odd to Meri-Ra. Why did they want to appear at the Aten temple when they were worshippers of Amun? *Perhaps it was to see where Nefertiti was found at the time of her death,* he thought. Without questioning the order, he directed them to the exterior of the majestic temple. Horemheb surveyed it from the ground up, paying close attention to the floor and walls of the structure.

"We can make good use of the limestone and gold," said Horemheb to Ay.

"I don't understand," said Meri-Ra.

"We're shipping the limestone and gold back to Thebes to use as building materials—"

"You'll do no such thing! I'll allow no one to desecrate this holy temple by ripping away its foundation," said Meri-Ra.

Horemheb continued speaking as if he didn't hear him. "After we remove it, you'll have fifty days to gather the rest of the people here and return to Thebes before I set fire to this entire city," said Horemheb. He left Meri-Ra speechless as he and Ay returned to their ferryboat for their journey back to their capital.

Though the Amun priests had changed Tut and Senpaten's names, when they were alone, they secretly called each other by the name their parents gave them—what they considered to be their true names.

The royal couple had adjusted well to their new exalted position in the palace of Thebes. They spent most of their time sailing the river in the royal canoe. Tut loved to hunt ostrich and Senpaten delighted in helping him, handing him arrows to load into his bow.

"Teach me this time, I want to try," said Senpaten as she held out another arrow.

Tut put the bow in her hand and wrapped his arms around her from behind, guiding her aim at an ostrich lurking in the river for food. He allowed her to release it but the arrow completely missed the target and skidded across the water. Senpaten laughed at her failed attempt.

"I hope to be a better queen than a hunter," she said. Tut took the bow away from her and loaded an arrow for himself.

"You are a good wife and a great queen. One day you'll be as great as the great Queen Nefertiti."

"I miss her so much," said Senpaten. "If I had but one wish, it would be to see her beautiful face just once more. If you had one wish Tut, what would it be?"

It took Tut a moment to ponder her question before he could give her an honest answer.

"Because I see Mother's face whenever I gaze upon yours, I would wish to see Father. I yearn to hear his voice."

Senpaten kissed Tut, and he gave into her affection with caresses.

"I like being your wife," she said. "Tell me you won't take another."

"I want no one else," he said.

"Do you mean that?"

"With all my heart."

"Promise?"

"I promise."

They embraced, enraptured by the first and only love of their youth. Tut handed her a lotus blossom he picked from the river. She in turn gave him a mandrake that she had brought with her on the canoe.

"Soon I will be the *true* pharaoh of Egypt," said Tut."

"But you are the pharaoh of Egypt," Senpaten replied.

"In title only. Until the Amun priests release me from their co-regency, Egypt will be bound by their decisions, not mine."

"At one time will their co-regency expire?"

"The day of my seventeenth birthday, if they decide to follow the law."

"Months and years pass quickly. That day will be upon us soon," said Senpaten. "Do you still possess the Aten amulet Father gave you?"

Tut reached inside the neck of his garment and pulled it out so that it was visible.

"I have to keep it hidden or the Amun priests might discover it and condemn me for it," he said.

Tut kissed the amulet for luck and released an arrow from his bow at another ostrich. It pierced the stomach of the animal before it collapsed in the water. Senpaten cheered him on as she had always done since their childhood.

Meri-Ra had only days before Horemheb would return to raze the Aten temple. Afraid that the general might also pillage the temple of its valuable treasures, Meri-Ra collected the sacred gold utensils into a burlap sack to hide them from the general's men.

After he sealed the inner sanctuary, something on the altar covered by a black cloth caught his attention. He had never seen it there before, nor the amulet of a scarab beetle that was lying next to it.

Meri-Ra picked it up and examined it. He had seen an amulet like it before in Thebes but could not quite recall where.

Meri-Ra placed the amulet inside the sack with the sacred utensils and tied it shut with string. When he removed the black cloth from the altar he gasped and stepped back. Under the cloth there appeared to be two severed hands crudely cut off at the wrists, stained in blood and infested with crawling maggots. He turned to flee the temple, but was confronted at the door by a man holding a wooden mask of the same scarab beetle on the amulet, over his face, concealing his identity.

Meri-Ra grabbed his priest wand from the altar. "Who are you?"

The masked man did not move nor respond. He stood there as still as a statue, his black pupils shifting about through the eye-holes of his mask.

"If you don't reveal yourself, the Amarna guards will do it for you," threatened Meri-Ra.

The man moved the mask away from his face. It was Sia.

Fear enveloped Meri-Ra. He pointed his priest wand at Sia's legs and shouted an incantation:

"You cannot stand against the Aten, you will fall at his feet and collapse because you have no legs to stand on," repeated Meri-Ra.

Sia screamed from the pain as he fell to his knees. He went silent, then a moment later, laughed hysterically.

At first Meri-Ra was perplexed until it occurred to him that Sia had pretended to be affected by his spell. Without effort, Sia stood up and faced Meri-Ra.

"I can and will stand against him."

Sia lunged forward and grabbed the flint knife from the altar and slit his own wrist with it.

Meri-Ra was bewildered at the sight of Sia's blood dripping on the floor.

"This is not my blood, Meri-Ra, it's yours, and it's draining out of *you*. You are growing weaker, Meri-Ra, and it's you that cannot stand," said Sia.

"Your gods are powerless without the illusions," replied Meri-Ra. "The contraptions they built underground for your rigged statues only work in your temples. It has no effect here in Amarna."

"Really? Is that what you believe?" said Sia, smiling at him.

"It is the truth," Meri-Ra answered.

"The truth is that the underground contraptions the engineers built had never worked. What you, my twin, and so many others witnessed—the blood dripping from the statue's mouth, the thunderous sounds it made were all real, and proof that Amun is the true and most powerful god of Egypt."

"I don't believe you."

"You don't? Then why are your legs weakening, Meri-Ra?"

Meri-Ra shook his head. "No."

His legs were weakening and suddenly snapped beneath him like a tree branch in a storm. He toppled over on the ground, fearing how he would survive a battle against a priest whose god was proving itself to be more powerful than his own.

Meri-Ra struggled, unable to prop himself to his feet. Sia was winning.

"The power of the Heka god is mightier than the Aten, but when it unites with the power of Amun, it is insuppressible," said Sia. "I am the master of the writings of Heka, you were only a student, Meri-Ra. If you renounce the Aten and convert to the worship of Amun, I will make you its highest ranking disciple."

Meri-Ra lifted his head and spat in Sia's direction. "I will never convert to a god of darkness, when I am enclosed and protected by the life-giving light of the Aten."

"What a pity," Sia replied. "There were so many things I myself could've taught you Meri-Ra—priest of the Aten. Unfortunately, your time has run out. Your insides have rotted and decayed."

"No, my insides are clean and protected by the Aten from your sorcery."

"By the power of Heka and Amun, your insides are rotted and decayed," Sia repeated.

Meri-Ra's subconscious capitulated to Sia's incantation, and he choked and gasped for air. His fear of the Amun priest had overtaken him.

In the midst of consternation, scenes and images from his life's past flashed before him and then faded away as if each one was being erased from his memory one-by-one. He trembled so violently that the pain in his organs rose into his heart. "I must meditate and be calmed. I must pray for the power of—" he murmured out loud in a frenzied voice trying to convince himself. He needed to be calm before he could recite the pertinent incantation that would halt Sia's advantage over him. But, before he was able to conjure up the words from his memory, Sia continued his incantation of sorcery against him.

"They are inside you, feeding on your decayed flesh, Meri-Ra. You want to vomit it out but you can't."

"The Aten protects me from your divination!" shouted Meri-Ra, "and I call upon—"

Meri-Ra suddenly couldn't speak. His body jerked back and forth as though he was about to vomit, and just as Sia told him, nothing came out. Curling up into a fetal position, he prayed silently to himself for the Aten god to save his life. It was then he convulsed, until he vomited out what he had ignored was moving about in his intestines the whole time. Meri-Ra's eyes widened as a slew of maggots poured out of his mouth.

"You were never alive, Meri-Ra. You were long dead before I even appeared," said Sia, as he took the black cloth from the altar and wrapped it around his wrist to stop the bleeding from his self-inflicted wound.

The next morning, an Aten priest entered the temple to find it ransacked and the image of the sun-disk defaced in camel-dung. The sacred gold utensils were gone, and the seal on the inner sanctuary was broken.

Inside, the priest found Meri-Ra dead on the floor, his eyes wide open and staring up at nothing. There were two amputated hands still lying on the altar in the identical manner Meri-Ra saw in his premonition. They were the same two bloody hands that were now missing from Meri-Ra's severed wrists.

CHAPTER

34

THREE YEARS LATER, on Tut's seventeenth birthday, the Amun priests' co-regency expired. Sia had been reluctant to release full control of Upper and Lower Egypt over to Tut citing his youth and inexperience as a valid reason to continue it. Horemheb told him of Tut's combat skills and of his extensive knowledge of Egyptian history in the ways of the great pharaohs, but when Sia still refused, Horemheb referenced his knowledge of Egyptian law to force the priest to comply.

Tut celebrated the momentous occasion by racing across the wide valley of Thebes in his most magnificent chariot, worked with electrum and gold, and anchored atop six-spoked wheels. His driver had spotted a gazelle fleeing to the northern side and Tut had instructed him to give chase. This was no picture target from his youth; they were chasing a living, breathing animal running for its life in the year 1327, and Tut basked in the excitement of it all. Archery thrilled him, but to practice it while traveling at incredible speeds in his favorite chariot went beyond exhilarating. Killing the animal would not be his reward.

Tut took careful aim at the gazelle, and at the precise moment, when the chariot traveled at its most stable point, he released the arrow. It pierced the animal in the belly, though stubbornly, it kept running. He nocked another arrow and signaled his driver to speed up. Tut steadied himself, closed one eye, and aimed for its head. The chariot made a second sharp turn and just as the gazelle seemed to have escaped his sight, an opening in the dust cloud appeared and he released it. The animal fell dead on its side with the arrow protruding from its head. He envisioned how proud his father would have been to see him in this moment.

Tut thought of his father often, more than he did his mother. What Akenaten taught him and his sisters about reading and writing hieroglyphics instilled in him the confidence that he could accomplish anything. Tut knew the writings of scribes, able to read his grandfather, Amenhotep's, stories of war written on the walls of his Colonnade Hall. He had spent days and nights there deciphering, learning, and memorizing his grandfather's war strategies and diplomatic victories that were ostentatiously displayed throughout the unfinished structure. Because of his youth and inexperience, these were all things from which Tut expected to be tested.

His knowledge of war was a necessary resource when he attended the State of Affairs meetings with Horemheb, Ay, Kafrem, and Maya.

The morning following the hunt, Tut found his advisers battling each other over how the harvest surplus should be used.

"It's urgent that the army is supplied with new shields, battle-axes, bows, and sandals to replace the old, inferior ones immediately," demanded Horemheb.

"Only you say it's urgent," Maya argued. "This war has no urgent purpose and it should be delayed until our treasury can support it."

"You had no aversion to war when it suited Queen Nefertiti's desire for gold," Horemheb quipped.

"This is not Amarna," said Maya.

"War is necessary and not just an item on a list you can schedule whenever you see fit. We don't dictate the time of war. War dictates its time to us," replied Horemheb.

"Perhaps you, my Pharaoh, should settle the matter," Ay said.

Tut didn't hesitate to respond. He had thoroughly studied both points of view days before he would appear in their presence.

"The Hittites have to be stopped now before they turn their attention to our most valuable tributary—the kingdom of Nubia," he said. "Once we collect the tribute from them, our treasury will triple."

"Yes, my Pharaoh, but—" said Maya. Tut cut him off.

"Horemheb will receive all that he requests," Tut went on. "If I am to fight, myself, I want each of my soldiers equipped with the best of what's available. Would you not want the same for someone who fights alongside you, Maya?"

"Without question, my Pharaoh," replied Maya.

Tut knew his father would be disgusted at knowing his only son wanted to use his skill in chariot archery to become a warrior king. Nevertheless, he surprised them all with his intention to fight in the war. Tut not only intended to fight, he yearned for it. He believed his archery skills could benefit their army and was more than willing to overlook the wish of his father and learn in battle what he could from the great General Horemheb.

Before Egypt waged war against the Hittites for their encroachment upon their northern tributaries, the Nubian tribute would be collected. Tut traveled to the kingdom of Kush with Horemheb and his army to personally retrieve it. The Nubians needed to see him in the flesh, Tut reasoned, and become familiar with his face.

Upon their arrival they were greeted with a thunderous welcoming salute of three hundred drummers beating rhythmic patterns on their cowhide-skinned drums that sounded more adversarial to Tut than friendly. The Nubians cheered for them and brought before Tut many talents of gold, ivory, and precious jewels. The Nubian king himself vowed his allegiance to Egypt, and in turn, Tut vowed to protect them from the Hittites, by appointing an Egyptian governor to reside there in Kush with the Nubian people.

Once they made their exchanges, Tut and the Egyptian army left Kush with chariots filled with Nubian treasures.

"He kept smiling at me while his guards filled our chariots with their gold and ivory," Tut said to Horemheb. "Under what circumstances is it ever a joyful occasion for a king to give his treasures away? Either he doesn't take me seriously as the anointed pharaoh of Egypt, or he's conspiring to do something against us."

"I commend your intuition, my Pharaoh. However, I think both scenarios are true. He certainly does not take you seriously because of your youth, and he indeed is conspiring against us as his spurious demeanor easily gives him away. The Nubians are no different than the Hittites—both are untrustworthy dogs and deserving of each other," replied Horemheb.

Their journey home from the Nubian kingdom was long and treacherous. Dust-filled windstorms enveloped the desert, creating unbearable heat. Horemheb's army lost many of their horses to dehydration and their food supplies had dwindled to almost nothing by the time they reached the boundaries of Egypt. Only the camels appeared unscathed.

Senpaten was waiting for Tut in her chamber when he returned. He had an aching in his shoulders pulsating outward to his extremities.

She helped him to his favorite chair and rubbed his body down in an aloe ointment.

"Tut, you have a fever," she said after caressing his forehead.

"It's nothing," he replied.

"I know your plan is to lead the army into battle, but your illness will put your life at risk. I beg you to let Horemheb take the lead," said Senpaten.

"Just because I haven't taken part in a war doesn't mean I'm incapable of fighting in one. I am a skilled archer and master of the chariot."

"Tut, you're the bravest man I know and will make a great warrior king. But think of us. What will we do if you don't return? How will I tell our child? It will need its father."

Senpaten placed Tut's hand on her swelled belly. It was her eighth month of pregnancy. Tut worried for her, but refused to forsake the calling set by his grandfather, Amenhotep. The glorious scenes of combat drawn on the walls throughout the Colonnade Hall had evoked an irresistible urge in him to lead their army in the war against the Hittites.

Tut pulled out his father's amulet from under his garment. "The Aten will protect me from my enemies," he said, "I'm not afraid."

Horemheb admired Tut's passion for learning the ways of war and his keen determination to lead the fight for his country, but physically the young pharaoh's body was much too slight for combat, and his prowess, grander than what his small frame allowed. A Hittite soldier could easily toss him from his chariot and crush every bone in his frail body with one blow of the battle ax. The pharaoh's position in the front line would be a liability, not an asset to his army. Tut's strength was his skill as an archer, and the challenge to keep him alive during the combat would be an unnecessary burden on Horemheb's men.

Traveling east through the fortress of T'aru, Horemheb tried his hand at convincing Tut to abandon the fight, with no success. He pleaded with Tut to at least take the position in the rear of the platoon where he would be more protected. Tut's resolve could not be shaken. Horemheb had no choice but to support Tut's decision by granting him the respect a general gives his pharaoh in allowing him to lead the charge.

At the break of dawn, in the valley of Kadesh, Tut ordered a surprise attack on a remnant of the Hittite army as they were encamped at the base of Mount Hor. Tut led the charge in his war chariot adorned with the engraved copper symbol of the Montu god. Behind him loomed three thousand of his soldiers in battle formation carrying spears, battle-axes, and leather shields.

The Hittite army was no less well-equipped. Bronze conical helmets covered their heads with earflaps that extended down their backs to protect their necks. Their powerful bows shot bronze-tipped arrows, and the Hittite warriors carried bronze daggers, lances, spears, and curved swords. The function of their chariots proved to be more effective as well. Instead of a bowman at the helm, some had javelin throwers. Still, the overwhelming number of Egyptian horses and chariots were enough to rip through the Hittite camp, leaving most of them with no time to mount their horses for a counterattack.

Tut's fever raged, and though disoriented, he was successful at striking down a large number of Hittites with his articulated arrows. Horemheb demonstrated immeasurable agility as well, despite his age, and his skill with the spear and battle-ax proved to be devastating for the Hittites.

The battle was going well for Tut when the left wheel of his chariot loosened from its axle. The wheel broke apart piece-by-piece as two vengeful Hittites on horseback focused their rage on Tut and chased after him. In an attempt to escape the bombardment of the enemy's spears and arrows, Tut signaled his driver to accelerate their speed well past the mechanical ability of the chariot.

The driver made a sudden turn, and before the wheel completely disintegrated, he and Tut jumped from it. The driver landed on his side uninjured as the carriage broke away from the horse's bridle and flipped three times. Tut landed on his leg, shattering his tibia bone so violently that it broke through the skin. The sight and shock of it deadened the pain. His driver rushed over to him, tore off a strip of his garment, and wrapped and tied it over his wound. After Tut was helped into another chariot, twenty-four of his soldiers formed a circular barrier around it, protecting their pharaoh with their arrows, axes, and shields. Not one Hittite was able to penetrate their defense.

The Hittite army struggled against the Egyptians but in the end conceded defeat. Those who survived retreated to their homeland of Hatti. Those injured or dead on the battlefield were mutilated. Horemheb ordered their uncircumcised genitals and hands severed and brought back to Egypt as trophies of their conquest. Their most prized trophy from the war was the captured Hittite General Callum.

Tut longed to bask in Egypt's triumph with his general, but was still suffering in great pain as he lay in the healing temple days after the battle. He watched the physicians meticulously clean and disinfect his wound with copper and honey, and shrieked when they set the bone and secured it with splints on both sides. Tut was ashamed that he hadn't kept control over his reactions. A pharaoh's inclination should always be of long-suffering and strength. He wondered if the people thought of him as he did in that moment—a failure to the memory of his grandfather Amenhotep.

Sia appeared with his priest wand and waved it over Tut's leg. He then recited a healing spell to the god Amun that Tut had no confidence would work. When Sia completed the incantation, he left Tut alone with Senpaten. She cried when she took hold of his hand. He masked the pain so as not to make it worse for her.

"The Amun priests say that your ailment was judged and treated, and that you'll be healed," said Senpaten.

"Then why are you crying?" asked Tut.

"It hurts me to see you like this."

"My leg will heal. It's not what I'm concerned about."

"Tell me. What is it?" she asked.

"The Aten amulet is gone," he said. "It must have broken away from my neck when I jumped from the chariot."

Senpaten reached under his garment to feel his chest. Nothing was there.

"I fear without it I have no protection," said Tut.
"You have no enemies here in Thebes," she said. "There's nothing to fear."

CHAPTER

35

AT LONG LAST, Egypt's most grand structure, the Colonnade Hall, was completed. Amenhotep had begun construction forty years before and Tut, along with Horemheb, had been determined to see it finished. Amenhotep's legacy as the great builder of Egypt would live on.

In the healing temple, Ay prepared a special mixture of the cure made of goat's milk and latex from three poppy capsules for Tut to drink. He assured him it would numb the pain so he could walk with his splints in time for the festivities. The potion made him vomit, but as Ay promised, it soothed his pain. The citizens of Thebes expected to see their pharaoh at the Colonnade Hall celebration no matter how wounded or ill he might be.

With the help of a cane and the hand of his pregnant wife, Senpaten, Tut approached the podium in front of the large gathering of his subjects, still burning with fever.

"People of Thebes, we have gathered here at Egypt's most grand structure: The Colonnade Hall. This hall was envisioned and commissioned to be built by my grandfather, Amenhotep the Third, the great builder of Egypt, and now today after many years of construction, I stand before you to dedicate the completed structure in his honor. Many praises to Amun—the mighty and benevolent god that lives in our midst!"

Aware that he was being monitored by the twelve Amun priests, Tut continued his declaration, saying what he thought would appease their senses.

"I have immolated the bull and the ox, offerings to the gods Amun, Montu, Khonsu, and Osiris, my gods and your gods. You will witness the spilling of their blood on the pillar of the Amun temple when the sun disappears from the horizon, but first we must pay homage to the greatest general Egypt has ever known. Because of his bravery, we have defeated the Hittites once again," Tut said turning toward Horemheb. "General, come to me."

Horemheb strode up to the podium and bowed before Tut.

"The victory over the Hittites was borne of your skill and bravery, general," said Tut. "With this gold collar, I promote you, General Horemheb, to the highest post in Egypt. From this day forward, you will be the Overseer of All Works of the Pharaoh."

Ay stared suspiciously at the general before he handed Tut the collar that he would place around Horemheb's neck.

"I'm honored to serve you, my Pharaoh," Horemheb replied, "and proud to present the Hittite General who goes by the name of Callum, for you and the peoples' amusement," the general said before turning to his guards. "Bring him forward!" he shouted.

There were hushed gasps as a stocky man with a groomed beard, dressed in a decorated tunic and the distinctive curled up shoes of the Hittites was shoved forward with his hands and ankles shackled. The people had never seen a Hittite general before, at least not one alive with his hands and genitals still attached. As General Callum was led across the hall in chains, the crowd whipped into a frenzy of jeering and shouting. From the pompous smirk on his face, the captive Hittite general looked amused at being paraded around, and he sneered back at the Egyptian people.

General Callum was a temporary trophy for Horemheb, but not the one he wanted most of all. Horemheb's greatest desire was to capture King Suppiluliumas himself. In truth, any prince of Hatti or anyone of Hittite royalty would do. With such a prize, he would keep the vow he made to Amenhotep, to avenge the murder of Lady Lupita. The Hittite general was mere entertainment Horemheb could bestow upon the Egyptian people until he fulfilled that promise. After the spectacle was over, he would allow the Hittite general to return to his country, knowing the shame he would no doubt endure from being captured.

As General Callum weathered the Egyptians' insults, Senpaten caught his eye, and he smiled at her, amused by her curiosity.

"Where is the prisoner from?" Senpaten whispered in Tut's ear.

"He's from a land called Hatti, ruled by a duplicitous king named Suppiluliumas," said Tut. Grandfather Amenhotep signed a peace treaty with them many years ago, yet they still attack our tributaries. Why do you ask?"

"I was only curious. Do I dare say there's something kind about his eyes?"

"There's nothing kind about him or his king," Tut corrected. "The heathens once murdered an Egyptian queen by the order of their King Suppiluliumas."

"How do you know?"

"The story was written in hieroglyphics on the Colonnade Hall."

"Are all stories inscribed on the Colonnade wall true?"

"Why would the scribes write a lie that would be read from a wall throughout eternity, Senpaten?" Tut snapped. "Besides, Horemheb told me it was he himself who retrieved her body—"

A searing pain shot from Tut's leg and spread up into his chest. The numbing effect of the cure had faded. The pain was so intense that the pharaoh doubled over, placing all of his weight onto his cane. It cracked before breaking in half, and Ay and Senpaten had to help him into the royal chariot where he was taken back to the healing temple of Amun.

Before Sia and the physicians appeared at the temple to treat Tut's illness, Senpaten and Mayati went to him first in private.

"Why won't you take more of the cure from Ay so you won't have to bear the pain?" asked Mayati.

"It makes me vomit. The cure can't remove an evil spirit that someone has conjured up," said Tut.

"Then Senpaten and I will pray to the Aten in secret for your protection."

"The amulet was my protection, as it was to Father and his brother. Do you think the Aten has abandoned me?" Tut asked, revealing his deepest fear of all.

"Don't ask such things," replied Senpaten. "You are a strong and wise king. You have survived what would have been a fatal accident for a mere mortal. I know the Aten will continue to protect you even without the amulet."

Senpaten was interrupted by the arrival of Sia and his entourage of physicians: one to treat Tut's bruises, one to treat his fever, and another to treat his pain. Senpaten and Mayati moved aside as the bruise physician unwrapped the bandages from Tut's leg and removed both splints.

Sia was curiously fixated on his leg. When Tut tried to sit up in bed to see it for himself, Sia forced him back down to a lying position. "Don't look at it," he warned.

"Why? Tell me." said Tut. "Is the wound not healing?"

"The wound has spread, my Pharaoh; gangrene has set in. We'll have to amputate the leg or the infection will spread and kill you."

Senpaten and Mayati both froze in fear.

Tut couldn't digest what Sia had just said to him. It was devastating, and the last thing he wanted Senpaten to hear. She was nearing her moment to give birth, and he was concerned about his inability to console her like a husband should at such a crucial time. Senpaten had experienced premature birthing pangs, and Tut worried about her and the health of their unborn child. Sia's diagnosis would only cause her more despair.

"You're mistaken. Bring me another physician!" Tut yelled. Another jolt of pain shot up his leg, and the pharaoh arched his back and screamed.

Senpaten cried and Mayati took her in her arms.

"It's not a mistake, my Pharaoh," Sia repeated. "The amputation must be performed before the infection spreads."

Senpaten rushed over to him and held his hand. Tut looked her in the eye. "I won't let them sever me," he murmured with defiance. "What sort of pharaoh has only one leg? I would be an embarrassment to Egypt, a symbol of weakness to all the other kingdoms."

"Tut, please. I don't care what other kingdoms think. Let them remove it before it's too late. If the leg is infected, it'll spread the poison to your heart if you don't stop it," said Senpaten.

Senpaten siding with the Amun priest made Tut's temper boil. He wanted them all to go away.

"Leave me!" he shouted.

Sia and the physicians gathered their utensils and left his chamber as ordered. Senpaten and Mayati remained standing next to him in tears.

"If I had been born with just one leg from the beginning," said Tut, "then I would have been divine like our father, perfect in his deformity from birth. An amputation is not godly, but a constant reminder of my incompetence.

Tut couldn't bear his sisters' sad faces anymore. Shame overwhelmed him.

"All of you! Leave me now!" Tut demanded.

Clutching each other's hands, Senpaten and Mayati rushed out of the healing temple leaving Tut alone in his desperation.

When Horemheb and Mundi attempted to visit him, he turned them away in the same manner, shouting that they leave his presence. The two were the closest thing to parents he had left, and the thought of them seeing him in such a vulnerable state made him feel like a failure, ashamed of being a son they couldn't be proud of.

Alone and in solitude, Tut closed his eyes and said a prayer to the god of his father and mother, the only god he knew—the Aten.

> *My god, the Aten, the sun-disk, you are the one and only god of Egypt and of the world. As my father, Akenaten, was your son, I, Tutankhaten, am also your son and the one that brings you glory. I come to you without the amulet of Aten, hoping that you will forgive me for losing it. There is only one that can save me and that is you, the Aten. Please strike from me the evil spirit that is infecting my leg. I desire your power to shine down upon me and my wife, Senpaten, and our child. My father—the Aten, I ask you to remove this evil disease from my leg and bless your son and his family with good health.*

Tut repeated his prayer seven times, knowing that such words spoken inside the Amun temple had little chance of reaching the ears of the Aten. Nevertheless, he envisioned his divine prayer being carried away on the wings of a crowned falcon, out from the dark blasphemous Amun temple and beyond to the bright shores of Amarna, the place where his father first saw the sun rise between the two mountains, the home where, with his sisters and parents, he once lived the joys of his childhood.

As soon as Senpaten and Mayati returned to the palace, Senpaten's birth pangs became so severe she lost consciousness and had to be revived with pungent incense. When she stood up, liquid from her womb burst and spilled out on the floor. The child was coming a month early. Mundi went to the palace to help Senpaten onto the birthing stool, but after two days in labor, the child still remained trapped in the womb. Mundi assumed that an evil spirit blocked the child's exit way, most likely a messenger of the god Sekhmet, and it would have to be removed with magic before the child's path could be cleared.

The Sacred Women of Bes were summoned to the palace. Despite their reputation of promiscuity, the voluptuous women were also known as spiritual fertility healers throughout the city because of their powerful magic rituals in child birthing. They were rushed into Senpaten's chamber dressed in their traditional blue-beaded fishnet dresses with their tattooed breasts exposed and their lips painted bright red. All four of them carried a sistrum in their hand: a musical instrument formed like a stick. The frame had small metal disks attached that shook and rattled as they circled Senpaten.

The queen breathed heavily, bearing down as hard as she could to help push the child free from her womb. One of the sacred women placed an amulet over Senpaten's neck to secure divine protection of her unborn child. The women danced around her in a circle, shaking their sistrums at her belly and repeating an incantation:

> *We will fill her womb with male and female children. We will save her from miscarrying and from giving birth to twins. Bear down, Senpaten! Bear down!*

Senpaten screamed from the labor pain as she tried to follow the women's order to bear down. Mayati held her hand as Mundi wiped the sweat from her brow. One of the women handed Mundi an ivory wand and instructed her to touch Senpaten's belly with it. While she touched her with the wand, the women repeated another incantation:

> *Come down, placenta, come down. I am Horus who conjures in order that she who is giving birth becomes stronger than she was before she delivered. Look, Hathor will lay her hand on her with an amulet of health. I am Horus who saves her and the child!*

After the fourth repetition, the child's head appeared. Exhausted, Senpaten pushed one last time as hard as her body allowed, and the newborn girl slipped out from her womb into Mundi's arms without a scream nor a cry.

Ramose, the pharaoh's butler, rushed to the entrance of the healing temple anxious and distressed. Ay cornered him before he entered.

"If you're here to see pharaoh Tut, I can tell you he's not in any condition to speak to you," said Ay.

"I'm aware the pharaoh is ill, but it's imperative he hears what I have to report to him," replied Ramose.

"And what is that?" asked Ay.

Ramose paused.

Ay found it insulting that the pharaoh's butler was reticent.

"I am the pharaoh's manservant and confidant, Ramose, a position more significant than yours as a butler. If there's anything of urgency, he would prefer you make me aware of it so I can prepare him. What is it?" Ay asked again.

Ramose handed him Tut's Aten amulet.

"I believe this belongs to the pharaoh. As it is a symbol of the Aten, I trust you will keep it secret from the Amun priests until you can return it to him," said Ramose.

"Certainly," said Ay as he placed the amulet away in his garment.

"Also," Ramose said leaning in and speaking more quietly, "I have evidence of someone replacing the pharaoh's chariot bolts with inferior ones. It would seem to be the cause of his accident. Inform him he should be very cautious of his surroundings until I find the one responsible," said Ramose.

Ay nodded and Ramose mounted his horse and sped away.

There existed a conspirator in the pharaoh's royal court. If anyone was keen enough to discover his identity, it would be Ay, but he had no intention of informing Tut of Ramose's warning nor returning his Aten amulet.

When he arrived at Tut's bedside that evening, his condition was critical. Gangrene had spread from his wounded leg up to his hip and he couldn't move the lower extremities of his body.

"My pharaoh, please let the physicians remove the infected leg so that your life will be spared," said Ay.

The fever clouded Tut's vision, yet he recognized the sound of Ay's voice.

"What kind of life would that be, Ay? It will never be written that I, Tutankhamun, a pharaoh of Egypt, became a one-legged pharaoh. I could never bring such shame against my father. You of all people should know that about me."

"It's true. I have watched you grow from a timid boy to a courageous king, my Pharaoh. Then at least allow me to give you the cure so that it will ease your pain."

"With the cure I feel no pain, but what's worse is that I feel nothing at all," Tut replied. "I need to *feel* something. Where is my Senpaten? Why hasn't she or even Mayati come to me?"

When Ay hesitated to answer, Tut knew he was withholding information. "Ay tell me! Where is Senpaten?"

"Queen Senpaten is very ill from childbirth. The physicians are trying to heal her. Mayati is there by her side," said Ay.

"My child is born? Where are they? Why did you not tell me this before so I could be there for her?"

"My pharaoh, you're incapable of standing on your feet. I didn't want to sicken you more."

"I have to go to them now," Tut replied. He tried to sit up in bed. The slight movement wracked his body with pain, and the pharaoh shrieked from the torment.

Ay helped Tut recline back into a lying position. "You must rest, my Pharaoh," said Ay. "The physicians are with Senpaten. Let them heal her."

"Promise me, Ay, that you'll care for my Senpaten. Tell her I'll come to her soon."

"She is my granddaughter, and I love her as much as you do. Of course I'll take care of her."

"What about our child? Is it a girl or a boy?"

"A girl." He paused for effect. "I'm sorry, my Pharaoh, the infant was stillborn," said Ay.

His words stunned Tut into silence. His child was dead. *Why? She did nothing wrong. Even if the Amun god had heard his prayer to the Aten, the child was innocent. What god could she have offended?*

"I want to see her. Bring me my daughter," Tut commanded.

"The infant is dead. It would be unclean to bring her here, my Pharaoh."

"I don't care if it's unclean. I want to hold her. Please, bring her to me, Ay."

At risk of being caught and exposed by the Amun priests, Ay retrieved the body of Tut's daughter from the embalming tent and brought her to him. Tut rocked her in his arms as if she was sleeping. Her face was beautiful like her mother's, a shade of shiny copper without a single blemish. Tut kissed her tiny forehead and sang a lullaby to her as his father had often done for him. It was agonizing to return his baby daughter to Ay. The pain of knowing she would never open her eyes and see how much her father loved her was a thousand times worse than the gangrene that was devouring his body.

The moment Ay left his bedside, Tut wept for Senpaten. If he could just see her face one last time it would bring him so much joy. To touch her perfumed skin and feel her embrace might offer him contentment in this last hour of his life.

When Ay and the physicians returned days later to forcibly amputate Tut's leg, it was too late. The muscle tissue had decomposed to a state of putrefaction and the odor from it overwhelmed the chamber. The infection had entered Tut's bloodstream and spread throughout his internal organs. In his desperation, Tut offered one final prayer to the Aten that the sun god show mercy for his dear Senpaten and keep her safe. It would be his last thought as a living mortal.

News of Tut's death had not yet reached General Horemheb because of his prolonged journey to Amarna. It had taken years before he had the resources to return to the land of the Aten with his guards and destroy what was left of the blasphemous city. Horemheb stared indifferently at the sight of the colossal statues of Akenaten and Nefertiti tumbling to the ground in the darkness of the night, and his eyes glowed in the flame as his men set about torching every building and monument until the entire city, with its thousands of homes and farms, was set ablaze.

CHAPTER

36

TUTANKHATEN, the only son of the pharaoh and Queen Nefertiti, husband and brother to Senpaten, the love of her existence, was dead. What made the pain unbearable was that he had died alone, without her there by his side to kiss his lips and hold his hand. She hadn't been able to tell him how much she truly loved him, nor comfort him before he embarked on his journey.

The times they had spent together sailing the river and sharing their most intimate thoughts and fears she would never forget. It was only a small part of how he had made her life meaningful and worth living. His untimely death pained her more than the stillborn birth of her child just days earlier. *Why should I remain alive? What sort of life is left for me?* She wondered.

Her heart fractured and bled for her husband and child. She wept alone, without her best friend and protector, defenseless and vulnerable to those in Thebes who secretly despised her because of her father's worship of the Aten god. Senpaten was now the queen of Egypt, and dubious about her unknown future. The memory of her mother's courage gave her the strength and inspiration she needed to continue.

Of the immediate royal bloodline, only two were left, she and her sister Mayati. Senpaten took refuge in her sister and sought her help as she entombed Tut and their infant daughter for their journey into the afterlife. After seventy-two days and nights, the bodies were mummified and prepared for The Opening of the Mouth ceremony.

As Tut's only male relative, Ay led the funerary procession. Eight pallbearers were chosen from the best warriors of Horemheb's army and they carried Tut's sarcophagus deep into the Valley of the Kings. His tomb had been hastily prepared because of his untimely death, and as a result it was much smaller than the other royal tombs that were built for pharaohs.

They carried his body through the stone-carved entrance and descended a stairway made of limestone. The inside walls were plastered, and a picture of a jackal with nine slaves that represented Tut's royalty was embedded into it. Farther into the tomb, an antechamber was stocked with hundreds of objects: baskets, chests, stools, beds, statues, and three animal head couches made of wood and gilded in gold that would follow Tut into the afterlife.

The treasury room contained fourteen boats as well. The boats were intended to float Tut through the twelve hours of night and darkness before the sun would rise again. These were all the necessary items the pharaoh would need in his daily existence.

The funerary procession came to a standstill at the burial chamber. Two life-sized statues of Tutankhamun stood guard at the entrance. The statues were black and positioned facing each other. They were dressed in golden head caps, sandals and kilts. The walls inside the burial chamber were colored a vibrant yellow and painted with a colorful mural depicting scenes of Tut with the gods Osiris, Isis, Anubis and Hathor, and ending with the scene of Ay performing the Opening of the Mouth ceremony on him. Dressed in the garment of an Amun priest, Ay raised a wand over Tut's mummified body and touched his mouth with it while reciting the words, *"You are young again, you live again, you live again forever."*

Tut's mummy was then placed in three staggered coffins nested inside one another with the innermost coffin made of solid gold. Tut's golden death mask depicted the young pharaoh wearing the striped nemes headdress and a false beard that connected him to the image of the Amun god, not the Aten, the god of his father that he truly revered. It rested directly on the shoulders of Tut's mummy inside the innermost coffin.

Lying next to Tut's coffin sat a miniature one containing the mummy of his stillborn daughter. After the lids to both coffins were closed and sealed, Senpaten placed a wreath and a lotus flower on both. Her grief suddenly overwhelmed her, and she collapsed to the ground. Mayati grabbed her by the arm and helped her back to her feet.

"Senpaten, you have to be strong like our mother," Mayati whispered in her ear.

It was the bit of encouragement Senpaten needed.

She regained her composure and placed Tut's favorite bow in the tomb with a hundred arrows so he could hunt and practice as much as he wanted. He would need his walking canes too, so she placed those inside as well, along with the throne he had used when he was just thirteen years old. Senpaten had every possession that Tut cherished put into the tomb for his enjoyment in the afterlife. Ay filled the remaining space with hundreds of objects of gold and valuable jewelry, things that were never important to her husband.

Tables were set up outside the entrance of the tomb covered with platters of geese, breads, fish, goat, and wine: a ritual last meal for royalty and palace officials. After they consumed the feast, the servants broke the dishes with mallets and placed the fragments along with scraps of food into storage jars that were then carried inside the tomb. After Horemheb followed with Tut's disassembled chariot and his cheetah-skin shield, everyone departed and Tut's tomb was officially sealed.

Senpaten returned to her palace bedchamber in deep mourning.

Before she could even have a day alone, Ay appeared at her door.

"I saw you speaking with Ramose during Tut's funerary rites," he said. "What has he told you that has caused you such anguish?"

Senpaten sat up from her bed alarmed at Ay's sudden intrusion.

"The anguish I suffer is because I mourn the death of my husband and child. I would prefer the next time you enter my chamber you announce yourself first by one of my maidservants."

"Why should I have to be announced at my own granddaughter's chambers? What has changed in you?" asked Ay.

Senpaten got up from the bed and handed Ay what Ramose had given to her at the funeral—Tut's broken chariot bolt.

"Why didn't you tell me that Ramose suspected sabotage? He says Tut's chariot was tampered with by someone in his royal court."

Outraged, Ay hurled the bolt across the room. Senpaten cringed as it clanged against the wall and fell to the floor.

"Because it's nonsense! Countless chariots are damaged in war. Of what significance is a broken chariot bolt?" Ay replied.

Senpaten looked terrified of him. So, Ay shifted to a softer tone when he approached her. "I kept silent about it," he said, "because I was thinking of your health and how I could help you overcome your mourning for Tut."

As he spoke, Ay caressed Senpaten's face with his hands. His fingers across her skin felt like the legs of a spider crawling on her.

All of a sudden, he lowered his head as if to kiss her. The move startled her, and she backed away from him before his lips made contact.

"Get out of my chamber or I'll have my royal guards arrest you!" said Senpaten.

Ay remained standing, ignoring her command for a moment before finally leaving her alone in her chamber.

Once she was certain he was gone, Senpaten went to her ablution tank and washed her face, arms and hands. Ay's attempt at intimacy sickened and repulsed her. Her next inclination was to call on her sister to tell her of the encounter, and when she went to the door to leave, she found Ay standing behind it. She gasped. There was an awfully frightening glint in his eye as he walked Senpaten slowly back into her chamber.

"Seventy-two days is more than enough time to mourn anyone," Ay said to her, grimacing.

Fearful as she was, Senpaten found her courage. "How dare you. Leave my chamber," she commanded.

"Listen closely, Senpaten. Today the mourning for Tut will end, and you and I will marry. I will become your husband and the pharaoh of Egypt. Royalty must remain in the bloodline; it's the right thing to do," said Ay cowing her with his stern and unrelenting gaze.

She had been right to fear her grandfather all those years. It was a premonition of what he had been planning all along. A chill went through Senpaten as she recalled the day she had told her mother about her fear of her grandfather, and how when she awoke the next morning, Nefertiti had been found dead. Ay was poison, and she would have to do everything in her power to get away from him.

"I will never marry a servant of mine," said Senpaten, returning his stare as best she could.

"I am not your servant. I'm the father of your mother. Either you'll marry me and continue our bloodline, or the Amun priests will strip you of your right to be queen and have you judged and punished for your secret allegiance to the Aten."

To show he had proof, Ay produced Tut's Aten amulet.

Senpaten's eyes widened in disbelief. "What are you doing with his amulet? How did you get it?"

"Either you marry me or I'll expose you with this to the Amun priests. The choice is yours, Senpaten." said Ay.

"You are a servant. You're not worthy of the throne of Egypt," she replied.

"Worthy? You are the one with no true knowledge of what you're speaking! For three generations I have remained silent as the pharaohs of Egypt ruled successfully because of the actions I took on their behalf. From Pharaoh Amenhotep down to your precious Tut. They all relied on my direction and advice because they were too weak and incompetent to rule on their own. Because of my divine wisdom, Egypt has flourished for over forty years. The one not worthy to lead Egypt was your Tut—a helpless boy."

Ay had finally betrayed the contempt he harbored for Tut. He had kept secrets, many secrets from everyone his entire life, patiently waiting years for the right moment to take what was due him. Senpaten was saddened as much as she was shocked at her grandfather's poisonous secret disdain for her brother and husband. But, as Mayati had reminded her, if she wanted to survive, she needed to be strong and to contain her emotions like her mother.

Senpaten yearned for Ay to continue his confession, so she could hear what she had always suspected but could never prove.

"Since you're now confessing the truth of what was in your heart, Grandfather, tell me: What did you do to my mother?"

"Who has whispered such absurdities in your ear? It's well known my daughter died from the disease."

"The disease leaves bruises on the body. There were none on hers. She's dead for no proven reason and my husband's chariot sabotaged. My heart tells me you're aware of what happened to them."

"Your heart is treacherous. I didn't sabotage Tut's chariot. His death was the will of Amun. The Amun god has ordained me to be pharaoh of Egypt and I will take my rightful place on the throne. As for my daughter's death, I warn you again, if you want to remain queen of Egypt, you will consent to our marriage and stop repeating absurd rumors."

After Ay left her room, Senpaten rushed to her sister's chamber, desperate for help and advice. When she reached Mayati she collapsed in her sister's arms crying.

"Help me. I feel as if I'm alone. You have to help me, please," she begged her.

Senpaten's sudden distress frightened Mayati. She helped her to a chair and gave her a jar of water to drink.

"You're not alone, my sister," Mayati replied. "Tell me what happened."

Senpaten told her of Ay's visit, his despicable demands and his threats. She sobbed as everything poured out of her.

"I don't want to marry my grandfather. He's old and frightening," Senpaten cried out.

"You don't have to marry him," consoled Mayati. "There has to be another way."

"What other way? Allow him to remove me as queen and banish me from Egypt?"

Mayati paused. "What if somehow he was poisoned?"

Senpaten looked in Mayati's eyes, stunned.

"No, Mayati. He's still the father of our mother, and if we're involved in his demise his mut spirit could return to curse us."

"Not if our hands are clean of it. We could have a servant—

Senpaten cut her off. "Stop speaking about devious things. It is the dark way of the Amun god. Our parents were of the Aten, the god of the light."

Mayati accepted what her sister told her and paused again to think. "Then if you don't mind the *idea* of a marriage, there could be another way," said Mayati.

Senpaten shook her head. "There aren't any other ways."

"Senpaten, you're the queen, and just as Tut chose you, you can choose your husband."

"A husband chooses his queen. The Amun priests will deny a queen to choose her husband."

"They cannot deny nor challenge your right to choose if you took a husband from another land; a king or a prince," said Mayati.

"Only male pharaohs marry foreigners. Never has an Egyptian queen done such a thing. I would be making a foreigner the king of Egypt."

"Yes, it's true, it has never happened," replied Mayati. "But not because it's unlawful. It's only because an Egyptian queen has never lost her husband in death without an heir to replace him."

Intrigued, Senpaten took her sister's hand and looked her straight in the eye. "How do you know this?"

"I heard it from Aunt Mundi," Mayati replied. "Her stepbrother is a royal scribe and talks to her often of Egypt's laws in marriage. You have every right as queen of Egypt to marry a foreign king or prince as long as he is willing to come and reside here with you in our land. It is written law by the Oracle himself."

Senpaten was suddenly hopeful. She knew of only one land that had a powerful enough king with sons. Tut had warned her about them when their general was captured and brought back to Egypt. It was the Hittite General Callum with the 'kind eyes.'

"What about the Hittites?" asked Senpaten. "I've heard Tut speak of King Suppiluliumas and his sons—*the three princes of Hatti*, many times. Perhaps I can send a message to him asking for one in marriage."

"The Hittites? They're an enemy of Egypt," replied Mayati.

"At times they were our ally. Tut told me that Egypt once had a peace treaty with King Suppiluliumas."

"Are you sure?" asked Mayati.

Senpaten stroked Mayati's hair as she contemplated their plan. "I am, but though it might be part of the law, there's a chance if we're caught, we'll be charged with treason. Are you still willing to help me?"

Mayati nodded her head in agreement, and with the assistance of a scribe, they hastily etched a letter into a clay tablet and sent it to

King Suppiluliumas by Egypt's most discreet and courageous messenger: Hani.

Unbeknownst to Senpaten, her future and the future of Egypt was already being discussed in the Colonnade Hall, at the meeting of the royal court. Ay, General Horemheb, Kafrem, Sia, and seven of his Amun priests were deliberating on who would be the one to replace Queen Senpaten as pharaoh of Egypt.

"She is too young and weak to rule Upper and Lower Egypt," said one of the Amun priests. "There needs to be a king chosen from among us. Our lector priest, Sia, is the wisest choice."

"Sia has no royal blood," Horemheb countered.

"Neither do you, general. Your convenient marriage to Nefertiti's sister does not completely qualify you as royalty. I, however, have the support of every Amun priest, and the respect of the Egyptian citizens as a sound leader," replied Sia.

"Indeed I have no royalty in my blood," said Horemheb, "but there is no Egypt without the mighty Egyptian army."

Horemheb's response silenced the Amun priests. Kafrem turned to Ay for his opinion.

"You were a friend to all pharaohs, Ay. What is your recommendation on how to settle this?" asked Kafrem.

Ay's plan was falling apart. He needed more time to fix it.

"It is written not to rush an important decision, but to give it seventy-five days to ponder," said Ay. "We'll return here after that time period and make the decision."

CHAPTER

37

THREE WEEKS into his journey, Senpaten's messenger, Hani, set foot on Hittite land. He was greeted instantly by a show of swords and drawn bows from one of King Suppiluliumas's regiments who then shackled him and brought him to the king's son, Prince Zenanza, near the outskirts of their capital city of Hattusas. At twenty-three years of age, the Hittite prince had grown into an ambitious young man, eager to prove to his father that he could be as emphatic and imperious as his three older brothers, Prince Telipinus, Prince Mursili II, and Prince Piyassilis.

Zenanza approached the Egyptian messenger intent on torturing him into submission.

"Before we cut you open, I'll give you a chance to tell me why you came to our country. Were you sent as a spy for your pharaoh?" asked Zenanza.

"Our pharaoh is dead. I came to deliver a letter to King Suppiluliumas from our queen, Senpaten. The clay tablet is in the sack your guard seized from me," said Hani.

The guard handed Hani's sack to Zenanza. He opened it and retrieved the tablet inscribed with Senpaten's letter to King Suppiluliumas. Zenanza was inclined to brush it aside as a hoax until he saw the familiar seal of Egyptian royalty at the bottom.

"You say your pharaoh is dead? Then why have we not heard of it?" asked Zenanza.

"The pharaoh died only recently and unexpectedly. It's urgent that your father read what the queen has to say. Please, my lord."

There was true sincerity in Hani's plea and Zenanza ordered the guards to release him from his shackles. The prince personally escorted the messenger into the Hatti palace and after finding Berbalis—King Suppiluliumas's personal steward and chamberlain, they walked directly to his father's chamber.

Inside, King Suppiluliumas was speaking privately with his wife, Tawanna. He was silenced at the sight of his son and the visitor.

"Who is this foreigner that you bring to my chamber unshackled?" asked Suppiluliumas, irritated by the interruption.

"Father, this is Hani, the messenger of Queen Senpaten of Egypt. He has brought with him a letter she has written to you. Berbalis can decipher it if you're willing to hear it," said Zenanza.

"And how do you know this man is not a liar and his letter a hoax?"

Berbalis stepped forward. "Because I have confirmed the authenticity of the letter myself, my lord," he replied.

"Examine the seal, Father," added Zenanza. "You'll see it's of genuine Egyptian royalty."

Despite his hard expression, Suppiluliumas was impressed by his son's assertiveness. He took the tablet and examined the seal closely.

"It does appear to be of Egyptian royalty," said Suppiluliumas, handing it back to Berbalis. "Go ahead, read it to me."

The chamberlain deciphered Senpaten's entire letter silently to himself before he repeated it out loud to the king:

[5] *My husband has died, and I have no son. Never will I take a servant of mine and make him my husband! I have written to no other kingdom. Only to you have I written. They say your sons are many, so I ask for you to give me one son of yours. To me he will be my husband, but in Egypt he will be king. Please send him quickly, I am afraid!*

"The letter is signed and sealed by Senpaten, queen of Egypt, my lord," said Berbalis.

"I have seen nothing like this in my entire life," replied Suppiluliumas, scratching his head. "It's certainly a trick to hold a Hittite prince hostage in Egypt when in fact there is an heir for your pharaoh," he said glaring at the Egyptian messenger, Hani. "You Egyptians think we're mindless brutes, don't you?"

"My lord, if the queen had a son from the pharaoh, would I have risked coming here to Hatti? Our pharaoh, Tut, has died unexpectedly without an heir. This is our country's shame, but our queen needs a husband and Egypt a king."

Suppiluliumas laughed. "Even if I believed such nonsense, I would never allow a son of mine to take such a foolish risk."

Moved by the urgency and innocence of Senpaten's letter, Zenanza stepped forward.

"I want to go, Father. Let me travel to Egypt to marry the queen."

Tawanna sprang up from her seat. "No!" she shouted. "They'll kill you!"

"Mother, I'm not a child, nor am I afraid. Berbalis has confirmed the letter's authenticity. The Egyptian queen is frightened and needs a husband. Who is more qualified to travel there than me? I am a prince and I'm unmarried."

---

[5] Ankh-Senpaten Letter translation: Journal of Cuneiform Studies Vol. 10 No.3 (1956) Frgm. 28 contains: The Deeds of Suppiluliuma as Told by His Son, Mursili II. Hans Gustav Guterböck.

"It's true, my lady. Queen Senpaten is as young in age as Prince Zenanza. They would appear to be compatible," said Hani.

"No," said Suppiluliumas. "It's surely a trap."

"It's not a trap. It's the truth my lord. I'm happy with my life, I would not risk it for a hoax," Hani countered.

Prince Mursili, who so far had remained silent, scoffed at Hani's justification. "Father, even if Zenanza was allowed to marry the Egyptian queen, my brother is unproven and much too young to lead such a magnanimous country as Egypt."

"You, Mursili, were not much older when you were appointed king and sent away to a distant land to rule. You know nothing about my capabilities," said Zenanza.

Tawanna shed her pride and kneeled in front of her husband, hoping it would garner his compassion.

"You have many sons from your mistresses, my blessed husband, but Zenanza is my only son. Please, don't allow him to risk his life for the Egyptians. They can't be trusted," she pleaded.

King Suppiluliumas gazed into his wife's eyes. The despair of her plea made it a grueling decision that Zenanza perceived was working in his mother's favor.

"Father, you have appointed my brothers Telipinus king of Halab and Piyassilis king of Carchemish and no harm has ever come to them. Mother is overreacting. Please, let me travel to Egypt and marry the Egyptian queen so that I will be a king in my own kingdom of Egypt," said Zenanza. "Allow me to have the equal respect that you give my brothers. I deserve no less."

Before King Suppiluliumas could answer his son, Hani offered his own final plea to the king.

"My lord, remember how your Storm-god endorsed a peace treaty between your country and our country of Egypt. This could be a new chance at everlasting peace between Hatti and Egypt with your son Zenanza as our pharaoh," said Hani.

The thought of his son ruling the Egyptian empire was too tempting for King Suppiluliumas to ignore. To his wife's dismay he gave in to his own ambitions.

"As the Storm-god endorsed the treaty between our countries, we will continue to be friendly with Egypt," replied Suppiluliumas. "You have my blessing, Zenanza. Go and marry the Egyptian queen."

Tears swelling in her eyes, Tawanna rose to her feet and stormed out of the room. King Suppiluliumas turned away from his momentary concern for her and embraced his son. "I'll have the best of my army shadow your convoy," he said.

"No, Father," replied Zenanza. "If the Egyptians see an obvious army of Hittites, they'll assume it's for war. I'll travel only with my convoy so they'll know I have come to them in peace."

Zenanza's confidence impressed King Suppiluliumas. It made it easier for him to ignore his paternal instincts to protect his son.

"As you wish, but my chamberlain Berbalis will accompany you on your journey," replied Suppiluliumas.

"May the next words you hear from me Father, be that the queen has accepted me as her husband and that I am the new king of Egypt."

Zenanza left his father's chamber and hurried to prepare a convoy for his journey while Hani was given food supplies and sent out ahead of the prince to alert Queen Senpaten.

CHAPTER

38

SENPATEN AND MAYATI spent most of their days playing Senet while they waited for Hani to return with a response from the Hittite king or possibly a husband for Senpaten. Thirty-eight days and nights had passed and she still had no word from King Suppiluliumas on whether he would allow one of his sons to journey to Egypt in order to marry her.

"Do you think a Hittite prince will really come? Or does a widowed queen bring shame to everyone she encounters?" asked Senpaten.

"My sister, you are an Egyptian queen and as beautiful as a lotus blossom," replied Mayati. "A prince from any kingdom would be enamored by you."

"Then why hasn't he come?"

"Be patient. He's traveling from a faraway land and it's possible their horses are not as fast and capable as the ones born and bred here in Egypt."

Mayati's speculation gave Senpaten a reason to be optimistic, and she smiled lovingly at her sister for being a source of light in her time of despair.

"The Aten will give you the husband you desire," said Mayati. "Don't worry, sleep now and I'll return at dawn to finish our game."

When Mayati stepped out of Senpaten's chamber, someone reached out and grabbed her by the arm. Her heart beat rapidly at the sight of her grandfather, Ay. She tried to pull away, but his grip was unrelenting as he yanked her out further into the palace corridor.

"What prince is coming?" he asked. "And what faraway land is he traveling from?"

Mayati was terrified. Ay must have secretly hid behind the entrance of Senpaten's chamber and eavesdropped on their conversation. He frightened Mayati speechless.

"Either you'll tell me what prince is coming to marry her, or I'll report Senpaten to the Amun priests as a follower of the Aten god and one who is treasonous of her country. She'll most certainly be banished from Egypt, if not executed," said Ay.

There was no way out. Mayati told her grandfather everything she knew.

Ay released her arm and left the palace for Horemheb's quarters.

The general would be appalled at the possibility of a Hittite claiming the right to rule Egypt and Ay was meticulous in choosing the words that would manipulate him into doing his bidding.

"Will you allow this Hittite prince to come upon Egyptian soil to marry our queen and take your place as the next pharaoh? Or will you cut him off at our border before he enters and becomes king himself?" Ay asked Horemheb.

Ay waited for Horemheb's response and was delighted to see the general burning with fury at the mention of a Hittite coming to Egypt to marry the queen. "There will never be a Hittite king of Egypt!" shouted Horemheb. "Never!"

After leaving Horemheb, Ay made it his priority to return to Senpaten's chamber to scold her. When he entered, again unannounced, he found her fastening her hair with jewels and rubbing herself down with sweet perfumes.

"Are you preparing yourself for me?" asked Ay.

Without turning to face him, she answered, "I'm not preparing for anyone. Is there any time of day or night that I can have privacy in my own chamber?"

"I'll grant you your privacy, but it ends when we unite in marriage at the end of ten days."

"I would rather relinquish my right to rule as queen than marry you."

"This arrogance is unbecoming of you, granddaughter. I suppose you think such behavior will be attractive to your Hittite prince," said Ay.

Senpaten stopped rubbing her skin, stood up, and faced Ay. It brought him immense satisfaction to see the dread in her eyes.

"Either you'll agree to marry me," said Ay, "or I'll expose your sister, Mayati, for her involvement in your scheme to deliver Egypt into the hands of our enemy, the Hittites. And you can be assured her banishment to a foreign land will be immediate and you will never see her again."

Senpaten trembled with fear as Ay turned to leave but stopped once more at the door of her chamber.

"And, as for your Hittite prince, General Horemheb is on his way to meet him. He'll be dead before he reaches our border."

Prince Zenanza and his convoy of seven men had reached the Ugarit Valley on their route to Egypt. Two covered chariots loaded with silver and gifts of cattle and sheep were attached to the rear with ropes. Berbalis, his father's chamberlain, directed their path as they traveled side-by-side on horseback.

"You seem convinced they'll welcome us. Do you fear at all what the Egyptians might do to us once we arrive?" asked Berbalis.

"What I fear is that Queen Senpaten may be in danger. The desperation in her letter worries me," replied Zenanza. "And look at us. We're moving much slower because of our gifts."

"If you're crowned king of Egypt, you'll be greater than all three of your brothers combined, and your kingdom grander than anything your father ever conquered. He would be indebted to you," said Berbalis.

Zenanza laughed. "You're my father's chamberlain, yet, you obviously don't *know* my father. If I could win the heart of the beautiful Queen Senpaten, how much greater my accomplishments would be."

"How do you even know if the queen is beautiful?"

"Have you not heard of the beauty of her mother Nefertiti? I have no doubt the young queen is a flower plucked from her mother's bosom."

"And I have no doubt that you, Prince Zenanza, are love-drunk."

The grin on their faces faded as an expansion formed on the far side of the valley. The image kept expanding until the line of cavalry approaching them at high speed became clear.

"What army is that?" asked Zenanza.

"From the shape of the chariots, I would say Egyptian."

"It should be obvious we're only a convoy. Why are they speeding toward us as if we're an army?"

"That's a good question," replied Berbalis.

Zenanza halted his convoy. His seven horsemen gathered next to him in a straight line, ready to give their life in his defense.

Kicking up dust, Horemheb stopped his cavalry just cubits away from Zenanza's convoy. There was a fiery look in the general's eyes as he stared them down one-by-one without uttering a single word. Each of the convoy's men wore the same tunic and not one of them appeared to be royalty. The sight of cattle and sheep further confused Horemheb.

"Who are you and why are you traveling with livestock?" asked Horemheb.

Berbalis stepped forward on his horse.

"My lord, please accept our entreaties. I am the chamberlain from Hatti," he said nervously, "and the sheep, cattle and silver are gifts to Queen Senpaten from our King Suppiluliumas."

"What other gift does a Hittite have for our Queen Senpaten?" asked Horemheb.

No one answered him.

"One of you is the son of King Suppiluliumas. The one who intends to marry our queen. Which one of you is it?" said Horemheb.

Still, no one spoke.

Horemheb glanced back at his cavalry and smiled. "Akure, take aim with your bow and shoot an arrow through one of them."

Without hesitation, Akure loaded his bow, and to the horror of Zenanza's convoy, released an arrow. It pierced the shoulder of one of Zenanza's men, and he fell off his horse to the ground, screaming from the pain.

"The next arrow released will be fatal. I'll ask you one last time. Which one of you is King Suppiluliumas's son?" demanded Horemheb.

One of Zenanza's men directed his horse forward, but the prince signaled him to return to his position.

"No," said Zenanza, as he dismounted his horse and stood in front of his convoy.

"I am Prince Zenanza, son of King Suppiluliumas and Queen Tawanna. I've come in peace to answer your Queen Senpaten's request to marry a prince of Hatti. I ask that you honor the ancient peace treaty between our two countries."

"You're speaking to the general of Egypt's army, and I'm well aware of the treaty. Your father broke it when he murdered our Egyptian princess, Lupita."

"So you're Horemheb. My father has informed me of our country's history. He didn't know that Lupita was an Egyptian princess. Our country was at war with Mitanni, and because she was dressed as a Mitannian and escorted by a Mitanni convoy, our soldiers naturally assumed she was lying about being an Egyptian princess. I ask that you forgive our country's mistake, it wasn't intentional," said Zenanza.

Horemheb smirked. "There has never been and will never be a marriage between an Egyptian queen and a Hittite. Suppiluliumas will pay blood-for-blood for the murder of Lupita," replied Horemheb.

The conviction in Horemheb's decree convinced Zenanza that it was the end of his journey. He had taken an enormous gamble and lost. As Horemheb and his men unsheathed their swords, he thought about how he could save his own life, or at the very least, the lives of his men.

"I'll concede blood-for-blood, general, but I ask that you consider that I am a prince, the son of a king and, at the least, should be granted a chance at an honorable redemption," said Zenanza.

"In what way?"

"A one-on-one fight to the death."

Horemheb smiled at the Hittite. "Now why would I agree to that?"

"I sense that you're an honorable man, General Horemheb, and you would agree to what is indeed honorable," said Zenanza.

"Is that really what you prefer? A tortuous battle in lieu of instant death? It could get painfully messy."

"Yet, it's the honorable way. Is it not?"

"There was no honor in the way you people slaughtered our princess. I have no obligation to grant you honor," Horemheb replied.

"True, but if your judgment is that I should pay the price for something my people have done, then wouldn't it be lawful that I be allowed to stand on my own to make a defense, whether I choose a verbal defense or a physical one? Is it not written in your law?"

Zenanza knew that it was. Besides being well versed in his own kingdom's laws, he was also proficient in the law of the Egyptians, the Mitannians, and the Assyrians. Before his journey, Zenanza had made a genuine effort to refresh his knowledge, particularly of Egyptian law. Bound by his own devotion to the law, Horemheb gave in as Zenanza had hoped.

"Very well," said Horemheb, returning his sword to its scabbard. "Choose which one of my warriors you would like to challenge."

Zenanza gazed across the front line of Horemheb's cavalry. They all appeared eager to be chosen.

"Quickly, which one will it be?" asked Horemheb.

Zenanza settled his gaze on Horemheb himself.

"The great and mighty General of Egypt . . . Horemheb!" he shouted.

Horemheb rolled with laughter. "You're insane."

"General, if I fall in battle, it will not be to a common soldier, but to you—the great Egyptian warrior Horemheb. I don't fear the challenge. Do you, General?"

Horemheb's laughter ceased. The Hittite Prince had challenged his honor, and in front of his men. He was now obligated to give Zenanza his one-on-one fight to the death. Horemheb removed his helmet.

"Give the Hittite prince a spear and a shield, the same as mine," ordered Horemheb to one of his soldiers.

One of the Egyptian soldiers equipped Zenanza with his war gear. The prince examined the tip of the spear by touching it to his finger. A drop of his blood fell to the earth.

"I think we should set terms," said Zenanza.

"What terms?" Horemheb mocked. "There are no 'terms,' in a one-on-one fight to the death."

"I propose that we have just one."

"You, Hittite prince, are challenging my patience," said Horemheb. "What is this term?"

"It's simple and fair. If I severely wound or kill you, your army must allow us safe passage to Thebes, and if you succeed in killing me, you will allow my convoy to return my body home to my father. I would do the same for you, general."

"That's preposterous!" shouted Horemheb's captain, Salitas.

"I'm inquiring of the general, not his soldiers!" shouted Zenanza, glaring at Salitas.

"Why would we allow you safe passage into our kingdom and not drag your dead body back to Egypt as our trophy?" asked Salitas.

"Salitas, I make the decisions here. Don't say another word," Horemheb corrected, before turning back to the prince. "It is agreed," he said.

Salitas spit and sheathed his own sword in disappointment.

"So I have your word and the word of your army," continued Zenanza, "that if I succeed at killing you, they'll not harm me or my convoy and will allow us to finish our journey into Egypt?"

"You have my word. And theirs," answered Horemheb, turning to glare at Salitas, before once again facing Zenanza. "I have sealed it here in front of my army, the war god Montu and our almighty god, Amun." he said.

CHAPTER

39

WITHIN THE HOUR Hani set foot back on Egyptian soil, he was apprehended and charged with treason. Ay had convinced Horemheb's royal guards that Senpaten's messenger had devised the plan himself to bring a Hittite prince to Egypt, and in her vulnerable state of mourning and despair of Tut's death, she lost control of her senses and went along with it. The story was meant to keep Senpaten secure as queen until he could marry her and take his position as pharaoh.

To frighten the young queen and her sister, Mayati, further into submission, Ay had them both escorted to the prison barracks where they were forced to witness Hani's decapitation.

Now that Horemheb was dispatched to the Ugarit Valley to eliminate the Hittite prince, there stood only one obstacle in the way of Ay's ascension to the throne of Egypt—Sia. The lector priest had become popular and wielded great influence over the citizens of Thebes. He was unanimously voted in as the sole leader of the Amun priesthood by all twelve Amun priests, and mere steps away from the throne of Egypt himself.

At dawn, before the first prayer to the Amun god was recited, Ay entered the temple dressed in a leopard skin cloak, carrying a scroll in his hand. He walked up to Sia with a conniving smile.

"Why are you dressed in a garment only fit for me, the lector priest of Amun?" Sia asked.

"Is it not a fitting garment for a pharaoh?" said Ay.

"You are not a candidate for pharaoh."

"On the contrary, I'm the only candidate and I'm here for your support."

Sia studied Ay. "Perhaps you've consumed too much of the cure yourself," he said.

"Hardly," replied Ay. "Do you understood what I just told you? You will withdraw your claim to the throne and support me as pharaoh. My marriage to Queen Senpaten seals my authority to rule."

"You have lost your senses! Never would I withdraw my claim to the throne and neither would Queen Senpaten take such an old man in marriage."

Ay handed Sia the scroll he was carrying.

"What is this?" asked Sia.

"Perhaps you should unroll it and read it," Ay replied. "You would be very interested in its contents. Your brother, Neper, gave it to me the day before you murdered him."

Sia looked up at Ay, startled. "What are you speaking about? I did not murder my twin."

"Of course you did. I saw you as I stood behind a column, you were tightening the rope around his neck, and I watched you inhale his last breath into your mouth. You didn't see me, Sia, but I certainly witnessed it along with your failed attempt to defeat Meri-Ra's magic."

Sia stopped voicing denials and went silent.

"It occurred to me to intervene, but how rude would that have been of me to interfere in a disagreement between brothers?" said Ay.

Sia turned his attention to the scroll and unrolled it.

"You and I have much in common, Sia," Ay continued, "except that you lack patience. Your need for instant gratification dooms you."

Sia studied the scroll, taking in every word. He shook his head in denial of the secrets it revealed, secrets he thought were long entombed with his twin, Neper.

"Did you see where it reveals the true identity of your mother?" asked Ay, "who interestingly enough turns out not to be of Egyptian lineage at all, but Libyan—Egypt's enemy in the west. And your father, Kerinac, was never a noble scribe of the pharaoh's royal court as you have your fellow Amun priests believe, but a Nubian slave with barely a drop of Egyptian blood in his veins. All lies, though clever ones, but lies nonetheless that you and your brother used to attain your lofty position above the citizens and alongside the pharaoh."

Sia rolled up the scroll and attempted to disguise his nervousness.

"Why have you stopped reading, Sia? There's more; a list of names of every farmer you and your brother stole grain and semiprecious jewels from as taxes in the name of Amun. Hardworking men reduced to living as beggars in the street while their wives and children died of starvation. You, Sia, of Libyan descent, prospered from the deaths of native Egyptian citizens. Can you imagine the enormity of your transgression if it was ever revealed to the royal court, your fellow priests, or even General Horemheb? Surely, it's grounds for your execution. Would you not agree?"

Sia didn't answer. Ay wondered what exactly he was thinking in that moment. Had he fully accepted that he was defeated or was he conjuring in his mind a scheme or a spell that would reverse his predicament?

"Your brother Neper was remorseful for his part in the mass deceit and wanted to redeem himself by confessing to me his part in your depravity."

"Enough!" Sia shouted. "It makes no difference. None of it."

"Oh, it makes quite a difference. Once the people are made aware that you are actually a Libyan imposter, and the farmers who paid your bribes come forward and testify against you, you'll be a disgrace to your fellow servants of Amun and be stripped of your position as lector priest. In the end, you will become like those impoverished farmers you forced into the streets begging for food, all before the day of your execution."

Sia finally exhaled the breath that he had been holding in for so long—a sign to Ay that the priest conceded defeat. "Who else has seen this scroll?" Sia asked.

"I don't see any reason why it needs to be shown to anyone else," replied Ay. "Since you will now, I assume, fully support my ascension as pharaoh, it's only fair I secure your position as head lector priest and forget the trivial things about imposters and Libyans. Feel free to keep the scroll for yourself Sia. I have your brother's original signed and sealed version hidden away in a safe place."

Ay was certain he had eviscerated Sia enough to gain his loyalty, but before he left the temple, he gave the priest one last warning.

"Don't bother with your spells and incantations against me, Sia. They won't work. Your twin taught me well on how to rebuff your illusions."

In the Ugarit valley, Horemheb and Zenanza circled each other, their spears poised for combat. To allot the general and the prince more space to maneuver, Horemheb's cavalry moved their horses back fifty cubits. Zenanza's convoy did the same, corralling the sheep and cattle to the side so the animals wouldn't enter the battle area.

Both men stepped around each other, locking eyes as they waited for the other to make the first move. Horemheb gave a volcanic growl and charged forward, planting his head into Zenanza's chest. The sudden pointed force knocked the prince flat on his back and the air from his diaphragm. Before Horemheb could follow up his attack, the prince recovered and rose to his feet.

They both struck at each other with their spears, back and forth, but each had only made contact with the other's shield. Horemheb was surprised at how quick and agile Zenanza was in deflecting his brute force. It would not be a quick and easy feat to subdue the young prince as he had assumed. The hand-to-hand combat was physically taxing and Horemheb felt his age. The general now understood that experience and skill may not be enough to defeat the Hittite prince if the battle lingered on for an extended period of time. A duel of brevity and brutality would be the general's course of attack if he wanted to be victorious over the young, and surprisingly agile, prince.

Horemheb's apprehension aided Zenanza in finding an opening, and the prince exploited it by thrusting his spear forward and slicing through the general's ear. Horemheb was more rattled by the prince's ability than from the searing pain. As his blood dripped to the ground, Salitas unsheathed his dagger. Horemheb put his hand in the air, signaling his captain not to interfere.

Inside, Horemheb raged from humiliation. He would not allow himself to be defeated by an adolescent Hittite. The internal anger made him patient and out of the corner of his eye he saw Zenanza circle behind him. At the moment the prince raised his spear behind his back to attack, Horemheb turned and charged like a wild boar. He plunged the blade of his spear through Zenanza's chest and the prince fell to the ground bleeding. The quick loss of blood made it hard for him to breathe and stand as he had done so quickly before, yet he refused to let the general see the anguish on his face.

"Get up!" shouted Horemheb.

Wheezing from the pain of a punctured chest, Zenanza got to his knees, grabbed his spear, and used it to force himself up from the ground. His strength was fading, and he could barely stay on his feet. In an effort that Horemheb thought was courageous, Zenanza had managed to face the general in a battle stance again.

"You want to go on?" asked Horemheb, recognizing the severity of Zenanza's wound.

The prince nodded, and both men circled each other again. Horemheb charged at the prince once more and kicked his shield into his chest, knocking him back to the ground. The general then walked up to Zenanza and plunged his spear through the prince's thigh. Zenanza squawked as Horemheb yanked the spear out, tearing the prince's flesh on the way out.

Horemheb and his cavalry were amazed as Zenanza, suffering in immense pain, staggered, but stood up on his feet again. He could only hold onto his spear and shield for a fleeting moment before dropping them and collapsing.

"What is there to be done on the ground?" shouted Horemheb. "Get up, prince of Hatti, son of the great King Suppiluliumas. Get up!"

Zenanza tried as hard as he could to stand, but there was no strength left in his body. He collapsed once more, covering his chest with his hand to tamp the bleeding. Horemheb picked up the prince's shield and threw it on him. It bounced off Zenanza's body and landed on the ground. Consumed by laughter, Horemheb turned his back on his opponent and faced the Hittite convoy.

"So this is your prince? The next great king of Egypt? How insulting that his pathetic death is not worth nearly that of our Lady Lupita," mocked Horemheb.

The general's mockery was contagious and soon his cavalry joined him in amusing themselves in laughter at the prince's expense. When Zenanza produced a dagger hidden beneath his belt and hurled it at Horemheb, and the blade sliced through the general's calf muscle, the laughter ceased.

Furious, Horemheb turned and faced Zenanza. Without a flinch, he pulled the blade from his calf and tossed it aside, then walked up to the prince and stood over him as the young man lay on the ground still writhing in pain.

"Beg for your life now or I will end it at this very moment," said Horemheb. He picked up the prince's spear from the ground and pointed it at his face. "Beg. Now," Horemheb repeated, "or I will take it."

Zenanza lifted his head and looked Horemheb in the eye. "I will not dishonor my father by begging a foreigner for my life," he said. "And yes, General Horemheb, I am the son of the great King Suppiluliumas. One day you will feel his wrath," replied Zenanza, his voice fading.

Horemheb sneered at him before thrusting the spear through the prince's heart, killing him instantly. The Hittite convoy gasped, afraid of what was to happen to them next.

Horemheb ripped a piece of Zenanza's tunic and tied the cloth around his calf to stop the bleeding, then turned and mounted his horse.

"You, chamberlain, and your convoy, return to your King Suppiluliumas and inform him that the great General Horemheb of Egypt, commanding general of the armies of Pharaoh Amenhotep and Tutankhamun, has avenged their Lady Lupita," said Horemheb.

Berbalis smirked. "You avenged no one, general. The only thing you've done was murder a love-struck prince who was brave beyond his years. Neither he nor my King Suppiluliumas had anything to do with the death of your Lady Lupita. It was our General Callum who took it upon himself to violate and kill her and her unborn child— the same Hittite general you captured in Kadesh but then foolishly released back to us."

Berbalis's revelation rendered Horemheb speechless. The euphoric look on the chamberlain's face revealed how pleased he was to have alarmed the general. He took the opportunity to further deepen Horemheb's internal wound.

"Not to worry," Berbalis continued. "Our General Callum died peacefully in his sleep from the disease only days ago. So you Horemheb, the great and powerful general of Egypt, will go to your grave without the vengeance you so desperately require, and every moment of your pitiful existence you glimpse the scar on your calf, you will remember our Prince Zenanza, the true courageous one who skillfully smote you as he lay wounded on the ground."

Miffed by the chamberlain's disrespect, Salitas aimed and released an arrow from his bow, striking Berbalis through his lung. He dropped from his horse and landed flat on his back in the sand, clutching the arrow as blood spilled from his fatal wound.

"Prince Zenanza's death is our revenge!" shouted Salitas.

As the Egyptian cavalry roared with cheering and beating of their swords against their shields, Horemheb languished inside over an empty revenge. The realization that he had Lady Lupita's murderer in his custody and unknowingly allowed the Hittite to return to his country alive, tortured him. Zenanza's death meant nothing now, and the audacity of his captain Salitas to kill another Hittite for his own personal pleasure compounded his anger.

"Now we will take his body back to Thebes so that all can ridicule this ridiculous prince of Hatti!" said Salitas.

Horemheb raised his hand in the air and the cheering stopped.

The general turned his cold gaze upon Salitas. "I don't recall giving you the order to kill the chamberlain. Do I need to remind you, Salitas, who gives the orders here?"

"He disrespected you in the face of your army. I merely upheld your honor. If anything, I should be rewarded."

"When have I ever needed you to uphold my honor? I decide who is executed and the timing of the execution, not you. Do you understand!?" shouted Horemheb.

"As you wish, General. I would only say one last thing on the matter. It would be a grave mistake to allow this Hittite convoy to return to Hatti with the prince's body. His appearance in his homeland will only fester rage and contempt against us for generations, just as we had for the death of Lady Lupita. Martyrs will surely be born of Zenanza's death," said Salitas.

"Whoever possesses the boldness to rise up against Egypt will be slaughtered. My word to the Hittite prince will be kept and you will not disrupt or change my orders again or I will strip you completely of your rank," replied Horemheb.

Salitas matched Horemheb's stare before reversing his horse, and racing back to Egypt alone. Horemheb and his army remained while the Hittite convoy loaded the bodies of their chamberlain and Prince Zenanza onto the carriage for the long journey back to their land of Hatti.

CHAPTER

40

AT THE FIRST sight of the morning sun, a crowd gathered in front of the Amun temple chanting Senpaten and Ay's names. Dancers and musicians flooded the main road encircling the temple, performing in celebration of the day's wedding festivities.

In the solitude of her bedchamber, Senpaten sat alone lamenting her fate. She wiped her tears away and applied double the amount of black kohl around her eyes to conceal it. Mayati entered her room just after she finished applying the last of the beet-colored paint to her cheeks.

"Ay forced me to tell him about the letter," confessed Mayati. "I'm so sorry."

"Don't cry, sister, it's what's meant to be. Perhaps, it's best to keep royal blood on Egypt's throne," replied Senpaten. "It may have been what Mother would have wanted."

"Mother would have never wanted you to marry her father. It was never her plan for us. Don't marry him, Senpaten. He's an evil man, and we should leave this evil city behind and travel away together."

"To where, Mayati? Thebes is our home now, there's no more Amarna. The fire has reduced it to ashes."

"What about T'aru? Father used to speak of it as his parents' place of refuge and contentment. With Halima's help, we could steal away in the late hour when no one would see us," said Mayati.

Senpaten stood up and kissed her on her cheek. "No, sister. It would destroy me to see what happened to Hani come upon Halima. It's too risky."

Despite the gloom brewing inside her, Senpaten's outward appearance was beautiful, as she was dressed in her best linen, and adorned with gold, silver, and lapis-lazuli jewels. Bead-net layered her body from head-to-toe.

Mayati smiled and gave her sister a hug. "You look so much like Mother," she said.

The mention of their mother brought up a question in Senpaten's mind she had longed to ask Mayati.

"Do you still believe in the afterlife?" asked Senpaten.

"What do you mean? Of course I do. It's what our parents, and their parents and even the Aten teaches us. How could you question it?"

"Then why have we not seen our mother, nor our father, or even our sister Meketa again? They should have completed their journey by now and returned to us. Something is wrong, Mayati."

"They could have lost their way, but it's only a matter of time before the Aten god will set them on the right path and sends us their message."

"Maybe the Aten is powerless here in this city of Amun, and maybe the afterlife doesn't exist, and all we really have left are just hopes and memories," said Senpaten.

"No, sister, you mustn't think that way. If there is no afterlife then we have nothing."

Senpaten embraced Mayati again. "We have each other."

"Forever through eternity," replied Mayati.

The sisters locked hands.

"Escort me to the ceremony. I don't want to go alone," said Senpaten.

The sisters boarded the royal chariot and were driven to the Amun temple, holding each other's hands for support the entire ride.

When they arrived, Sia and Kafrem were already inside prepared to bear witness to the ceremony. Senpaten was despondent at the first sight of Ay and his wife, Teyla, entering the temple. Ay approached her with a lotus blossom and Senpaten accepted it without looking at his face. Once they stepped up to the altar together, Sia unrolled the marriage contract that he and Ay had written prior to the ceremony and read it aloud:

"This man, Ay, son of Yuya and Tuyu, comes before us today in the year thirteen hundred twenty-two to form a union of marriage with Queen Senpaten, daughter of Akenaten and Nefertiti, queen of Upper and Lower Egypt. They stand before the god Amun and I, Sia, his lector priest. This marriage contract validates the authority of Ay to rule as pharaoh and it prohibits you, Queen Senpaten, from divorcing him and marrying another—"

Senpaten looked over at her sister. They both shared the same distressed expression. Not even a divorce now could help her escape the claws of her grandfather.

While Sia read the rest of the marriage contract, Senpaten allowed her thoughts to roam free as she focused away in the distance, her attention not in the present, but faraway in her past, to the time when her mother would shower her with little kisses on the bank of the river, and her father would sing her favorite lullaby before putting her and her sisters to bed. Maybe her parents, Tut and her sister Meketa were all together in the afterlife enjoying each other's company so much that they had forgotten about her and Mayati, and decided to remain there without ever returning.

Sia interrupted Senpaten's daydream. "Do you understand, queen?"

She didn't know what she was expected to have understood, but she replied "yes," anyway.

"Then I will continue," said Sia. "Upon your death, your royal treasures will be divided among your husband, Ay, or any children you might conceive with him. Ay will move from his home with Teyla into the royal palace chamber to reside with you, Queen Senpaten. This will take place in the eyes of Amun and in front of the witnesses, Kafrem and Teyla. Now, as I have ordained you husband and wife, you will both sign and seal this document."

Ay took the reed brush from Sia and signed his name to the papyrus. When he finished, he handed the reed to Senpaten. Hesitating before the scroll, she turned and gazed at her sister. Mayati shook her head "no" with tears in her eyes. Senpaten shifted her focus away from Mayati and dipped the brush in ink and signed the contract.

Outside the temple, Horemheb and his soldiers had returned from their confrontation with Zenanza and his convoy. Surprised by the riotous crowd celebrating in the streets, Horemheb dismounted his horse and approached a blind musician playing his harp in the courtyard.

"Why is there a celebration today? Is there a new festival in honor of Amun?" asked Horemheb.

"It's not a festival. It is a royal union taking place now in the Amun temple."

"What royal union?"

"We celebrate the marriage of our Queen Senpaten to her grandfather, Ay, our new pharaoh," explained the musician.

Horemheb was stunned. *It can't be true,* he thought.

The general ordered his men to remain in the courtyard as he hurried into the entrance of the temple. He entered the moment Sia placed the crown of Upper and Lower Egypt upon Ay's head.

"You are now husband to Queen Senpaten and pharaoh of the glorious kingdom of Egypt. May you and your queen reign for a thousand years under the guidance of Amun, Osiris, and Anubis," Sia decreed, unaware of Horemheb's presence.

Ay turned to Horemheb and smiled. "General, it is good to see you. I'll need you to report to me at dawn on Egypt's state of affairs with our tributaries. I believe there is gold owed to us that needs to be collected."

Horemheb had no choice but to nod and prostrate himself before the new pharaoh. Ay had won, proving himself to be more devious and clever than the general had estimated, and for that, the Amun god had rewarded him.

Before Mayati took a step to leave the temple with Horemheb, Senpaten embraced her as if it would be their last. Ay had promised Senpaten that her sister would neither be harmed nor banished from Egypt as long as she went along with the marriage, but he also made it clear that Mayati was no longer welcome inside the royal palace. She would now have to reside in Horemheb's and Mundi's home.

Senpaten told her sister she loved her and would see her again soon. Once Mayati left the ceremony with Horemheb, Ay grabbed Senpaten's arm and pulled her close.

"I am your only family now and I expect you to conceive my heir," he whispered in her ear. "Return to your chamber and prepare yourself for me."

Senpaten was repulsed by the thought of copulation with Ay. Though the threat was imminent, she refused to believe it could ever be enforced. Nonetheless, she was determined to maintain her dignity by not shedding a tear in his presence as she walked out from the Amun temple with her head held high.

In the sacred temple of Arinna, a lamb was brought forward by a Hittite servant and placed into a pit at the base of the Sun-goddess statue—the most powerful god of the land of Hatti. Plated in gold, the towering structure portrayed a woman seated on her throne, and around her shoulders, a long flowing robe made of a purple cloth. King Suppiluliumas stepped into the pit, forced the head of the lamb against the ground, and slashed its neck in an upward motion so as to direct the flow of blood directly into a golden beaker handed to him by the servant. Once it was filled, he set the beaker on the ground before the Sun-goddess, and allowed the remainder of the lamb's blood to drain out into the pit. The servant then carried the lamb carcass out of the temple to be butchered and eaten by the sons of Suppiluliumas, while two additional servants brought loaves of bread and placed them into the blood-filled pit.

King Suppiluliumas was dipping pieces of the bread in the lamb's blood and consuming it when his wife, Tawanna, burst into the temple's inner sanctuary.

"What are you doing here?" he asked, wiping the blood away from his mouth.

She didn't answer. She trudged straight to the altar and knelt in front of him, face-to-face, her lips close to his as if she was contemplating kissing him. There was something unnerving about her blank expression and the one tear that formed in her eye and rolled down her cheek. Tawanna suddenly slapped Suppiluliumas across his face.

"I begged you not to let him go," she said. "I begged you!"

Before the king could react, Tawanna stormed out of the sanctuary past the guard carrying Zenanza's body. He carried the boy over to his father and placed him in his arms. King Suppiluliumas held his dead son in disbelief. A piercing wail rose to his lips and the grieving father screamed at the top of his lungs.

Suppiluliumas rested Zenanza's limp body on the altar of the Sun-Goddess and knelt beside him, caressing his son's withered gray face. "Oh goddess of Arinna," he prayed. "You did no evil to the people of Egypt, yet look what they have done to me!"

When Ay entered Senpaten's bedchamber, he was delighted to find her sitting up under the bedcover prepared to consummate their marriage. Ay removed his garments. Tut's Aten amulet momentarily drew Senpaten's attention away from the old man's sagging, wrinkled skin hanging from his arms, chest, and abdomen.

"You are as beautiful to me as your mother," said Ay as he crawled into bed with her.

Senpaten flinched at what he said but kept her eyes locked on the amulet. Her eyelids appeared heavy, and she struggled to keep them open.

"What's wrong with you? Are you intoxicated?"

When she didn't answer, Ay became suspicious and reached under the bedcover to touch her. There was a dampness, thick and slippery, that met his hand. He snatched the bedcover off of her and was horrified by what he saw.

Senpaten sat calmly, drenched in her own blood with a dagger buried deep in her abdomen. Only the handle was visible. As Ay searched her eyes for an explanation, Senpaten lunged forward, grabbed a hold of Tut's amulet and ripped it from Ay's neck.

"I am a queen of Egypt and my body belongs to me. You are nothing but a lowly servant and I will never be a wife to you, because I am, and will forever be, the wife of my beloved Tutankhaten."

Senpaten took in a deep breath, but it was her last. Still clutching Tut's Aten amulet in her hand, she drifted off to an endless sleep, quietly onward to her journey.

On a clear, sunny morning, Sia walked to the Amun temple to prepare a sacrifice for the gods Mut and Khonsu. All was calm in Thebes. The disease that had ravaged much of the Egyptian empire had disappeared as mysteriously as it had first emerged in the Theban village.

Out on the river, Sia caught a glimpse of the royal canoe with its single sail expanding in the wind. It had been some time since Sia had spoken with the pharaoh. Since Queen Senpaten's death, her entombment in the Valley of the Kings and the pharaoh's subsequent official coronation, Sia had interacted very little with Egypt's new ruler.

After the sacrifice, Sia went into the temple's inner sanctuary. He put on his high priest leopard skin cloak and knelt before the Amun statue. The new edifice, built after Akenaten's guards destroyed the original many years before, was not as tall. It was identical to the old statue and bore the same ram's head, but with no built-in contraptions that allowed blood to flow on command or the statue to spontaneously rumble.

Sia retrieved a clay pot and filled it with twigs and grass. In it, he placed a wax figurine formed into the likeness of a man and wrapped in a piece of the pharaoh's nemes head cloth. He torched the contents of the pot and it silently burned to ashes. Sia grabbed a nearby vase where he had collected blood from a bull calf and poured a generous amount of the coagulated blood into the clay pot. He then smeared some of the blood mixture across the back of his left thigh.

Carrying the pot, Sia left the inner sanctuary, descended the steps of the temple, and went to the bank of the river. He spat into the pot and set it on the ground. Sia unearthed a stone halfway buried in the mud and with it smashed the pot to pieces. This was the same ritual the Oracle had taught Sia in his youth.

After reciting an incantation, he scattered the pieces into the fast-moving current of the river, the same river that Ay and his wife

Teyla were sailing that day. The newly ordained pharaoh and queen were admiring the beauty of Thebes as they did every morning. On his head, Ay wore the nemes head cloth and around his neck, Tut's Aten amulet hidden underneath his garment. He wore it not because he admired it, but because it had been a possession of a pharaoh, one of true royal lineage, a position he envied.

As Ay and Teyla sailed in their royal canoe, Ay, as he always did, dipped fruit in the river to cleanse it before feeding it to himself and his wife. When Ay turned to retrieve more berries from the fruit basket, Teyla saw a mark on his leg, partially hidden by the hem of his garment.

"What is that on your thigh?" she asked.

Her concern alarmed him. "Where?"

"Pull your garment above your knee."

Ay pulled up his garment. A purplish bruise the size and shape of an olive was on the back of his left thigh. Ay couldn't believe what he was seeing.

"It's an illusion. The disease perished years ago," said Ay.

"It cannot be an illusion if we both see it, my husband. It's more sinister than a disease. It is an unrelenting plague, and it has found you," cried Teyla.

Nine years later, citizens of Thebes gathered in the courtyard of the Colonnade Hall to hear their pharaoh speak. Pharaoh Horemheb was now in his fifth year of reign. Ay, whose reign had lasted only four years, was long buried, his life cut short by the mysterious disease that had killed thousands before in Amarna. Buried with Ay was the knowledge that he deliberately left Amenhotep with the fatal doses of the cure, knowing the pharaoh would consume it all at once to his demise. It was the first step he had taken to secure his position as pharaoh, but what happened in the unexplained death of his daughter, Queen Nefertiti, remained a mystery.

Ay's death had cleared the path for Horemheb's ascension, and to prevent Sia, Ay's staunchest enemy of the two, from succeeding him as pharaoh, Ay had turned over Neper's scroll (that contained Sia's illicit secrets), to Horemheb just before his death, and the general used it as collateral to quash any ambition Sia might have had for the position of pharaoh. As a token for his cooperation, Horemheb gave Sia his blessing to become the new oracle of Egypt.

On the day of the festival commemorating Sia's new position as oracle, Pharaoh Horemheb appeared at the podium side-by-side with Sia, wearing his copper war helmet in place of the customary nemes head cloth. His wife, Mundi, stood directly behind him, admiring the enthusiasm of the crowd for her husband.

A young sturdy man in a soldier's uniform escorted Mayati to her royal position next to Mundi. The soldier was well-built, tall and muscular, as Pharaoh Horemheb had been in his youth. The pharaoh welcomed him to stand by his side opposite of Sia.

"Praises to the almighty god Amun and to Osiris, Montu, Isis, and Horus," shouted Horemheb, his voice amplified and echoing off the surrounding cliffs. "Egypt has flourished with law, order, peace, and abundance now that the heretic Pharaoh Akenaten and his god, the Aten have perished. Their blasphemous names have been erased from the Colonnade Hall and from every monument and statue in Egypt. I have destroyed their city of Amarna by fire so neither their works nor the Aten will be remembered. The names of Akenaten, Senpaten, Ay, Nefertiti and Tut have been stricken from the history of Egypt and of the world forever. They will be forgotten, but my name, Pharaoh Horemheb, will last until the end of time!"

The crowd applauded. Horemheb turned to his wife, proud of the adulation pouring out from the Egyptian people. Instead of joining the crowd in praising her husband, Mundi's concern was for Mayati, who had tears in her eyes because of the curse Horemheb had just pronounced against her parents and siblings by erasing their names from the Colonnade Hall—a curse that could forever prevent their return from the afterlife.

Horemheb waited for the crowd to grow quiet before he continued his pronouncements.

"And now," he said, nodding to the young soldier next to him, "just as you have welcomed Sia, our newly ordained Oracle, you must welcome your new ordained general of the Egyptian army . . . General Ramesses!"

As the crowd erupted in applause again, Horemheb spotted Salitas approaching in his chariot. The pharaoh's military captain was furious he had been passed over for the position he believed was rightfully his. The disdain he harbored toward Horemheb distorted the fake pleasant expression on the captain's face.

Salitas halted his chariot next to the crowd and nodded at Mayati. Horemheb watched aghast as Mayati left her position next to his wife and entered Salitas' chariot. Salitas embraced her and smirked at Horemheb before speeding away from the festival with Mayati by his side.

Confused by what he just witnessed, Horemheb turned to his wife and spoke directly in her ear in order to keep their conversation private. "Why did she go with him?"

Mundi looked straight ahead and didn't answer.

"Answer me, Mundi. Why has Mayati spited me by leaving with Salitas?"

"They're lovers," she answered, still looking straight ahead ignoring his stare. "And if you had been paying the slightest bit of attention to her, you would have known that it was you and only you who drove her into his arms."

Burning with anger, Horemheb gripped Mundi's chin with one hand forcing her to look him in the eye, while he caressed her shoulder with the other. His teeth clenched as he spoke to her. "You allowed this, and now he'll soon exploit her because of her royalty in order to stake a claim as pharaoh. And when he has attained his position, he will discard her in the same manner he defecates. Is that what you want for your niece?"

"The same has been said about you," Mundi replied, shoving his hand away from her chin, "as you have used for your benefit in becoming pharaoh, the royal relation of my dear sister, Queen Nefertiti. And contrary to what you've told these people, my sister's legacy is ingrained in the earth as deep as the roots of a sycamore tree. Not even you nor the battle axes from a thousand of your men could cut it off," she said, undeterred by his anger or concerned that she could be heard by the people around them.

Her response silenced Horemheb. He turned away from Mundi's unyielding gaze and focused his attention back on the crowd to avoid having to assault her in their presence.

Ramesses stepped forward onto the podium, and Horemheb removed his war helmet and placed it upon his new general's head. The citizens chanted and cheered their names, unaware that their celebration was being watched.

Hidden among the hills surrounding Thebes, a massive army moved into battle formation. After years of waiting for the perfect moment to strike, King Suppiluliumas had used the secret trade route and was staring down into the Egyptian capital with the same blazing rage he felt the day his son Zenanza was laid into his arms, slaughtered by the hand of Horemheb.

On horseback, next to Suppiluliumas, sat Shattiwaza grinning from ear-to-ear with his Mitanni army, and behind them stood a Hittite and Nubian alliance of thousands of soldiers from as far as the eye could see. And just as the Nubian prisoner who killed Tuthmosis over forty years before had predicted—the Hittites, the Nubians, and the Mitannians had all united as one force against Egypt that day for war. The story of Ramesses and the 19th dynasty had just begun.

*****

TUT/Tutankhaten

Bust of Tutankhamun, museum of Cairo/Egypt.

Source: Jean-Pierre Dalbéra from Paris, France. November 1, 2002.
This photo is licensed under the Creative Commons Attribution
Generic license.

Replica of Akhenaten's model head, that was found in the
workshop of the sculptor Djehutimes at Akhet-Aton.

The original is in the Egyptian Museum, Cairo. Picture taken at
VAM Design Center, Budapest, on 'Tutankhaton's Treasures'
exhibition April 22, 2010. Source: HoremWeb (Az Ókori
Egyiptom website). Permission is granted under the terms of the
GNU Free Documentation License.

NEFERTITI

Nefertiti Bust, Berlin Museum August 13, 2006

QUEEN TY

Queen Ty bust, Ägyptisches Museum Berlin June 28, 2011

Source: Einsamer Schütze
Permission is granted under the terms of the GNU Free
Documentation License.

AMENHOTEP III

Red Granite Head from a colossal statue of a Pharaoh Amenhotep III from the Temple of Mut in Thebes (Waset). circa 1390 BCE.
June 8, 2013
Source: Avrand6

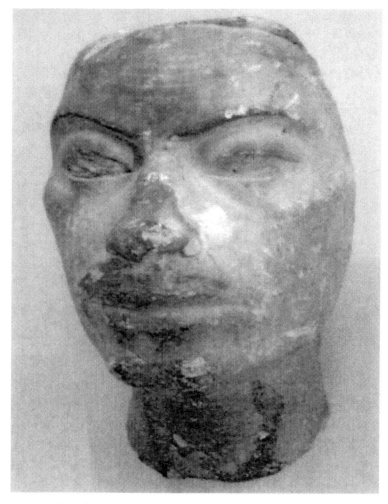

Portrait study of a man thought to be of Ay (attribution is not certain). Amarna, 18th dynasty. Catalog #21350.
Image taken at the Altes Museum, Berlin. November 8, 2006
Source: Keith Schengili-Roberts
Permission is granted under the terms of the GNU Free Documentation License.

HOREMHEB

Partial profile of Horemheb, from a statue of him with the God
Horus made of limestone, 18th dynasty, reign of Horemheb (circa
1343-1315 BCE) November 13, 2010
Source: Captmondo

TERRANCE COFFEY

VALLEY
— OF —
THE KINGS

The 18ᵗʰ Dynasty

Reader's Guide

HELM HOUSE
PUBLISHING

Questions & Topics for Discussion

Please note: the questions below contain spoilers. You should wait to read them until you've finished the book.

1. What character(s) in the novel do you believe were not part of the actual historical record?

2. Now that you have viewed photos of some of the major characters' likenesses, how close was it to your preconceived notion of how they might have looked?

3. Which character in the novel did you sympathize with the most?

4. Did you agree with Teppy that leaving the capital city of Thebes to build his own city away from the Amun priests was the only way to maintain his sovereignty as pharaoh?

5. What did the *afterlife* mean to the characters? And why and how did Senpaten's feelings about it change in the end?

6. What shared experience brought Nefertiti and Queen Ty closer together?

7. What effect did Teppy's childhood disability have on his character as an adult?

8. Did you feel Horemheb was justified in killing Zenanza?

9. What or who do you believe caused Nefertiti's mysterious death?

10. Did Shattiwaza have a legitimate reason to kill his father King Tushratta, or was it done just to satisfy his own ambition for power?

11. How did Teppy tell the identical twin Amun priests Sia and Neper apart?

12. Are there any parallels in the novel to our modern day times in terms of the process in gaining political power?

13. What were the most emotional scenes?

14. What were the most interesting practices about the way of life for the ancient Egyptians? Were there any similarities to our way of life today?

15. The novel is told from a close third-person POV in which we get the perspective of the character with the most dramatic stakes in the scene. Which character POV did you find the most compelling, and why?

A Conversation with Terrance Coffey

Valley of The Kings: The 18th Dynasty is an historical fiction novel. What attracted you to the historical fiction genre?

Since early childhood I shared a genuine love for history and historical biography. Real people of the past who have experienced real-life tragedies and triumphs I find fascinating and relatable.

This novel is part of a Dynastic trilogy, tell us about the series.

'VALLEY OF THE KINGS' is a book series that chronicles the turbulent lives of some of the most known and sometimes lesser known pharaohs of ancient Egypt. Told in story-form, it's a fictional biography based on historical facts and events. *The 18th Dynasty* is Book 1 of the trilogy which recounts the reign of pharaohs in that particular dynasty. The next installment is *The 19th Dynasty* that will focus on the pharaoh Ramesses and the pharaohs that followed his reign.

Tell us about the cover and the inspiration for it.

My idea for the cover was to incorporate the one object that proved to be eminent for the main characters in the novel—the Aten amulet.

You've built a career working in marketing, and as a music branding consultant. When did you start writing prose?

I actually started writing fifteen years ago when a friend challenged me to co-write a screenplay with him. The collaboration experience gave me the confidence to do something I had never done before and from that point on I was hooked.

Over the years, when and how did you find time to write?

Because I worked as an independent consultant through my own company, I was able to set my own working schedule. I would maneuver my hours so that I had time to write daily, and I would work into the early morning hours at it as much as I could.

While Valley of the Kings is your debut novel, you've tried your hand at screenplays, teleplays, television pilots and short stories. Did you ever try to publish, or sell, any of those projects?

Prior to Kindle Scout selecting 'Valley Of The Kings' for publication, I had never tried to publish anything before. A screenplay that I co-wrote and a television pilot that I wrote myself was optioned by two different production companies. Both still have yet to be produced.

When did you start working on Valley of the Kings? What was your process, in terms of writing the book?

I asked a friend to read and then give me his comments on a television series pilot script I wrote back in 2003. He loved it but felt the story deserved to be told in its entirety first, and suggested that I write a novel based on the series outline. At first I didn't take the suggestion seriously because I had never written a book before, but because he was so tenacious in his opinion that it would make a great novel, I decided to give it a try. Once I started writing it in early 2014, I literally couldn't stop. I worked on it at least 6 days a week, spending 5 to 8 hours on it a day. It was as if the characters were telling the story themselves. It took me about a year to actually complete the first draft and an additional six months for the 2nd and 3rd drafts. The editing took a total of five months before I passed the final manuscript on to the publisher.

The novel takes place in 1400 B.C.E.—and seems to have required quite a bit of research. Was that daunting, or was the research what initially drew you to writing the book? When and how did you start researching?

I actually started researching the story for *Valley of The Kings* in 2001, after stumbling across a televised biography about king Tut. Though the bio focused mainly on the young pharaoh, I was more intrigued by the story it wasn't telling—the story of his father, the pharaoh Akenaten. The untimely death of the young pharaoh Tut was ominously tied to the life of his father who at the time of his reign was considered a heretic and it was his actions and decisions that almost destroyed the Egyptian superpower. I was fascinated by just the little I knew of his story and from that spark, I really got into researching the history of the 18th and 19th dynasty pharaohs. After two years of research, I wrote a fifty-page outline for a television mini-series based on my story and from that I wrote a one-hour pilot episode. I then put the whole thing away and would periodically update it whenever new information or recent discoveries in the tombs of Egypt were documented. I did this up until I actually began writing the book in 2014.

ACKNOWLEDGMENTS

The recent discovery of the Hittite and Amarna letters has provided access to the actual correspondence between the 18ᵗʰ dynasty pharaohs and the surrounding kingdoms of Mesopotamia who battled them for prominence. This important finding has helped to unlock some of the many mysteries of the ancient Egyptian superpower. Our lives today and those of the ancient Egyptians are separated by thousands of years and cultural differences, yet we seem to have shared similar hopes and dreams, and most notably, triumphs and tragedies. Writing this book was more than fulfilling, it was my therapy. I felt privileged and obliged to share the story of these provocative characters whose voices deserve a chance to be heard by more than just its author. The anecdote has always been there, waiting for those willing to take on the research and the responsibility of unearthing it. I hope you will continue this journey with me into the next installment of the 'Valley of the Kings' dynastic trilogy; *The 19ᵗʰ Dynasty: Book 2.*

I would like to thank my family: Tony, Yolonda, Rick, and my mother—Yvonne, for their continued support during the writing process. It was just the push I needed to keep moving forward. Thanks to Megan, Ernesto, and the entire Kindle Scout team for acknowledging my work and giving it a chance to live and thrive via Kindle Press.

They say a book can only be as good as the ability of its editor, so my mission from the beginning was to find the best possible editor around. I am fortunate to have found such an awesome team in Ronit Wagman & Dustin Schwindt, and my proof editor Samantha Gordon. You guys have taught me so much and I bow to your expertise. Many thanks to my friend and fellow author Marsha Jenkins-Sanders, whose critique, encouragement, and advice were invaluable in the writing and publishing of this book, and to Doriano Carta, who insisted that I write it when I wasn't convinced that I could. Thanks to Damon Za for such an intriguing cover. Also, thanks to Donnie Demers for championing my literary endeavors from the start, and a special thanks to Larry, Janet, and Damon Stout for their help and support in making this book the best that it could be.

ABOUT THE AUTHOR

Terrance 'Terry' Coffey is an award-winning author, screenwriter, and music composer-producer with a predilection for Egyptian history. He has written numerous short stories, screenplays, television pilots, and even Coca-Cola music jingles. Born in Chicago, Illinois, Terrance now lives in an ambitious little town near Atlanta, Georgia, where he constantly dreams of ancient Egypt.

Join the mailing list at
www.TerranceCoffey.com
@terry_coffey

If you enjoyed this book, please take a few moments to write a review using the url below. Thanks!

https://goo.gl/220mfb

CPSIA information can be obtained
at www.ICGtesting.com
Printed in the USA
LVOW08s1456040117
519724LV00003B/386/P

9 780692 756584